John Timbs

Things to be Remembered in Daily Life

SALZWASSER
VERLAG

John Timbs

Things to be Remembered in Daily Life

Reprint of the original, first published in 1863.

1st Edition 2022 | ISBN: 978-3-37500-319-7

Verlag (Publisher): Salzwasser Verlag GmbH, Zeilweg 44, 60439 Frankfurt, Deutschland
Vertretungsberechtigt (Authorized to represent): E. Roepke, Zeilweg 44, 60439 Frankfurt, Deutschland
Druck (Print): Books on Demand GmbH, In de Tarpen 42, 22848 Norderstedt, Deutschland

THINGS
TO BE REMEMBERED
IN DAILY LIFE.

THINGS

TO BE REMEMBERED

In Daily Life.

WITH PERSONAL EXPERIENCES AND RECOLLECTIONS.

By JOHN TIMBS, F.S.A.

LONDON:

MDCCCLXIII.

TO THE READER.

TIME and Human Life are the staple subjects of the following pages. These are great matters for so small a book, and may remind you of the philosophical scheme of compressing the world into a nutshell. Now, although we have as yet no means of determining exactly what relation this latter idea has to truth,—it is certain that the rapid multiplication of books incessantly presses upon us, that "condensation is the result of time and experience, which reject what is no longer essential." Such is the treatment adopted in the present volume, in which, by *focusing* great truths from the Living and the Dead, is sought to be exemplified the moral couplet:

> Honour and shame from no condition rise;
> Act well your part—there all the honour lies.

As a companion volume to *Things not Generally Known*, it is hoped that *Things to be Remembered* may be as popularly received as its predecessor. To render the present work more directly of practical application, the sketches of character which it contains have been drawn in great measure from our own time, so as to give the book a current interest. Meanwhile, historic gossip has not been eschewed; but its piquancy has been sparingly used.

The present is, in many respects, a more reflective volume than its predecessor: for it is scarcely possible to illustrate the Ages of Man without

> Thoughts that do often lie too deep for tears.

This is one of the byways of the book: its highway lies through the crowded city, and upon "the full tide of human affairs;" and the Experiences here set down are, in common parlance, *original*, and have been chiefly garnered throughout a long life, in which truthful observation has been the cardinal aim.

With these few words of introduction, I commend to your indulgence this volume of *Things to be Remembered in Daily Life*, in the hope that its contents may be considered worthy of the reminiscence.

London, March 1863.

ERRATUM.

Page 20. The Terrace, New Palace-yard, Westminster, was taken down in the spring of 1863; the Sun-dial had previously been removed.

CONTENTS.

Time.

Life, and Length of Days.

The School of Life.

Business-Life.

Home Traits.

The Spirit of the Age.

World-Knowledge.

Conclusion.

THINGS TO BE REMEMBERED.

Time.

The conventional personification of Time, with which every one is familiar, is the figure of Saturn, god of Time, represented as an old man, holding a scythe in his hand, and a serpent with its tail in its mouth, emblematical of the revolutions of the year: sometimes he carries an hour-glass, occasionally winged; to him is attributed the invention of the scythe. He is bald, except a lock on the forehead; hence Swift says: "Time is painted with a lock before, and bald behind, signifying thereby that we must take him (as we say) by the forelock; for when it is once passed, there is no recalling it."

The scythe occurs in Shirley's lines, written early in the seventeenth century:

> The glories of our blood and state
> Are shadows, not substantial things;
> There is no armour against fate;
> Death lays his icy hand on kings.
> Sceptre and crown
> Must tumble down,
> And in the dust be equal made
> With the poor crooked scythe and spade.

Shakspeare prefers the scythe:

> Time doth transfix the flourish set on youth,
> And delves the parallels in beauty's brow,
> Feeds on the rarities of nature's truth,
> And nothing stands but for his scythe to mow.

The stealthiness of his flight is also told by Shakspeare:

> Let's take the instant by the forward top;
> For we are old, and our quick'st decrees
> The inaudible and noiseless foot of Time
> Steals ere we can effect them.

Mayne thus quaintly describes his flight:

Time is the feather'd thing,
And whilst I praise
The sparklings of thy locks, and call them rays,
Takes wing—
Leaving behind him, as he flies,
An unperceived dimness in thine eyes.

Gascoigne also thus paints the flight:

The heavens on high perpetually do move;
By minutes' meal the hour doth steal away,
By hours the days, by days the months remove,
And then by months the years as fast decay;
Yea, Virgil's verse and Tully's truth do say,
That Time flieth, and never clasps her wings;
But rides on clouds, and forward still she flings.

Shakspeare pictures him as the fell destroyer:

Misshapen time, copesmate of ugly night;
Swift subtle post, carrier of grisly care;
Eater of youth, false slave to false delight,
Base watch of woes, sin's pack-horse, virtue's snare:
Thou nursest all, and murderest all that are.

And Spenser brands him as

Wicked Time, that all good thoughts doth waste,
And workes of noblest wits to naught outweare.

The present section partakes much of the aphoristic character, which has its recommendatory advantages.—Bacon says: "Aphorisms representing a knowledge broken do invite men to inquire further; whereas methods, carrying the show of a total, do secure men as if they were at farthest." Again: "Nor do apophthegms only serve for ornament and delight, but also for action and civil use, as being the edge-tools of speech, which cut and penetrate the knots of business and affairs."

Coleridge is of opinion that, exclusively of the Abstract Sciences, the largest and worthiest portion of our knowledge consists of Aphorisms; and the greatest and best of men is but an Aphorism.

"Truths, of all others the most awful and interesting, are too often considered as so true, that they lose all the power of truth, and lie bedridden in the dormitory of the soul, side by side with the most despised and exploded errors.

"There is one way of giving freshness and importance to

the most commonplace maxims,—that of reflecting on them in direct reference to our own state and conduct, to our own past and future being."

Mature and sedate wisdom has been fond of summing up the results of its experience in weighty sentences. Solomon did so; the wise men of India and Greece did so; Bacon did so; Goethe in his old age took delight in doing so.

Lucretius has his philosophical view of Time, which Creech has thus Englished:

> Time of itself is nothing, but from Thought
> Receives its rise, by lab'ring fancy wrought
> From things consider'd, while we think on some
> As present, some as past, or yet to come.
> No thought can think on Time,
> But thinks on things in motion or at rest.

Ovid has some illustrations, which Dryden has thus translated:

> Nature knows
> No steadfast motion, but or ebbs or flows.
> Ever in motion, she destroys her old,
> And casts new figures in another mould.
> Even times are in perpetual flux, and run,
> Like rivers from their fountains rolling on.
> For Time, no more than streams, is at a stay,—
> The flying hour is ever on her way;
> And as the fountain still supplies her store,
> The wave behind impels the wave before;
> Thus in successive course the minutes run,
> And urge their predecessor minutes on,
> Still moving, ever anew; for former things
> Are set aside, like abdicated kings;
> And every moment alters what is done,
> And innovates some act till then unknown.
>
> * * * *
>
> Time is th' effect of motion, born a twin,
> And with the worlds did equally begin:
> Time, like a stream that hastens from the shore,
> Flies to an ocean where 'tis known no more:
> All must be swallow'd in this endless deep,
> And motion rest in everlasting sleep.
>
> * * * *
>
> Time glides along with undiscover'd haste,
> The future but a length behind the past,
> So swift are years.
>
> * * * *
>
> Thy teeth, devouring Time! thine, envious Age!
> On things below still exercise your rage;
> With venom'd grinders you corrupt your meat,
> And then, at ling'ring meals, the morsels eat.

The comparison to a river is more amply developed by a modern poet:

The lapse of time and rivers is the same:
Both speed their journey with a restless stream;
The silent pace with which they steal away,
No wealth can bribe, no prayers persuade to stay:
Alike irrevocable both when past,
And a wide ocean swallows both at last.
Though each resembles each in every part,
A difference strikes, at length, the musing heart:
Streams never flow in vain; where streams abound,
How laughs the land with various plenty crown'd!
But time, that should enrich the nobler mind,
Neglected, leaves a dreary waste behind.

An old playwright makes him a fisher by the stream:

Nay, dally not with time, the wise man's treasure,
Though fools are lavish on't—the fatal fisher
Hooks souls, while we waste moments.

Horace has some lines, thus paraphrased by Oldham:

Alas! dear friend, alas! time hastes away,
Nor is it in your power to bribe its stay;
The rolling years with constant motion run,
Lo! while I speak, the present minute's gone,
And following hours still urge the foregoing on.
'Tis not thy wealth, 'tis not thy power,
'Tis not thy piety can thee secure;
They're all too feeble to withstand
Gray hairs, approaching age, and thy avoidless end.
When once thy glass is run,
When once thy utmost thread is spun,
'Twill then be fruitless to expect reprieve;
Could'st thou ten thousand kingdoms give
In purchase for each hour of longer life,
They would not buy one gasp of breath,
Nor move one jot inexorable death.

Perhaps there is no illustration in our language more impressive than Young's noble apostrophe, commencing:

The bell strikes one. *We take no note of time*
But from its loss: to give it, then, a tongue
Is wise in man. As if an angel spoke,
I feel the solemn sound. If heard aright,
It is the knell of my departed hours.
Where are they? With the years beyond the flood.
* * * * *

O time! than gold more sacred; more a load
Than lead to fools, and fools reputed wise.
What moment granted man without account?
What years are squandered, wisdom's debt unpaid!
Our wealth in days all due to that discharge.
* * * * *

Youth is not rich in time; it may be poor;
Part with it as with money, sparing; pay
No moment, but in purchase of its worth;
And what's it worth, ask death-beds; they can tell.
Part with it as with life, reluctant; big
With holy hope of nobler time to come.

* * * * *

But why on time so lavish is my song?
On this great theme kind Nature keeps a school
To teach her sons herself. Each night we die—
Each morn are born anew; each day a life;
And shall we kill each day? If trifling kills,
Sure vice must butcher. Oh, what heaps of slain
Cry out for vengeance on us; time destroyed
Is suicide, where more than blood is spilt.

Throw years away!
Throw empires, and be blameless: moments seize;
Heaven's on their wing: a moment we may wish,
When worlds want wealth to buy. Bid day stand still,
Bid him drive back his car, and re-impart
The period past, regive the given hour.
O for yesterdays to come!

How exquisite is this beguiling of time in *Paradise Lost*.

With thee conversing I forget all time;
All seasons, and their change, all please alike.

How beautifully has Burns alluded to these influences, in his "Lines to Mary in Heaven:"

Time but the impression deeper makes,
As streams their channels deeper wear.

The Hon. W. R. H. Spencer has something akin to this in his "Lines to Lady A. Hamilton:"

Too late I stay'd; forgive the crime;
Unheeded flew the hours;
How noiseless falls the foot of Time
That only treads on flow'rs!

Edward Moore, in one of his pleasing Songs, thus points to these charming influences:

Time still, as he flies, adds increase to her truth,
And gives to her mind what he steals from her youth.

The best lessons of life are to be learnt in his school:

Taught by time, my heart has learn'd to glow
For others' good, and melt at others' woe.

How well has Shakspeare expressed this work of the great reconciler:

Time's glory is to calm contending kings,
To unmask falsehood, and bring truth to light,
To stamp its seal on aged things,
To wake the morn, and sentinel the night,
To wrong the wronger, till he render right.

Elsewhere Shakspeare paints him as the universal balm:

Cease to lament for that thou can'st not help,
And study help for that which thou lament'st.
Time is the nurse and breeder of all good.

It is notorious to philosophers, that joy and grief can hasten and delay time. Locke is of opinion that a man in great misery may so far lose his measure, as to think a minute an hour; or in joy make an hour a minute. Shakspeare's "divers paces" of Time is too familiar for quotation here.

Time's Garland is one of the beauties of Drayton's "Elysium of the Muses:"

The garland long ago was worn
As Time pleased to bestow it:
The Laurel only to adorn
The conqueror and the poet.

The Palm his due who, uncontroll'd,
On danger looking gravely,
When fate had done the worst it could,
Who bore his fortunes bravely.

Most worthy of the Oaken wreath
The ancients him esteemed,
Who in a battle had from death
Some man of worth redeemed.

About his temples grave they tie,
Himself that so behaved,
In some strong siege by th' enemy,
A city that hath saved.

A wreath of Vervains heralds wear,
Amongst our garlands named,
Being sent that dreadful news to bear,
Offensive war proclaimed.

The sign of peace who first displays,
The Olive wreath possesses;
The lover with the Myrtle sprays
Adorns his crisped tresses.

In love the sad forsaken wight
The Willow garland weareth;
The funeral man, befitting night,
The baleful Cypress beareth.

To Pan we dedicate the Pine,
Whose slips the shepherd graceth;
Again the Ivy and the Vine
On his front Bacchus placeth.

They who so stanchly oppose innovations, should remember Bacon's words: "Every medicine is an innovation, and he that will not apply new remedies must expect new evils; for time is the greatest innovator; and if time of course alter things to the worse, and wisdom and counsel shall not alter them to the better, what shall be the end?"

How much time has to do with our successes is thus solemnly told by the Preacher: "The race is not to the swift, nor the battle to the strong, neither yet bread to the wise, nor yet riches to men of understanding, nor yet favour to men of skill; but time and chance happeneth to them all."—*Ecclesiastes* ix. 11.

How truthfully has Dr. Johnson said: "So little do we accustom ourselves to consider the effects of time, that things necessary and certain often surprise us like unexpected contingencies. We leave the beauty in her bloom, and, after an absence of twenty years, wonder, at our return, to find her faded. We meet those whom we left children, and can scarcely persuade ourselves to treat them as men. The traveller visits in age those countries through which he rambled in his youth, and hopes for merriment in the old place. The man of business, wearied with unsatisfactory prosperity, retires to the town of his nativity, and expects to play away the last years with the companions of his childhood, and recover youth in the fields where he once was young."

Dr. Armstrong, the friend of Thomson, has left this solemn apostrophe on the Wrecks and Mutations of Time:

What does not fade? the tower that long had stood
The crush of thunder and the warring winds,
Shook by the slow but sure destroyer Time,
Now hangs in doubtful ruins o'er its base,
And flinty pyramids and walls of brass
Descend. The Babylonian spires are sunk;
Achaia, Rome, and Egypt moulder down.
Time shakes the stable tyranny of thrones,
And tottering empires rush by their own weight.
This huge rotundity we tread grows old,
And all these worlds that roll around the sun;
The sun himself shall die, and ancient night
Again involve the desolate abyss,
Till the Great Father, through the lifeless gloom,
Extend his arm to light another world,
And bid new planets roll by other laws.

We remember a piece of stage sentiment, beginning

"Time! Time! Time! why ponder o'er thy glass,
And count the dull sands as they pass?" &c.

It was touchingly sung, but had too much of gloom and despondency for the theatre: possibly it may have reminded some of its hearers of their own delinquency.

With what solemnity has our great Dramatic Bard foreshadowed Time's waning:

To-morrow, and to-morrow, and to-morrow,
Creeps in this petty pace from day to day,
To the last syllable of recorded time;
And all our yesterdays have lighted fools
The way to dusty death.

His departure is again sketched in *Troilus and Cressida:*

Time is like a fashionable host,
That slightly shakes his parting guest by th' hand,
But with his arms outstretch'd, as he would fly,
Grasps the incomer.

Sir Walter Scott thus paints Time's evanescence:

Time rolls his ceaseless course.—The race of yore,
Who danced our infancy upon their knee,
And told our marvelling boyhood legends store
Of their strange 'ventures happ'd by land or sea,
How are they blotted from the things that be!

Cowley has this significant couplet:

To things immortal Time can do no wrong,
And that which never is to die for ever must be young.

Yet, what a treasure is this:

My inheritance! how wide and fair!
Time is my estate; to Time I'm heir.
Wilhelm Meister: Carlyle.

"Time is almost a human word, and change entirely a human idea: in the system of nature we should rather say progress than change. The sun appears to sink in the ocean in darkness, but rises in another hemisphere; the ruins of a city fall, but they are often used to form more magnificent structures, as at Rome; but even when they are destroyed, so as to produce only dust, nature asserts her empire over them, and the vegetable world rises in constant youth, and in a period of annual successions, by the labours of man, providing food, vitality, and beauty upon the wreck of monuments which were once raised for purposes of glory, but which are now applied to objects of utility."

As this beautiful passage was written by Sir Humphry Davy nearly three-and-thirty years since, the above use of the word *progress* had nothing to do with the semi-political sense in which it is now commonly employed. Nevertheless, there occur in the writings of our great chemical philosopher occasional views of the advancement of the world in knowledge, and its real authors, with which the progressists of the present day fraternise.

At the above distance, Davy wrote in the following vein: "In the common history of the world, as compiled by authors in general, almost all the great changes of nations are confounded with changes in their dynastics; and events are usually referred either to sovereigns, chiefs, heroes, or their armies, which do, in fact, originate entirely from different causes, either of an intellectual or moral nature. Governments depend far more than is generally supposed upon the opinion of the people and the spirit of the age and nation. It sometimes happens that a gigantic mind possesses supreme power, and rises superior to the age in which he is born: such was Alfred in England, and Peter in Russia. Such instances are, however, very rare; and in general it is neither amongst sovereigns nor the higher classes of society that the great improvers and benefactors of mankind are to be found."—*Consolations in Travel*, pp. 34, 35.

Brilliant as was Davy's own career, it had its life-struggles: his last days were embittered with sufferings, mental as well as physical; and in these moments he may have written these somewhat querulous remarks.

TIME: PAST, PRESENT, AND FUTURE.

Harris, in his *Hermes*, in his disquisition on Time, gives the distinction between the grammatical or conventional phrase, "Present Time," and the more philosophical and abstract "Now," or "Instant." Quoting Nicephorus Blemmides, Harris would define the former as follows: "Present Time is that which adjoins to the Real Now, or Instant, on either side being a limited time made up of Past and Future;

and from its vicinity to that Real Now, said to be Now also itself." Whilst upon the latter term he remarks: "As every Now or Instant always exists in Time, and without being Time is Time's bound; the Bound of Completion to the Past, and the Bound of Commencement to the Future; and from hence we may conceive its nature or end, which is to be the medium of continuity between the Past and the Future, so as to render Time, through all its parts, one Intire and Perfect Whole."

Thus, logically, "Time Present" must be regarded as a mathematical point, having no parts or magnitude, being simply the end of the Past, and the beginning of the Future. Thus, perishing in action and eluding the grasp of thought, it is a nonentity, of which, at best, an intangible and shadowy existence can be predicated:

> Dum loquimur fugerit invida
> Ætas. *Hor.*

And we may ask of it, with its *carpe diem*, its manifold attributes, and imputed influences, as the poet Young does of the King of Terrors:

> Why start at Death? Where is he? Death *arrived*
> Is *past;* not *come*, or *gone*, he's never *here*.
> *Night Thoughts*, iv.

It is, however, in the more conventional sense that the phrase "Present Time" is generally made use of in writing and conversation. So Johnson, in his well-known passage: "Whatever withdraws us from the power of our senses, whatever makes the *past*, the *distant*, or the *future*, predominate over the *present*, advances us in the dignity of thinking beings," &c. Here we have "the Present" invested with the dignity of individual existence, and compared with the Past and the Future, as having duration or extension with these; as if we should speak of a series of numbers, ascending on each side of nothing to infinity, as being divisible into negative, zero, and positive.

Among coincident forms of expression, on the part of writers who have spoken of the "Present Time" in its more precise and philosophical sense, is the following by Cowley, in a note to one of his "Pindarique Odes:" "There are two sorts of Eternity; from the Present backwards to Eternity, and from the present forwards, called by the Schoolmen

Æternitas à parte ante, and *Æternitas à parte post.* These two make up the whole circle of Eternity, which *Present Time* cuts like a *Diameter*."

Carlyle, in his *Essays* ("Signs of the Times"), has this knowledgeful passage: "We admit that the present is an important time; as all present time necessarily is. *The poorest day that passes over us is the conflux of two Eternities*, and is made up of currents that issue from the remotest Past, and flow onwards into the remotest Future. We were wise, indeed, could we discover truly the signs of our own times; and, by knowledge of its wants and advantages, wisely adjust our own position in it. Let us, then, instead of gazing idly into the obscure distance, look calmly around us for a little on the perplexed scene where we stand. Perhaps, on a more serious inspection, something of its perplexity may disappear, some of its distinctive characters and deeper tendencies more clearly reveal themselves; whereby our own relations to it, our own true aims and endeavours in it, may also become clearer."*

Lord Strangford has left these pathetic stanzas:

Time was—when all was fresh, and fair, and bright,
My heart was bounding with delight,
It knew no pain, it felt no aching:
But o'er it all its airy woes
As lightly passed, or briefly staid,
Like the fleet summer-cloud which throws
On sunny lands a moment's shade,
A momentary darkness making.

Time is—when all is drear, and dim, and wild,
And that gay sunny scene which smiled
With darkest clouds is gloomed and saddened;
When tempest-toss'd on passion's tide
Reason's frail bark is madly driven,
Nor gleams one ray its course to guide
From yon o'ercast and frowning heaven,
Till peace is wreck'd and reason maddened.

Time come—but will it e'er restore
The peace my bosom felt before,
And soothe again my aching, tortured breast?
It will, for there is One above
Who bends on all a Father's eye;
Who hears with all a Father's love
The broken heart's repentant sigh,
Calms the vexed heart, and bids the spirit rest.

* Abridged from an excellent Communication, by William Bates, to *Notes and Queries*, 2d series, vol. x. p. 245.

MEASUREMENT OF TIME.

Sir Thomas Browne, treating of Errors regarding Numbers, observes: "True it is that God made all things in number, weight, and measure; yet nothing by them, or through the efficacy of either. Indeed, our days, actions, and motions being measured by time (which is but *motion measured*), whatever is observable in any, falls under the account of some number; which, notwithstanding, cannot be denominated the cause of these events. So do we unjustly assign the power of action even unto time itself; nor do they speak properly who say that time consumeth all things; for time is not effective, nor are bodies destroyed by it, but from the action and passion of their elements in it; whose account it only affordeth, and, measuring out their motion, informs us in the periods and terms of their duration, rather than effecteth or physically produceth the same."*

Time can only be measured by motion: were all things inanimate or fixed, time could not be measured. A body cannot be in two places at the same instant; and if the motion of any body from one point to another were regular and equal, the divisions and subdivisions of the space thus marked over would mark portions of time.

The sun and the moon have served to divide portions of time in all ages. The rising and setting of the sun, the shortening and lengthening of the shadows of trees, and even the shadow of man himself, have marked the flight of time. The phases of the moon were used to indicate greater portions; and a certain number of full moons supplied us with the means of giving historical dates.

Fifteen geographical miles, east or west, make one minute of time. The earth turning on its axis produces the alternate succession of day and night, and in this revolution marks the smallest division of time by distances on its surface.

If each of the 360 degrees into which the circumference of the earth is divided, be subdivided into twenty-four hours, it will be found that 15 degrees pass under the sun during each hour, which proves that 15 degrees of longitude mark one hour of time: thus, as Berlin is nearly 15 degrees east

* *Vulgar and Common Errors*, book iv. chap. xii.

of London, it is almost one o'clock when it is twelve at London.

Time, like bodies, is divisible nearly *ad infinitum.* A second (a mere pulsation) is divided into four or five parts, marked by the vibrations of a watch-balance; and each of these divisions is frequently required to be lessened an exact 2880th part of its momentary duration. It is, however, impossible to see this; for Mr. Babbage, speaking of a piece of mechanism which indicated the 300th part of a second, tells us that both himself and friend endeavoured to stop it twenty times successively at the same point, but could not be confident of even the 20th part of a second.

It has been said that many simple operations would astonish us, did we but know enough to be so; and this remark may not be inapplicable to those who, having a watch losing half a minute per day, wish it corrected, though they may not reflect that as half a minute is the 2880th part of 24 hours, each vibration of the balance, which is only the fifth part of a second, must be accelerated the 2880th part of its instantaneous duration; while to make a watch, losing one minute per week, go correctly, each vibration must be accelerated the 1008th part of its duration, or the 50,400th part of a second.*

Among the early methods of measuring Time, we must not omit to notice Alfred's "Time-Candles," as they have been called. His reputed biographer, Asser, tells us that Alfred caused six tapers to be made for his daily use: each taper, containing twelve pennyweights of wax, was twelve inches long, and of proportionate breadth. The whole length was divided into twelve parts, or inches, of which three would burn for one hour, so that each taper would be consumed in four hours; and the six tapers, being lighted one after the other, lasted twenty-four hours. But the wind blowing through the windows and doors and chinks of the walls of the chapel, or through the cloth of his tent, in which they were burning, wasted these tapers, and consequently they burnt with no regularity; he therefore designed a lantern made of ox or cow horn, cut into thin plates, in which he enclosed the tapers; and thus protecting them from the wind, the period of their burning

* *Time and Timekeepers.* By Adam Thomson, 1842.

became a matter of certainty. But the genuineness of Asser's work is doubted,—so the story is discredited. Nevertheless, there is nothing very questionable in Alfred's reputed method; and it is curious to see that an "improvement" was patented so recently as 1859, which consists in graduating the exterior of candles, either by indentation or colouring at intervals, and equal distances apart, according to the size of the candles. The marks are to consist of hours, half-hours, and, if necessary, quarter-hours; the distance to be determined by the kind of candle used.

Bishop Wilkins, in his *Mathematical Magic*, in the chapter relating to "such engines as did receive a regular and lasting motion from something belonging to their own frame, whether weights or springs, &c.," quotes Pancirollus, "taken from that experiment in the multiplication of wheels mentioned in Vitruvius, where he speaks of an instrument whereby a man may know how many miles or paces he doth go in any space of time, whether or no he pass by water in a boat or ship, or by land in a chariot or coach. They have been contrived also into little pocket instruments, by which, after a man hath walked a whole day together, he may easily know how many steps he hath taken." More curious is "the alarum, mentioned by Walchius, which, though it were but two or three inches big, yet would both wake a man and of itself light a candle for him at any set hour of the night. And those great springs, which are of so great force as to turn a mill (as some have contrived), may be easily applied to more various and difficult labours."

Occasionally, in these old curiosities, we trace anticipations of some of the scientific marvels of the present day. Thus, when the Grand Duke of Tuscany, in 1669, visited the Royal Society at Arundel House, he was shown "a clock, whose movements are derived from the vicinity of a loadstone; and it is so adjusted as to discover the distance of countries, at sea, by the longitude." The analogy between this clock and the electrical clock of the present day is not a little remarkable. The Journal-book of the Society for 1669 contains many allusions to "Hook's magnetic watch going slower or faster according to the greater or less distance of the loadstone, and so moving regularly in every posture."

On the occasion of the visit of illustrious strangers, this clock and Hook's magnetic watches were always exhibited as great curiosities.*

PERIODS OF REST.

The terrestrial day, and consequently the length of the cycle of light and darkness, being what it is, we find various parts of the constitution both of animals and vegetables which have a periodical character in their functions, corresponding to the diurnal succession of external conditions; and we find that the length of the period, as it exists in their constitution, coincides with the length of the natural day.

Man, in all nations and ages, takes his principal rest once in twenty-four hours; and the regularity of this practice seems most suitable to his health, though the duration of the time allotted to repose is extremely different in different cases. So far as we can judge, this period is of a length beneficial to the human frame, independently of the effect of external agents. In the voyages made into high northern latitudes, where the sun did not rise for three months, the crews of the ships were made to adhere, with the utmost punctuality, to the habit of retiring to rest at nine, and rising a quarter before six; and they enjoyed, under circumstances apparently the most trying, a state of salubrity quite remarkable. This shows that, according to the common constitution of such men, the cycle of twenty-fours is very commodious, though not imposed on them by external circumstances.

The succession of exertion and repose in the muscular system, of excited and dormant sensibility in the nervous, appears to be fundamentally connected with the muscular and nervous powers, whatever the nature of these may be. The necessity of these alternations is one of the measures of the intensity of these vital energies; and it would seem that we cannot, without assuming the human powers to be altered, suppose the intervals of tranquillity which they require to be much changed. This view agrees with the opinion of the most eminent physiologists. Thus, Cabanis notices the periodical and isochronous character of the desire

* See Weld's *History of the Royal Society*, vol. i. pp. 220, 221.

of sleep, as well as of other appetites. He states that sleep is more easy and more salutary, in proportion as we go to rest and rise every day at the same hours; and observes that this periodicity seems to have a reference to the motions of the solar system.

Now, how should such a reference be at first established in the constitution of man, animals, and plants, and transmitted from one generation of them to another? If we suppose a wise and benevolent Creator, by whom all the parts of nature were fitted to their uses and to each other, this is what we might expect and understand. On any other supposition, such a fact appears altogether incredible and inconceivable.*

RECKONING DISTANCE BY TIME.

In Oriental countries, it has been the custom from the earliest ages to reckon distances by *time*, rather than by any direct reference to a standard of measure, as is commonly reckoned in the present day. In the Scriptures we find distances described by "a day's journey," "three days' journey," and other similar expressions. A day's journey is supposed to have been equal to about thirty-three British statute miles, and denoted the distance that could be performed without any extraordinary fatigue by a foot-passenger; "a Sabbath day's journey" was peculiar to the Jews, being equal to rather less than one statute mile. It may not be in exact accordance with our habits of thought, and usual forms of expression, thus to describe distances by time; yet it seems to possess some advantages. A man knowing nothing of the linear standards of measure employed in foreign countries, would receive no satisfactory information on being told that a particular city, or town, was distant from another a certain number of miles† or leagues,‡ as the case might happen to be. But if he were told that such city or town was distant from another a certain number of *hours* or *days*, there would be something in the account that would com-

* Abridged from Whewell's *Bridgwater Treatise.*

† In Holland a *mile* is nearly equal to three and three-quarters; in Germany it is rather more than four and a half; and in Switzerland it is about equal to five and three-quarters British miles.

‡ A *league* in France is equal to two and three-quarters; in Spain to four; in Denmark to four and three-quarters; in Switzerland to five and a half; and in Sweden to six and three-quarters British miles.

mend itself to his understanding. A sea-voyage is oftener described by reference to time than to *distance.* We frequently hear persons inquire how many *weeks* or *months* it will occupy to proceed to distant parts of the world, but they rarely manifest any great anxiety about the number of *miles.* This mode of computation seems especially applicable to steam navigation: a voyage by a steam-packet, under ordinary circumstances, being performed with such surprising regularity, that it might, with greater propriety, be described by minutes, or hours, or days, than by miles.

SUN-DIALS.

Sun-dials are little regarded but as curiosities in these days; although the science of constructing Sun-dials, under the name of Gnomonics, was, up to a comparatively recent period, part of a mathematical course. As long as watches were scarce, and clocks not very common, the dial was an actual time-keeper. Of the mathematical works of the seventeenth century which are found on book-stalls, none are so common as those on Dialling.

Each of the old dials usually had its monitory inscription; and although the former have mostly disappeared, the mottoes have been preserved, so that all their good is not lost.

The stately city of Oxford, which Waagen declared it was worth a special journey from Germany to see, has, upon its churches and colleges, and in their lovely gardens, several dials. Christopher Wren, when a boy of fifteen at Wadham College, designed on the ceiling of a room a reflecting dial, embellished with various devices and two figures, Astronomy and Geometry, with accessories, tastefully drawn with a pen, and bearing a Latin inscription; but his more elaborate work is the large and costly dial which he erected at All Souls' College, of which he was a Fellow.

The Rev. W. Lisle Bowles was a sincere respecter of dials. In the garden of his parsonage at Bremhill he placed a Sun-dial—a small antique twisted column, gray with age, and believed to have been the dial of the abbot of Malmesbury, and counted his hours at the adjoining lodge; for it was taken from the garden of the farmhouse, which had originally been the summer retirement of this mitred lord: it is of monastic character, but a more ornate capital has been added, which bears the date of 1688; it has the following inscription by the venerable Canon·

To count the brief and unreturning hours,
This Sun-dial was placed among the flowers,
Which came forth in their beauty—smiled and died,
Blooming and withering round its ancient side.
Mortal, thy day is passing—see that Flower,
And think upon the Shadow and the Hour.

From beneath a venerable yew, which has seen the persecution of the loyal English clergy, you look into the adjoining churchyard of Bremhill, on an old Sun-dial, once a cross. Bowles tells us: "The *cross* was found broken at its foot, probably by the country iconoclasts of the day. I have brought the interesting fragment again into light, and placed it conspicuously opposite to an old Scotch fir in the churchyard, which I think it not unlikely was planted by Townson on his restoration. The accumulation of the soil of centuries had covered an ascent of four steps at the bottom of this record of silent hours. These steps have been worn in places, from the act of frequent prostration or kneeling by the forefathers of the hamlet, perhaps before the church existed." Upon this old dial Bowles wrote one of his most touching poems, of which these are the opening verses:

So passes silent o'er the dead thy shade,
  Brief Time! and hour by hour, and day by day,
The pleasing pictures of the present fade,
  And like a summer-vapour steal away.

And have not they, who here forgotten lie
  (Say, hoary chronicler of ages past),
Once more thy shadow with delighted eye,
  Nor thought it fled,—how certain and how fast?

Since thou hast stood, and thus thy vigil kept,
  Noting each hour, o'er mould'ring stones beneath,
The Pastor and his flock alike have slept,
  And "dust to dust" proclaim'd the stride of death.

Any thing that reminds us of the lapse of time should remind us also of the right employment of time in doing whatever business is required to be done.

A similar lesson is solemnly conveyed in the Scripture motto to a Sun-dial: "The night cometh, when no man can work." Another solemn injunction is conveyed in the motto to a Sun-dial erected by Bishop Copleston in a village near which he resided: "Let not the sun go down upon your wrath" (*Ephesians* iv. 26).

A more subtle motto is, "Septem sine horis;" signifying that there are in the longest day seven hours (and a trifle over) during which the Sun-dial is useless.

Upon the public buildings and in the pleasure-grounds of Old London the Sun-dial was placed as a silent monitor to those who were sailing on the busy stream of time through its crowded haunts and thoroughfares, or seeking meditation in quiet nooks and plaisances of its river mansions and garden-houses. Upon churches the dial commonly preceded the clock: Wren especially introduced the dial in his churches.

Sovereigns and statesmen may have reflected beside the palace-dials upon the fleetingness of life, and thus have learned to take better note of time. Whitehall was famous for its Sun-dials. In Privy Garden was a dial set up by Edward Gunter, professor of astronomy at Gresham College (and of which he published a description), by command of James I., in 1624. A large stone pedestal bore four dials at the four corners, and "the great horizontal concave" in the centre; besides east, west, north, and south dials at the sides. In the reign of Charles II. this dial was defaced by an intoxicated nobleman of the Court; upon which Marvell wrote:

> This place for a dial was too unsecure,
> Since a guard and a garden could not defend;
> For so near to the Court they will never endure
> Any witness to show how their time they misspend.

In the court-yard facing the Banqueting-house was another curious dial, set up in 1669 by order of Charles II. It was invented by one Francis Hall, *alias* Lyne, a Jesuit, and professor of mathematics at Liège. This dial consisted of five stages rising in a pyramidal form, and bearing several vertical and reclining dials, globes cut into planes, and glass bowls; showing, "besides the houres of all kinds," "many things also belonging to geography, astrology, and astronomy, by the sun's shadow made visible to the eye." Among the pictures were portraits of the king, the two queens, the Duke of York, and Prince Rupert. Father Lyne published a description of this dial, which consists of seventy-three parts: it is illustrated with seventeen plates: the details are condensed in No. 400 of the Mirror. About

1710, William Allingham, a mathematician in Canon-row, asked 500*l.* to repair this dial: it was last seen by Vertue, the artist and antiquary, at Buckingham House.

The bricky towers of St. James's palace had their Sun-dials; and in the gardens of Kensington palace and Hampton Court palace are to this day superb dials.

Upon a house-front in the Terrace, New Palace Yard, Westminster, is a Sun-dial, having the motto from Virgil, "Discite justitiam, moniti," which had probably been inscribed upon the old clock-tower of the palace, in reference to its having been built with a fine that had been levied on the Chief Justice of the King's Bench for altering a record.

The Inns of Court, where time runs its golden sand, have retained a few of their Sun-dials. In Lincoln's Inn, on two of the old gables, are: 1. A southern dial, restored in 1840, which shows the hours by its gnomon, from 6 A.M. to 4 P.M., and is inscribed, "Ex hoc monumento pendet æternitas." 2. A western dial, restored in 1794 and 1848, from the different situation of its plane, only shows the hours from noon till night: inscription, "Quam redit nescitis horam." And in Serle's-court (now New-square), on the west side, was a dial inscribed, "Publica privatis secernite, sacra prophanis."

Gray's Inn has lost its Sun-dials: but in the gardens was a dial, opposite Verulam Buildings, not far from Bacon's summer-house; and the turret of the great Hall had formerly a southern declining dial, with this motto, "Lux diei, lex Dei."

Furnival's Inn had its garden and dial, which disappeared when the old Inn buildings were taken down in 1818, and the Inn rebuilt.

Staple Inn had upon its Hall a well-kept dial, above a luxuriant fig-tree.

Clement's Inn had, in its small garden, a kneeling figure supporting a dial,—one of the leaden garden embellishments common in the last century. In New Inn, adjoining, the Hall has a large vertical Sun-dial, motto: "Time and Tide tarry for no man."

Lyon's Inn, which had been an Inn "since 1420, or sooner," had, in 1828, an old Sun-dial, which had lost its gnomon and most of its figures.

The Temple garden, Inner and Middle, has each a large pillar Sun-dial; the latter very handsome. There are vertical dials in various courts; but the old dial of Inner Temple terrace, with its "Begone about your business,"—in reality the reply of a testy bencher to the painter who teased him for an inscription,—disappeared in the year 1828. There remain three dials with mottoes: Temple-lane, "Pereunt et imputantur;" Essex-court, "Vestigia nulla retrorsum;" Brick-court, "Time and tide tarry for no man;" and in Pump-court and Garden-court are two dials without mottoes. Charles Lamb has this charmingly reflective passage, suggested by the Temple dials:

What an antique air had the now almost effaced sun-dials, with their moral inscriptions, seeming coevals with that Time which they measured, and to take their revelations of its flight immediately from heaven, holding correspondence with the fountain of light! How could the dark line steal imperceptibly on, watched by the eye of childhood, eager to detect its movement, never catched, nice as an evanescent cloud, or the first arrests of sleep!

> And yet doth beauty like a dial-hand
> Steal from his figure, and no pace perceived!

What a dead thing is a clock, with its ponderous embowelments of lead and brass, its pert or solemn dulness of communication, compared with the simple altar-like structure and silent heart-language of the old dial! It stood as the garden god of Christian gardens. Why is it almost every where vanished? If its business be superseded by more elaborate inventions, its moral uses, its beauty, might have pleaded for its continuance. It spoke of moderate labours, of pleasures not protracted after sunset, of temperance and good hours. It was the primitive clock, the horologe of the first world. Adam could scarce have missed it in Paradise. It was the measure appropriate for sweet plants and flowers to spring by, for the birds to apportion their silver warblings by, for flocks to pasture and be led to fold by. The shepherd 'carved it out quaintly in the sun,' and, turning philosopher by the very occupation, provided it with mottoes more touching than tombstones. It was a pretty device of the gardener, recorded by Marvell, who, in the days of artificial gardening, made a dial out of herbs and flowers:

> How well the skilful gardener drew,
> Of herbs and flowers, this dial new!
> Where from above, the milder sun
> Does through a fragrant zodiac run:
> And, as it works, the industrious bee
> Computes its time as well as we.
> How could such sweet and wholesome hours
> Be reckon'd, but with herbs and flowers?
>
> *From "The Garden."*

Another noted dial gave name to a locality of the metropolis, which has known many mutations, viz. Seven Dials, built in the time of Charles II. for wealthy tenants. Evelyn notes, 1694: "I went to see the building near St. Giles's, where Seven Dials make a star from a Doric pillar placed in the middle of a circular area, said to be by Mr. Neale (the introducer of the late lotteries), in imitation of Venice, now set up here for himself twice, and once for the state."

> Where famed St. Giles's ancient limits spread,
> An in-rail'd column rears its lofty head:
> Here to seven streets seven dials count their day,
> And from each other catch the circling ray:
> Here oft the peasant, with inquiring face,
> Bewilder'd trudges on from place to place;
> He dwells on every sign with stupid gaze,
> Enters the narrow alleys' doubtful maze,
> Tries every winding court and street in vain,
> And doubles o'er his weary steps again.
>
> Gay's *Trivia*, book ii.

The seven streets were Great and Little Earl, Great and Little White Lion, Great and Little St. Andrew's, and Queen; though the dial-stone had but six faces, two of the streets opening into one angle. The column and dials were removed in June 1773, to search for a treasure said to be concealed beneath the base. They were never replaced; but in 1822 were purchased of a stone-mason, and the column was surmounted with a ducal coronet, and set up on Weybridge Green as a memorial to the late Duchess of York, who died at Oatlands in 1820. The dial-stone is now a stepping-stone at the adjoining Ship inn.*

The Sun-dial was also formerly used with a compass. The Hon. Robert Boyle relates, "that a Boatman one day took out of his pocket a little Sun-dial, furnished with an excited needle to direct how to set it, such dials being used among mariners, not only to show them the hour of the day, but to inform them from what quarter the wind blows."

A Cape Town Correspondent of *Notes and Queries* describes a Sun-dial and compass in his possession, made by "Johann Willebrand, in Augsburg, 1848:" it has a curious perpetual calendar attached, and is of highly finished work in silver, parcel-gilt. Another Sun-dial and compass is mentioned as made by Butterfield, at Paris: it is small, of silver, and horizontal; upon its face are engraved dials for several latitudes, and at the back a table of principal cities; it is set by a compass, and the gnomon adjusted by a divided

* The *Town and Country Magazine*, edited by Albert Smith.

arc. The N. point of the compass-box is *fixed* in a position to allow for variation, probably at Paris; and, judging from this, it would appear to have been made about 1716.*

We should also notice the pocket ring-dial, such as that which gave occasion to the Fool in the Forest of Arden to "moral on the time:"

> And then he drew a dial from his poke,
> And, looking on it with lack-lustre eye,
> Says, very wisely, "It is ten o'clock."

This is a ring of brass, much like a miniature dog-collar, and has, moving in a groove in its circumference, a narrower ring with a boss, pierced by a small hole to admit a ray of light. The latter ring is made movable, to allow for the varying declination of the sun in the several months of the year, and the initials of these are marked in the ascending and descending scale on the larger ring, which bears also the motto:

> Set me right, and use me well,
> And i ye time to you will tell.

The hours are lined and numbered on the opposite concavity. When the boss of the sliding ring is set, and the ring is suspended by the ring directly towards the sun, a ray of light passing through the hole in the boss impinges on the concave surface, and the hour is told with fair accuracy. Mr. Thomas Q. Couch, of Bodmin, thus describes this Dial in *Notes and Queries*, 3d series, No. 36. Mr. Charles Knight, in his *Pictorial Shakspeare*, has engraved a dial of this kind, as an illustration of *As you like it.*

Mr. Redmond, of Liverpool, describes the old pocket ring-dial as common in the county of Wexford some twenty-five years ago: there was hardly a farm-house where one could not be had. The same Correspondent of *Notes and Queries*, 3d series, No. 39, describes a door-sill marked with the hour for every day in the year: the sill had a full southern aspect, so that when the sun shone, the time could be read as correctly as by any watch.

Another Correspondent of *Notes and Queries*, 2d series, No. 38, has an ingenious pocket-dial, sold by one T. Clarke: it is merely a card, with a small plummet hanging by a thread, and a gnomon, which lies flat on the card, but, when

* N. T. Heineken; *Notes and Queries*, 3d series.

lifted up, casts the shadow to indicate the hour of the day, and also the hours of sunrise and sunset.

In the United Service Museum, Whitehall, is a Sun-dial, with a burning-glass arranged to fire a small gun at noon; also a large Universal Dial, with a circle showing minutes; and another large Universal Dial, with horizontal plate and spirit-level.

Suppose we collect a few of the monitory inscriptions on dials in various places. Hazlitt, in a graceful paper "On a Sun-dial," tells us that

Horas non numero nisi serenas

is the motto of a Sun-dial near Venice; and the same line is painted in huge letters over the Sun-dial in front of an old farmhouse near Farnworth, in Lancashire.

At Habden Bridge, in Yorkshire, is this quaint motto:

Quod petis, umbra est.

Canon Bowles, in his love of the solemn subject, prescribed the following, with paraphrastic translations:

Morning Sun.—Tempus volat.
Oh! early passenger, look up—be wise,
And think how, night and day, *time onward flies.*

Noon.—Dum tempus habemus, operemur bonum.
Life steals away—this hour, oh! man, is lent thee.
Patient to work the work of Him who sent thee.

Setting Sun.—Redibo, tu nunquam.
Haste, traveller, the sun is sinking now:
He shall return again, but never thou.

Over the Sun-dial on an old house in Rye:

Tempus edax rerum.*

Underneath it:

That solar shadow,
As it measures life, it life resembles too.

In Brading churchyard, Isle of Wight, on a Sun-dial fixed to what appears originally to have been part of a churchyard cross, is the motto:

Hora pars vitæ.

Near the porch of Milton church, Berks, is:

Our Life's a flying Shadow; God's the Pole,
Death, the Horizon, where our sun is set;
The Index, pointing at him, is our Soul,
Which will, through Christ, a Resurrection get.

* We remember this motto for many years beneath a large figure of Time, executed in Coade and Seeley's composition, and placed at the corner of the lane leading from Westminster Bridge Road to Pedlar's Acre.

Butler has this couplet:

> True as the dial to the sun,
> Although it be not shin'd upon.
> *Hudibras*, part iii. canto 2.

Upon this Dr. Nash notes: "As the dial is invariable, and always open to the sun whenever its rays can show the time of day, though the weather is often cloudy, and obscures its lustre: so true loyalty is always ready to serve its king and country, though it often suffers great afflictions and distresses."

There cannot be a more faithful indicator, according to Barton Booth's song:

> True as the needle to the pole,
> Or as the dial to the sun.

After all, the *sun*-dial is but an occasional timekeeper; a defect which the pious Bishop Hall ingeniously illustrates in the following beautiful Meditation "On the Sight of a Dial:" "If the sun did not shine upon this dial, nobody would look at it: in a cloudy day it stands like an useless post, unheeded, unregarded; but, when once those beams break forth, every passenger runs to it, and gazes on it.

"O God, while thou hidest thy countenance from me, methinks all thy creatures pass by me with a willing neglect. Indeed, what am I without thee? And if thou have drawn in me some lines and notes of able endowments; yet, if I be not actuated by thy grace, all is, in respect of use, no better than nothing; but when thou renewest the light of thy loving countenance upon me, I find a sensible and happy change of condition: methinks all things look upon me with such cheer and observance, as if they meant to make good that word of thine, *Those that honour me, I will honour:* now, every line and figure, which it hath pleased thee to work in me, serve for useful and profitable direction. O Lord, all the glory is thine. Give thou me light: I will give others information: both of us shall give thee praise."

The Pyramids of Egypt, the most ancient and the most colossal structures on the earth,—the purpose and appropriation of which has been much controverted by antiquaries and men of science,—have been considered by some to have served as Sun-dials. Sir Gardner Wilkinson does not pretend to explain the real object for which these stupendous monuments were constructed, but feels persuaded that they have served for tombs, and have also been intended for astronomical purposes. " The form of the exterior might lead to many useful calculations. They stand exactly due north and south; and while the direction of the faces to the east and west might serve to fix the return of a certain period of the year, the shadow cast by the sun, or the time of its coinciding with their slope, might be observed for a similar purpose."

There is an interesting association of the Great Pyramid with the ambitious dream of one of the world's celebrities, which may be noticed here. When Napoleon I. was in Egypt, in 1799, he rode on a camel to the Great Pyramid and the Sphinx, that relic of mystic grandeur. Karl Girardet has painted this impressive visit; and the picture has been engraved by Gautier, and inscribed, " Forty Centuries look down upon him."

Charles Mackay has written a graceful poem as a pendent to this print; in which the poet makes the young Napoleon thus invoke the colossal monuments:

Ye haughty Pyramids !
Thou Sphinx, whose eyeless lids
On my presumptuous youth seem bent in scorn !
What though thou'st stood
Coeval with the flood,
Of all earth's monuments the earliest born,
And I so mean and small,
With armies at my call,
Am recent in thy sight as grass of yestermorn !

Yet in this soul of mine
Is strength as great as thine,
O dull-eyed Sphinx that wouldst despise me now;
Is grandeur like thine own,
O melancholy stone,
With forty centuries furrow'd on thy brow;
Deep in my heart I feel
What time shall yet reveal,
That I shall tower o'er men, as o'er these deserts thou.

The dreamer of empire proceeds, bespeaking:

Nations yet to be,
Surging from Time's deep sea,
Shall teach their babes the name of great Napoleon.

But hear the reply of the decaying oracle:

Over the mighty chief
There came a shadow of grief.
The lips gigantic seemed to move and say,
"Know'st thou his name that bid
Arise yon Pyramid?
Know'st thou who placed me where I stand to-day?
Thy deeds are but as sand
Strewn on the heedless land:
Think, little mortal, think, and pass upon thy way!

Pass, little mortal, pass!
Grow like the vernal grass—
The autumn sickle shall destroy thy prime.
But nations shout the word
Which ne'er before they heard,
The name of glory, fearful yet sublime.
The Pharaohs are forgot,
Their works confess them not:
Pass, hero! pass,—poor straw upon the gulf of Time!"

t will be remembered how Napoleon's disastrous Egyp- campaign ended; and how he secretly embarked for ıce, and read during his passage both the Bible and Koran with great assiduity.

ımong the interesting memorials of Mary Queen of s at Holyrood Palace, Edinburgh, there remains the -dial placed in the centre of the palace-garden, and ılly denominated "Queen Mary's Dial."

; is the apex of a richly-ornamented pedestal, which rests upon a gonal base, consisting of three steps. The form of the 'horologe' is angular; for though its principal sections are pentagonal, yet from terminating in pyramidal points, and being diametrically opposed ch other, again connected by triangular interspaces, it presents no than twenty sides, on which are placed twenty-two dials, inserted circular, semicircular, and triangular cavities. Between the dials he royal arms of Scotland, with the initials M. R., St. Andrew, St. ge, *fleurs-de-lis*, and other emblems. This memorial carries us back y three centuries, when Holyrood was a palace

Where "Mary of Scotland" kept her court.

THE HOUR-GLASS.

The use of the Hour-glass can be traced to ancient ece. In Christie's Greek Vases, one is engraved from a abæus of sardonyx, in the Towneley collection: it is tly like the modern hour-glass. The first mention of it rs in a Greek tragedian named Bato. On a bas-relief ıe Mattei Palace, of the marriage of Thetis and Peleus, pheus holds an hour-glass; and from Athenæus it ap- s that persons, when going out, carried it about with them, as we do a watch. In a woodcut in Hawkins's *History of Music*, the frame is more solid, and the glass probably slipped in and out. There is another cut of one in Boissard, held by Death, precisely of the modern form.

The hour or sand-glass is liable to the objection, that it requires a horary attendant, as is intimated in the glee:

Five times by the taper's light
The hour-glass we have turned to-night.

But the Hour-glass is a better measurer of time than is generally imagined. The flow of the sand from one bulb to another is perfectly equable, whatever may be the quantity of sand above the aperture. The stream flows no faster when the upper bulb is almost full than when it is almost empty; the lower heap not being influenced by the pressure of the heap above.* Bloomfield, in one of his rural tales, "The Widow to her Hour-glass," sings:

I've often watched thy streaming sand,
And seen the growing mountain rise,
And often found life's hope to stand
On props as weak in wisdom's eyes:
Its conic crown
Still sliding down,
Again heaped up, then down again:
The sand above more hollow grew,
Like days and years still filtering through,
And mingling joy and pain.

Ford, contemporary with Massinger, has this impressive picture of the primitive time-keeper:

Minutes are number'd by the fall of sands,
As, by an hour-glass, the span of time
Doth waste us to our graves; and we look on it.
An age of pleasures, revell'd out, comes home
At last, and ends in sorrow: but the life,
Weary of riot, numbers every sand,
Wailing in sighs, until the last drop down;
So to conclude calamity in rest: numbering wasted life.

How cleverly the old dramatist, Shirley, illustrates this philosopher in glass:

Let princes gather
My dust into a glass, and learn to spend
Their hour of state, that's all they have; for when
That's out, Time never turns the glass again.

The Hour-glass has almost entirely given place to the

* Le Jeune has painted two children watching with wonder the sand flowing in the hour-glass.

more useful, because to a greater extent self-acting, instrument; and it is now seldom seen except upon the table of the lecturer or private teacher, in the study of the philosopher, in the cottage of the peasant, or in the hand of the old emblematic figure of Time.* We still sometimes see it in the workshop of the cork-cutter. The half-minute glass is still employed on board ship; and the two and a half or three minute glass for boiling an egg with exactness.

Preaching by the Hour-glass was formerly common; and public speakers are *timed*, in the present day, by the same means. In the churchwardens' books of St. Helen's, Abingdon, date 1599, is a charge of fourpence for an hour-glass for the pulpit; in 1564, we find in the books of St. Katherine's, Christ Church, Aldgate, "paid for an hour-glass that hangeth by the pulpit when the preacher doth make a sermon, that he may know how the hour passeth away—one shilling;" and in the books of St. Mary's, Lambeth, 1579 and 1615, are similar entries. Butler, in *Hudibras*, alludes to pulpit hour-glasses having been used by the Puritans: the preacher having named the text, turned up the glass; and if the sermon did not last till the sand was out, it was said by the congregation that the preacher was lazy; but if, on the other hand, he continued much longer, they would yawn and stretch till the discourse was finished. At the old church of St. Dunstan-in-the-West, Fleet-street, was a large hour-glass in a silver frame, of which latter, when the instrument was taken down, in 1723, two heads were made for the parish staves. Hogarth, in his "Sleepy Congregation," has introduced an hour-glass on the west side of the pulpit. A very perfect hour-glass is preserved in the church of St. Alban, Wood-street, Cheapside; it is placed on the right of the reading-desk within a frame of twisted columns and arches, supported on a spiral column: the four sides have angels sounding trumpets; and each end has a line of crosses *patées* and fleurs-de-lis, somewhat resembling the imperial crown.

CLOCKS AND WATCHES.

The clock was also the horologe of our old poets, from the Latin *horologium:*

> He'll watch the horologe a double set,
> If drink rock not his cradle.—*Othello,* act ii. sc. 3.

Drayton calls the cock the country horologe.

Rabelais thus capriciously ridicules the use of the clock: "The greatest loss of time that I know, is to count the hours. What good comes of it? Nor can there be any greater dotage in the world, than for one to guide and direct his course by the sound of a bell, and not by his own judgment and discretion." In similar exuberance has this gay satirist said: "There is only one quarter of an hour in

* The Hour-glass is the sign of Calvert's Brewery, in Upper Thames-street.

human life passed ill, and that is between the calling for the reckoning and paying it."

With more serious purpose has Sir Walter Scott, in his "Lay of the Imprisoned Huntsman," thus anathematised the clock and the dial:

> I hate to learn the ebb of time
> From yon dull steeple's drowsy chime,
> Or mark it as the sunbeams crawl
> Inch after inch along the wall.

Richard II., in the dungeon of Pomfret Castle, soliloquises more solemnly:

> Now hath Time made me his numb'ring clock:
> My thoughts are minutes, and with sighs they jade
> Their watches on to mine eyes, the outward watch
> Whereto my finger, like a dial's point,
> Is pointing still, in cleansing them from tears.
> Now, sir, the sound that tells what hour it is,
> Are clamorous groans, that strike upon my heart,
> Which is the bell: so sighs, and tears, and groans
> Show minutes, times, and hours.

Lucian, who died A.D. 180, refers to an instrument, mechanically constructed with water, which reported the hours by a bell. "Before the time of Jerome" (born A.D. 332), says Browne, "there were horologies that measured the hours, not only by drops of water in glasses, called *clepsydra*, but also by sand in glasses, called *clepsummia*." It was the clepsydra to which Lucian alludes. When the water, which was constantly dripping out of the vessel, reached a certain level, it drew away, by means of a rope connected with the piston in the water-vessel, the ledge on which a weight rested; and the falling of this weight, which was attached to a bell, caused it to strike. This, perhaps, was the earliest kind of striking clock.

A public striking clock may well be termed the regulator of society: it reminds us of our engagements, and announces the hours for exertion or repose; and in the silence of night it tells us of the hours that are past, and how many remain before day.

The earliest public clock set up in England was that with three bells, which was placed in the clochard or bell-tower of the Palace at Westminster, built by Edward III. in 1365-6: the palace was then the most frequent residence of the king and his family; and the three bells were "usually rung at Coronations, Triumphs, Funeralls of Princes, and their Obits."* This bell-tower stood very near to the site of the great clock-tower of the new palace; the gilding of the exterior of which cost no less than 1500*l.*

A public clock is a public monitor; and the dimensions of its dial, and works, and striking-bell add much to the solemnity of its proclaiming the march of time. The great clocks in the International Exhibition of 1862 were among its colossal marvels.

The clocks of St. Paul's Cathedral, Westminster Palace, and the Royal Exchange, are three of the largest clocks in London. The St. Paul's hour-hands are the height of a tall man; the hour struck by this clock has been heard at midnight on the terrace of Windsor Castle; and from the telegraph station on Putney-heath the hour has been read by the St. Paul's clock-face without the aid of a telescope: the hour-numerals are 2 feet 2½ inches in height. This clock once struck thirteen, which being heard by a sentinel, accused of being asleep at his post at that hour, was the means of saving his life; this striking thirteen was caused by the lifting-piece holding on too long.

The former church of St. Paul, Covent Garden, built by Inigo Jones, contained within the pediment a pendulum-clock, made by Richard Harris in 1641, and stated by an inscription in the vestry to be the first pendulum-clock made.†

The Horse Guards Clock is properly described by Mr. Denison as "a superstitiously venerated and bad clock;" it is minutely described by Mr. B. L. Vulliamy in the *Curiosities of London*, pp. 378-380.

St. James's Palace Clock, made by Clay, clockmaker to George II., strikes the hours and quarters upon three bells; it requires to be wound up every day, and originally had

* *Archæologia*, vol. xxxvii.

† Cunningham's *Handbook*, 2d edit. p. 386. If this inscription be correct, it negatives the claim of Huyghens to having first applied the pendulum to the clock, about 1657; although Justus Bergen, mechanician to the Emperor Rodolphus, who reigned from 1576 to 1612, is said to have attached one to a clock used by Tycho Brahe. Inigo Jones, the architect of St. Paul's, having been in Italy during the time of Galileo, it is probable that he communicated what he heard of the pendulum to Harris. Huyghens, however, violently contested for the priority; while others claimed it for the younger Galileo, who, they asserted, had, at his father's suggestion, applied the pendulum to a clock in Venice which was finished in 1649.—Adam Thomson's *Time and Timekeepers*, pp. 67, 68.

but one hand. We were told by the late Mr. B. L. Vulliamy, that when the gatehouse was repaired in 1831, the clock was removed, and not put up again, on account of the roof being reported unsafe to carry the weight. The inhabitants of the neighbourhood then memorialised William IV. for the replacement of the timekeeper: the King, having ascertained its weight, shrewdly inquired how, if the tower-roof was not strong enough to carry the clock, it was safe for the number of persons occasionally seen upon it to witness processions, &c. The clock was forthwith replaced, and a minute-hand was added, with new dials: the original dials were of wainscot, in a great number of very small pieces curiously dovetailed together.

Trinity College, Cambridge, has a double-striking clock, put up by the famous Dr. Bentley; striking, as it used to be said, once for Trinity and once for his former college, St. John's, which had no clock.

The clock of St. Clement's Danes, in the Strand, strikes twice; the hour being first struck on a larger bell, and then repeated on a smaller one; so that if the first has been miscounted, the second may be more correctly observed.

Wren has introduced the gilt projecting dial in several of the City churches: that at St. Magnus, London Bridge, was the gift of Sir Charles Duncomb, who, it is related, when a poor boy, had once to wait upon London Bridge a considerable time for his master, whom he missed through not knowing the hour; he then vowed that if ever he became successful in the world, he would give to St. Magnus a public clock, that passengers might see the time; and this dial proves the fulfilment of his vow. It was originally ornamented with several richly gilded figures: upon a small metal shield inside the clock are engraven the donor's arms, with this inscription: "The gift of Sir Charles Duncomb, Knight, Lord Major, and Alderman of this ward; Langley Bradley fecit, 1709."

The former church of St. Dunstan-in-the-West, Fleet-street, within memory possessed one of London's wonders: it had a large gilt dial overhanging the street, and above it two figures of savages, life-size, carved in wood, and standing beneath a pediment, each having in his right hand a club, with which he struck the quarters upon a suspended bell, moving his head at the same time. To see the men strike was considered very attractive; and opposite St. Dunstan's was a famous field for pickpockets, who took advantage of the gaping crowd. So it had long been; for Ned Ward, in his *London Spy*, says: "We added to the number of fools, and stood a little, making our ears do penance to please our eyes, with the conceited notion of their (the puppets') heads and hands, which moved to and fro with as much deliberate stiffness as the two wooden horologists at St. Dunstan's when they strike the quarters." Cowper thus describes them in his *Table-Talk:*

> When labour and when dulness, club in hand,
> Like the two figures at St. Dunstan's, stand,
> Beating alternately, in measur'd time,
> The clockwork tintinnabulum of rhyme,
> Exact and regular the sounds will be,
> But such mere quarter-strokes are not for me.

These figures and the clock were put up in 1671. Among those who were struck by their oddity was the third Marquis of Hertford, born in 1777: "When a child, and a good child, his nurse, to reward him, would take him to see *the giants* at St. Dunstan's; and he used to say that when he grew to be a man *he would buy those giants*" (Cunningham's *Handbook of London*). Many a child of rich parents may have used the same words; but in the present case the Marquis kept his word. When the old church of St. Dunstan was taken down, in 1830, Lord Hertford attended the second auction-sale of the materials, and purchased the clock, bells, and figures for 200*l.*; he had them placed at the entrance to the grounds of his villa in the Regent's Park, thence called St. Dunstan's Villa; and here the figures do duty to the present day.

These automata remind us of the Minute-Jacks in Shakspeare's *Timon of Athens*, generally interpreted as Jacks of the Clock-house:

> You fools of fortune, trencher friends, time's flies,
> Cap and knee slaves, vapours, and minute-jacks.

Still, the Minute-Jacks only struck hours and quarters; and the term is rather thought to mean "fellows that watch their minutes to make their advantage, time-servers." There is no doubt that by the "Jack that keeps the stroke," in *Richard III.*, is meant the Jack of the Clock-house.*

A much more noteworthy sight than the Fleet-street clock-figures is possessed by the Londoners of the present day in the Time-ball Signal upon the roof of the Electric Telegraph Office, No. 448 West Strand.

The signal consists of a zinc ball, 6 feet in diameter, supported by a rod, which passes down the centre of a column, and carries at the base a piston, which, in its descent, plunges into a cast-iron air-cylinder; the escape of the air being regulated so as at pleasure to check the momentum of the ball, and prevent concussion. The raising ot the ball, half-mast high, takes place daily at 10 minutes to 1 o'clock; at 5 minutes to 1 it is raised to the full height; and at 1 precisely, and simultaneously with the fall of the Time-ball at Greenwich Observatory (by which navigators correct their chronometers), it is liberated by the galvanic current sent from the Observatory, through a wire laid for that purpose. The same galvanic current which liberates the Ball in the Strand moves a needle upon the transit-clock of the Observatory, the time occupied by the transition being about 1-3000th part of a second; and by the unloosing of the machinery which supports the ball, less than one-fifth part of a second. The true moment of one o'clock is therefore indicated by the first appearance of the line of light between the dark cross over the ball and the body of the ball itself. There is a similar Time-ball upon the roof of a clockmaker's in Cornhill.

At Edinburgh, also, is a Time-ball connected with a Time-gun signal, consisting of a large iron cannon, in the Half-moon Battery, at the Castle; which cannon, having been duly loaded and primed some time between twelve and one o'clock, is fired off precisely at the latter hour by an electric influence from the corrected Mean-time of the Royal Observatory, at a distance of three-quarters of a mile; which, however, first passes to another clock close to the gun, and thus affords a short fraction of a second *before* one o'clock for the train of processes; so that the actual final flash of the exploding gun in the Castle occurs absolutely coincidently with the tick of the sixtieth second of the corrected mean-time clock in the Royal Observatory. The whole is well described by Professor Piazzi Smith, Astronomer-Royal for Scotland, in *Good Words*, 1862, part iv.

We now return to the details of the great London Clocks. Mr. Dent undertook the construction of the Royal Exchange Clock in 1843: it was required to be superior to any public clock in England, and to satisfy certain conditions

* Nares's *Glossary*.

proposed for the first time by the Astronomer-Royal, and such as could not be satisfied by any clock of the common construction. Mr. Dent had then no factory of his own for making large clocks, and he could not get the clock made for him; "but with the energy and genius by which that remarkable man raised himself from a tallow-chandler's apprentice to the position of the first horologist in the world, he set up a factory for himself at a great expense, and made the clock there; and of this, the first turret-clock he had ever made, the Astronomer-Royal certified, in 1845, that it not only satisfied his conditions, but that Mr. Dent had made some judicious improvements upon his suggestions, and that he had no doubt it was the best public clock in the world."* It is true to a second of time, and has a compensation-pendulum.

The Westminster Palace Clock, designed by Mr. Denison, has four dials, each 22½ feet wide: they are not the largest in the world, being considerably less than the dial at Mechlin; but there is no other clock in the world which has to work four dials of such great width, especially a clock going 8½ days. St. Paul's Clock has only two 17-feet dials, and is wound up every day, which makes a vast difference in the power and strength required. Each pair of hands weighs above 2 cwt.: they are made of gun-metal, instead of sheet-iron or copper. The hour-sockets are iron tubes, 5 inches in diameter; the dials are of cast-iron framework, filled with opal glass, and stand out 5 feet from the main walls.

The size of public dials is often very inadequte to their height, and the distance at which they are intended to be seen. They ought to be at least one foot in diameter for every ten feet of height above the ground, and in many cases more, whenever the dial will be seen far off. Now, the clock-dials of St. Pancras, Euston-square, are but 6½ feet in diameter, though at the height of 100 feet, and therefore are much too small.

The Clock, of silver-gilt, presented by Henry VIII. to Anne Boleyn on the morning of their marriage, is one of the earliest chamber-clocks in the kingdom: the case is richly chased and engraved, and on the weights are the initial letters of Henry and Anne, with true-lovers' knots.

* *Denison on Clocks.*

This clock was purchased at the Strawberry Hill sale in the year 1842, for 110*l.*, and is now in the collection of Queen Victoria.

We may here mention that the late Duke of Sussex possessed, at Kensington Palace, an invaluable collection of the early as well as the most perfect specimens of Timekeepers, among which was "Harrison's first Clock, the forerunner of that invaluable machine, without which the compass itself would be but an imperfect guide to the mariner."*

John Harrison received for his improved chronometers, in 1749, the Copley Medal; and, thus encouraged by the Royal Society, and by the hope of sharing the reward of 20,000*l.* offered by Parliament for the discovery of the longitude, Harrison produced in 1758 a time-keeper, which was sent for trial on a voyage to Jamaica. After 161 days, the error of the instrument was only one minute five seconds, and the maker received from the nation 5000*l.* For other chronometers, subjected, with perfect success, to a trial in a voyage to Barbadoes, Harrison received 10,000*l.* more. Dr. Stukeley writes of this ingenious man: "I passed by Mr. Harrison's house at Barrow, that excellent genius of clock-making, who bids fair for the golden prize for the discovery of the longitude. I saw his famous clock last winter at Mr. George Graham's: the sweetness of its motion, the contrivances to take off friction, to defeat the lengthening and shortening of the pendulum through heat and cold, and to prevent the disturbance of motion by that of the ship, cannot be sufficiently admired."—*Ms. Journal.*†

An exact measure of time is of the utmost importance to many of the sciences. Horology is indispensable to astronomy, in which the variation even of two or three seconds is of the greatest consequence. By means of a clock the Danish astronomer, Roemer, was enabled to discover that the eclipses of Jupiter's satellites took place a few seconds later than he had calculated, when the earth was in that part of its orbit the farthest from Jupiter. Speculating on the cause of this phenomenon, he calculated that light was

* *Adam Thomson.*

† There is an odd traditionary story told of a Watch at Somerset House. A little above the entrance-door to the Stamps and Taxes is a white watch-face,—of which it is told, that when the wall was being built, a workman had the misfortune to fall from the scaffolding, and was only saved from destruction by the ribbon of his watch, which caught in a piece of projecting work. In thankful remembrance of his wonderful preservation, he is said to have inserted his watch into the face of the wall. Such is the popular belief, and hundreds of persons go to Somerset House to see this fancied memento, and hear the above tale. But the watch-face was placed in its present position many years ago by the Royal Society, as a meridian mark for a portable transit instrument in one of the windows of the anteroom. Captain Smyth assisted in mounting the instrument, and perfectly recollects the watch-face placed against the opposite wall.

not propagated instantaneously, but took time to reach us; and, from calculations founded on this theory, light has been discovered to dart through space with a velocity of about 192,000 miles in a second: thus, the light of the sun takes eight minutes to reach the earth.

Horology has also enabled us to discover that when the wind passes one mile per hour, it is scarcely perceptible; while at the rate of one hundred miles per hour it acquires sufficient force to tear up trees, and destroy the produce of the earth. And, without the aid of a seconds-clock, it would have been scarcely possible to ascertain that a cannon-ball flies at the rate of 600 feet in a second.

The use of Chronometers in geography and navigation is well known; since it is only necessary to ascertain the exact difference in time between two places, to determine their distance east or west of each other.

Graham applied the motion of a Clock showing sidereal time to make a telescope point in the direction of any particular star, even when before the horizon.

Alexander Cummins made a Clock for George III. which registered the height of the barometer during every day throughout the year. This was effected by a circular card, of about 2 feet in diameter, being made to turn round once in a year. The card was divided by radii lines into 365 divisions, the months and days of the month being marked round the edge, while the usual range of the barometer was indicated in inches and tenths by circular lines described from the centre. A pencil with a fine point pressed on the card by a spring, and, held by an upright rod floating on the mercury, faithfully marked the state of the barometer; the card, being carried forward by the clock, brought each day to the pencil. Wren proposed to have a clock constructed on a similar principle, to register the position and force of the wind; which idea has been adopted.

In the Armoury of George IV. was a model of a small cannon, with a clock attached to the lock in such a manner that the trigger could be discharged at any desired time by setting the clock as an alarum.

Breguet contrived a Clock to set a Watch to time. This clock is of the size of a chamber-clock, and has a fork and support on a top to carry the watch. When the clock strikes twelve, a piece of steel like a needle rises, and entering a hole in the rim of the watch-case, comes in contact with a piece which carries the minute-hand, and by pressure makes the hand of the watch correspond with that of the clock, provided the difference be not more than twenty minutes.

The same artist constructed for George IV. a Chronometer which had two pendulums, one making the machine show mean time, the other to make it act as a metronome by beating the time for music. This pendulum was merely a small ball attached to a slight chain carried round a pulley, on the centre of which was an index, which, when brought to any of the musical measures engraved on the scale, shortened or lengthened the chain, so as to cause the pendulum to perform its oscillations in the time required, and a hammer struck on a bell the beats contained in each bar; these would be silently struck by placing a piece of wood between the hammer and the bell; the musical time was also indicated by the seconds-hand of the clock.

A certain dynamical theory of chemistry has been propounded, founded upon precipitations and decompositions taking place in a definite space. Time forms, too, the very key by which alone we can be admitted to a proper view of the archives of the ancient world. Want of time for the due development of the geological periods, for a long season, hindered men's conceptions upon this subject from taking a sharp, clear cast of thought. Linnæus constructed a *Clock of Flora*—a dial of flowers, each opening and shutting at an appointed time.*

By a series of comparisons with Pendulums placed at the surface and the interior of the earth, the Astronomer-Royal has ascertained the variation of gravity in descending to the bottom of a deep mine, as the Harton coal-pit, near South Shields. By calculations from these experiments, he has found the mean density of the earth to be 6·566, the specific gravity of water being represented by unity. In other words, it has been ascertained by these experiments that if the earth's mass possessed every where its average density, it would weigh, bulk for bulk, 6·566 times as much as water. The immediate result of the computations of the Astronomer-Royal is: supposing a clock adjusted to go true

* *The Relations of Science*, by J. M. Ashley.

time at the top of the mine, it would gain $2\frac{1}{4}$ seconds per day at the bottom. Or it may be stated thus: that gravity is greater at the bottom of a mine than at the top by $\frac{1}{19190}$th part.*

The Electric Clock is an invention of our own time. An ordinary clock consists essentially of a series of wheels acting on each other, and carrying round, as they revolve, the hands which mark the seconds, minutes, and hours. The wheels are moved by the falling of a weight, or the unwinding of a spring; and the rate at which they revolve is determined by the length of a pendulum made to oscillate by the wheels. In electric or (as they should rather be called) electro-magnetic clocks, there are neither weights nor springs; so that they never run down, and never require to be wound up. To produce motion, electricity is employed alternately to make and remake an electro-magnet, or alternately to reverse the poles of a permanent magnet, which, by lifting up and letting fall, or attracting and repelling a lever, moves the wheels.

M. Bouilly endeavoured to show that character was much influenced by Time-keepers. He describes two young persons who were allowed to select Watches for themselves: one chose a plain watch, being told that its performance could be depended on; the other, attracted by the elegance of a case, decided upon one of inferior construction. The possessor of the good Watch became remarkable for punctuality; while the other, although always in a hurry, was never in time, and discovered that, next to being too late, there is nothing worse than being too early.

The choice of a good Watch is, however, a difficult matter: none but a good workman is capable of forming a correct opinion; and a Watch must be bad indeed for an inexperienced eye to detect the errors either of the principle or its construction; even a trial of a year or two is no proof, for wear seldom takes place within that time; and while a good Watch can but go well, a bad one, by chance, may occasionally do so.

A Watch must not only be well constructed, and on a

* *Letter to James Mather, Esq., South Shields.* See also *Professor Airy's Lecture*, 1854. Baily approximately weighed the earth by another contrivance, described and illustrated in *Things not generally Known*, First Series, which see.

good principle, but the brass must be hard, and the steel properly tempered. The several parts must be in exact proportion, and well finished, so as to continue in motion with the least possible wear. It must also be so made that, when taken to pieces, all its parts may be replaced as firmly as before.

A bad Watch is one in which no more attention has been paid to the proportion of the parts, or durability of the material, than was necessary to make it perform for a time: it is either the production of inefficient workmen, or of those who, being limited in price, are unable to give sufficient time to perfect the work. In some instances these Watches will go well for a time; but as they wear, from friction, they require frequent repair, which cannot be effectually done.

The most useful lesson is, that low price is not exactly another word for cheapness. If you wish to possess a good Watch, apply to a maker of known honesty and ability in the art he professes, and who, therefore, should be implicitly trusted.

It has been said, that "no man ever made a true circle, or a straight line, except by chance;" and the same may be said of any machine which measured time exactly; indeed, positive accuracy can never be attained until an unchangeable material is discovered, of which the works may be constructed. These practical instructions are by Mr. Adam Thomson.

How beautifully has Lord Herbert of Cherbury sung "to his Watch when he could not sleep:"

Uncessant minutes, whilst you move you tell
  The time that tells our life, which though it run
  Never so fast or far, your new begun
Short steps shall overtake: for though life well
May 'scape his own account, it shall not yours.
  You are Death's auditors, that both divide
And sum whate'er that life inspir'd endures,
  Past a beginning; and through you we bide
The doom of fate, whose unrecall'd decree
  You date, bring, execute; making what's new,
  Ill, and good, old; for as we die in you,
You die in time, time in eternity.

EARLY RISING.

Get up, sweet slug-a-bed, and see
The dew-bespangling herb and tree;
Each flower has wept and bowed towards th' east
Above an hour since, yet you are not drest;
Nay, not so much as out of bed,
When all the birds have matins said,
And sung their thankful hymns.—*Herrick.*

"Up with the sun" implies, in common parlance, very early habits, of difficult attainment. But, "we rise with the sun at Christmas: it were but continuing to do so till the middle of April, and without any perceptible change we should find ourselves then rising at five o'clock; at which hour we might continue till September, and then accommodate ourselves again to the change of season, regulating always the time of retiring in the same proportion. They who require eight hours sleep would, upon such a system, go to bed at nine during four months."

Thus wrote Southey, in his loved sojourn upon the Derwent, of which he says:

Hither I came in manhood's active prime,
And here my head hath felt the touch of time.

In our great Public Schools, Early Rising appears to have been practised from very remote periods. A manuscript document, showing the system at Eton College about the year 1560, records that the boys rose at five to the loud call of "Surgite;" they repeated a prayer in alternate verses as they dressed themselves, and then made their beds, and each swept the part of the chamber close to his bed. They then went in a row to wash, and then to the school, where the under-master read prayers at six; then the præpositor noted absentees, and one examined the students' faces and hands, and reported any boys that came unwashed.

The great Lord Burghley, when at St. John's College, Cambridge, was distinguished by the regularity of his conduct, and the intensity of his application: that he might early devote several hours to study, without any hazard of interruption, he was called up by the bell-ringer every morning at four o'clock. Such was the educational basis upon which Cecil laid the foundation of his brilliant but sound reputation; and by which means, conjoined with the strong natural gift of sagacity, and a mind tinctured with piety, he acquired the esteem and confidence successively of three sovereigns, and held the situation of prime minister of England for upwards of half a century.

Of Sir Edward Coke's laborious course of study at the Inner Temple, we have some interesting records. Every morning at three, in the winter season lighting his own fire, he read Bracton, Littleton, the Year Books, and the folio Abridgments of the Law, till the courts met at eight. He then went by water to Westminster, and heard cases argued till twelve, when pleas ceased for dinner. After a short repast in the Inner Temple Hall, he attended "readings" or lectures in the afternoon, and then resumed his private studies till five, or supper-time. This meal being ended, the *moots* took place, when difficult questions of law were proposed and discussed,—if the weather was fine, in the garden by the river-side; if it rained, in the covered walks near the Temple Church. Finally, he shut himself up in his chamber, and worked at his common-place book, in which he inserted, under the proper heads, all the legal information he had collected during the day. When nine o'clock struck, he retired to bed, that he might have an equal portion of sleep before and after midnight.*

Bishop Ken, when a scholar at William of Wykeham's College at Winchester, in the words of his fellow Wykehamist, the Rev. W. Lisle Bowles, on the glimmering and cold wintry mornings, would perhaps repeat to himself—watching the slow morning through the grated window—one of the beautiful ancient hymns composed for the scholars on the foundation:

Jam lucis ordo sydere
   Deum precemur supplices,
Ut in diurnis actibus
   Nos servet a nocentibus.

Now the star of morning light
Rises on the rear of night;
Suppliant to our God we pray,
From ills to guard us through this day.

Rising before the others, he had little to do except apply a candle to a large fagot, in winter, which had been already laid.

* See *School-days of Eminent Men*, by the Author of the present volume. Second edition, 1862.

Ken composed a devotional Manual for the use of the Winchester scholars; but his most interesting compositions are those affecting and beautiful hymns which were sung by himself, and written to be sung in the chambers of the boys, before chapel in the morning, and before they lay down on their small boarded beds at night. Of Ken's own custom of singing his hymn to the Creator at the earliest dawn, Hawkins, his biographer, relates, "that neither his (Ken's) study might be the aggressor on his hours of instruction, nor what he judged duty prevent his improvement, he strictly accustomed himself to but one hour's sleep, which obliged him to rise at one or two o'clock in the morning, or sometimes earlier; and he seemed to go to rest with no other purpose than the refreshing and enabling him with more vigour and cheerfulness to sing his Morning Hymn, as he used to do, to his lute, before he put on his clothes." When he composed those delicious hymns, he was in the fresh morn of life; and who does not feel his heart in unison with that delightful season, when such a strain as this is heard?

> Awake, my soul, and with the sun
> Thy daily stage of duty run;
> Shake off dull sloth, and early rise
> To pay thy morning sacrifice.
>
> * * * *
>
> Lord, I my vows to thee renew;
> Disperse my sins as morning dew.

May we not also say that when the evening hymn is heard, like the sounds that bid farewell to evening's parting plaint, it fills the silent heart with devotion and repose?

> All praise to thee, my God, this night
> For all the blessings of the light;
> Keep me, oh, keep me, King of kings,
> Under thine own almighty wings.
>
> Forgive me, Lord, for thy dear Son,
> The ills that I this day have done;
> That with the world, myself, and thee,
> I, ere I sleep, at peace may be.

Ken died, Bishop of Bath and Wells, in 1711, in his 74th year, and was carried to his grave, in Frome churchyard, by six of the poorest men of the parish, and buried under the eastern window of the church, at *sunrise*, in reference to the words of his Morning Hymn:

Awake, my soul, and *with the sun.*

The same words are sung, to the same tune, every Sunday, by the parish children, in the church of Frome, and over the grave of him who composed the words, and sung them himself, to the same air, nearly two centuries since.

Rubens, the consummate painter, enlightened scholar, skilful diplomatist, and accomplished man of the world, was in the habit of rising very early,—in summer at four o'clock; and he made it a law of his life to begin the day by prayer. After this he went to work, and before his first meal made those beautiful sketches known by the name of *breakfast sketches.* While painting, he habitually employed a person to read to him from one of the classical authors (his favourites being Livy, Plutarch, Cicero, Seneca), or from some eminent poet. This was the time when he generally received his visitors, with whom he entered willingly into conversation on a variety of topics in the most animated and agreeable manner. An hour before dinner was always devoted to recreation; which consisted either in allowing his thoughts to dwell, as they listed, on subjects connected with science or politics,—which latter interested him deeply,—or in contemplating his treasures of art. As work was his great happiness, he indulged but sparingly in the pleasures of the table, and drank but little wine. After working again till the evening, he usually mounted a spirited Andalusian horse, and rode for an hour or two. On his return home, he customarily received a few friends, principally men of learning, or artists, to partake of a frugal supper, and passed the evening in conversation. This active and regular mode of life could alone have enabled Rubens to satisfy all the demands which were made upon him as an artist; for, including copies, the engravings from works of Rubens amount to more than 1500; and the astonishing number of his works, the genuineness of which is beyond all doubt, can only be accounted for by his union of extraordinary diligence with the acknowledged fertility of his productive powers.

John Wesley, at an early age, was sent to the Charterhouse, where he suffered under the tyranny which the elder boys were permitted to exercise. The boys of the higher forms were then in the practice of taking their portion of meat from the younger ones, by the law of the strongest; and during great part of the time that Wesley remained there, a small daily portion of bread was his only food. He strictly performed an injunction of his father's, that he should run round the Charter-house playing-green, of three acres, three times every morning; and to this early practice he attributed his great length of days.

Wesley satisfied himself of the expediency of rising early by experiment, which he describes thus:

> I waked every night about twelve or one, and lay awake for some time. I readily concluded that this arose from my being longer in bed than nature required. To be satisfied, I procured an alarum, which waked me the next morning at seven (near an hour earlier than I rose the day before), yet I lay awake again at night. The second morning I rose at six; notwithstanding this I lay awake the second night. The third morning I rose at five; nevertheless I lay awake the third night. The fourth morning I rose at four, as I have done ever since; and I lay awake no more. And I do not now lie awake, taking the year round, a quarter of an hour together in a month. By the same experiment, rising earlier and earlier every morning, may one find out how much sleep he really wants.

But Wesley's moderation in sleep, and his rigid constancy in rising early, admit of explanation. Mr. Bradburn, who travelled with him almost constantly for years, said that Wesley generally slept several hours in the course of the day; that he had himself seen him sleep three hours together often enough. This was chiefly in his carriage, in which he accustomed himself to sleep on his journeys as regularly, as easily, and as soundly, as if he had gone to bed.

When at Oxford, he formed for himself a scheme of studies: Mondays and Tuesdays were allotted for the Classics; Wednesdays to logic and ethics; Thursdays to Hebrew and Arabic; Fridays to metaphysics and natural philosophy; Saturdays to oratory and poetry, but chiefly to composition in those arts; and the Sabbath to divinity. It appears by his diary, also, that he gave great attention to mathematics. Full of business as he now was, he found time for writing by rising an hour earlier in the morning, and going into company an hour later in the evening: he had generally from ten to twelve hours in the day which he could devote to study: and thus he became alike familiar with the literature of his day, as well as with that of past ages.

Dr. Philip Doddridge attributes the production of his

various writings to his rising early; adding, "the difference between rising at five and seven o'clock in the morning for the space of forty years, supposing a man to go to bed at the same hour at night, is nearly equivalent to the addition of ten years to his life."

Through life, Gibbon the historian was a very early riser. Before the first volume of his *Decline and Fall* had given him celebrity, six o'clock was his usual hour of rising: fashionable parties and the House of Commons brought him down to eight.

The day of the profound German philosopher, Immanuel Kant, was begun early. Precisely at five minutes before five o'clock, winter or summer, Lampe, Kant's servant, who had formerly served in the army, marched into his master's room with the air of a sentinel on duty, and cried aloud in a military tone, "Mr. Professor, the time is come." This summons Kant invariably obeyed without one moment's delay, as a soldier does the word of command—never, under any circumstances, allowing himself a respite, not even under the rare accident of having passed a sleepless night. As the clock struck five, Kant was seated at the breakfast-table, where he drank what he called *one* cup of tea, and no doubt he thought it such; but the fact was, that, in part from his habit of reverie, and in part also for the purpose of refreshing its warmth, he filled up his cup so often, that in general he is supposed to have drunk two, three, or some unknown number. Immediately after, he smoked a pipe of tobacco; during which operation he thought over his arrangements for the day, as he had done the evening before during the twilight.

Thomson, who has advocated early rising more eloquently than any other writer, was himself an indolent man; he usually lay in bed till noon, and his principal time for composition was midnight. One of his early pictures is:

When from the opening chambers of the east,
The morning springs, in thousand liveries drest,
The early larks their morning tribute pay,
And in shrill notes salute the blooming day.
* * * * *
The crowing cock and chattering hen awakes
Dull sleepy clowns, who know the morning breaks.
In his Golden Age of Innocence—
The first fresh dawn then waked the gladdened race

Of uncorrupted man, nor blushed to see
The sluggard sleep beneath its sacred beam,
Then, his charming Summer morn:
Falsely luxurious, will not man awake,
And, springing from the bed of sloth, enjoy
The cool, the fragrant, and the silent hour,
To meditation due, and sacred song?
For is there aught in sleep can charm the wise?
To lie in dead oblivion, losing half
The fleeting moments of too short a life,—
Total extinction of the enlightened soul!
Or else to feverish vanity alive,
Wildered, and tossing through distempered dreams!
Who would in such a gloomy state remain
Longer than Nature craves; when every muse
And every blooming pleasure wait without,
To bless the wildly-devious morning walk?

Lord Chatham, writing to his nephew, January 12, 1754, says: *Vitanda est improba Syren, Desidia*, I desire may be affixed to the curtains of your bedchamber. If you do not rise early, you can never make any progress worth mentioning. If you do not set apart your hours of reading, if you suffer yourself or any one else to break in upon them, your days will slip through your hands unprofitably and frivolously, unpraised by all you wish to please, and really unenjoyed by yourself.

Harford relates of Dr. Burgess, Bishop of Salisbury:

Of his literary labours and self-denying life, writes a clergyman, "few can have any conception. I was frequently admitted to see him on business, even as early as six in the morning, when, rather than detain me, he has seen me in his dressing-room. Often he kindly remarked, 'Your time is not your own, and is as precious to you as mine; scruple not to send to me when you really want to see me.' On one of my early morning visits, about eight o'clock, in the winter, I found him seated in his greatcoat and hat, writing at a table, in a room without a carpet, the floor covered with old folios, and his candles only just extinguished. 'I have been writing and reading,' he said, 'since five o'clock.' At another time I breakfasted with him one morning, by appointment, at his hotel in town; and found him at eight o'clock, about Christmas, writing by candlelight; the whole room being strewed with old books, collected from various places in the metropolis. The untiring perseverance with which he prosecuted his researches for evidence on any particular subject is inconceivable."

Sir Astley Cooper, in one of his Lectures to his pupils, used to say: "The means by which I preserve my own health are: temperance, early rising, and sponging my body every morning with cold water,—a practice I have pursued for thirty years; and though I go from this heated theatre into the squares of the Hospital in the severest winter-nights, with merely silk stockings on my legs, yet I scarcely ever have a cold. An old Scotch physician, for whom I had a great respect, and whom I frequently met professionally in the City, used to say, as we were entering the patient's room, 'Weel, Mister Cooper, we ha' only twa things to keep in meend, and they'll sarve us for here and herea'ter: one is always to have the fear of the Laird before our ees, that 'ill do for herea'ter; and the t'other is to keep your booels open, and that will do for here.' "

William Cobbett, who had great contempt for conventionalities, was an early riser from his boyhood,—when his first occupation was driving the small birds from the turnip-seed and the rooks from the peas; when he trudged with his wooden bottle and his satchel, and was hardly able to climb the gates and stiles; when he weeded wheat, and had a single horse at harrowing barley; drove the team, or held the plough—which employments he apostrophises as "Honest pride, and happy days!" He tells us that to the husbanding well of his time he owed his extraordinary promotion in the army. He says: "I was always ready: if I had to mount guard at ten, I was ready at nine; never did any man or any thing wait one moment for me. Being at an age under twenty years, raised from Corporal to Sergeant-Major at once, over the heads of thirty Sergeants, I naturally should have been an object of envy and hatred; but the habit of early rising really subdued these passions; because every one felt that what I did he had never done, and never could do. Before my promotion, a clerk was wanted to make out the morning report of the regiment. I rendered the clerk unnecessary; and long before any other man was dressed for the parade, my work for the morning was all done, and I myself was on the parade, walking, in fine weather, for an hour perhaps. My custom was this: to get up in summer at daylight, and in winter at four o'clock; shave, dress, and even to the putting of the sword-belt over my shoulder, and having the sword lying on the table before me, ready to hang by my side. Then I ate a bit of cheese, or pork, and bread. Then I prepared my report, which was filled up as fast as the companies brought me in the materials. After this I had an hour or two to read, before the time came for my duty out of doors, unless when the regiment, or part of it, went out to exercise in the morning. When this was the case, and the matter was left to me, I always had it on the ground in such time as that the bayonets glistened in the rising sun; a sight which gave me delight, of which I often think, but which I should in vain endeavour to describe. When I was commander, the men had a long day of leisure before them: they could ramble into the town or into the woods; go to get raspberries, to catch birds, to catch fish, or to pursue any other recreation; and such of them as chose and were qualified, to work at their trades. So that here, arising solely from the early habits of one very young man, were pleasant and happy days given to hundreds."

Elsewhere Cobbett addresses this advice "to a lover:" "Early rising is a mark of industry; and though, in the higher situations of life, it may be of no importance in a mere pecuniary point of view, it is, even there, of importance in other respects: for it is, I should imagine, pretty difficult to keep love alive towards a woman who never sees the dew, never beholds the rising sun, and who constantly comes directly from a reeking bed to the breakfast-table, and there chews about without appetite the choicest morsels of human food. A man might, perhaps, endure this for a month or two without being disgusted; but that is ample allowance of time. And as to people in the middle rank of life, where a living and a provision for children is to be sought by labour of some sort or other, late rising in the wife is certain ruin; and never was there yet an early-rising wife who had been a late-rising girl. If brought up to late rising, she will like it; it will be her habit; she will, when married, never want excuses for indulging in the habit: at first she will be indulged without bounds; to make change afterwards will be difficult; it will be deemed a wrong done to her; she will ascribe it to diminished affection; a quarrel must ensue, or the husband must submit to be ruined, or, at the very least, to see half the fruit of his labour snored and lounged away. And is this being rigid? is it being harsh? is it being hard upon women? Is it the offspring of the frigid severity of the age? It is none of these: it arises from an ardent desire to promote the happiness, and to add to the natural, legitimate, and salutary influence of the female sex. The tendency of this advice is to promote the preservation of their health; to prolong the duration of their beauty; to cause them to be beloved to the last day of their lives; and to give them, during the whole of their lives, weight and consequence, of which laziness would render them wholly unworthy."

When Cobbett had become a public writer, he constantly inveighed against those who

O'er books consumed the midnight oil.

In country or in town, at Barn Elms, in Bolt-court, or at Kensington, he wrote his Registers early in the morning: these, it must be admitted, had force enough; for he said truly, "Though I never attempt to put forth that sort of stuff which the intense people on the other side of the Channel call *eloquence*, I bring out strings of very interesting facts; I use pretty powerful arguments; and I hammer them down so closely upon the mind, that they seldom fail to produce a lasting impression." This he owed, doubtless, to his industry, early rising, and methodical habits.

Daniel Webster, the famous American statesman, unlike most men of his day, usually went to bed by nine o'clock, and rose very early in the morning. General Lynian had heard Webster say, that while in Washington, there were periods when he shaved and dressed himself for six months together by candlelight. The morning was his time for study, writing, thinking, and all kinds of mental labour: from the moment when the first streak of dawn was seen in the east, till nine or ten o'clock in the forenoon, scarcely a moment was lost; and it was then that his work was principally done. Persons who occasionally called upon him as early as ten in the morning, and found him ready to converse with them, wondered when he did his work; for they knew that he did work, yet they rarely, if ever, found him, like other men of business, engaged. The truth was, that when their day's work began, his ended; and while they were indulging in their morning dreams, Webster was up, looking "quite through the deeds of men." This habit, followed from his youth, enabled him to make those remarkable acquisitions of knowledge on all subjects, and afforded him so much leisure to devote to his friends.

The college-life of Albert, Prince Consort of Queen Victoria, presents us with some of the beneficial results of the habit of early rising. The people of England were not a little surprised, at first, to hear that the Queen and the royal Consort were seen walking together at a very early hour on the morning of the very day after their marriage. But, while at Bonn, Prince Albert was particularly distinguished from the other students of the same rank for the salutary habit of getting up early, one which he had uniformly persevered in from his boyhood: therefore, it is very natural that he should have adhered to it after he had come of age, whether in England or in any other country, and be likely to do so all the days of his life. At Bonn, the prince generally rose about half-past five o'clock in the morning, and never prolonged his repose after six. From that hour up to seven in the evening, he assiduously devoted his whole time to his studies, with the exception of an interval of three hours, which he allowed himself for dinner and recreation. At seven he usually went out, and paid visits to those individuals or families who were honoured with his acquaintance.*

To these instances of the remarkable labours which have been accomplished by rising early, it can scarcely be considered necessary to add any thing to enforce the benefits to be derived from the practice. Nevertheless, something has been said on the other side. An able essayist has urged that most people who get up unusually early find that there is nothing to do when they are dressed There are comparatively few mornings in the year when it is pleasant to take an hour's walk before breakfast in the country. Then, if the early riser stays within doors, the sitting-rooms are not ready for his reception. Among the physical inconveniences, this writer shows that the early riser, if not tormented with a consequent headache, is often troubled with a feeling of sleepiness and heaviness through the latter part of the day; and, as far as time goes, he is apt to lose afterwards much more, while he in some way or other compensates himself for his activity, than he gained by the extra hour we are supposing him to have had early in the morning. Then, the moral effect on the early riser,

* *History of the University of Bonn.*

it is said, is to cause in him an exuberant feeling of conscious goodness: he has performed a feat which raises him, by his moral self-approval, above ordinary people, who merely come down to breakfast. There is some truth in all this, which, however, we think to be the exception rather than the rule; for if early rising be the general practice in a house, these minor inconveniences will soon disappear. The above writer is inclined to allow that the objections to early rising may too exclusively rest on exceptional cases. He admits, with great fairness, in favour of the practice, that "if the spare hour can be turned to serious profit, so much the better. Coming at the beginning of the day, it finds the mind tranquil, sanguine, and fresh. The time it gives is likely to be free from interruptions; and the good effect of the study will tell more powerfully than when it has, as it were, the whole day in its grasp, than if it were merely slipt in among the other thoughts and occupations of busier hours. Health, too, is said to profit by early rising; and so many people have stated this as a fact, that it may perhaps be taken for granted."*

THE ART OF EMPLOYING TIME.

The Aristotelian philosopher has well expressed its value by saying, "Nothing is more precious than time; and those who misspend it are the greatest of all prodigals."

Again:

The time of life is short:
To spend that shortness basely, were too long
If life did ride upon a dial's point,
Still ending at the arrival of an hour.

Fuller has this quaint instruction upon our present topic: "Lay down such rules to thyself, of observing stated hours for study and business, as no man shall be able to persuade thee to recede from. For when thy resolutions are once known, as no man of ingenuity will disturb thee, so thou wilt find this method will become not only more practicable, but of singular benefit in abundance of things.

"He that loseth his morning studies, gives an ill precedent to the afternoon, and makes such a hole in the beginning

* *Saturday Review*, March 26, 1859.

of the day, that all the winged hours will be in danger of flying out thereat: think how much work is behind; how slow thou hast wrought in thy time that is past; and what a reckoning thou shouldst make, if thy Master should call thee this day to thine account.

"There is no man so miserable as he that is at a loss how to spend his time. He is restless in his thoughts, unsteady in his counsels, dissatisfied with the present, solicitous for the future.

"Be always employed; thou wilt never be better pleased than when thou hast something to do. For business, by its motion, brings heat and life to the spirits; but idleness corrupts them like standing water.

"Make use of time, if thou valuest eternity. Yesterday cannot be recalled; to-morrow cannot be assured; to-day only is thine, which if thou procrastinatest, thou losest; which loss is lost for ever."

Dr. South, in one of his nervous Discourses, speaking of the uncertainty of the present, says: "The sun shines in his full brightness but the very moment before he passes under a cloud. Who knows what a day, what an hour may bring forth? He who builds upon the present, builds upon the narrow compass of a point; and where the foundation is so narrow, the superstructure cannot be high and strong too."

Sir William Jones, the profound scholar, of whom it was said that if he were left naked and friendless on Salisbury-plain he would nevertheless find the road to fame and riches, left among his manuscripts the following lines on the management of his time, which he had written in India, on a small piece of paper:

Sir Edward Coke:

Six hours in sleep, in law's great study six;
Four spend in prayer—the rest on nature fix.

Rather:

Seven hours to law, to soothing slumbers seven;
Ten to the world allot, and all to heaven.

Dr. Johnson has moralised on Money and Time as "the heaviest burdens of life;" adding, "the unhappiest of mortals are those who have more of either than they know how to use. To set himself free from these incumbrances, one hurries to Newmarket; another travels over Europe; one pulls down his house, and calls architects about him; another buys a seat in the country, and follows his hounds over hedges and through rivers; one makes collections of shells; and another searches the world for tulips and carnations."

Elsewhere Johnson has these pertinent remarks: "Among those who have contributed to the advancement of learning, many have risen to eminence in opposition to all the obstacles which external circumstances could place in their way,—amidst the tumults of business, the distresses of poverty, or the dissipation of a wandering and unsettled state. A great part of the life of Erasmus was one continued peregrination: ill supplied with the gifts of fortune, and led from city to city and from kingdom to kingdom by the hopes of patrons and preferment, hopes which always flattered and always deceived him, he yet found means, by unshaken constancy and a vigilant improvement of those hours which in the midst of the most restless activity will remain unengaged, to write more than another in the same condition could have hoped to read. Compelled by want to attendance and solicitation, and so much versed in common life that he has transmitted to us the most perfect delineation of the manners of his age, he joined to his knowledge of the world such application to books, that he will stand for ever in the first rank of literary heroes. Now, this proficiency he sufficiently discovers, by informing us that the *Praise of Folly*, one of his most celebrated performances, was composed by him on the road to Italy, lest the hours which he was obliged to spend on horseback should be tattled away, without regard to literature."

These are two memorable instances of the employment of minute portions of time. We are told of Queen Elizabeth, that, except when engaged by public or domestic affairs, and the exercises necessary for the preservation of her health and spirits, she was always employed in either reading or writing, in translating from other authors, or in compositions of her own; and that, notwithstanding she spent much of her time in reading the best writings of her own and former ages, yet she by no means neglected that best of books, the Bible; for proof of which, take the Queen's own words: "I walk many times in the pleasant fields of the

Holy Scriptures, where I pluck up the godlisome herbs of sentences by pruning, eat them by reading, digest them by musing, and lay them up at length in the high seat of memory by gathering them together; that so, having tasted their sweetness, I may the less perceive the bitterness of life." Her piety and great good sense were undeniable.

The Chancellor of France, D'Aguesseau, finding that his wife always kept him waiting a quarter of an hour after the dinner-bell had rung, resolved to devote the time to writing a book on jurisprudence; and putting the subject in execution, in course of time produced a work in four quarto volumes. His literary tastes greatly distinguished him from the mass of mere lawyers.

He whose mind the world wholly occupies imagines that no time can be spared for divine duties. But many circumstances in the lives of good men inform him that he is mistaken. The wise statesman, the sound lawyer, the eminent merchant, the skilful physician, the most profound mathematician, astronomer, or general student, will rise up in judgment against the man who endeavours to excuse the observance of his religious duties under the plea of learned or professional employment. Addison, Hale, Thornton, Boerhaave, Bacon, Boyle, Newton, Locke, and many others, prove that while the most important of worldly studies and occupations employed their outward attention, *God rested at their hearts*. The Ethiopian treasurer read Isaiah in his chariot, and Isaac meditated in the fields. The friends of the good Hooker, when they went to visit him at his parsonage, found him with a book in his hand, tending his own sheep. In short, the true Christian will neither want place nor opportunity for devotion, nor for the cultivation of those useful and general talents which may contribute to the benefit or happiness of man.

Lord Woodhouselee, in his *Life of Lord Kames*, has well remarked, that the professional occupations of the best-employed lawyer or the most distinguished judge cannot fill up every interval of his time. The useful respite of vacation, the hours of sickness, the surcease of employment from the infirmities of age,—all necessarily induce seasons of languor, against which a wise man would do well to provide a store in reserve, and an antidote and cordial to cheer and support his spirits. In this light the pursuits of science and literature afford an unbounded field and endless variety of useful occupations; and even in the latest hours of life the reflection on the time thus spent, and the anticipation of an honourable memorial in after ages, are sources of consolation of which every ingenuous mind must fully feel the value. How melancholy was the reflection uttered on his deathbed by one of the ablest lawyers and judges of the last age, but whose mental stores were wholly limited to the ideas connected with his profession, "*My life has been a chaos of nothing!*"

Sir Matthew Hale, one of the most upright judges that ever sat upon the English bench, was of a benevolent and devout, as well as righteous disposition; and in addition to his great legal works, found time to write several volumes on natural philosophy and divinity. His *Contemplations Moral and Divine*, written two centuries since, retain their popularity to this day. Bishop Burnet, his biographer, tells us that "his whole life was nothing else but a continual course of labour and industry; and when he could borrow any time from the public service, it was wholly employed either in philosophical or divine meditation." . . . "He that considers the active part of his life, and with what unwearied diligence and application of mind he despatched all men's business that came under his care, will wonder how he could find time for contemplation; he that considers, again, the various studies he passed through, and the many collections and observations he made, may as justly wonder how he could find any time for action. But no man can wonder at the exemplary piety and innocence of such a life so spent as this was, wherein, as he was careful to avoid every evil word, so it is manifest *he never spent an idle day.*"

At every turn we are defeated through want of due regard to this preciousness of time. "In early life we lay long plans of conduct. After a considerable interval, we find most of our plans unexecuted; we then begin to reflect that if they *are* to be accomplished, a far smaller portion of our time than we had originally allotted to them can be employed in their execution; and, what is perhaps more fatal to our schemes, that portion is uncertain. An awful thought for those who have in their possession many of the chief blessings of life, and are approaching, by a rapid progress, that mortal bourn from whence no traveller returns."*

How much of our time would be saved by the cultivation of the habit of being content to be ignorant of certain subjects! Nothing can be more beneficial to the mind than this habit; since it has thereby a more free and open access to matters of the highest importance.

How much of our time is wasted in paying visits of insincerity! Boileau being one day visited by an indolent person of rank, who reproached him with not having returned his former call; "You and I," replied the satirist, "are upon unequal terms: I lose my time when I pay you a visit; you only get rid of yours when you pay me one."

One of the most familiar methods of taking note of time is by what are usually termed family parties. When these are given on public holidays, the effect is doubtless beneficial. Southey has well remarked: "Festivals, when duly observed, attach men to the civil and religious institutions of their country: it is an evil, therefore, when they fall into disuse." They do more,—in reminding us of the fewer anniversaries we have to witness.

Boyle has these wholesome reflections upon *profuse talkers:* he tells us "that easiness of admitting all Kind of Company, provided men have boldness enough to intrude into ours, is one of the uneasiest Hardships (not to say Martyrdoms) to which Custom has expos'd us, and does really do more Mischief than most Men take notice of; since it does not only keep impertinent Fools in countenance, but encourages them to be very troublesome to Wise Men. The World is pester'd with a certain sort of Praters, who make up in Loudness what their Discourses want in Sense; and because Men are so easie natur'd as to allow the hearing to their Impertinencies, they presently presume that the things they speak are none; and most Men are so little able to discern in Discourse betwixt Confidence and Wit, that to any that will but talk loud enough they will be sure to afford answers. And (which is worse) this readiness to hazard our Patience, and certainly lose our Time, and thereby incourage others to multiply idle

* Brewster's *Meditations for the Aged.*

words, of which the Scripture seems to speak threateningly, is made by Custom an Expression, if not a Duty, of Civility; and so even a Virtue is made accessory to a Fault.

"For my part, though I think these Talkative people worse publick Grievances than many of those for whose prevention or redress Parliaments are wont to be assembled and Laws to be enacted; and though I think their Robbing us of our time a much worse Mischief than those petty Thefts for which Judges condemn Men, as a little Money is a less valuable good than that precious Time, which no sum of it can either purchase or redeem; yet I confess I think that our great Lords and Ladies, that can admit this sort of Company, deserve it: For if such Persons have but minds in any measure suited to their Qualities, they may safely, by their Discountenance, banish such pitiful Creatures, and secure their Quiet, not only without injuring the Reputation of their Civility, but by advancing that of their Judgment."

Sir John Harrington, the epigrammatic poet in the reign of Elizabeth, and a dangler at her court, appears, by the following confession, from his *Breefe Notes and Remembrances*, to have been a disappointed man: "I have spente my time, my fortune, and almost my honestie, to buy false hope, false friends, and shallow praise;—and be it remembered, that he who casteth up this reckoning of a courtlie minnion, will sette his summe like a foole at the ende, for not being a knave at the beginninge. Oh, that I could boaste, with chaunter David, *In te speravi Domine!*"

Many ill-regulated persons thoughtlessly waste their own time simultaneously with that of others. Lord Sandwich, when he presided at the Board of Admiralty, paid no attention to any memorial that extended beyond a single page. "If any man," he said, "will draw up his case, and will put his name to the bottom of the first page, I will give him an immediate reply: where he compels me to turn over the page, he must wait my pleasure."

George III., though always willing and ready for business, disliked (as who does not?) long speeches out of season; and grievously lamented the well-informed but verbose and ill-timed eloquence of his minister, Grenville. "When," such were the King's own words to Lord Bute, "he has wearied me for two hours, he looks at his watch to see if he may not tire me for one hour more."

Paley had an ingenious mode of economising his time, and keeping off these time-wasters. The Earl of Ellenborough is in possession of the only original portrait of the Doctor, which was painted for the earl's father by Romney. Paley was painted with the fishing-rod, by his own particular desire; not because he cared much about fishing, but because while he was so occupied he could keep intruders at a distance, and give his mind to uninterrupted thought. He kept people away, not because they disturbed the fish, but because they disturbed him. *He composed his works while he seemed to fish.**

Sterne, in one of his fascinating Letters, writes: "Time wastes too fast: every letter I trace tells me with what rapidity life follows my pen: the days and hours of it more precious, my dear Jenny, than the rubies about thy neck, are flying over our heads like light clouds of a windy day, never to return more. Every thing presses on; whilst thou art twisting that lock,—see, it grows gray; and every time I kiss thy hand to bid adieu, and every absence which follows it, are preludes to that eternal separation which we are shortly to make."

Thomson's habit of composition while he lay in bed has been mentioned. We knew a reverend vicar who usually composed his sermon in bed, and committed it to paper next morning. Dr. Wallis, who nearly two centuries ago was professor of geometry at Oxford, attained the power of making arithmetical calculations "without the assistance of pen and ink, or aught equivalent thereunto," to such an extent, that he extracted the square root of three down to twenty places of decimals. We must indeed suppose him to have had originally some peculiar aptitude for such calculations; but he describes himself to have acquired it by practising at night and in the dark, when there was nothing to be seen, and nothing to be heard, that would disturb his attention. It is in such uninterrupted intervals that we best learn to think; and Sir Benjamin Brodie† acknowledges

* Communication to *Notes and Queries*, 3d series, No. 47.

† *Psychological Inquiries*, part ii. 1862. The Author died in the autumn of 1862, at his beautiful retreat, Broome Park (formerly Tranquil Dale), at the foot

that in these ways he had not unfrequently derived ample compensation for the wearisome hours of a sleepless night.

Division of time is the grand secret of successful industry. Lockhart, in his *Life of Scott*, shows how effectually the illustrious subject of his memoir found opportunity for unequalled literary labour, even while enjoying all the amusements of a man of leisure. "Sir Walter rose by five o'clock, lit his own fire when the season required one, and shaved and dressed with great deliberation; for," says his biographer, "he was a very martinet as to all but the mere coxcombries of the toilet, not abhorring effeminate dandyism itself so cordially as the slightest approach to personal slovenliness, or even those 'bed-gown and slipper tricks,' as he called them, in which literary men are so apt to indulge. Arrayed in his shooting-jacket, or whatever dress he meant to use till dinner-time, he was seated at his desk by six o'clock, all his papers arranged before him in the most accurate order, and his books of reference marshalled around him on the floor, while at least one favourite dog lay watching his eye just beyond the line of circumvallation. Thus, by the time the family assembled for breakfast, between nine and ten, he had done enough (in his own language) 'to break the neck of the day's work.' After breakfast a couple of hours more were given to his solitary tasks, and by noon he was, as he used to say, 'his own man.' When the weather was bad, he would labour incessantly all the morning; but the general rule was to be out and on horseback by one o'clock at the latest; while, if any more distant excursion had been proposed overnight, he was ready to start on it by ten; his occasional rainy days of unintermitted study forming, as he said, a fund in his favour, out of which

of the fine range of the Betchworth Hills, in Surrey. In the *Inquiries* are some interesting traces of the work having been written in the tranquillity of Broome, and its picturesque characteristics of noble cedars, elms, and chestnuts, stream and sheet of water, and mineral spring. In the opening pages, "the fresh air and quiet of his residence in the country" evidently refers to Broome; and throughout the volume are occasional references to the geniality of the place for the group of philosophers who keep up the mode of dialogue. Sir Benjamin Brodie was some time President of the Royal Society; and it may be worthy of notice, that his two volumes of "Inquiries," in their thoughtful tone and reflective colour, bear some resemblance to the two volumes produced in the retirement of his illustrious predecessor in the Chair of the Royal Society—Sir Humphry Davy; but with this difference,—that Sir Benjamin Brodie's Researches are of more practical application than the speculative Dialogues of our great chemical philosopher, Davy.

he was entitled to draw for accommodation whenever the sun shone with special brightness."

Sir Walter Scott, writing to a friend who had obtained a situation, gave him this excellent practical advice: "You must be aware of stumbling over a propensity, which easily besets you from the habit of not having your time fully employed; I mean what the women very expressively call *dawdling*. Your motto must be *Hoc age*. Do instantly whatever is to be done, and take the hours of recreation after business, and never before it. When a regiment is under march, the rear is often thrown into confusion because the front does not move steadily and without interruption. It is the same thing with business. If that which is first in hand is not instantly, steadily, and readily despatched, other things accumulate behind, till affairs begin to press all at once, and no human brain can stand the confusion. Pray mind this: this is a habit of mind which is very apt to beset men of intellect and talent, especially when their time is not regularly filled up, and left at their own arrangement. But it is like the ivy round the oak, and ends by limiting, if it does not destroy, the power of manly and necessary exertion. I must love a man so well, to whom I offer such a word of advice, that I will not apologise for it, but expect to hear you are become as regular as a Dutch clock,—hours, quarters, minutes, all marked and appropriated. This is a great cast in life, and must be played with all skill and caution."

Coleridge observes: "It would, indeed, be superfluous to attempt a proof of the importance of Method in the business and economy of active or domestic life. From the cotter's hearth, or the workshop of the artisan, to the palace or the arsenal, the first merit, that which admits neither substitute nor equivalent, is, that *every thing is in its place*. Where this charm is wanting, every other merit loses its name, or becomes an additional ground of accusation and regret. Of one by whom it is eminently possessed, we say proverbially, he is like clockwork. The resemblance extends beyond the point of regularity, and yet falls short of the truth. Both do, indeed, at once divide and announce the silent and otherwise undistinguishable lapse of time. But the man of methodical industry and honourable pursuits does more: he realises its ideal divisions, and gives a character and individuality to its moments. If the idle are described as killing time, he may be justly said to call it into life and moral being, while he makes it the distinct object not only of the consciousness, but of the conscience. He organises the hours, and gives them a soul; and that the very essence of which is to fleet away, and ever more *to have been*, he takes up into his own permanence, and communicates to it the imperishableness of a spiritual nature. Of the good and faithful servant, whose energies, thus directed, are thus methodised, it is less truly affirmed, that he lives in time, and that time lives in him. His days, months, and years, as the stops and punctual marks in the records of duties performed, will survive the wreck of worlds, and remain extant when time itself shall be no more."* This is admirable reasoning.

A great deal has been said against routine and red tape, or rather the abuse of the latter; but its proper use has much to do with success. Curran, when Master of the Rolls, once said to Grattan, "You would be the greatest man of your age, Grattan, if you would buy a few yards of red tape, and tie up your bills and papers;" though another version of the anecdote has, "*tie up your thoughts*." This was the fault and misfortune of Sir James Mackintosh: he never knew the use of red tape, and was utterly unfit for the common business of life. That a guinea represented a quantity of shillings, and that it would barter for a quantity of cloth, he was well aware; but the accurate number of the baser coin, or the just measurement of the manu-

* Coleridge, however, was a better preacher than practitioner of what he so urgently recommends. When in his younger days he was offered a share in the *London Journal*, by which he could have made two thousand pounds a year, provided he would devote his time seriously to the interest of the work, he declined,—making the reply, so often praised for its disinterestedness, "I will not give up the country, and the lazy reading of old folios, for two thousand times two thousand pounds; in short, beyond three hundred and fifty pounds a year, I consider money a real evil." The "lazy reading of old folios" led to laziness, the indolent gratification of mind and sense. Degenerating into an opium-eater, and a mere purposeless theoriser, Coleridge wasted time, talents, and health; came to depend, in old age, on the charity of others; and died at last, with every one regretting, even his friends, that he had done nothing worthy of his genius. The world is full of men having Coleridge's faults, without Coleridge's abilities; men who cannot, or will not, see beyond the present; who are too lazy to work for more than a temporary subsistence, and who squander, in pleasure or idleness, energy and health, which ought to lay up a capital for old age.

factured articles to which he was entitled for his gold, he could never learn, and it was impossible to teach him. Hence his life was often an example of the ancient and melancholy struggle of genius with the difficulties of existence.

The tying-up thoughts corresponds with Fuller's aphorism, "Marshall thy thoughts into a handsome method. One will carry twice more weight trussed and perched up in bundles, than when it lies untoward, flapping and hanging about his shoulders. Things orderly fardled up under heads are most portable." This is the plan adopted by lawyers upon their tables. The Duke of Wellington had a table upon which his papers were thus arranged; and, during his absence for any length of time, a sort of lid was placed upon the table and locked, so as to secure the papers without disturbing their arrangement.

The Duke of Wellington is also known to have been an early riser; the advantages of which were illustrated throughout his long life. His service of the Sovereigns and the public of this country for more than half a century,—in diplomatic situations and in councils, as well as in the army,—has scarcely a parallel in British history. His Despatches are the best evidence of his well-regulated mind in education. No letters could ever be more temperately or more perspicuously expressed than those famous documents. They show what immense results in the aggregate were obtained by the Duke, solely in virtue of habits which he had sedulously cultivated from his boyhood—early rising, strict attention to details, taking nothing ascertainable for granted, unflagging industry, and silence, except when speech was necessary, or certainly harmless. His early habit of punctuality is pleasingly illustrated in the following anecdote: "I will take care to be punctual at five to-morrow morning," said the engineer of New London Bridge, in acceptance of the Duke's request that he would meet him at that hour the following morning. "Say a quarter before five," replied the Duke, with a quiet smile; "I owe all I have achieved to being ready a quarter of an hour before it was deemed necessary to be so; and I learned that lesson when a boy."

Whoever has seen "the Duke's bedroom" at Apsley-house, and its plain appointments, will not regard it as a chamber of indolence. It was, a few years since, narrow, shapeless, and ill-lighted; the bedstead small, provided only with a mattress and bolster, and scantily curtained with green silk; the only ornaments of the walls were an unfinished sketch, two cheap prints of military men, and a small portrait in oil: yet here slept the Great Duke, whose "eightieth year was by." In the grounds and shrubbery he took daily walking exercise, where with the garden-engine he was wont to enjoy exertion; reminding one of General Bonaparte at St. Helena, "amusing himself with the pipe of the fire-engine, spouting water on the trees and flowers in his favourite garden."

TIME AND ETERNITY.

Sir Thomas More, when a youth, painted for his father's house in London a hanging with nine pageants, with verses over each. There were Childhood, Manhood, Venus and Cupid, Age, Death, and Fame. In the sixth pageant was painted the image of Time, and under his feet was lying the picture of Fame that was in the sixth pageant. And over this seventh pageant was (spelling modernised):

TIME.

I whom thou seest with horologe in hand
Am named Time, the lord of every hour:
I shall in space destroy both sea and land.
O simple Fame, how darest thou man honour,
Promising of his name an endless flower!
Who may in the world have a name eternal,
When I shall in process destroy the world and all?

In the eighth pageant was pictured the image of Lady Eternity, sitting in a chair under a sumptuous cloth of state, crowned with an imperial crown. And under her feet lay the picture of Time that was in the seventh pageant. And above this eighth pageant was written as follows:

ETERNITY.

Me needeth not to boast: I am Eternity,
The very name signifieth well
That mine empire infinite shall be.
Thou mortal Time, every man can tell,
Art nothing else but the mobility
Of sun and moon changing in every degree;
When they shall leave their course, thou shalt be brought,
For all thy pride and boasting, unto naught.

Life, and Length of Days.

LIFE—A RIVER.

PLINY has compared a River to Human Life; and Sir Humphry Davy was a hundred times struck with the analogy, particularly among mountain scenery. A full and clear River is the most poetical object in nature; and contemplating this, Davy wrote: "The river, small and clear in its origin, gushes forth from rocks, falls into deep glens, and wantons and meanders through a wild and picturesque country, nourishing only the uncultivated tree or flower by its dew or spray. In this, its state of infancy and youth, it may be compared to the human mind, in which fancy and strength of imagination are predominant; it is more beautiful than useful. When the different rills or torrents join, and descend into the plain, it becomes slow and stately in its motions; it is applied to move machinery, to irrigate meadows, and to bear upon its bosom the stately barge;—in this mature state, it is deep, strong, and useful. As it flows on towards the sea, it loses its force and its motion; and at last, as it were, becomes lost and mingled with the mighty abyss of waters."

Again, Life is often compared to a River, because one year follows another, and vanishes like the ripples on its surface. A flood, without ebb, bears us onward: "we can never cast anchor in the river of life," as Bernardin de St. Pierre finely and profoundly observes.

But the comparison can be still further developed. "It is taking a false idea of life," says Cuvier, "to consider it as a single link, which binds the elements of the living body together, since, on the contrary, it is a power which moves and sustains them unceasingly. These elements," he adds, "do not for an instant preserve the same relations and connexions; or, in other words, the living body does not for an instant keep the same state and composition."

But this is only the new enunciation of a very old idea in science. Long before Cuvier, Leibnitz said, "Our body is in a perpetual flux, like a river; particles enter and leave it continually." And long before Leibnitz, physiologists had compared the human body to the famous ship of Theseus, which was always the same ship, although, from having been so often repaired, it had not a single piece with which it was originally constructed. The truth is, that the idea of the continued renovation of our organs* has always existed in science; but it is also true that it has always been disputed.

M. Flourens has proved by direct experiment that the mechanism of the development of the bones consists essentially in a continual irritation of all the parts composing them. But it is the change of *matérial;* for its *form* changes very little. Cuvier has further developed this fine idea:

> In living bodies no molecule remains in its place; all enter and leave it successively: life is a continued whirlpool, the direction of which, complicated as it is, remains always constant, as well as the species of molecules which are drawn into it, but not the individual molecules themselves; on the contrary, the actual material of the living body will soon be no longer in it; and yet it is the depository of the force which will constrain the future material in the same direction as itself. So that the form of these bodies is more essential to them than the material, since this latter changes unceasingly, while the other is maintained.

THE SPRING-TIME OF LIFE.

The Spring-time of Life,—the meeting-point of the child and the man,—the brief interval which separates restraint from liberty,—has a warmth of life, which Dr. Temple thus pictures with glowing eloquence. "To almost all men this period is a bright spot to which the memory ever afterwards loves to recur; and even those who can remember nothing but folly,—folly, of which they have repented, and relinquished,—yet find a nameless charm in recalling such folly as that. For indeed even folly at that age is sometimes the

* One may well say of a given individual, that he lives and is the same, and is spoken of as an identical being from his earliest infancy to old age, without reflecting that he does not contain the same particles, which are produced and renewed unceasingly, and die also in the old state, in the hair and in the flesh, in the bone and in the blood,—in a word, in the whole body.—*Plato; The Banquet.*

cup out of which men quaff the richest blessings of our nature,—simplicity, generosity, affection. This is the seed-time of the soul's harvest, and contains the promise of the year. It is the time for love and marriage, the time for forming life-long friendships. The after-life may be more contented, but can rarely be so glad and joyous. Two things we need to crown its blessings,—one is, that the friends whom we then learn to love, and the opinions which we then learn to cherish, may stand the test of time, and deserve the esteem and approval of calmer thoughts and wider experience; the other, that our hearts may have depth enough to drink largely of that which God is holding to our lips, and never again to lose the fire and spirit of the draught. There is nothing more beautiful than a manhood surrounded by the friends, upholding the principles, and filled with the energy of the spring-time of life. But even if these highest blessings be denied, if we have been compelled to change opinions and to give up friends, and the cold experience of the world has extinguished the heat of youth, still the heart will instinctively recur to that happy time, to explain to itself what is meant by love and what by happiness."*

THE FIRST TWENTY YEARS OF LIFE.

It is a saying of Southey's, "that, live as long as you may, the first twenty years are the longest half of your life. They appear so while they are passing; they seem to have been so when we look back to them; and they take up more room in our memory than all the years that succeed them."

But in how strong a light has this been placed by the American teacher, Jacob Abbott, whose writings have obtained so wide a circulation in England. "Life," he says, "if you understand by it the season of preparation for eternity, is more than half gone; life, so far as it presents opportunities and facilities for penitence and pardon,—so far as it bears on the formation of character, and is to be considered as a period of probation,—is unquestionably more than half gone to those who are between fifteen and twenty.

* *Education of the World.*

In a vast number of cases it is more than half gone even *in duration;* and if we consider the thousand influences which crowd around the years of childhood and youth, winning us to religion, and making a surrender of ourselves to Jehovah easy and pleasant,—and, on the other hand, look forward beyond the years of maturity, and see these influences losing all their power, and the heart becoming harder and harder under the deadening effects of continuance in sin,—we shall not doubt a moment that the years of immaturity make a far more important part of our time of probation than all those that follow."

That pious man, who, while he lived, was the Honourable Charles How, and might properly now be called the honoured, says, that "twenty years might be deducted for education from the threescore and ten, which are the allotted sum of human life; this portion," he adds, "is a time of discipline and restraint, and young people are never easy till they are got over it."

There is indeed during those years much of restraint, of weariness, of hope, and of impatience; all which feelings lengthen the apparent duration of time. Sufferings are not included here; but with a large portion of the human race, in all Christian countries (to our shame be it spoken), it makes a large item in the account; there is no other stage of life in which so much gratuitous suffering is endured,—so much that might have been spared,—so much that is a mere wanton, wicked addition to the sum of human misery, arising solely and directly from want of feeling in others, their obduracy, their caprice, their stupidity, their malignity, their cupidity, and their cruelty.*

PASSING GENERATIONS.

"The deaths of some, and the marriages of others," says Cowper, "make a new world of it every thirty years. Within that space of time the majority are displaced, and a new generation has succeeded. Here and there one is permitted to stay longer, that there may not be wanting a few grave dons like myself to make the observation."

* *The Doctor.*

Man is a self-survivor every year;
Man, like a stream, is in perpetual flow.
Death's a destroyer of quotidian prey:
My youth, my noontide his, my yesterday;
The bold invader shares the present hour,
Each moment on the former shuts the grave.
While man is growing, life is in decrease,
And cradles rock us nearer to the tomb.
Our birth is nothing but our death begun,
As tapers waste that instant they take fire.—*Young.*

Yet, infinitely short as the term of human life is when compared with time to come, it is not so in relation to time past. A hundred and forty of our own generations carry us back to the Deluge, and nine more of antediluvian measure to the Creation,—which to us is the beginning of time; "for time itself is but a novelty, a late and upstart thing in respect of the ancient of days."* They who remember their grandfather, and see their grandchildren, have seen persons belonging to five out of that number; and he who attains the age of threescore, has seen two generations pass away. "The created world," says Sir Thomas Browne, "is but a small parenthesis in eternity, and a short interposition, for a time, between such a state of duration as was before it, and may be after it." There is no time of life, after we become capable of reflection, in which the world to come must not to any considerate mind appear of more importance to us than this; no time in which we have not a greater stake there. When we reach the threshold of old age, all objects of our early affections have gone before us, and in the common course of mortality a great proportion of the later. Not without reason did the wise compilers of our admirable Liturgy place next in order after the form of Matrimony, the services for the Visitation and Communion of the Sick, and for the Burial of the Dead.†

A home-tourist, halting in the quiet churchyard of Mortlake, in Surrey, about half a century since, fell into the following reflective train of calculation of generations:

"I reflected that, as it is now more than four hundred years since this ground became the depository of the dead, some of its earliest occupants might, without an hyperbole, have been ancestors of the whole contemporary English nation. If we suppose that a man was buried in this

* Dr. Johnson. † *The Doctor.*

churchyard 420 years ago, who left six children, each of whom had three children, who again had, on an average, the same number in every generation of thirty years; then, in 420 years, or fourteen generations, his descendants might be multiplied as under:

1st generation	6	8th generation	13,122
2d "	18	9th "	39,366
3d "	54	10th "	118,098
4th "	162	11th "	354,274
5th "	486	12th "	1,062,812
6th "	1458	13th "	3,188,436
7th "	4374	14th "	9,565,308

That is to say, nine millions and a half of persons; or, as nearly as possible, the exact population might at this day be descended in a direct line from any individual buried in this or any other churchyard in the year 1395, who left six children, each of whose descendants have had on the average three children! And, by the same law, every individual who has six children may be the root of as many descendants within 420 years, provided they increase on the low average of only three in every branch. His descendants would represent an inverted triangle, of which he would constitute the lower angle.

"To place the same position in another point of view, I calculated also that every individual now living must have had for his ancestor every parent in Britain living in the year 1125, the age of Henry I., taking the population of that period at 8,000,000. Thus, as every individual must have had a father and mother, or two progenitors, each of whom had a father and mother, or four progenitors, each generation would double its progenitors every thirty years. Every person living may, therefore, be considered as the apex of a triangle, of which the base would represent the whole population of a remote age.

1815.	Living individual	1
1785.	His father and mother	2
1755.	Their fathers and mothers	4
1725.	" "	8
1695.	" "	16
1665.	" "	32
1635.	" "	64
1605.	" "	128
1575.	" "	256
1545.	" "	512
1515.	" "	1,024

1485.	Their fathers and mothers . .	2,048
1455.	,, ,, . .	4,096
1425.	,, ,, . .	8,192
1395.	,, ,, . .	16,384
1365.	,, ,, . .	32,768
1335.	,, ,, . .	65,536
1305.	,, ,, . .	131,072
1275.	,, ,, . .	262,144
1245.	,, ,, . .	524,288
1215.	,, ,, .	1,048,576
1185.	,, ,, .	2,097,152
1155.	,, ,, .	4,194,304
1125.	,, ,, .	8,388,608

That is to say, if there have been a regular co-mixture of marriages, every individual of the living race must of necessity be descended from parents who lived in Britain in 1125. Some districts or clans may require a longer period for the co-mixture, and different circumstances may cut off some families, and expand others; but, in general, the lines of families would cross each other, and become interwoven, *like the lines of lattice-work*. A single intermixture, however remote, would unite all the subsequent branches in common ancestry, rendering the contemporaries of every nation members of one expanded family, after the lapse of an ascertainable number of generations."*

AVERAGE DURATION OF LIFE.

The Assurance of Lives has often been regarded, by weak-minded persons, as an interference with the ways of Providence, which is highly reprehensible. But it can be shown that calculation of lives can be averaged with certainty. Mr. Babbage, in his work on the Assurance of Lives, observes: "Nothing is more proverbially uncertain than the duration of human life, where the maxim is applied to an individual; yet there are few things less subject to fluctuation than the average duration of a multitude of individuals. The number of deaths happening amongst persons of our own acquaintance is frequently very different in different years; and it is not an uncommon event that this number shall be double, treble, or even many times larger in one year than in the next succeeding. If we consider larger societies of individuals, as the inhabitants of a village or

* Sir Richard Phillips's *Morning's Walk from London to Kew.*

small town, the number of deaths is more uniform; and in still larger bodies, as among the inhabitants of a kingdom, the uniformity is such, that the excess of deaths in any year above the average number seldom exceeds a small fractional part of the whole. In the two periods, each of fifteen years, beginning at 1780, the number of deaths occurring in England and Wales in any year did not fall short of, or exceed, the average number one-thirteenth part of the whole; nor did the number dying in any year differ from the number of those dying in the next by a tenth part."

In a paper on Life Assurance, in the *Edinburgh Review*, the Average Mortality of Europe is thus stated: "In England 1 person dies annually in every 45; in France, 1 in every 42; in Prussia, 1 in every 38; in Austria, 1 in every 33; in Russia, 1 in every 28. Thus England exhibits the lowest mortality; and the state of the public health is so improved, that the present duration of existence may be regarded (in contrast to what it was a hundred years ago) as, in round numbers, *four to three*."

The Registrar-General gives the following statistical results: "The average age of life is 33½ years. One-fourth of the born die before they reach the age of seven years, and the half before the seventeenth year. Out of 100 persons, only six reach the age of 60 years and upwards, while only 1 in 1000 reaches the age of 100 years. Out of 500, only 1 attains 80 years. Out of the thousand million living persons, 330,000,000 die annually, 91,000 daily, 3730 every hour, 60 every minute, consequently 1 every second. The loss is, however, balanced by the gain in new births. Tall men are supposed to live longer than short ones. Women are generally stronger than men until their fiftieth year, afterwards less so. Marriages are in proportion to single life (bachelors and spinsters) as 100 : 75. Both births and deaths are more frequent in the night than in the day."

PASTIMES OF CHILDHOOD RECREATIVE TO MAN.

Paley regarded the pleasure which the amusements of childhood afford as a striking instance of the beneficence of the Deity. We have several instances of great men descending from the more austere pursuits to these simple but innocent pastimes. The Persian ambassadors found Agesilaus, the Lacedæmonian monarch, riding on a stick. The ambassadors found Henry the Fourth playing on the carpet with his children; and it is said that Domitian, after he had possessed himself of the Roman empire, amused himself by catching flies. Socrates, if tradition speaks truly, was partial to the recreation of riding on a wooden horse; for which, as Valerius Maximus tells us, his pupil Alcibiades laughed at him. (Is not this the origin of our rocking-horse?) Did not Archytas,

> He who could scan the earth and ocean's bound,
> And tell the countless sands that strew the shore,

as Horace says, invent the children's rattle? Toys have served to unbend the wise, to occupy the idle, to exercise the sedentary, and to instruct the ignorant. To come to our own times: we have heard of a Lord-Lieutenant of Ireland, a man of grave years and thoughts, being surprised playing at leap-frog with his young nephews.

The same desire to unstring the bow, as old Æsop taught, impels sturdy workmen, let loose from their toil, to seek diversion in the amusements of boyhood. Often have we seen scores of men break forth from a factory or printing-office for their dinner-hour, and in great measure disport themselves like schoolboys in a playground.

PLEASURES OF THE IMAGINATION LATE IN LIFE.

Dugald Stewart, in his *Essay on the Cultivation of Intellectual Habits*, predicates, in persons of mature age, what may be termed the enjoyment of a second season of enjoyments far more refined than the first. Thus he says: "Instances have frequently occurred of individuals in whom the power of imagination has, at an advanced period of life, been found susceptible of culture to a wonderful degree. In such men, what an accession is gained to their most refined pleasures! What enchantments are added to their most ordinary perceptions! The mind, awakening, as if from a trance, to a new existence, becomes habituated to the most interesting aspects of life and of nature; the intellectual eye is 'purged of its film;' and things the most familiar and unnoticed disclose charms invisible before. The same objects and events which were lately beheld with indifference occupy now all the powers and capacities of the soul, the contrast between the present and the past serving only to enhance and to endear so unlooked-for an acquisition. What Gray has so finely said of *the pleasures of vicissitude* conveys but a faint image of what is experienced by the man who, after having lost in vulgar occupations and vulgar amusements his earliest and most precious years, is thus introduced at last to a new heaven and a new earth:

> The meanest floweret of the vale,
> The simplest note that swells the gale,
> The common sun, the air, the skies,
> To him are op'ning Paradise."

Nothing can be more deplorable than a man who has outlived the likings, and perchance the innocence, of his early life; which is by no means rare, if they have not grown out of the study and love of nature, for this clings to the heart in all the vicissitudes of life,—in adversity as well as in prosperity; in sickness as well as in health; even to extreme old age, when almost every other worldly source of pleasure is dried up. Hear the testimony of Hannah More, at the age of eighty-two: "The only one of my youthful fond attachments," says she, "which exists still in full force, is a passion for scenery, raising flowers, and landscape gardening." Well indeed will it be for the young if they follow the example of this venerable woman, and early acquire a passion for scenery and flowers. For as they pass through life, they will find the world often frowning upon them, but the flowers will always smile. And it is sweet, in the day of adversity, to be met with a smile.

We remember a touching instance of the love of flowers lighting up the last hours of a botanist who had wooed nature in the picturesque vale of Mickleham, in Surrey. A few short hours before his death, he turned to his niece and said: "Mary, it is a fine morning; go and see if *Scilla verna* is come in flower."

WHAT IS MEMORY?

Man possesses a nervous system pervaded by a nervous force, the modification of which manifests itself to our consciousness in the varied phenomena of what we call Sensation. From Sensation, the next step is to Perception. Sensation, we know, as such, dies away from the consciousness, or rather is obliterated by fresh impressions upon the sensorium. We cannot retain a feeling in perpetuity. But when a definite sensation has been excited, or a distinct experience has been acquired, something remains behind; and upon these *residua*, left in the structure of the nerves, or the cerebral tissues, or the animating soul, and on the permanence of these *residua*, rests the whole possibility of reminiscence. Upon this blending and organisation round the centre of mind-life follows the faculty of Memory, or that power which the mind possesses of making a peculiar representation of an object for itself, of creating a special idea of it by giving greater prominence to some features, and letting others sink away unthought of, till there remains an image, the product of its own free activity, which it can mentally connect with other trains of ideas, and thus multiply, as it were, the bridges by which it can return to it at any period.*

Byron has beautifully personified this paramount image:

> She was a form of life and light,
> That seen became a part of sight;
> And rose, where'er I turned mine eye,
> The Morning-star of Memory!

"Mere abstraction, or what is called absence of mind, is often attributed, very unphilosophically, to a want of memory. La Fontaine, in a dreaming mood, forgot his own child, and, after warmly commending him, observed how proud he should be to have such a son. In this kind of abstraction external things are either only dimly seen, or are utterly overlooked; but the memory is not necessarily asleep. In fact, its too intense activity is frequently the cause of the abstraction. This faculty is usually the

* See an admirable paper on Dr. Morell's *Introduction to Mental Philosophy*, in *Saturday Review;* also *Mysteries of Life, Death, and Futurity*, for the following articles: "What is Memory?" "How the Function of Memory takes place;" "Persistence of Impressions;" "Value of Memory;" "Registration;" and "Decay of Memory;" pp. 69-75.

strongest when the other faculties are in their prime, and fades in old age, when there is a general decay of mind and body. Old men, indeed, are proverbially narrative; and from this circumstance it sometimes appears as if the memory preserves a certain portion of its early acquisitions to the last, though in the general failure of the intellect it loses its active energy. It receives no new impressions, but old ones are confirmed. The brain seems to grow harder. Old images become fixtures. It is recorded of Pascal, that, till the decay of his health had impaired his memory, he forgot nothing of what he had done, read, or thought in any part of his rational age. The Admirable Crichton could repeat backwards any speech he had made. Magliabecchi, the Florentine librarian, could recollect whole volumes; and once supplied an author from memory with a copy of his own work, of which the original was lost. Pope has observed that Bolingbroke had so great a memory, that if he was alone and without books he could refer to a particular subject in them, and write as fully on it as another man would with all his books about him. Woodfall's extraordinary power of reporting the debates in the House of Commons without the aid of written memoranda is well known. During a debate he used to close his eyes and lean with both hands upon his stick, resolutely excluding all extraneous associations. The accuracy and precision of his reports brought his newspaper into great repute. He would retain a full recollection of a particular debate a fortnight after it had occurred, and during the intervention of other debates. He used to say that it was put by in a corner of his mind for future reference."*

CONSOLATION IN GROWING OLD.

Montaigne said of Cicero *On Old Age*, "It gives one an appetite for old age." Its persuasive eloquence is the inspiration of an elevated philosophy. Flourens has cleverly said, "The moral aspect of old age is its best side. We cannot grow old without losing our *physique*, nor also without our *morale* gaining by it. This is a noble compensation."

* *Literary Leaves*, by D. L. Richardson.

M. Reveillé-Parise says: "In a green old age, when from fifty-five to seventy-five years, and sometimes more, the life of the mind has a scope, a consistence, and remarkable solidity, man having then truly attained to the height of his faculties."

Patience is the privilege of age. A great advantage to the man who has lived is, that he knows how to wait. Again, experience is an old man's memory.

Buffon was seventy years of age (this was young for Buffon, he lived to eighty-one) when he wrote *The Epochs of Nature*, in which he calls old age a prejudice. Without our arithmetic we should not, according to Buffon, know that we were old. "Animals," he says, "do not know it; it is only by our arithmetic that we judge otherwise."

Buffon having settled on his estate at Montbard, in Burgundy, there pursued his studies with such regularity that the history of one day seems to have been that of all the others through a period of fifty years. After he was dressed, he dictated letters, and regulated his domestic affairs; and at six o'clock he retired to his studies in a pavilion in his garden, about a furlong from the house. This pavilion was only furnished with a large wooden secretary and an arm-chair; and within it was another cabinet, ornamented with drawings of birds and beasts. Prince Henry of Prussia called it the cradle of natural history; and Rousseau, before he entered it, used to fall on his knees, and kiss the threshold. Here Buffon composed the greater number of his works. At nine o'clock he usually took an hour's rest; and his breakfast, a piece of bread and two glasses of wine, was brought to him. When he had written two hours after breakfast, he returned to the house. At dinner he enjoyed the gaieties and trifles of the table. After dinner he slept an hour in his room; took a solitary walk; and during the rest of the evening he either conversed with his family or guests, or examined his papers at his desk. At nine o'clock he went to bed, to prepare himself for the same routine of judgment and pleasure. He had a most fervid imagination; and his anxious solicitude for a literary immortality, "that last infirmity of noble minds," continually betrayed him to be a vain man.

"Every day that I rise in good health," said Buffon to a conceited young man, "have I not the enjoyment of this day as fully as you? If I conform my actions, my appetites, my desires, to the strict impulses of wise nature, am I not as wise and happy as you are? And the view of the past, which causes so much regret to old fools, does it not afford me, on the contrary, the pleasures of memory, agreeable pictures of precious images, which are equal to your objects of pleasure? For these images are sweet; they are pure; they leave upon the mind only pleasing remembrances; the uneasiness, the disappointments, the sorrowful troop which accompanies your youthful pleasures, disappear from the picture which presents them to me. Regrets must disappear also; they are the last sparks of that foolish vanity that never grows old.

"Some one asked Fontenelle, when ninety-five years old, which were the twenty years of his life he most regretted. He replied that he had little to regret; but the age at which he had been most happy was that from forty-five to seventy-five. He made this avowal in sincerity, and he proved what he said by natural and consoling truths. At forty-five, fortune is established; reputation made; consideration obtained; the condition of life established; dreams vanished or fulfilled; projects miscarried or matured; most of the passions calmed, or at least cooled; the career in the work that every man owes to society nearly completed; enemies, or rather the enemies, are fewer, because the counterpoise of merit is known by the public voice," &c.

Galen, speaking of Hippocrates, and wishing to represent in one word the man who, in his eyes, constitutes the most perfect type of slowly matured wisdom and profound experience, simply calls him *the old man.*

The first rule of the Art of Preserving Life is to know how to be old. "Few men know how to be old," said La Rochefoucauld. Voltaire has—

> Qui n'a pas l'esprit de son âge,
> De son âge a tous les malheurs.

The first rule is more philosophic than medical, but is perhaps none the less valuable.

The second rule is to know yourself well; which is also a philosophical precept applied to medicine.

The third rule is properly to conform to regular habits. Old men, who spend one day like another, with the same moderation, the same appetites, live always. "My miracle is existence," said Voltaire; and if that foolish vanity which never grows old had not induced him, when eighty-four years of age, to make a ridiculous journey to Paris, his miracle would have continued a century, as was the case with Fontenelle.

"Few would believe," said M. Reveillé-Parise, "how far a little health, well managed, may be made to go." And Cicero said: "To use what we have, and to act in every thing according to our strength,—such is the rule of the sage."

Most men die of disease, very few die of mere age. Man has made for himself a sort of artificial life, in which the moral is often worse than the physical; and the physical itself often worse than it would be with habits more serene and calm, more regularly and judiciously exercised.

Haller, the physiologist, says: "Man should be placed among the animals that live the longest: how very unjust, then, are our complaints of the brevity of life!" He then inquires what can be the extreme limit of the life of man; and he gives it as his opinion that man might live not less than two centuries. M. Flourens,* however, decides on a century of ordinary life; and at least half a century of extraordinary life is the prospect science holds out to man. Still, as these inferences are drawn from the exceptions of Jenkins and Parr, the opinions must be received accordingly.

Haller, who has collected a great number of examples of Longevity, says that he has found more than

1000	who have	lived from	100 to 110	years
60	„	„	110 to 120	„
29	„	„	120 to 130	„
15	„	„	130 to 140	„
6	„	„	140 to 160	„

and one who reached the astonishing age of 169 years.

LENGTH OF DAYS.

There are few records so generally interesting as those of human existence being protracted beyond "threescore years and ten," and the Psalmist's limit of "fourscore years." It is natural to expect every man, woman, and child to take a kindred interest in such matters: the girl or boy reads with wonder the dates upon the tombstones of very aged persons; and old men and women approach these memorials with awe, in proportion to their fancied distance from the same earthly bourn. All cannot alike read the story of the pictured urn, or the mysteries of the inverted torch or the winged mundus; but the uneducated young and old are sensible of the

* *Human Longevity and the Amount of Life upon the Globe.* By P. Flourens, Perpetual Secretary to the Academy of Sciences, Paris, 1855.

solemnity of the line, "Aged 102 years;" whilst the more pretentious "Hic jacet" only teaches the comparatively few that

The paths of glory lead but to the grave.

We are not, therefore, surprised at the implicit belief in such records in times gone by, when no populous village in England was without a man or woman of fourscore years old. It has, however, become of late a matter of some moment to inquire into the authority on which statements of extreme old age have usually rested; and the result has been to shake the testimony of many recorded cases of great longevity.

Lord Bacon, in his *History of Life and Death*, quotes as a fact unquestioned, that a few years before he wrote, a morris-dance was performed in Herefordshire, at the May-games, by eight men, whose ages in the aggregate amounted to eight hundred years! In the seventeenth century, some time after Bacon wrote, two Englishmen are reported to have died at ages greater than almost any of those which have been attained in other nations. According to statements which are printed in the *Philosophical Transactions* of the Royal Society, as well as his epitaph in Westminster Abbey, Thomas Parr lived 152 years and 9 months; Henry Jenkins, 169 years. The testimony in these extraordinary instances is, however, considered by the Registrar-General by no means conclusive, as it evidently rests on uncertain tradition, and on the very fallible memories of illiterate old men; for there is no mention of documentary evidence in Parr's case, and the births date back to a period (1538) before the parish registers were instituted by Cromwell.

Yet parish registers are sometimes astounding; for in that of Evercreech, in Somersetshire, occurs this entry: "1588, 20th Dec., Jane Britton, of Evercriche, a Maidden, as she afirmed, of the age of 200 years, was buried."

Here is a difficulty of belief cleared up. In the register of the parish of St. Leonard, Shoreditch, is entered, among the "Burialles, Thomas Cam, ye 22d inst. of January 1588 (curiously enough the date of the Somersetshire entry), Aged 207 years, Holywell-street. George Garrow, parish clerk." In a newspaper paragraph of 1848, this entry is stated to add: "he was born in the year 1381, in the reign of King Richard II., and lived in the reigns of twelve kings and queens." These words are not, however, in the register; and it is evident that some mischievous person has altered the figure 1 into 2. Sir Henry Ellis, in his *History of Shoreditch*, gives the entry correctly as follows: "Thomas Cam, aged 107, 28 January 1588."

Another instance, less known, but better authenticated, is that of Sir Ralph Vernon, of Shipbrooke, who was born some time in the thirteenth century, died at the great age of 150; and is said to have been succeeded by his descendant in the sixth generation; he was called "Old Sir Ralph," or Sir R. "the long-liver." A deed of settlement by him was the cause of long litigation; and it is said that the papers respecting this law-suit still exist, to prove the fact of the old knight's patriarchal age.*

In Conway churchyard is the tombstone of Lowry Owens, stated to have died "May the 1st, 1766, aged 192;" but the inscription has evidently been recut, and, it is presumed, with a difference, especially as the round of the "9" is above the date-line.

In the church of Abbey Dore, Herefordshire, is a slab to the memory of Elizabeth Lewis, who died "aged 141 years," which is stated to be confirmed by the parish register.

In the churchyard of Cheve Prior, Worcestershire, is a record of a man who died at the age of 309; doubtless meant for 39, the blundering stonecutter having put the 30 first and 9 afterwards.

In these and similar cases our belief should be in proportion to the trustworthiness of the record, allowance being made for the imperfect state of documents of times when writing was a comparatively rare accomplishment. It is curious to contrast this state of things with the chronicle of our times, when, occasionally, one day's newspaper records several instances of longevity:

In the *Morning Post*, January 30th, 1858, out of thirty-five deaths recorded, with the ages, there were five upwards of 60 and under 70; 70 and under 80, seven; in 80th year and upwards, nine; one female, 95; and Mrs. E. Miles, of Bishop Lidyard, near Taunton, 112.

In the obituary of the *Times*, February 20th, 1862, were recorded the deaths of persons who had attained the following ages: one of 103,

* See Burke's *Peerage and Baronetage*, ed. 1848.

one of 94, two of 90, one of 85, one of 84, one of 82, and eight of 70 years and upwards. And, on April 20th of the same year, were recorded the deaths of ten persons, whose united ages amount to 828 years, or an average of nearly 83. They comprise one of 100 and one of 99.

HISTORIC TRADITIONS THROUGH FEW LINKS.

Of late years considerable interest has been added to the attraction of records of Longevity, by showing through how few individuals may be traced the evidence of far-distant events and incidents in our history.

Mr. Sidney Gibson, F.S.A., relates some curious instances of this class. A person living in 1847, then aged about 61, was frequently assured by his father that, in 1786, he repeatedly saw one Peter Garden, who died in that year at the age of 127 years; and who, when a boy, heard Henry Jenkins give evidence in a court of justice at York, to the effect that, when a boy, he was employed in carrying arrows up the hill before the battle of Flodden Field.

This battle was fought in		1513
Henry Jenkins died in 1670, at the age of	169	
Deduct for his age at the time of the battle of Flodden Field	12	
		157
Peter Garden, the man who heard Jenkins give his evidence, died at	127	
Deduct for his age when he saw Jenkins	11	
		116
The person whose father knew Peter Garden was born shortly before 1786, or seventy years since		70
		A.D. 1856

So that a person living in 1786 conversed with a man that fought at Flodden Field.

Mr. Gibson then passes on to some remarkable instances of longevity from the Scrope and Grosvenor Roll, the record of the celebrated cause in the reign of Richard II., when, among the noble and knightly deponents who gave evidence in the following year, 1386, were:

Sir John Sully, Knight of the Garter and a distinguished soldier of the cross, who had served for eighty years, was then, by his own account, 105 years of age, and who is supposed to have died in his 108th year.

But, more remarkable, John Thirlwall, an esquire of an

ancient Northumbrian house, deposes to what he heard from his father, who died forty-four years before, at the age of 145.

Not far from Thirlwall Castle, at Irthington, Mr. B. Gibson has seen the register of the burial of Robert Bowman, one of the most remarkable of the long-lived yeomen of that parish, who died in the year 1823, at the age of 118.

Mr. John Bruce, F.S.A., has also illustrated our subject by the following curious evidence. Lettice, Countess of Leicester, was born in 1539 or '40, and was consequently 7 years old at the death of Henry VIII. She may very well have had a recollection of the bluff monarch, who cut off the head of her great-aunt, Anne Boleyn. She was thrice married, and had seen six English sovereigns, or seven if Philip be counted; her faculties were unimpaired at 85; and until a year or two of her death, on Christmas-day 1634, at the age of 94, she "could yet walk a mile of a morning." Lettice was one of a long-lived race: her father lived till 1596; two of her brothers attained the ages of 86 and 99.

There is nothing (says Mr. Bruce) incredible, or even very extraordinary, in Lettice's age; but even her years will produce curious results if applied to the subject of possible transmission of knowledge through few links. I will give one example: "Dr. Johnson, who was born in 1709, might have known a person who had seen the Countess Lettice, If there are not now (1857), there were amongst us within the last three or four years, persons who knew Dr. Johnson. There might, therefore, be only two links between ourselves and the Countess Lettice, who saw Henry VIII."*

Mr. John Pavin Philips writes from Haverfordwest: "A friend of mine, now (1857) in his 80th year, knew an old woman resident in his parish who remembered her grandmother, who saw Cromwell when he was in Pembrokeshire, in 1648. I myself, when a student in Edinburgh in 1837, knew a centenarian lady, named Butler, who well recollected being taken by her mother to witness the public entry of Prince Charles Edward into the city in 1745." And in Haverfordwest might be seen daily walking, in 1857, in perfect health, a man who was born four years previous to the death of George II.†

* See *Notes and Queries*, 2d series, Nos. 51 and 53. † Ibid. No. 58.

Mary Yates, of Shiffnal, Salop, who died 1776, aged 128, well remembered walking to view the ruins of the Great Fire of London, 1666.

In the *News Letter* of June 1st, 1724, Bodl. Mss., Rawl. C., it is related, that on the King's birthday, as the nobility and others of distinction passed through Pall Mall to Court at St. James's, there sat in the street one Elinor Stuart, being 124 years old. She had kept a linen-shop at Kendal, and had nine children living at the time King Charles I. was beheaded, and was undone by adhering to the royal cause. "She is reckoned," says the account (Jane Skrimshaw, who was now dead, being 128), "the oldest woman in London."*

Margaret Mapps, of Eaton, near Leominster, who died in 1800, aged 109, had so retentive a memory, that to her last hours she could relate many incidents which she had witnessed in the reign of Queen Anne.

In 1858 died Mrs. Milward, of Blackheath, at the age of 102. She was, consequently, born four years previous to the accession of George III.; she saw the separation of the American colonies from the mother country; the three French revolutions, and the great war with France; she well remembered the London riots of 1780, and was placed in some jeopardy in Hyde-park in one of the incidents.

Jane Forrester, of Cumberland, is stated in the *Public Advertiser*, March 9th, 1766, as then living in her 138th year: she remembered Cromwell's siege of Carlisle, in 1646; and in 1762 she gave evidence in a Chancery-suit of an estate having been enjoyed by the ancestors of the then heir 101 years.

One Evans, of Spitalfields, who died 1780, is stated to have reached the age of 139 years: he remembered the execution of Charles I., at which time he was 7 years old.

In the London newspapers of November 7th, 1788, is recorded the celebration of the centenary of the Revolution, at which was present a person who remembered that glorious event; he was 112 years old, and belonged to the French Hospital, Old Street-road, where were then ten persons whose ages together were 1000 years.

In 1826 there died at Corby, near Carlisle, aged 102, one

* W. D. Macray; *Notes and Queries*, 2d series, No. 23.

Joseph Liddle, a shoemaker, who was at work in his shop, in the market-place of Carlisle, when the Scotch rebels entered the town, in 1745; he was very fond of horticulture, and, with little help, kept in order a large garden nearly until the day of his death.

Samuel Rogers, the banker-poet, who died on December 18th, 1855, aged 96, among many accomplishments possessed a most retentive memory; and his sweep of recollections was very wide.

He remembered when one of the Rebels' heads remained on Temple Bar; when schoolboys chased butterflies in the fields in cocked hats; when gentlemen universally wore wigs and swords; when Ranelagh was in all its glory, and ladies going thither had head-dresses so preposterously high that they had to sit on stools placed in the bottom of the coach; when Garrick crowded the theatre, Reynolds crowded the lecture-room, and Johnson crowded the club; he had heard the Duke of York relate how he and his brother George, when young men, were robbed by footpads on Hay-hill, Berkeley-street; he had shaken hands with John Wilkes, dined with Lafayette, Condorcet, &c. at Paris, before the great Revolution began, and been present at Warren Hastings' trial in Westminster Hall; he had seen Lady Hamilton go through her "attitudes" before the Prince of Wales, and Lord Nelson spin a teetotum with his *one* hand for the amusement of children.—*R. Carruthers.*

Mr. Peter Cunningham noted, a few days after the death of our Poet: "When Rogers made his appearance as a poet, Lord Byron was unborn—and Byron has been dead thirty-one years! When Percy Bysshe Shelley was born, Rogers was in his 30th year—and Shelley has been dead nearly thirty-four years! When Keats was born, *The Pleasures of Memory* was looked upon as a standard poem—and Keats has been dead thirty-five years! When this century commenced, the man who died but yesterday, and in the latter half too of the century, had already numbered as many years as Burns and Byron had numbered when they died. Mr. Rogers was born before the following English poets: Scott, Southey, Wordsworth, Coleridge, Byron, Moore, Campbell, Bloomfield, Cunningham, Hogg, James Montgomery, Shelley, Keats, Wilson, Tom Hood, Kirk White, Lamb, Joanna Baillie, Felicia Hemans, L. E. L.; and he outlived them all."

On April 24th, 1858, died Mr. James Nolan, at Auchindrane, Carlow, Ireland, aged 115 years and 9 months. There is something more interesting than his being the oldest subject of her Majesty, who had lived in the reigns of five sovereigns of England; and no doubt it is curious to be carried back by two lives—Mr. Nolan and his father—to the reign of Charles II., and almost to the time of Cromwell.

Here is a remarkable instance: Commander Pickernell, R.N., who died April 20th, 1859, aged 87, knew well in his youth a man who was a soldier encamped on Hounslow-heath at the time of the Revolution in 1688. This same man played an instrument in the band at Queen Anne's coronation, and served through Marlborough's wars; in his old age he returned to the neighbourhood of his native place, Whitby, where he died, considerably over a century, when Commander Pickernell was a boy about 7 or 8 years old.*

The venerable President of Magdalen College, Oxford, Dr. Routh, who died 1855, in his hundredth year, brought up old memories of times and men long passed away. Dr. Routh had known Dr. Theophilus Lee, the contemporary of Addison; had seen Dr. Johnson "in his brown wig scrambling up the steps of University College;" and had been told by a lady of her aunt who had been present when Charles II. walked round the parks at Oxford.

Dr. Routh had maintained an immediate and personal connexion with the University of Oxford for upwards of 80 years; and his long life supplied many instructive links between the present and the past. He was born in the reign of King George II., before the beginning of the Seven Years' War; before India was conquered by Clive, or Canada by Wolfe; before the United States ever dreamt of independence; and before Pitt had impressed the greatness of his own character on the policy of Britain. The life of this college student comprehended three most important periods in the history of the world. Martin Routh saw the last years of the old state of society which introduced the political deluge; he saw the deluge itself—the great French Revolution, with all its catastrophes of thrones and opinions; and he lived to see the more stirring but not less striking changes which forty years of peace had engendered. It is therefore not a little curious to read of such a man, that the times on which his thoughts chiefly dwelt were those of the Stuarts; which is not, however, altogether surprising, as he might himself have shaken hands with the Pretender. This Prince did not die till young Routh was ten years of age; so that, if accident had put the chance in his way, he might easily have had an interview with the representative of James II.† What an interval was there

* *Notes and Queries*, 2d series, No. 169.
† Condensed from the *Times* journal.

between this epoch and Dr. Routh sitting for a photograph on his hundredth birthday!

LONGEVITY IN FAMILIES.

The long life of different members of the same family is remarkable. In 1836, Mrs. H. P., residing near the Edgeware-road, attained her 103d year: she had three sisters,—one 107, another 105; and the other, who died about 1834, 100.

Mr. Bailey records the death of Widow Stephenson, of Wolverton, Durham, in 1816, aged 104: her mother lived to be 106, two sisters 106 and 107, and a brother 97; making an aggregate of 519 years as the age of these five relatives.

Edward Simon, 81 years a dock-labourer in Liverpool, died 1821, aged 101: his mother lived to 103; his father 101; and a brother 104.

Gilbert Wakefield states that his wife's great-grandfather and great-grandmother's matrimonial connexion lasted seventy-five years: they died nearly at the same time, she at the age of 98, he at the age of 108. He was out hunting a short time before his death. His portrait is in the hall of Mr. Legh, of Lyme.

Mary Tench, of Cromlin, Ireland, who died 1790, aged 100, was of aged parents her father attained 104, and her mother 96; her uncle reached 110 and she left two sisters, whose aggregate ages made 170.

In the year 1811, within four miles of the house at Alderbury formerly occupied by Parr, there died, in the month of September, four persons, whose ages were 97, 80, 96, and 97. There were then living in the neighbourhood a man aged 100, and two others of 90.

The Costello family, county Kilkenny, lived to very great ages. On June 12, 1824, died Mary Costello, aged 102; her mother died at precisely the same age; her grandmother at 120; her great-grandmother exceeded 125: long before her death, she had to be rocked in a cradle, like an infant. Mary Costello's brother lived beyond 100 years; and when 90, cut down half an acre of grass in a day.*

In Appleby churchyard is a tombstone in memory of

* *Dublin Warder*, 1824.

three persons named Hall: the grandfather died in 1716, aged 109, and the father aged 86; and the son died in 1821, aged 106. "So that the father had seen a man (his father) who saw James I., and also a man (his son) who saw me, or might have done so."*

The Countess of Mornington, who died in 1831, attained the age of 90: her eldest son, the Marquis Wellesley, ennobled for his administration in India, reached 82; his brother, Lord Maryborough, 83; Lady Maryborough, 91; and their brother, the Great Duke of Wellington, 83. We possess a small portrait of Lady Mary Irvine, aunt to Lady Maryborough, painted in her 82d year; the face is without a wrinkle, but of *riant* beauty.

The London bankers, Joseph and William Joseph Denison, exceeded 80; and the sister of the latter, Dowager Marchioness of Conyngham, 90.

Lady Blakiston, died, November 1862, in her 102d year; and her eldest son, Sir Matthew Blakiston, died December following, in his 82d year.

"On 8th April 1860, Mr. S. Cronesberry died at Farmer's Bridge, aged 99. His grandfather died in 97th year; his father died in 97th year; his mother in 98th year."†

Archibald, 9th Earl of Dundonald, died 1831, aged 83; and his son, 10th Earl, 1860, reached 82: both in the naval service, and distinguished by their scientific attainments.

FEMALE LONGEVITY.

One of the most celebrated personages in the history of Female Longevity is the Countess of Desmond, who is usually said to have died early in the 17th century, aged 140 years. Bacon, in his *Natural History*, describes her as "the old Countess of Desmond, who lived till she was sevenscore years old, that she did *dentire* (produce teeth) twice or thrice." Sir Walter Raleigh, in his *History of the World*, says: "I myself *knew* the old Countess of Desmond of Inchiquin, in Munster, who lived in the year 1589, and many years since, who was married in Edward IV.'s time, and held her jointure from all the Earls of Desmond since

* Letter of Baron Alderson, in his *Life*, by his Son, date Feb. 19, 1833.
† *Kilkenny Moderator.*

then: and that this is true, all the noblemen and gentlemen in Munster can witness."* Sir William Temple was told by Robert Earl of Leicester of the Countess married in Edward IV.'s time, "and who lived far in King James's reign, and was counted to have died some years above 140." There has been much controversy respecting the portraits of this lady which are said to exist: that in the possession of the Knight of Kerry, and engraved in 1806, is reputed authentic; and after much discussion, the Countess has been identified as Katharine, second wife of Thomas 12th Earl of Desmond, who died in 1534. Fynes Morrison, the traveller, who was in Ireland from 1599 to 1603, tells of the Countess living to the age of about 140 years; of her walking four or five miles weekly to the market-town in her last years; and of her death by falling out of a tree which she had climbed to gather nuts. There is a tradition which might be true, of her having danced at Court with the Duke of Gloucester (Richard III.), of whom she affirmed that he was the handsomest man in the room, except his brother Edward, and was very well made.†

Of Margaret Patten, stated to have died 136 and 138 years old, a curious portrait was found at Glasgow, amongst some family papers, in 1853. She was born in the parish of Locknugh, near Paisley, in Scotland, and is described beneath the portrait as "now living in the workhouse of St. Margaret's, Westminster, aged 138." And in the Boardroom of St. Margaret's workhouse is another portrait of Margaret (there stated to be 136), the gift of the overseers of the parish in 1737. The old woman was buried in the burial-ground of the Broadway church, now Christ-church, Westminster, where a stone is inscribed, "Near this place lieth Margaret Patten, who died June 26, 1739, in the Parish Workhouse, aged 136." "She was brought to England to prepare Scotch broth for King James II.; but owing to the abdication of that monarch, fell into poverty, and died in St. Margaret's workhouse. Her body was followed to the grave by the parochial authorities and many of the principal inhabitants, while the children sung a hymn before it reached its last resting-place."‡

* *History of the World,* book i. chap. 5.
† Chambers's *Book of Days,* vol. i.
‡ Walcott's *Westminster,* p. 238.

In the Dublin Exhibition of 1853 was a print with this inscription: "Mary Gore, born at Cottonwith in Yorkshire, A.D. 1582; lived upwards of one hundred years in Ireland, and died in Dublin, aged 145 years. This print was done from a picture *taken* (the word is torn off) when she was one hundred and forty-three. Vanluych *pinxit*, T. Chambers *del.*"*

The following instances of long widowhoods are interesting: the widow of Thomas, second Lord Lyttleton, who died in 1779, survived his lordship in a state of widowhood sixty-one years, dying in 1840, aged 97.

The widow of David Garrick died in 1822, in the same house, on the Adelphi-terrace, wherein her celebrated husband died forty-three years previously. We remember a small etching of the old lady appearing in the print-shops just after her death, portraying her characteristic dignified deportment. Among the legacies bequeathed to her husband's family was a service of pewter used by him when a bachelor, and having the name of Garrick engraven on it.

The widow of Charles James Fox, the statesman, died in 1842, aged 96, having survived her husband thirty-six years.

Amelia Opie, the amiable novelist, died in 1853, in her 85th year, having survived her husband, the painter, forty-six years. He painted a remarkable picture of Mrs. Opie,—two portraits, full-face and profile, upon the same canvas; they are said to be faithful likenesses.

Some years since, writes the editor of the *Quarterly Review*, "we beheld the strange sight of an old woman, aged 102, bent double, crooning over the fire, and nursing in her lap an infant a few days old. The infant was the grandchild of the old woman's grandchild. The only remarkable circumstance in the veteran's history was, that she had nursed Wordsworth in his infancy. She had lived the greater part of her life in Westmoreland, near the poet's residence, and there her descendants had been chiefly born and lived."

Here are a few instances of women of remarkable talent attaining great ages:

Caroline Lucretia Herschel, who discovered seven comets, and passed years of nights as amanuensis to her brother, Sir William Herschel, in his astronomical labours, attained the

* Eironnach; *Notes and Queries*, No. 215.

age of 97, with her intellect clear, and princes and philosophers alike striving to do her honour.

Miss Linwood, whose Needlework Pictures were exhibited nearly sixty years, died in 1844, at the age of 90. No needlework of ancient or modern times has ever surpassed these productions. The collection consisted of sixty-four pictures, mostly of large or gallery size; the finest work, from the "Salvator Mundi," by Carlo Dolci, was bequeathed by Miss Linwood to Queen Victoria; for this picture 3000 guineas had been refused.

Dr. Webster, F.R.S., who takes great interest in records of Longevity, in 1860 contributed to the *Athenæum* a copy of the certificate of birth of a lady in her 100th year, living at Hampstead, namely, the surviving sister of the authoress Miss Joanna Baillie, who died 1851, aged 89. This document is as follows:

> Copy of an entry in a separate register of the Presbytery of Hamilton, under the head "Shotts."—That Mr. James Baillie had a daughter named Agnes, born 24th September 1760, attested and signed at Hamilton the 25th day of November 1760, in presence of the Presbytery.—Signed, James Baillie; John Kirk, Clerk; Patrick Maxwell, Moderator.

In the same year, 1859, died Lady Morgan, the novelist, at 76; Leigh Hunt, the poet and *littérateur*, at 75; Washington Irving, at 77; and Thomas de Quincey, at 76.

Lady Charlotte Bury, the novelist, attained the age of 88, retaining her beauty and conversational accomplishments to the last; she died 1861.

The Dowager Countess of Hardwicke, who died in 1858, in her long life brought points of time together which, at first, seem separated by impassable spaces. She was born in 1763, and was consequently 95 years of age; but her father, the Earl of Balcarres, having been advanced in years at the time of her birth, their two lives extend back to before the beginning of the eighteenth century; and it was strange to hear, in 1858, that a person just dead could speak of her father as having been "out in the Fifteen" (1715) with Lord Derwentwater and Forster, and having been begged off by the great Duke of Marlborough. Yet such was the fact; and not only so, but having been born in 1649, the three lives of grandfather, son, and granddaughter stretched over a period of 200 years; and, when her grandmother was married,

Charles II. gave away the bride! When this venerable lady was born, Pitt the younger was 4 years old; Fox, a lad of 14; and Sheridan of 12,—so that they were strictly her contemporaries; Burke was turned of 30; she was 21 years old when Dr. Johnson died, and a well-grown girl when Goldsmith died, so that she might have known them both; and Sir Joshua Reynolds may have painted her, as she was near 30 when he died. All the literature of this century, running back to the birth of Scott and Wordsworth, eight or nine years after her own, was as much hers as ours. She was married and 26 before the French Revolution began; and the whole of the American Revolution must have been within her personal recollection.

Then there was Viscountess Keith, who died at about the same age, 95, and who had been "the plaything often, when a child," of Johnson, and who received his last blessing on his death-bed. She was the daughter of Mrs. Thrale, and was a link that directly connected us with the Literary Club at its foundation, all the members of which she must have seen, and most of whom she was old enough to know well as a grown-up young lady.

Lady Louisa Stuart, the daughter of the Marquess of Bute, actually remembered her grandmother, Lady Mary Wortley Montague, who died in 1762. She herself died 1851, aged 94, and was the intimate friend of Scott, and one of the few original depositaries of the Waverley secret.

And Mary Berry, aged 89, and her sister Agnes, 88, both died in 1852, having lived in the best of London society for sixty years. For the amusement of these ladies, Horace Walpole wrote his most delightful *Reminiscences*.

LONGEVITY AND DIET.

It may now be as well to glance at the modes of living of a few of the patriarchal folks. Cornaro, who is one of the *penates* of healthful longevity, was born at Venice in 1464, of a noble family. In early life he injured his health by intemperance, and by indulging his propensity to anger; but he succeeded in acquiring such a command over himself, and in adopting such a system of temperance, as to recover his health and vigour, and to enjoy life to an extreme old age. At 83 he wrote a comedy "abounding with innocent mirth and pleasant jests." At 86 he wrote: "I contrive to spend every hour with the greatest delight and pleasure." He was fond of literature and the conversation of men of sense and good manners, and his principal delight was to be of service to others. Every year he travelled, visited architects, painters, sculptors, musicians, and husbandmen; and he was especially fond of natural scenery. "Being freed, by God's grace, from the perturbations of the mind and the infirmities of the body," he no longer experienced any of those contrary emotions which torment a number of young men, and many old ones destitute of strength and health, and every other blessing. His diet consisted of bread, meat, eggs, and soup, not exceeding in the day three-quarters of a pound of food, and a pint of new wine. He passed with health and comfort beyond his hundredth year; and at Padua, in 1566, sitting in his arm-chair, he died, as he had lived for his last threescore years, exempt from pain and suffering.

Thomas Parr* was an early riser. Taylor, the Water-poet, quaintly sings of his mode of living:

> Good wholesome labour was his exercise,
> Down with the lamb, and with the lark would rise;
> In wise and toiling sweat he spent the day,
> And to his team he whistled time away;
> The cock his night-clock, and till day was done,
> His watch and chief sun-dial was the sun.
> He was of old Pythagoras' opinion,
> That new cheese was most wholesome with an onion;
> Coarse meslin bread; and for his daily swig,
> Milk, butter-milk, and water, whey and whig;
> Sometimes metheglin, and, by fortune happy,
> He sometimes sipped a cup of ale most nappy,
> Cider or perry, when he did repair
> To a Whitson ale, wake, wedding, or a fair,
> Or when in Christmas-time he was a guest,
> At his good landlord's house among the rest;
> Else he had little leisure-time to waste,
> Or at the alehouse buff-cup ale to taste;
> His physic was good butter, which the soil
> Of Salop yields, more sweet than Candy-oil;
> And garlic he esteemed above the rate
> Of Venice treacle, or best mithridate;

* In the Ashmolean Collection at Oxford is a portrait of Old Parr, presumed to have been painted from the life, and, we believe, not engraved. The portrait by Rubens is well known.

He entertained no gout, no ache he felt,
The air was good and temperate where he dwelt;
Thus living within bounds of Nature's laws,
Of his long-lasting life may be some cause.

Taylor thus describes the person of Parr:

From head to heel, his body had all over
A quick-set, thick-set, natural hairy cover.

The Vegetarians maintain that their system of living conduces highly to longevity. We find in the *Gentleman's Magazine*, 1774, this recorded instance: "At Brussels, Elizabeth de Val, aged 103, who was remarkable for never having eaten a bit of meat in her life."

An advocate of vegetable diet adduces the Norwegian and Russian peasantry as the most remarkable instances of extreme longevity: "The last returns of the Greek Church population of the Russian empire give (in the table of the deaths of the male sex) more than one thousand above 100 years of age, many between 140 and 150. . . . Slaves in the West Indies are recorded from 130 to 150 years of age." Widow Rogers, of Penzance, Cornwall, who died 1779, aged 118, for the last sixty years lived entirely on vegetable diet.

Among the Pythagoreans of our time should be mentioned Sir Richard Phillips, who from his twelfth year conceived an abhorrence of the slaughter of animals for food; and from that period to his death, at the age of 72, he lived entirely on vegetable products, enjoying such robust health that no stranger could have suspected his studious and sedentary habits.* Sometimes this Pythagorean principle was strongly enunciated; as, when about to take his seat at a supper-party, perceiving a lobster on the table, he loudly denounced the cruelty of his friends' sitting down to eat a creature which had been boiled alive! and the offensive dish had to be removed. Sir Richard often published his Reasons for not eating Animal Food; his abstinence drew upon him the harmless ridicule of a writer in the *Quarterly Review*, observing that, although he would not eat meat, he was addicted to gravy over his potatoes.

One Wilson, of Worlingworth, Suffolk, who died 1782,

* The portrait of Sir Richard Phillips as Sheriff, painted by Saxon, shows him as above described. The picture is of gallery size, and in the possession of his grandson and representative, Mr. Bacon Phillips, M.R.C.S., of Brighton. The bust of Sir Richard, by Turnerelli, conveys a similar *personnel*.

aged 116, for the last forty years of his life supped off roasted turnips, to which he ascribed his long life.

The Hon. Mrs. Watkins, of Glamorganshire, who died 1790, aged 110, for her last thirty years lived principally on potatoes. The year before her death she came from Glamorgan to London to see Mrs. Siddons play, and attended the theatre nine nights; and one morning she mounted to the Whispering-gallery of St. Paul's Cathedral.

It is rarely that table-wits attain such longevity as did Captain Morris, the Anacreon of the Beef-steak Club, who wrote lyrics at the age of 90. He died three years afterwards. He was of short stature, and usually wore a buff waistcoat, such as he apostrophised in one of his latest lyrics, "The old Whig Poet to his old Buff Waistcoat." He lies in the churchyard of Betchworth, Surrey,—his grave simply marked by a head and foot stone, 1838.

Civic annals present few such instances of long life as that of Richard Clark, Chamberlain of London, who died 1831, in his 92d year. He was one of the latest of the contemporaries of Dr. Johnson, whom he had known from his 15th year: when sheriff, he took the Doctor to a "Judges' Dinner" at the Old Bailey, the judges being Blackstone and Eyre.

In the autumn of 1831 died the Rev. Dr. Shaw, aged 83, of Chesley, Somerset, said to have been the last surviving friend of Dr. Johnson.

Few persons addicted to riotous living attain great ages. A remarkable exception is recorded of George Kirton, Esq., of Oxcrop Hall, Yorkshire, who died in 1762, aged 125. He was a stanch foxhunter, and hunted till after he was 80; thenceforth, till his hundredth year, he attended the "breaking cover" in his single chair. He was a heavy drinker till within a few years of his death.

Thomas Whittington, who died at Hillingdon, Middlesex, in 1804, aged 104, retained his faculties to the last, and could walk two or three miles; yet he was a great drinker, gin being the only fluid he took into his stomach, and of this a pint and a half daily, until a fortnight of his death. He remembered William III. and Queen Anne; and in 1745 he conveyed troops and baggage from Uxbridge to London. His father died at exactly the same age (104) as the son, and both lie in Hillingdon churchyard.

LONGEVITY AND LOCALITIES.

With respect to the atmosphere most favourable to health and longevity, Sir John Sinclair says, "More depends upon a current of pure air than mere elevation. There is no place in Scotland, proportionably with its population, where a greater number of aged people are to be found than in the neighbourhood of Loch Lomond." The purest atmosphere, Sir John maintains, is in the neighbourhood of a small stream running over a rocky or pebbly bottom.

Mr. Thomas Bailey, in his *Records of Longevity*, states that "Nottinghamshire has the driest atmosphere of any district in England, the depth of rain which falls there being something like 50 per cent below what falls in Lancashire, Devonshire, and one or two of the northern counties;" yet the records show that it enjoys no superiority, in point of the longevity of its inhabitants, over those moister districts. Hence it is concluded that moderately moist air is most conducive to great age. The reason Hufeland assigns for this is, that moist air, being in part already saturated, has less attractive power over bodies,—that is to say, consumes them less. Besides, in a moist atmosphere there is always more uniformity of temperature, fewer rapid revolutions of heat being possible than in a dry atmosphere. Lastly, an atmosphere somewhat moist keeps the muscular tissue of the body longer pliable, whereas that which is dry or arid brings on much sooner rigidity of the muscles and vessels of the body, and all the characteristics of old age. It is this very dry air, joined with the heat of the sun, which gives to the dried and shrivelled skin of the face of some old men, in the felicitous humour of Charles Dickens, "the appearance of a walnut-shell."

We now proceed to cite instances of Long Life from various localities. On the fly-leaves of a book named *Long Livers*, published in 1722, were written the following notes of several old persons in Yorkshire: Ursula Chicken, at Holderness, 120 years in 1718, and she lived some years later. In Firbeck churchyard were buried a brother and son, one 113 and the other 109 years old, both of whom had lived in caves at Roche Abbey. Mr. Philip, of Thorner, born in Cleveland (the birthplace of Old Jenkins), had his picture taken when he was 116 years old, with all his senses perfect. Thomas Rudyard, Vicar of Everton, in Bedfordshire, died in King Charles's time, aged 140 years, as appears by the parish register. Early in June 1768 died, at Burythorpe, near Malton, Francis Consit, aged 150 years. A few years previously there were three women, each 100 years old, or upwards, who lived in and about Whitwell, met at that town and danced a Yorkshire reel. About 1758 a woman died at Sutton 107 years old. "Old Robinson's father, at Boltby, lived to 108," and he himself beyond 98.*

The register of Middleton Tyas, adjoining, contains, in sixteen years, entries of 230 persons buried, of whom seventy-six had reached the age of 70 years or upwards. In 1813, of fifteen deceased, three were 90, 91, and 92; in 1815 a person died 97; and thirty-three of the number specified were 80 years old and upwards; and in the churchyard are buried two persons of 103 and 101 years. But within the last thirty-five years instances of longevity in this parish, once so common, form the exception.

Mr. Durrant Cooper, F.S.A., has communicated to *Notes and Queries*, No. 212, these interesting records from the burial register of Skelton-in-Cleveland, in the North Riding of Yorkshire:

Out of 799 persons buried between 1813 and 1852, no less than 263, or nearly one-third, attained the age of 70. Of these, two were respectively 101. Nineteen others were 90 years of age and upwards, viz. one 97, one 96, one 95, four 94, one 93, five 92, three 91, and three 90. Between the ages of 80 and 90 there died 109; and between 70 and 80 there died 133. In one page of the register, containing eight names, six were above 80, and in another five were above 70.

In the parish of Skelton there was then living a man named Moon, 104 years old, who was blind, but managed a small farm till nearly or quite 100; and a blacksmith, named Robinson Cook, aged 98, who worked at his trade until within six months of this age.

In the chapelry of Brotton, adjoining Skelton township, the longevity was even more remarkable. Out of 346 persons buried since the new register came into force in 1813, down to Oct. 1, 1853, more than one-third attained the age of 70. One Betty Thompson, who died in 1834, was 101; nineteen were more than 90, of whom one was 98, two 97, three 95, one 93, four 92, five 91, and three 90; forty-four died between 80 and 90 years old, and fifty-seven between 70 and 80, of whom thirty-one were 75 and upwards. That celibacy did not lessen the chance of life was proved by a bachelor named Simpson, who died at 82, and his maiden sister at 91.

* Edward Hailstone, Horton Hall; *Notes and Queries*, 2d series, No. 230.

Gilling, in Richmondshire, shows also a very great length of life, and in persons above 90 years of age a larger proportion even than in the Cleveland parishes. Between 1813 and 1853, of 701 persons buried, 207, or rather more than one-third, attained the age of 70 and upwards. Three were 100, or upwards; between 90 and 100, twenty-one; one 96, 95, and 94; two 92, six 91, and ten 90. Between 80 and 90 there died 87; between 70 and 80, ninety-six.

George Stephenson, a farm-labourer, of Runald-Kirk, near Barnard-Castle, Durham, who died 1812, aged 105, was a very early riser; he used to reprove (for lying a-bed) his daughter and her husband, both about 70 years of age, but who rose before six o'clock in the morning,—George saying, "if they would not work while they were *young*, what would they do when they became old?"

Mr. Carruthers, of Inverness, whose evidence is entitled to respect, wrote in 1836, that "the patriarchs of the glen of Stratchcarron have been gathered to their fathers. The primitive manners of the olden time are disappearing even in that remote corner, and human life is dwindling down to its ordinary brief limits." This experience is the converse of the opinion that civilisation and refinement tend to lengthen life.

The Western Isles of Scotland have long been noted for persons of great age. Martin describes a male native of Jura, who had kept 180 Christmas festivals in his own house, and this marvellous account was confirmed to Pennant; but the evidence is not given, and the man died fifty years before Martin's visit. Buchanan, in his *History of Shetland*, gives an account of one Laurence, a Shetlander, who lived to 140; Dr. Derham, in his *Physico-Theology*, confirms this, and Martin received from Laurence's family particulars of his fishing to the last year of his life. At Orkney Martin heard of a man aged 112; and that one William Muir, of Westra, lived to be near 140. Tarquis M'Leod, near Stornoway, in the island of Lewis, died in 1787, aged 113; he had fought at Killiecrankie, Sheriffmuir, and Culloden, under the Stuarts.

In the *Aberdeen Journal* we find this evidence: Died, at Strichen, Widow Reid, aged 81; and in the following fortnight, Christian Grant, aged 97 years. The surviving resident paupers number only twenty-five, and among them there are seven individuals whose respective ages are 92, 90, 88, 86, 83, 82, and 80 years—making a total of 601 years, and an average of nearly 86 years to each. These statistics, in a parish containing a population of only 947, are perhaps unparalleled in Scotland.

A well-authenticated instance is that of Mrs. Elizabeth Gray, who died at Edinburgh on the 2d of April 1856, at the age of 108, having been born in May 1748, as chronicled in the register of her father's parish. Her mother attained 96, and two of her sisters died at 94 and 96 respectively. In 1808 died the Hon. Mrs. Hay Mackenzie, of Cromartie, at the age of 103. The well-known Countess Dowager of Cork died in 1840, having just completed her 94th year; she was to the last accustomed to dine out every day when she had not company at home. Mr. Francis Brokesby, in 1711, wrote of a woman then living near the Tower of London, aged about 130, and who remembered Queen Elizabeth; to the last there was not a gray hair on her head, and she never lost memory or judgment. Mr. Brokesby also records the death, about 1660, of the wife of a labouring man at Hedgerow, in Cheshire; she is said to have attained the age of 140.*

Reflecting upon this record, Mr. Robert Chambers observes, with poetic feeling, "When we think of such things, the ordinary laws of nature seem to have undergone some partial relaxation; and the dust of ancient times almost becomes living flesh before our eyes." We confess to the weakness of being occasionally depressed in the society of some very aged persons. We remember Louis Pouchée to have died about twenty years since, considerably above 100 years old: his voice was a childish treble, and there was at last a sort of forced gaiety in his manner which was any thing but cheerful; his piping of "I've kissed and I've prattled with fifty fair maids" was a lugubrious rendering of that lively lyric.

In White's *Suffolk Directory* for 1844, the following living instances are recorded. "W. A. Shuldham, Esq., resides at the Hall, in which, on July 18, 1843, he celebrated the hundredth anniversary of his birthday. Mrs. Susan Godbold,

* Condensed from Chambers's *Book of Days*, vol. i.

who was born at Flixton, has resided at Metfield eighty years, and walked round the village on her 104th birthday, Sept. 13, 1843. Thomas Morse, Esq., of Lound, is now in his 99th year." Dr. Smith, residing at Bawdsea, a few years since completed his 109th; when, in the fulness of his spirits, he expressed a belief that he should live for some years to come.

Here is an instance of remarkable memory. George Kelson ("the Woodman," in illustration of Cowper's poem) died near Bath in 1820, aged 101; he gave evidence before the Commissioners of Public Charities, deposing, with great clearness, to facts which had occurred ninety years before his examination.

The parish register of Bremhill, Wiltshire, records: "Buried, September the 29th, 1696, Edith Goldie, Grace Young, Elizabeth Wiltshire. Their united ages make 300 years."*

Two centuries ago, the now sleepy town of Woodstock, Oxon., was proverbial for its long livers. The Rev. John Ward, Vicar of Stratford-upon-Avon, in his Diary, 1648-9, records: "Old Bryan, of Woodstock, a taylor by profession, and a fiddler by present practice, of age 90, yet very lively, and will travail well. George Green and Cripps, each 90, very hard labourers. Thomas Cock, *alias* Hawkins, 112 years of age when he died. Woodstock men frequently long lived. Goody Jones, of Woodstock, and old Bryan, two such old people as it is thought England does not afford, nor two such travailors of their age."

In 1637 there was living in Blackboy-lane, Oxford, "Mother George," who, although 120 years of age, could thread a fine needle without the help of spectacles.†

Between February and May 1767, there died in Oxford seven persons whose ages together amount to 616, viz. 88, 93, 86, 87, 90, 82, and 90. In the same year is recorded the death of Francis Ange, in Maryland, aged 130; he was born at Stratford-upon-Avon, remembered the death of King Charles I., and left England soon after.‡

The heads of Colleges in Oxford have frequently attained great ages: we have mentioned Dr. Routh, President

* Britton's *Wilts.* vol. iii.

† *Walks in Oxford*, 1817.

‡ *Select. Gent. Mag.* iv.

of Magdalen, who died in his 100th year. There are generally very old people living in Oxford; and at Iffley the ages recorded in the churchyard commonly exceed 70.

Midhurst, in Sussex, must be a healthy locality; for, according to the *Dublin Chronicle*, December 2, 1788, the town, then containing only 140 houses and cottages, had seventy-eight inhabitants whose ages were above 70; thirty-two were 80 and upwards; and five were between 90 and 100; and the seventy-eight persons, except four, were in some business or occupation.

Wye, near Ashford, Kent, is another noted locality for long life; the ages of 70, 80, and even 90, being by no means rare in the parish register.

In 1800 twenty-two men died in England and Wales who had reached or passed the age of 100, and forty-seven women. The oldest woman, 111 years of age, died in Glamorganshire. With the men there was a tie: a man aged 107 died in Hampshire, and another of the same age in Pembrokeshire. Four of the centenarians died in London, two others at Camberwell, one also at Greenwich, and one at Lewisham. More men died in the year than women; but of the 595 persons who had reached the age of 95 or upwards before they died, nearly two-thirds were women.

Great longevity is attained in some of the murky streets, lanes, and alleys of London. In 1767 died Widow Prossen, of Oxford-road, in her 102d year, having passed nearly her whole life among old clothes in a pawnbroker's shop, accumulating a large fortune. In the same year died her neighbour, Benjamin Perryn, aged 103.

In 1767 also we find Widow Waters, of Saffron-hill, dying at the age of 103; and one Wood, of Markam-court, Chandos-street, at 100.

In 1846 there died in grimy Holywell-street, Strand, one Harris, a Jew clothesman, who had lived in the same street more than seventy years: his wife died a few years before him, at the age of 93; and his eldest son was 73 at the time of his father's death. In 1780 there died in St. Martin's workhouse Widow Pettit, aged 114; and next year, Widow Parker, of White-Hart-yard, Drury-lane, aged 108, with all her faculties unimpaired.

In 1788 there died at Hoxton, aged 121, a widow, who, up to a very advanced period, cried gray peas for sale about the streets of London; and was well remembered by many aged persons as a woman apparently beyond the middle stage of life, full twenty years before the time of her decease.*

Occasionally we find very old persons almost *growing to the spot* on which they were born. In 1780 died at Englefield, Hants, James Hopper, an agricultural labourer, aged 108, who had never quitted his native Englefield even for a few miles. And in 1799 died Mr. Humphries, a carpenter, born at Newington, Surrey, aged 102, and who would never go more than two or three miles from the house in which he was born. One Trundle, a farmer of Rotherhithe, who died 1766, aged 100, had lived in the same house eighty-two years. Sometimes this takes the turn of misanthropic seclusion: Christopher Tarran, of Sutton, near Richmond, Yorkshire, who died 1827, aged 93, shut himself up in his chamber, from which he never stirred during the last twenty years of his life, and only twice admitted any one into the room. In 1811 there died at Desford, Leicestershire, one John Upton, aged 100; he had been a worsted framework-knitter for one firm in Leicester for ninety-three years.

Widow Richardson, of Holwell, Leicestershire, who died 1806, aged 97, kept school in the parish 75 years, and was never five miles from home during her long life.

We remember two stalwart millers, brothers, Joseph and John Saunders, aged 79 and 73, born at Pixham-mill, and then of Pixham-house, hard by, near the foot of Box-hill, Surrey, where they died, at the above ages.

LONGEVITY OF CLASSES.

Deep-thinking philosophers have at all times been distinguished by their great age, especially when their philosophy was occupied in the study of Nature, and afforded them the divine pleasure of discovering new and important truths,—the purest enjoyment; a beneficial exaltation of ourselves, and a kind of restoration which may be ranked among

* Bailey's *Records of Longevity*, p. 249.

the principal means of prolonging the life of a perfect being. The most ancient instances are to be found among the Stoics and the Pythagoreans, according to whose ideas subduing the passions and sensibility, with the observation of strict regimen, were the most essential duties of a philosopher. Thus, we have the examples of a Plato and an Isocrates. Apollonius of Tyana, an accomplished man, endowed with extraordinary powers both of body and mind, who by the Christians was considered as a magician, and by the Greeks and Romans as a messenger of the gods, in his regimen a follower of Pythagoras, and a friend to travelling, was above 100 years of age. Xenophilus, a Pythagorean also, lived 106 years. The philosopher Demonax, a man of the most severe manners and uncommon stoical apathy, lived likewise 100. Even in modern times philosophers seem to have obtained this preëminence; and the deepest thinkers appear in that respect to have enjoyed, in a higher degree, the fruits of their mental tranquillity. Kepler and Bacon both attained to a great age; and Newton, who found all his happiness and pleasure in the higher spheres, attained to the age of 84. Euler, a man of incredible industry, whose works on the most abstruse subjects amount to above three hundred, approached near to the same age; and Kant, who reached the age of 80, showed that philosophy not only can preserve life, but that it is the most faithful companion of the greatest age, and an inexhaustible source of happiness to one's self and to others. Academicians, in this respect, have been particularly distinguished. We need only mention the venerable Fontenelle,* who wanted but one year of a hundred, and that Nestor, Formey; both perpetual secretaries, the former of the French, and the latter of the Berlin Academy.

We find also many instances of long life among schoolmasters; so that one might almost believe that continual intercourse with youth may contribute something towards our renovation and support. But poets and artists, in short all those fortunate mortals whose principal occupation leads

* Fontenelle attributed his longevity to a good course of strawberry eating every season: his only ailment was fever in the spring; when he used to say, "If I can only hold out till strawberries come in, I shall get well." His long life may, however, rather be attributed to his insensibility, of which he himself boasted: he was rarely known to laugh or cry.

them to be conversant with the sports of fancy and self-created worlds, and whose whole life, in the properest sense, is an agreeable dream, have a particular claim to a place in the history of longevity. Anacreon, Sophocles, and Pindar attained a great age. Young, Voltaire, Bodmer, Haller, Metastasio, Gleim, Utz, and Oeser, all lived to be very old; and Wieland, the prince of German poets, lived to the age of 80. (See *Wilson on Longevity.*)

Among the clergy are several remarkable instances. The venerable Bishop Hough, the Cato of Sir Thomas Bernard's *Comforts of Old Age*, through an extraordinary degree of health of body and mind, attained the age of 92. "Blessed be God for his great mercies to me! I have to-day entered my ninetieth year, with less infirmity than I could have presumed to hope, and certainly with a degree of calmness and tranquillity of mind, which is gradually increasing as I daily approach the end of my pilgrimage. I think, indeed, that my life must now be but of short duration; and, I thank God, the thought gives me no uneasiness."*

Sancroft, Archbishop of Canterbury, after he had been deprived and ejected from Lambeth, for refusing to take any new oaths to William and Mary, retired to his paternal estate, of 50*l.* a year, at Fresingfield, in Suffolk, his birthplace. He was then approaching fourscore; and here he was visited by Bishop Hough, in 1693.

> I found him (says the Bishop) working in his garden, and taking advantage of a shower of rain which had fallen to transplant some lettuces. I was struck with the profusion of his vegetables, the beauty and luxuriance of his fruit-trees, and the richness and fragrance of his flowers, and noticed the taste which had directed every thing. "You must not compliment too hastily (says he) on the *directions* which I have given. Almost all you see is the work of my own hands. My old woman does the weeding, and John mows my turf and digs for me; but all the nicer work,—the sowing, grafting, budding, transplanting, and the like,—I trust to no other hand but my own; so long, at least, as my health will allow me to enjoy so pleasing an occupation. And in good sooth (added he) the fruits here taste more sweet, and the flowers have a richer perfume, than they had at Lambeth." I looked up to our deprived metropolitan with more respect, and thought his gardening-dress shed more splendour over him, than ever his robes and lawn-sleeves could have done when he was the first subject in this great kingdom.†

The Rev. Mr. Sampson, Incumbent of Keyham, Leicestershire, who died 1655, is stated by Thoresby to have held the

* Bishop Hough; *Comforts of Old Age.* † Ibid.

living of his parish 92 years; so that he could scarcely be less than 116 years old.

The Rev. R. Lufkin, Rector of Ufford, Suffolk, died September 1678, aged 110, having preached the Sunday before he died.

Morton, Bishop of Lichfield and Coventry, who died 1695, aged 95, constantly rose at four o'clock to his studies when he was 80 years old; he usually lay upon a straw bed, and seldom exceeded one meal a day.

Here are two lengthy incumbencies: "1753, December 22. Rev. Mr. Braithwaite, of Carlisle, [died] aged 110. He had been 100 years in the cathedral, having commenced singing-boy in the year 1652." "1763. Rev. Peter Alley (Rector of Donamow, Ireland, 73 years), [died] in the 111th year of his age. He did his own duty till within a few days of his death; he was twice married, and had thirty-three children."*

The Rev. John Bedwell, Rector of Odstock, near Salisbury, according to the Bishop's registry, held that benefice 73 years; and, by the parish register, died at the age of 108.

The Rev. S. W. Warneford, the munificent benefactor to colleges and schools, died 1855, aged 92; and Maltby, Bishop of Durham, 1859, at 90.

Soldiers who survive the chances of war are proverbial for long life: there are several instances recorded in the Chelsea Hospital burial-ground. The lists of the survivors of England's great battles present instances ranging from 100 to 120 years.† The oldest General of our time was Marshal Count Joseph Radetzsky, who died January 5, 1858, in his 92d year.

"History only mentions a single man who, at such an advanced age, commanded an army in the field; and that was Dandolo, the Doge of Venice, who was 95 years of age, and almost blind, when he commanded the Venetians in the great Crusade, and who was the first to enter Constantinople at the time of the assault on it in 1203. Talbot, Earl of Shrewsbury, was 83 years old when he commanded in Guienne, in 1453; but he was killed in the same year at the battle of Chatillon. Fuentes, General of the Spanish

* *Selections Gent. Mag.* vol. iv. p. 299.

† See *Choice Notes* (History), pp. 170-177; and Military Centenarians, *Notes and Queries*, 2d series, No. 232, pp. 238, 239, for several well-authenticated records.

troops at the battle of Rocroy, in 1643, was 82; but he was gouty, and was carried in an arm-chair. He fell in that battle, and with him disappeared the glory of the Spanish arms. The Prussian Field-Marshal Mollendorf was present, in his 82d year, at the defeat of Auerstadt, but not as commander-in-chief. One octogenarian of modern times has been more fortunate than the preceding, and that is Marshal de Villars, who, in his 81st year, undertook the campaign of 1712, crowned by the victory of Denain, which saved the French monarchy."*

Quakers attain great ages. In the Obituary of the *Friend* Magazine, 1860, we find the following ages of some deceased members of the Society of Friends: 84, 84, 85, 85, 85, 86, 86, 87, 87, 88, 88, 89, 89, 89, 91, 91, 91, 91, 91, 91, 92, 92, 93, 93—making a total of 2128 years, with an average for each life of rather more than 88½ years. Fifty lives in the same period give 4258 years, with an average of 85 per life. The average duration of life in the Society of Friends during 1860 was 58 years and 6 months; but one girl died under 6 months old; five girls and thirteen boys—in all eighteen out of the 324, or 5½ per cent—did not reach the age of one year.

Hard-workers are often long livers. Hobson, the noted Cambridge carrier, died on New-year's Day, 1630-1, it is said in his 86th year. His visits to London were suspended on account of the Plague, and during this cessation he died; whereupon Milton remarked that Death would never have hit him had he continued dodging it backwards and forwards between Cambridge and the Bull Inn, Bishopsgate.

One John King, of Nokes, Oxon, died in 1766, at the age of 130: he was a farm-labourer, and at the age of 128 walked to and from the market at Oxford—twelve miles. One Wilks, a farm-labourer, of Stourbridge, Worcestershire, who died 1777, aged 109, was suspected by his ignorant neighbours of having purchased the secret of long life from a witch with whom he had become acquainted.

An Irish fisherman, Jonas Warren, who died 1787, Mr. Bailey states, at 167, had for ninety-five years drawn his subsistence from the ocean. Another fisherman, Worrell, of Dunwich, Suffolk, died 1789, aged 119, having fished till he was 107.

* *Morning Advertiser.*

On June 3, 1862, there died at his farm, Tullyskerra, near Castleblayney, Gilbert Hand, at the advanced age of 105 years. Two days before his death deceased travelled round his farm, apparently taking his last farewell of the fields in which he so often toiled.

Of Ephraim Pratt, who was living at Shaftesbury, U.S., in 1803, aged 116 years, the Rev. Timothy Dwight relates that he had mown grass 101 years successively. He drank large quantities of milk, and in his latter years it was almost his sole sustenance. His descendants, to the fifth generation, it was publicly stated, numbered more than 1500 persons.

Margaret Woods, of Great Waltham, who died 1797, aged 100, had, with her ancestors, lived in the service of one Essex family for 400 years.

Here is well-authenticated evidence of long service from Sussex. At Battle is the gravestone of Isaac Ingoll, who died April 2, 1798, aged 120 years; his register is to be seen in the parish, and he lived 101 years in the service of the Webster family, of Battle Abbey, having entered it at the age of 19.*

Philip Palfreman, who had been box-keeper at the first Covent Garden Theatre in Garrick's time, died in 1768, aged 100: he almost lived in the theatre, and by his thrift saved a fortune of 10,000*l.* In 1845 died William Ward, aged 98, of the Sun Fire Office, London, where he had filled a situation seventy years.

Jockeys, from the severe effects of training, are proverbially short-lived; yet John Scott, of Brighton, once a jockey, reached the age of 96.

Great pedestrian feats have been performed by very old men. Mr. M'Leod, of Inverness, who died 1790, aged 102, two years previously walked from Inverness to London (five hundred miles) in nineteen days: he had served in Marlborough's wars.

On May 28, 1802, a lunatic named James Coyle, 47 years old, was admitted a patient into St. Patrick's (Swift's) Hospital, Dublin: he continued there upwards of fifty-eight years, and eventually died July 17, 1860, at the age of 105 There can surely be no mistake as to this great age.

* *Notes and Queries*, 2d series, No. 250.

Peter Breman, of Dyott-street, St. Giles's, London, is one of the few instances on record of long life attained by tall men: he stood 6 feet 6 inches high, and was in the army from the age of 18 nearly until his decease, in 1769, at the age of 104 years. Another tall man, Edmund Barry, of Watergrass-hill, Ireland, died 1822, aged 113: he was 6 feet 2 inches in height, and walked well to the last.

One John Minniken, of Maryport, Cumberland, who died 1793, aged 112, was remarkable for the fast growth and profusion of his hair, which he sold, in successive croppings, to a hairdresser of the town, for a penny a day, during the remainder of his life; and more than seventy wigs were made of Minniken's hair.

Among aged persons of diminutive stature was Mary Jones, of Wem, Salop, who died 1773, aged 100: she was only 2 feet 8 inches in height. Elspeth Watson, of Perth, who died 1800, aged 115, did not exceed 2 feet 9 inches in height, but was bulky in person.

Old age can rarely withstand intense grief. John Tice, of Hagley, Worcestershire, having recovered from a fall out of a tree when he was 80 years old, and from being much burned when he was 100, after the death of his patron, Lord Lyttleton, became so depressed in spirits, that he took to his bed and died. Sir Francis Burdett had withstood the storms and tumults of political life for more than half a century, and had reached the age of 74, when his dear wife died, Jan. 10, 1844: from that instant Sir Francis refused food or nourishment of any kind, and he died of intense grief on the 23d of the same month: both were buried in the same vault, in the same hour, on the same day, in the church of Ramsbury, Wilts.

Cardinal Fleury, the great French minister, who died in 1743, had attained the age of 90. For fourteen years he essentially contributed to the peace and prosperity of France; but the three last years of his administration were unfortunate. On the death of the Emperor Charles XI., in 1740, without male issue, a war ensued respecting the imperial succession, the calamitous events of which preyed on the Cardinal's mind and occasioned his death.

Sir John Floyer, Physician to Queen Anne, seems to have found the golden mean of happiness. He died in

1734; four years previous to which he visited Bishop Hough, at Hartlebury. "Sir John Floyer (writes the Bishop to a friend) has been with me some weeks; and all my neighbours are surprised to see a man of eighty-five, who has his memory, understanding, and all his senses good; and seems to labour under no infirmity. *He is of a happy temper, not to be moved with what he cannot remedy;* which I really believe has, in a great measure, helped to preserve his health and prolong his days." This is the grand secret. Sir John wrote a curious Essay on Cold Bathing, among the benefits of which he does not omit long life.

Dr. Cheyne, the Scottish physician, of this period, in his well-known Essay, advocates strict regimen for preventing and curing diseases: by milk and vegetable diet he reduced himself from thirty-two stone weight almost a third, recovered his strength, activity, and cheerfulness, and attained the good age of 72.

Jeremy Bentham, the eminent philosophical jurist and writer on legislation, died in 1832, in Queen-square-place, Westminster, where he had resided nearly half a century, in his 85th year. Up to extreme old age he retained much of the intellectual power of the prime of manhood, the simplicity and freshness of early youth; and even in the last moments of his existence the serenity and cheerfulness of his mind did not desert him. "He was capable," says Dr. Southwood Smith, to whom he bequeathed his body for purposes of anatomical science, in the lecture delivered over his remains, "of great severity and continuity of mental labour. For upwards of half a century he devoted seldom less than eight, often ten, and occasionally twelve hours of every day to intense study. This was the more remarkable as his physical constitution was by no means strong. His health during the periods of childhood, youth, and adolescence was infirm; it was not until the age of manhood that it acquired some degree of vigour; but that vigour increased with advancing age, so that during the space of sixty years he never laboured under any serious malady, and rarely suffered even from slight indisposition; and at the age of 84 he looked no older, and constitutionally was not older, than most men are at 60; thus adding another illustrious name to the splendid catalogue which establishes the fact, that severe and constant mental labour is not incompatible with health and longevity, but conducive to both, provided the mind be unanxious and the habits temperate.

"He was a great economist of time. He knew the value of minutes. The disposal of his hours, both of labour and of repose, was a matter of systematic arrangement; and the arrangement was determined on the principle that it is a calamity to lose the smallest portion of time. He did not deem it sufficient to provide against the loss of a day or an hour; he took effectual means to prevent the occurrence of any such calamity to him. But he did more: he was careful to provide against the loss of even a single minute; and there is on record no example of a human being who lived more habitually under the practical consciousness that his days are numbered, and that 'the night cometh in which no man can work.'"

It should, however, be added, that Mr. Bentham's lot in life was a happy one. Even though he did not enjoy a widely diffused reputation in his own country, and his peculiar views exposed him to the attacks of contemporary writers, his easy circumstances and excellent health enabled him to devote his whole time and energies to those pursuits which exercised his highest faculties, and were to him a rich and unfailing source of the most delightful excitement. His retired habits likewise preserved him from personal contact with any but those who valued his acquaintance; and as for the writers who spoke of him with ridicule and contempt, he never read them, and therefore they never disturbed the serenity of his mind, or ruffled the tranquil surface of his contemplative and happy life.

It would be well for public writers if they possessed more of such equanimity as Mr. Bentham's, to shield them from the venom of adverse criticism and the attacks of those dishonest critics who abuse every indication of success which they conceive to stand in the way of their own advancement. We have something of the old leaven of Grub-street in our times, though the name is blotted out from our metropolitan streetology. It is true that the patronage of great men is no longer valued by men of letters,—it is but as dust in the balance against the weight of public opinion,—but something of the old trade of factious criticism which Swift, Pope, and Warburton so mercilessly exposed, has survived even to our days.

Mr. Thackeray, to our thinking one of the most masculine and unaffected writers of his day, has well described the Grub-street association of "author and rags—author and dirt—author and gin," such as were the literary hacks of the reign of George II.; but literature now takes its rank with other learned professions.

To return to Longevity. The following additional instances are mostly of our own time:

Among Lawyers, Francis Maseres, fifty years Cursitor-Baron of the Court of Exchequer, died 1824, at the age of 93: he was a ripe classical scholar, and one of the ablest mathematicians of his day. The Eldon family present three noteworthy examples: Mr. Scott, the Newcastle merchant, father of Lord Stowell and the Earl of Eldon, died 1800, at the age of 92: the two eminent sons, Stowell, 1836, at 91, and Eldon, 1838, at 87. Lord Plunket, the statesman and lawyer, who died 1854, had reached 90. Lord Chancellor Campbell, who in his busy law-life wrote many volumes of biography, attained the age of 81.

Sir William Blizard, the Surgeon, who died in 1835, in his 94th year, rose to eminence under many disadvantages. With all his activity and industry, except a fever caught by working night and day in the dissecting-room, his health never failed him till the last; he was temperate; and the only wine he drank was Cape. Sir William Burnett, the physician and scientific inventor, reached 82.

In 1862 two eminent Mathematicians died within a month of each other: Jean Baptiste Biot, aged 88; and Peter Barlow, 86. Prof. Narrien, of Sandhurst, died 1860, at 77; and, same year and age, Finlaison, the actuary.

Francis Place, the Westminster Politician, who died 1854, had reached 82. The Duc de Pasquier, the celebrated French statesman, attained the great age of 96: he died 1862, and was the oldest statesman of our time. Talleyrand, next to Napoleon the most extraordinary man of the revolutionary period of France, died 1838, aged 84.

The oldest Poets of our time were W. L. Bowles, 1850, aged 88; same year, Wordsworth, poet-laureate, 80; James Montgomery, 1854, at 82; Samuel Rogers, 1855, aged 96; Arndt, the German poet, 1860, at 91; and Dr. Croly, the poet and divine, 86.

Mitscherlich, the German Philologist, died 1854, at 94; same year, Gresnall, biographer, 89, and Faber, theologian, 80. Hamner-Purgstall, the Oriental historian, who died 1856, had attained 87; 1857, Hincks, the Orientalist, 90.

Sir John Stoddart, the Newspaper editor, who died 1855, had reached 85,—a rare age for a public journalist. John Sharpe, the tasteful *littérateur*, who died 1860, reached 83.

Dr. Lingard, the Historian, died 1851, aged 82. In 1859, Hallam, the historian; same year, Elphinstone, the historian of India, aged 81.

John Britton, the Topographer and antiquary, who died 1857, had reached 86: he was cheerful and chirping almost to the end. His brother topographer, Brayley, died 1854, aged 85. John Adey Repton, the architect and archæologist, died 1860, aged 86; Joseph Hunter, archæologist, 1861, 78.

Kirby, the Entomologist, who died 1850, had reached 91. Professor Jameson, the naturalist, died 1854, aged 81. Brunel, the engineer of the Thames Tunnel, died 1849, aged 81. Captain Manby, who invented apparatus for saving shipwrecked persons, and who died 1854, had reached 89. Sir John Ross, the Arctic navigator, died 1856, at 79. The chemists, Andrew Ure, at 79, and Thenard, at 80, died 1857. Baron Humboldt, who died 1859, reached 92; same year, Sir G. Staunton, the Chinese scholar, at 79. Colonel Leake, the geographer, 1860, at 83; and in the same year Carl Ritter, the geographer, 81; and Bishop Rigaud, astronomer, 85.

In 1858 died an unusually large number of Men of Science and Letters, and Artists, at great ages. Count Radetzsky, at 92; Creuzer, the German antiquary, 87; Thomas Tooke, political economist, 85; three musical composers, Neukomm, 80; J. B. Cramer, 88; and Horsley, 84;—Esenbach, botanist, 82; Aimé de Bonpland, 85; Robert Brown, botanist, 84; Bunting, Wesleyan preacher, 80; Mrs. Marcet, educational writer, 89; Edward Pease, "the Father of Railways," 92; Robert Owen, socialist, 87; Richard Taylor, of the *Philosophical Magazine*, 77.

In 1860 we lost the following eminent Engineers: Vicat (France), aged 75; General Pasley, 80; Eaton Hodgkinson, 72; Sir Howard Douglas, 86. In 1862 there died General Tulloch, at 72; and James Walker, at 81; and in 1860, Jesse Hartley, 80.

Charles Macklin, the oldest English Actor and playwright, who died 1797, had reached the age of 107: for his last twenty years he never took off his clothes, except to change them, or to be rubbed over with warm brandy or gin; he ate, drank, and slept without regard to set times, but according to his inclination.

M. Delphat, the French Musician, who died 1855, had reached 99; and in the same year died Robert Linley, the violoncellist, at 83. John Braham lived far beyond the usual age of singers, namely, to his 82d year: he died February 17, 1856; he first sung in public when ten years old. Ludwig Spohr, the German composer, died 1859, at 80.

Some aged persons have literally fallen asleep in death. Sir Christopher Wren passed his latter years at Hampton Court, and his town-house in St. James's-street. He caught cold, and this hastened his death. He was in town; he was accustomed to sleep a short time after dinner; and on February 25, 1723, his servant, thinking his master had slept longer than usual, went into his room, and found Wren dead in his chair: he was in his 91st year. James Elmes, who wrote Wren's life, died 1862, aged 80.

Copley, the Painter, died 1815, aged 78; his son, Lord Lyndhurst, in 1863, attained his 91st year: his mother lived to see her son a second time Lord High Chancellor. Stothard, for several months before his decease, though his bodily infirmities prevented his attending to his labours as an artist, would not relinquish his attendance at the meetings and lectures of the Royal Academy and in the library, notwithstanding extreme deafness prevented his hearing what was passing. Mr. Constable, in a letter to a friend, written in 1838, says: "I passed an hour or two with Mr. Stothard on Sunday evening. Poor man! the only elysium he has in this world he finds in his own enchanting works. His daughter does all in her power to make him happy and comfortable." Leslie remarks that Stothard must have possessed great constitutional serenity of mind; he was also, no doubt, much supported by his art. His easel, indeed, bore evidence of the many years he had passed before it; the lower bar, on which his foot rested, being nearly worn through. He died April 27, 1834, in his 80th year, at his house in Newman-street, where he had resided more than forty years.

Sir M. A. Shee, Painter, P.R.A., died 1850, at the age of 80. J. M. W. Turner, the greatest landscape painter, R.A., 1851, at 77; and 1854, Geo. Clint, painter of humour, 82; Wachter, the famous historical painter, who died 1852, reached 90. Two aged Frenchmen died 1853: Fontaine, the architect, 90; and Renouard, bibliographer, 98. James Ward, the animal painter, who died 1859, reached 91; Alfred Chalon, 1860, at 80; and in 1859, David Cox, founder of our Water-Colour School, 76.

In 1850 died Schadow, the Hungarian Sculptor, 86. In 1856, Sir R. Westmacott, the sculptor, R.A.; and next year, Christian Rauch, the German sculptor, at 80.

Matthew Cotes Wyatt, the Sculptor of the colossal Wellington statue, died 1862, at 86. The oldest engraver of the above period was John Landseer, who died 1852, aged 90.

Sir John Soane, R.A., the Architect, died 1837, having reached the age of 84, bequeathing his museum, in Lincoln's-inn Fields, to the nation. Sir John was the son of a Berkshire bricklayer, and by his own energy rose to eminence as an architect: he designed a greater number of public edifices than any contemporary. His last work (1833), the State-Paper Office, in St. James's-park, was very unlike any other of his designs; it was taken down in 1862.

Foster, the Artist, of Derby, celebrated the hundredth anniversary of his birthday on November 8, 1862, when he was entertained by his friends in the county hall. Mr. Foster served under Abercrombie in Egypt, and left the army on the day on which Nelson died. He has been five times married; and his youngest child, born sixty-eight years after his eldest, is now (1862) only ten years of age.

The great ages in the following records must be considered very remarkable:

Mr. Henry H. Breen, writing from St. Lucia, states that Louis Mutal, a Negro, died in the island in 1851, at the age of 135 years. Mutal was a native of Macouba, in the island of Martinique, and about 1785 settled in St. Lucia as a dealer in trade; after his death was found among his papers his marriage contract with his slave, Marie Catherine, in 1771, which establishes the fact of his being then 55 years of age, and consequently of his having been born in 1716. This is followed by a certificate, showing that the marriage contract was published and recorded in 1772. The date of his death in the parish register has been carefully verified by Mr. Breen, who adds: "There are now living in this island several persons of the age of 90, or upwards," in a population of about 26,000 souls. The particulars are:

Madame Toraille, coloured	aged	90
Madame Morel, coloured	„	90
Madame Jacob, coloured	„	92
Madame St. Philip, white	„	92
Madame Guy de Mareil, white	„	93
Mademoiselle Vitalis, white	„	96
Madame Anne, black	„	102
Madame Coudrey, coloured	„	106
Madame Baudoin, white	„	106*

* Communicated to *Notes and Queries*, August 4, 1855.

Another Correspondent, writing from Malta in 1855, states that Tony Proctor, a free coloured man, died at Tallahasse, Florida, June 16, 1854, aged 112. He was at the battle of Quebec, as the servant of an English officer, in 1759; and he was at the beginning of the revolutionary war in the vicinity of Boston, at the time the tea was thrown overboard; and was afterwards present at the battle of Lexington.*

THE HAPPY OLD MAN.

The wisest and best productions of the human intellect, says Dr. Moore,† have proceeded from those who have lived through the bustling morning and meridian periods of their day, and calmly sat down to think and instruct others in the meditative evening of life. Even when the brilliancy of reason's sunset yields to the advancing gloom, there is an indescribable beauty haunting the old man still, if in youth and vigour his soul was conversant with truth; and even when the chill of night is upon him, his eye seems to rest upon the glories for awhile departed; or he looks off into the stars, and reads in them his destiny with a gladness as quiet and as holy as their light.

How instructive is the usual state of memory and hope in advanced life! As the senses become dull, the nervous system slow, and the whole body unfit for active uses, the old man necessarily falls into constant abstraction. Like all debilitated persons, he feels his unfitness for action, and, of course, becomes querulous if improperly excited. Peacefulness, gentle exercise among flowers and trees, unstimulating diet, and the quiet company of books and philosophic toys, are suitable for him. With such helps his heart will beat kindly, and his intellect, however childlike, will maintain a beautiful power to the last. Objects of affection occasionally move him with more than their accustomed force. Young children are especially agreeable to him. When approaching him with the gentle love and reverence which unspoiled childhood is so apt to exhibit, his heart seems suddenly to kindle as the little fingers wander over his shrivelled hand and wrinkled brow. He smiles, and at once goes back in spirit to his childhood, and finds a world of fun, frolic, and liveliness before him;

* *Notes and Queries*, September 8, 1855.
† *The Use of the Body to the Mind.*

and he has tales of joy and beauty, which children and age and holy beings can best appreciate. Next to the children of his children, the old man, whose thoughts have been directed by the Bible, loves the society of persons of holy habits; and as he finds these more frequently among females, such are generally his associates. But all aged and infirm persons he deems fit company, because they, like himself, are busied in reviewing past impressions, rather than planning or plotting for a livelihood, or reasoning about ways and means. The past is his own, and he cons it over like a puzzling but at least an interesting lesson. If his soul have been trained to delight in truth, his will becomes weaned from this world of effort in proportion as he feels the weakness that disqualifies him from struggling on in it. Yet *in our ashes live their wonted fires:* he feels an internal, a spiritual energy, awakening in a new manner the sympathies that belong to his being, and he feels as if his affections had been laid by to ripen into an intensity out of keeping with the usages and objects about him. He realises most fully the facts of a coming life, and even now lives apart from the present; and if his habits of reflection be not distracted, and his heart broken by hard and ignorant treatment, and if his soul have not been wedded to care by a love of gold without the possibility of divorce, and mammon have not branded his spirit with indelible misery, then is the old man ready to enter on a purely spiritual existence with alacrity and joy.

PREPARATORY TO DEATH.

Jeremy Taylor, in his *Holy Dying* (General Considerations Preparatory to Death), has this memorable passage, in which he illustrates the daily experiences of every thoughtful mind:

And because this consideration is of great usefulness and of great necessity to many purposes of wisdom and the spirit, all the succession of time, all the changes in nature, all the varieties of light and darkness, the thousand thousands of accidents in the world, and every contingency to every man and to every creature, doth preach our funeral sermon, and calls us to look and see how the old sexton Time throws up the earth and digs a grave where we must lay our sins or our sorrows, and sow our bodies till they rise again in a fair or in an intolerable eternity. Every revolution which the sun makes about the world divides between life and death; and death possesses both those portions by the next morrow, and we are dead to all those months which we have already lived, and we shall never live them over again: and still God makes little periods of our age. First we change our world, when we come from the womb to feel the warmth of the sun. Then we sleep and enter into the image of death, in which state we are unconcerned in all the changes of the world [who hath not felt this when stretched upon his bed at the close of day?]: and if our mothers or our nurses die, or a wild boar destroy our vineyards, or our king be sick, we regard it not, but during that state are as disinterested as if our eyes were closed with the clay that weeps in the bowels of the earth. At the end of seven years our teeth fall and die before us, representing a formal prologue to the tragedy; and still every seven years it is odds but we shall finish the last scene: and when nature, or chance, or vice, takes our bodies in pieces, weakening some parts and loosing others, we *taste the grave* and the solemnities of our own funerals, first in those parts that ministered to vice, and next in them that served for ornament; and in a short time even they that served for necessity become useless, and entangled like the wheels of a broken clock. *Baldness* is but a dressing to our funerals, the proper ornament of mourning, and of a person entered very far into the regions and possession of death: and we have many more of the same signification: gray hairs, rotten teeth, dim eyes, trembling joints, short breath, stiff limbs, wrinkled skin, short memory, decayed appetite. Every day's necessity calls for a reparation of that portion which death fed on all night when we lay in his lap and slept in his outer chambers. The very spirits of a man prey upon the daily portion of bread and flesh, and every meal is a rescue from one death, and lays up for another: and while we think a thought we die; and the clock strikes, and reckons on our portion of eternity; we form our words with the breath of our nostrils, we have the less to live upon for every word we speak.

Thus nature calls us to meditate of death by those things which are the instruments of acting it: and God by all the variety of his Providence makes us see death every where, in all variety of circumstances, and dressed up for all the fancies and the expectation of every single person.

Nature hath given us one harvest every year, but death hath two: and the spring and the autumn sends throngs of men and women to charnel-houses; and all the summer long men are recovering from their evils of the spring, till the dog-days come, and then the Syrian star makes the summer deadly; and the fruits of autumn are laid up for all the year's provision, and the man that gathers them eats and surfeits, and dies and needs them not, and himself is laid up for eternity; and he that escapes till the winter only stays for another opportunity, which the distempers of that quarter minister to him with great variety. Thus death reigns in all the portions of our time. The autumn with its fruits provides disorders for us, and the winter's cold turns them into sharp diseases, and the spring brings flowers to strew our hearse, and the summer gives green turf and brambles to bind upon our graves. Calentures and surfeit, cold and agues, are the four quarters of the year, and all minister to death; and you can go no whither but you tread upon a dead man's bones.

DEATH BEFORE ADAM.

Two hundred years ago, long before the science of Geology called for the belief that mortality had been stamped on creation, and had manifested its proofs in the animal races previously to Adam's appearance, Jeremy Taylor could write as follows regarding Adam himself before the Fall. He considers him to have been created mortal; not merely liable to become mortal, but actually mortal.

"For 'flesh and blood,' that is, whatsoever is born of Adam, 'cannot inherit the kingdom of God.' And they are injurious to Christ who think that from Adam we might have inherited immortality. Christ was the giver and preacher of it; 'he brought life and immortality to light through the Gospel.'"

Again: "For that Adam was made mortal in his nature is infinitely certain, and proved by his very eating and drinking, his sleep and recreation, &c."

And in another passage, quoted by Professor Hitchcock: "That death which God threatened to Adam, and which passed upon his posterity, is not the going out of this world, but the manner of going. If he had stayed in innocence, he should have gone placidly and fairly, without vexatious and affective circumstances; he should not have died by sickness, defect, misfortune, or unwillingness." These sentiments Archdeacon Pratt* quotes, not as necessarily approving them, but to show that so good and learned a man as Jeremy Taylor had a view regarding death and mortality no less unusual than that which Geology demands.

FUTURE EARTHLY EXISTENCE OF THE HUMAN RACE.

Regarding Man, independently of any revealed knowledge of his future destiny, but simply with reference to his relations with the physical world about him, Mr. Hopkins, the able geologist, asks: "Do we see in his character and position here any indication that this earth is his destined abiding place for indefinite periods of time? We conceive that a negative answer to the question is suggested at least by the fact that the extent of the earth's surface and its powers of production are *finite*, whereas the tendency in human population to increase is unlimited. It is undoubt-

* *Science and Scripture not at Variance*, 2d ed. 1858.

edly easy to conceive this tendency to be arrested, but not probably by causes consistent with the moral and physical well-being of the race. Whether human population may have increased or not during the last two thousand years, is a matter of little import, we conceive, to the question before us. We know that it is now spreading itself over many parts of the globe, under influences far different from those under which it has heretofore extended,—the influence of Christianity, and of that higher civilisation which must attend the pure doctrines of our religion. We believe that this extension and increase of the civilised races of mankind will continue; and, however it may be temporarily checked by the hardships and evils to which man is subject, we can hardly understand how this tendency can be effectively and finally arrested before the population of the globe shall have approximated to that limit which must be necessarily imposed upon it by the finite dimensions of man's dwelling-place. We know not what might be the views of political economists on this ultimate condition of human population; but we feel it difficult to conceive its existence, under merely human influences, independently of physical want, and possibly of that moral debasement which so frequently attends it. In fact, those who regard man simply in his human character and in his relations to *nature*, and not in his relations to God, must find in his earthly future the most insoluble problem which can offer itself to the speculative philosopher. It would seem equally difficult to assign to the human race an indefinite term of existence, or to sweep it away by natural causes from the face of the earth. But it is in such questions as this that a steady faith in man's Creator and Redeemer affords to the embarrassed mind a calm and welcome resting-place. Those who believe man's introduction on the earth to have been a direct act of his Almighty Creator, will not think it necessary to look for his final earthly destiny in the operation of merely secondary causes, but will refer it to the same Divine Agency as that to which he refers the origin of the race."*

* *Geology*, by William Hopkins, M.A., F.R.S.; *Cambridge Essays*, 1857.

The School of Life.

WHAT IS EDUCATION?

BISHOP BURNET seems to have given the reply in the fewest words when he observes: "The education of youth is the foundation of all that can be performed for bettering the next age."

"Education," says Paley, "in the most extensive sense of the word, may comprehend every preparation that is made in our youth for the sequel of our lives; and in this sense I use it. Some such preparation is necessary for all conditions, because without it they must be miserable, and probably will be vicious, when they grow up, either from the want of the means of subsistence, or from want of rational and inoffensive occupation. In civilised life, every thing is affected by art and skill. Whence a person who is provided with neither (and neither can be acquired without exercise and instruction) will be useless, and he that is useless will generally be at the same time mischievous, to the community. So that to send an uneducated child into the world is injurious to the rest of mankind; it is little better than to turn out a mad dog or a wild-beast into the streets."

Who are the uneducated? is a question not easily to be answered in a time when books have come to be household furniture in every habitation of the civilised world. All that men have contrived, discovered, done, felt, or imagined, is recorded in books; wherein whoso has learned to spell printed letters may find such knowledge, and turn it to advantageous account.

D'Israeli the younger, in one of his politico-economic speeches, remarks: "As civilisation has gradually progressed, it has equalised the physical qualities of man. Instead of the strong arm, it is now the strong head that is the moving principle of society. You have disenthroned Force, and placed on her high seat Intelligence; and the necessary consequence of this great revolution is, that it has become the duty and the delight equally of every citizen to cultivate his faculties."

TEACHING YOUNG CHILDREN.

Coleridge relates that Thelwall thought it very unfair to influence a child's mind by inculcating any opinions before it should have come to years of discretion, and be able to choose for itself. "I showed him my garden," says Coleridge, "and told him it was my botanical garden." "How so?" said he; "it is covered with weeds." "Oh!" I replied, "that is only because it has not yet come to its age of discretion and choice. The weeds you see have taken the liberty to grow, and I thought it unfair in me to prejudice the soil towards roses and strawberries."

Madame de Lambert, in her work *Sur l'Education d'une jeune Demoiselle*, says: "The greatest enemy that we have to combat in the education of children is self-love; and to this enemy we cannot give attention too early. Our business is to weaken it, and we must be careful not to strengthen it by indiscriminate praise. Frequent praise encourages pride, induces a child to value herself as superior to her companions, and renders her unable to bear any reproach or objection however mild. We should be cautious, even in the expression of affection, not to lead children to suppose that we are constantly occupied with them. Timid children may be encouraged by praise; but it must be judiciously bestowed, and for their good conduct, not for personal graces. Above all things, it is necessary to inspire them with a love of truth; to teach them to practise it at their own expense; and to impress it upon their minds that there is nothing so truly great as the frank acknowledgment, 'I am wrong.'"

Harriet Martineau observes: "It is a matter of course that no mother will allow any ignorant person to have access to her child who will frighten it with goblin stories or threats of the old black man. She might as well throw up her charge at once, and leave off thinking of household education altogether, as permit her child to be exposed to such maddening inhumanity as this. The instances are not few of idiotcy or death from terror so caused."

Children should not be hedged-in with any great number of rules and regulations. Such as are necessary to be established, they should be required implicitly to observe. But there should be none that are superfluous. It is only in rich families, where there is a plentiful attendance of governors and nurses, that many rules can be enforced; and it is believed that the constant attention of governors and nurses is one of the greatest moral disadvantages to which the children of the rich are exposed.

Coleridge has well said: "The most graceful objects in nature are little children—before they have learned to dance."

"Grace," says Archbishop Whately, "is in a great measure a natural gift; elegance implies cultivation, or something of more artificial character. A rustic, uneducated girl may be graceful, but an elegant woman must be accomplished and well trained. It is the same with things as with persons; we talk of a graceful tree, but of an elegant house or other building. Animals may be graceful, but they cannot be elegant. The movements of a kitten or a young fawn are full of grace; but to call them 'elegant' animals would be absurd. Lastly, 'elegant' may be applied to mental qualifications, which 'graceful' never can. Elegance must always imply something that is made or invented by man. An imitation of nature is not so; therefore we do not speak of an 'elegant picture,' though we do of an elegant pattern for a gown, an elegant piece of work. The general rule is, that elegance is the characteristic of art, and grace of nature."

EDUCATION AT HOME.

Education at Home has been thus aptly illustrated: History and Geography should begin at home. If we want a boy to know some day the families of the Herods and the Cæsars, let him start by learning who was his own grandfather. The Church Catechism rightly commences by making the child tell his own name; it would be in many cases almost puzzling, but in all cases and senses a most proper question, to ask him, further, the names of his godfathers and godmothers; and so carrying him gradually onward, he would know, what seldom happens, the kings of England before he attempts those of Israel and Judah. This principle holds as true of places as of persons. The things that touch us nearest interest us most. Geography should begin from the school-walls: "Which side of this room does the sun rise on?" "Does Church-lane run west or north?" "Whither does the brook flow that rises on Squash-hill?" In this way the young scholar would in time be brought to comprehend the round world and his own position on it, and probably with some clearer perception of the truth and relation of things than if he had begun by rote: "The earth is a terraqueous globe, depressed at the poles, consisting of," &c. But we are all taught on the contrary plan. We begin at the wrong end; for, in the ladder of learning, *Ego*, not Adam, is the true No. 1. We start from the equator instead of High-street, and the result is the lamentable fact, that even educated men are strangers in their own country, and thousands die within the sound of Bow-bells who have never seen the inside of St. Paul's. Topography, then, should precede geography. Yet perhaps there is not a schoolroom in England where a county map is to be found hung up on the wall. Frightened by the remembrance of having been once the deluded subscriber to a Topographical Dictionary, even students have a horror of the word; and the subject is consigned, in expensive folios, to a few professed antiquaries, or to some eccentric member of a county family, who emerges every third or fourth generation to preserve a provincial dignity which he would not willingly let die.*

TENDERNESS OF YOUTH.

Leaving home the first time, for school, has been thus pathetically described by Southey: "The pain which is felt when we are first transplanted from our native soil, when the living branch is cut from the parent tree, is one

* *Quarterly Review.*

of the most poignant griefs which we have to endure through life. There are after-griefs which wound more deeply, which leave behind them scars never to be effaced, which bruise the spirit, and sometimes break the heart: but never do we feel so keenly the want of love, the necessity of being loved, and the utter sense of desertion, as when we first leave the haven of home, and are, as it were, pushed off upon the stream of life." Nelson, when he was sent a boy first to rough it out at sea, felt this loneliness most acutely: he paced the deck most of the day without being noticed by any one; and it was not till the second day that somebody, as he expresses it, "took compassion on him." Nelson had a feeble body and an affectionate heart, and he remembered through life his first days of wretchedness in the service.

Humanity to animals has been thus eloquently enjoined upon children by Dr. Parr: "He that can look with rapture upon the agonies of an unoffending and unresisting animal, will soon learn to view the sufferings of a fellow-creature with indifference: and in time he will acquire the power of viewing them with triumph, if that fellow-creature should become the victim of his resentment, be it just or unjust. But the minds of children are open to impressions of every sort, and indeed wonderful is the facility with which a judicious instructor may habituate them to tender emotions. I have therefore always considered mercy to beings of an inferior species as a virtue which children are very capable of learning, but which is most difficult to be taught if the heart has been once familiarised to spectacles of distress, and has been permitted either to behold the pangs of any living creature with cold insensibility, or to inflict them with wanton barbarity."

BUSINESS OF EDUCATION.

Among the many recommendations which will always attach to a public system of education, the value of early emulation, the force of example, the abandonment of sulky and selfish habits, and the acquirement of generous, manly dispositions, are not to be overlooked. To begin at the beginning is the only royal road to learning; and this is only to be reached by attention to elementary truths. Yet this is difficult, even for cultivated men. "In reality," says Dr. Temple, "elementary truths are the hardest of all to learn, unless we pass our childhood in an atmosphere thoroughly impregnated with them; and then we imbibe them unconsciously, and find it difficult to perceive their difficulty."* Yet how few children have this advantage: so many false impressions are received in childhood, that the first business of education proper is to *unlearn*.

The superior influence of example over precept is thus eloquently illustrated by Carlyle: "Is not love, from of old, known to be the beginning of all things? And what is admiration of the great but love of the truly lovable? The first product of love is imitation, that all-important peculiar gift of man, whereby mankind is not only held socially together in the present time, but connected in like union with the past and future; so that the attainment of the innumerable departed can be conveyed down to the living, and transmitted with increase to the unborn. Now, great men, in particular spiritually great men (for all men have a spirit to guide, though all have not kingdoms to govern and battles to fight), are the men universally imitated and learned of, the glass in which whole generations survey and shape themselves."

Lord Jeffrey has remarked upon the necessity of early restraint, that

> Young people who have been habitually gratified in all their desires will not only more indulge in capricious desires, but will infallibly take it more amiss when the feelings or happiness of others require that they should be thwarted, than those who have been practically trained to the habit of subduing and restraining them; and consequently will in general sacrifice the happiness of others to their own selfish indulgence. To what else is the selfishness of princes and other great people to be attributed? It is in vain to think of cultivating principles of generosity and beneficence by mere exhortation and reasoning. Nothing but the *practical habit* of overcoming our own selfishness, and of familiarly encountering privations and discomfort on account of others, will ever enable us to do it when required. And therefore I am firmly persuaded that indulgence infallibly produces selfishness and hardness of heart, and that nothing but a pretty severe discipline and control can lay the foundation of a magnanimous character.

THE CLASSICS.

Especially was Dr. Arnold an orthodox Oxonian in his

* *Education of the World.*

belief of the indispensable usefulness of Classical Learning, not only as an important branch of knowledge, but as the substantial basis of education itself, the importance of which he thus forcibly illustrates: "The study of Greek and Latin, considered as mere languages, is of importance mainly as it enables us to understand and employ well that language in which we commonly think and speak and write. It does this because Greek and Latin are specimens of language at once highly perfect and incapable of being understood without long and minute attention: the study of them, therefore, naturally involves that of the general principles of grammar; while their peculiar excellences illustrate the points which render language clear and forcible and beautiful. But our *application* of this general knowledge must naturally be to our own language: to show us what are its peculiarities, what its beauties, what its defects; to teach us, by the patterns or the analogies offered by other languages, how the effect we admire in them may be produced with a somewhat different instrument. Every lesson in Greek or Latin may and ought to be made a lesson in English; the translation of every sentence in Demosthenes or Tacitus is properly an extemporaneous English composition; a problem, how to express with equal brevity, clearness, and force, in our own language, the thought which the original author has so admirably expressed in his."

In other words, Dr. Arnold was the first English commentator who gave life to the study of the Classics, by bringing the facts and manners which they disclose to the test of real life.

Mr. Buckle, siding with the anti-classicists, remarks that, "With the single exception of Porson, not one of the great English scholars has shown an appreciation of the beauties of his native language; and many of them, such as Parr (in all his works) and Bentley (in his mad edition of Milton) have done every thing in their power to corrupt it. And there can be little doubt that the principal reason why well-educated women write and converse in a purer style than well-educated men, is because they have not formed their taste according to those ancient classical standards, which, admirable as they are in themselves, should never be introduced into a state of society unfitted for them. To this may be added, that Cobbett, the most racy and idiomatic of all our writers, and Erskine, by far the greatest of our forensic orators, knew little or nothing of any ancient language; and the same observation applies to Shakspeare."*

Our author has been just to Porson, to whom chiefly English scholarship owes its accuracy and its certainty; and this as a branch of education—as a substratum on which to rest other branches of knowledge often infinitely more useful in themselves—really takes as high a rank as any of those studies which can contribute to form the character of a well-educated English gentleman.

LIBERAL EDUCATION.

Dean Hook has written the following able defence of a Liberal Education, as distinguished from the special training for a profession:

A Liberal Education is to the present time the characteristic of what is called a University Education. By a liberal education is meant a non-professional education. By a non-professional educational is meant an education conducted without reference to the future profession, or calling, or special pursuit for which the person under education is designed. It is an education which is regarded not merely as a means, but as something which is in itself an end. The end proposed is not the formation of the divine, or the physician, or the lawyer, or the statesman, or the soldier, or the man of business, or the botanist, or the chemist, or the man of science, or even the scholar; but simply of the thinker.

It is admitted that the highest eminence can only be attained by the concentration of the mind, with a piercing intensity and singleness of view, upon one field of action. In order to excel, each mind must have its specific end. A man may know many things well, but there is only one thing upon which he will be preëminently learned, and become an authority. The professional man may be compared to one whose eye is fixed upon a microscope. The rest of the world is abstracted from his field of vision, and the eye, though narrowed to a scarcely perceptible hole, is able to see what is indiscernible by others. When he observes accurately, he becomes, in his department, a learned man; and when he reveals his observations, he is a benefactor of his kind. All that the university system does is to delay the professional education as long as possible; it would apply to the training of the mind a discipline analogous to that which common sense suggests in what relates to bodily exercise. A father, ambitious for his son that he might win the prize at the Olympian games or in the Pythian fields, devoted his first attention not to the technicalities of the game, but to the general condition and morals of the youth. The success of the athlete depended upon his first becoming a healthy man. So the university system trains the

* *History of Civilisation in England.*

man, and defers the professional education as long as circumstances will permit. It makes provision, before the eye is narrowed to the microscope, that the eye itself shall be in a healthy condition; it expands the mind before contracting it; it would educate mind as such before bending it down to the professional point; it does not regard the mind as an animal to be fattened for the market, by cramming it with food before it has acquired the power of digestion, but treats it rather as an instrument to be tuned, as a metal to be refined, as a weapon to be sharpened.

This is the system which the old universities of Europe have ininherited.

Philology, logic, and mathematics are still the instruments employed for the discipline of the mind, which is the end and object of a Liberal Education.*

The best education has been thus bodied forth: "Let a man's pride be to be a gentleman: furnish him with elegant and refined pleasures, imbue him with the love of intellectual pursuits, and you have a better security for his turning out a good citizen and a good Christian, than if you have confined him by the strictest moral and religious discipline, kept him in innocent and unsuspecting ignorance of all the vices of youth, and in the mechanical and orderly routine of the severest system of education."†

DR. ARNOLD'S SCHOOL REFORM.

Dr. Arnold, from his entering upon the head-mastership of Rugby, threw himself into the great work of school reform, based upon the associations of his boyhood, and the convictions of his more mature experience. "To do his duty was the height of his ambition,—those truly English sentiments by which Nelson and Wellington were inspired; and, like them, he was crowned with victory; for soon were verified the predictions of the Provost of Oriel, that *he would change the face of education through the public schools of England*. He was minded, *virtute officii*, to combine the care of souls with that of the intellects of the rising generation, and to realise the Scripture in principle and practice, without making an English school a college of Jesuits. His principles were few: the fear of God was the beginning of his wisdom; and his object was not so much to teach knowledge, as the means of acquiring it; to furnish, in a word,

* *Lives of the Archbishops of Canterbury.* † *Quarterly Review*, No. 103.

the key to the temple. He desired to awaken the intellect of each individual boy, and contended that the main movement must come from within and not from without the pupil; and that all that could be, should be *done by* him and not *for* him. In a word, his scheme was to call forth in the little world of school those capabilities which best befitted the boy for his career in the great one."*

SCHOOL INDULGENCE.

Nothing is more prejudicial to after-success in life than indulgence to youth when at school. Sir James Mackintosh felt and acknowledged this error. He tells us that when he left school he could only imperfectly construe a small part of Virgil, Horace, and Sallust: he adds, "Whatever I have done beyond, has been since added by my own irregular reading. But no subsequent circumstance could make up for that invaluable habit of vigorous and methodical industry which the indulgence and irregularity of my school-life prevented me from acquiring, and of which I have painfully felt the want in every part of my life."

Another mistake is a profuse allowance of Pocket-money at School: we once heard an old Westminster declare that to his unlimited supply of money when at the college he attributed over-indulgence in luxuries which had injured his health, and often rendered him the dupe of mean and designing persons—full-grown parasites—mischievous as the plants of that name, which bear down the trees they attack, and rob them of the food intended for their own leaves and fruit.

UNSOUND TEACHING.

The general unsoundness of what is termed an English education is, to a great extent, accounted for by the little attention paid in the Universities, Colleges, and Schools to teaching our native language, and especially to the proper teaching of English in schools for the people. The results of this neglect of the mother-tongue are multitudinous. "The

* *Quarterly Review*, No. 204. In the latter sentence is conveyed the advantage which education in a large school has over education at home.

mass of our population, in spite of all that has been done, must be considered densely ignorant. Millions never open a book. Nearly fifteen millions never enter church or chapel. Other causes may operate, but the want of a knowledge of language is a potent one. People whose vocabulary is limited to about three hundred words cannot follow a sermon, and clergymen who have never been taught the value of plain Saxon English cannot preach one. Then, amongst the middle and upper classes, how superficial is the knowledge of English. How few can write a common letter without faults in grammar, choice of words, or spelling. Punctuation is absolutely ignored by many. What are the speeches at public meetings, or rather, how would they appear in print but for the talent of the reporters, who bring order out of chaos? The results of the Civil-Service Examinations abundantly prove the justice of these strictures; and the fruits of University training, or rather non-training, are too patent to require illustration. Our clergy often carry into the prayer-desk and pulpit all the defects of early life,—the provincial accent, the sing-song tone, the nasal twang, the lisp, or burr, or stammer; indistinct utterance, inaudible reading and vociferation, wrong emphasis, undue stress on enclitics, and many other faults. Good sermons are the exception rather than the rule; for if sound in doctrine and full of zeal, the style is often obscure or pedantic or inflated, and the delivery monotonous and soporific. In the Senate, though most of the Members are University men, there are but few really effective speakers. Were our senators trained to speak well—that is, to the point—much time would be saved, and public business despatched more rapidly."

The remedies suggested by the Rev. Dr. D'Orsey are:

1. Training-schools for nursery governesses, who, without knowing or pretending to know French and Italian, should speak English without vulgarisms. 2. Greater attention in our present training colleges for schoolmasters to due instruction in English, especially in correct and fluent speaking. 3. More encouragement to men of talent and education to become and to remain schoolmasters, by holding out the prospect of honourable offices to distinguished teachers. Why should Inspectorships of Schools be always given to clergymen and barristers, to the exclusion of the schoolmaster? 4. The appointment of a thoroughly accomplished scholar as English Master in every great public school, of equal rank with the other masters. 5. The endowment of at least one Professorship in every University. 6. The recognition of English as a subject in every examination not strictly scientific, and

rewarding distinction in composition or oratory in the same substantial manner as eminence in classics or mathematics.

Sir John Coleridge relates the following inefficient examples of school-teaching which have come under his observation: "An Examiner was about, and he had a class before him—the first class in arithmetic. They were able to answer questions; they had gone through all the higher branches of arithmetic, and were prepared to answer any thing. But he said, 'I will give you a sum in simple addition.' He accordingly dictated a sum, and cautiously interspersed a good many ciphers. Suppose, for instance, he said, 'a thousand and forty-nine.' He found there was not one in the class who was able to put down that sum in simple addition; they could not make count of the ciphers. That showed him the boys had been suffered to pass over far too quickly the elementary parts of arithmetic. The examiner took them in grammar, and quoted a few lines from Cowper—

I am monarch of all I survey,
My right there is none to dispute.

'What governs right?' There was not a boy could say, till it was put to them, 'none to dispute my right.'

"Let me impress upon you that the best motto you can take for yourselves in this respect is that which was taken by a most eminent man who made his way from a hair-dresser's shop to be Chief Justice Tenterden. What was his motto? When a man is made a judge, he is made a serjeant; and as serjeant he gives rings to some of the great officers of State, with a motto upon each. His motto was 'Labore.' He did not refer to his own talents. It was not 'Invita Minerva.' To his immortal honour be it said—from the hair-dresser's shop in Canterbury to the Free School in Canterbury; from the Free School in Canterbury to Corpus Christi College; from Corpus Christi College to the bar; from the bar to the bench; from the bench to the peerage—he achieved all with unimpeachable honour, and always practising that which was his motto at last. One of the most gratifying scenes I have ever witnessed was when that man went up to the House of Peers in his robes for the first time, attended by the whole bar of England."

SELF-FORMATION.

The one great object—the finality—of rational Education is Self-instruction. In mind as well as body we are children at first, only that we may afterwards become men; dependent upon others, in order that we may learn from them such lessons as may tend eventually to our edification on an independent basis of our own. The knowledge of facts, or what is generally called learning, however much we may possess of it, is useful so far only as we erect its materials into a mental framework; but useless, utterly, as long as we suffer it to lie in a heap, inert and without form. The instruction of others, compared with self-instruction, is like the law compared with faith; a discipline of preparation, beggarly elements, a schoolmaster to lead us on to a state of greater worthiness, and there give up the charge of us.

"Every man," says Gibbon, "who rises above the common level, receives two educations—the first from his instructors; the second, the most personal and important, from himself." Almost all Lord Eldon's legal education was from himself, without even the ordinary helps, which he disdainfully flung from him; and of no one could it be more truly predicated, that he was not "rocked and dandled" into a lawyer.

The Rev. Sydney Smith has thus sketched a scheme, in which he deems it of the highest importance that the education of a British youth were directed to the true principles of legislation: what effect laws can produce upon opinions, and opinions upon laws; what subjects are fit for legislative interference, and when men may be left to the management of their own interests. The mischief occasioned by bad laws, and the perplexity which arises from a multiplicity of laws; the causes of national wealth; the relations of foreign trade; the encouragement of agricultures and manufactures; the fictitious wealth occasioned by paper-credit; the use and abuse of monopoly; the theory of taxation; the consequences of the public debt: these are some of the subjects and some of the branches of civil education, to which we would turn the minds of future judges, future senators, and future noblemen. After the first period of life had been given up to the cultivation of the classics, and the remaining powers were beginning to evolve themselves, these are some of the propensities in study which we would endeavour to inspire.

PRACTICAL DISCIPLINE.

The want of Practical Discipline has been thus put by a writer in *Blackwood's Magazine*: "What is the use of battering a man's brains full of Greek and Latin pothooks, that he forgets before he doffs his last round-jacket or puts on his first long-tailed blue, if ye don't teach him the old Spartan virtue of obedience, hard living, early rising, and them sort of classics? Where's the use of instructing him in hexameters or pentameters, if you would leave him in ignorance of the value of a pennypiece? What height of stupidity it is to be fillin' a boy's brains with the wisdom of the ancients, and then turn him out like an *omadhaum*, to pick up his victuals among the moderns!"

With equal truth, but finer humour, has Sydney Smith, at his own expense, exposed this neglect of the practical as a fair indication of the mode of English education. He is writing to his publisher, whom he tells: "I have twice endeavoured to write the word *skipping*—'*skipping spirit.*' Your printer first printed it 'stripling,' and then altered it into *stripping*. The fault is entirely mine. I was fifteen years at school and college—I know something about the Romans and the Athenians, and have read a good deal about the præter-perfect tense—but I cannot do a sum in simple addition, or *write a handwriting which any body can read.*"

"CRAMMING."

Cramming, which in our time was a cant term in the Universities for the art of preparing a student to pass an examination by furnishing him beforehand with the requisite answers, has travelled far beyond the tether of Oxford or Cambridge. Its abuse is well described by Watts: "As a man may be eating all day, and for want of digestion is never nourished, so these endless readers may cram themselves in vain with intellectual food." It reminds one also of the Baconian saw—of those who can pack the cards, yet know not how to play them.

A president Examiner of articled clerks at the Law Institution has observed upon this forcing system:

I for one, and I am glad of the opportunity of expressing it, abhor all Cramming; and I hold very cheaply the system of Competitive Examination, which is nowadays begun almost in the nursery, and thought so highly of in some quarters as a test. It is not to be expected, without inverting the natural order of things, that a youth of twenty or twenty-one should have exhausted those stores of learning which Coke speaks of as requiring not less than the *lucubrationes viginti annorum;* and remember that those twenty years would begin at that period of life on which most of you are now but entering. In this view the papers before you have been prepared, and our aim as examiners has been to set such questions as will prove you to possess the elements of a liberal education; and that you have so far acquired the principles of common law, equity, conveyancing, criminal law, and bankruptcy, that you are entitled to enter upon the practice of your profession, leaving its complete mastery to that experience which time alone can supply. I need not remind you of the men who, beginning as attorneys, have attained to high positions in the State. The portrait of Lord Chancellor Truro hangs before you on these walls. I had the privilege of knowing him personally; his example may well stimulate your ambition, and animate your exertions, for never man won high place with more unremitting labour than he did; not, however, at the expense of his childhood or of his youth, not by the sacrifice of all else for mere mental culture, but by the full-grown energies, by the well-directed vigour and power of the man, for he was between thirty and forty years of age before he was called to the bar.

MATHEMATICS.

Mathematics drew from Edmund Gurney the odd definition, that "a mathematician is like one that goes to market to buy an axe to break an egg."

Bacon complains that men do not sufficiently understand the excellent use of the Pure Mathematics, in that they do remedy and cure many defects in the wit and faculties intellectual. For if the wit be too dull, they sharpen it; if too wandering, they fix it; if too inherent in the sense, they abstract it. So that as tennis is a game of no use in itself, but of great use in respect it maketh a quick eye, and a body ready to put itself into any postures; so in the mathematics, that use which is collateral and intervenient is no less worthy than that which is principal and intended. And as for the Mixed Mathematics, I only make this prediction, that there cannot fail to be more kinds of them, as nature grows further disclosed;" thus foretelling the advance of Natural Philosophy.

However, the understanding of Applied Mathematics is not unattainable under ordinary circumstances. Lord Rosse has observed that, without any special mathematical knowledge, a well-informed man may often, in the results announced, and from the observations elicited, obtain very interesting glimpses of the nature of mathematical processes, and some general idea as to the progress making in that direction. In applied mathematics there is much more of general interest, and the results are often perfectly intelligible without special education. In proof of this Lord Rosse adduces, that "at the meeting of the British Association at Oxford, the general results of a very abstruse investigation in applied mathematics in physical astronomy were made very interesting. The subject was so brought forward as to rivet the attention of the whole section, and there were many ladies present. The paper was given in by M. Leverrier, and the subject was the identification of a comet. How wonderful from its origin has been the progress of mathematical science! Beginning perhaps three thousand years ago almost from nothing—one simple relation of magnitude suggesting another, and those relations gradually becoming more complicated, more interesting, I may add more important, till at length in our day it has expanded into a science which enables us to *weigh the planets*, and, more wonderful still, to calculate the course they will take when acted continually upon by forces varying in magnitude and direction."

We trace in Porson's habits of thought the influence which the study of mathematics had upon him.* He was to his dying day fond of these studies. There are still preserved many papers of his scribbled over with mathematical calculations; and when the fit seized him in the street which caused his death, an equation was found in his pocket.

ARISTOTLE.

Aristotle's Philosophy, from its being upheld by the Roman Catholic theology, was lowered in a corresponding degree by the Reformation. Hence it fell into undeserved

* In enabling him to give to English scholarship its accuracy and certainty,—as a substratum on which to rest other branches of knowledge often more useful in themselves. See Mr. Luard's able *Cambridge Essay*.

neglect during the latter part of the seventeenth and the whole of the eighteenth century. Of late years, however, the true worth of his writings has been more fully appreciated, and the study of his best treatises has been much revived. Dr. Holland remarks: "The whole of Aristotle's writings on Sleep, and other collateral topics, deserve much more frequent perusal than is given to them in the present day." The geological theory of Lyell, viz. that the causes which produce geological phenomena are in constant and gradual operation, is the theory of Aristotle and John Ray brought down to our present state of knowledge.

It has been well said that Solomon, Aristotle, and Bacon are the only three men, since our race appeared on earth, who would have been justified in saying that "they took all knowledge for their province."

GEOLOGY IN EDUCATION.

The genius of Werner, of De Saussure, and of Cuvier, laid the foundations on which Geology now rests. They gave us the first glimpse of the fauna and flora of the earlier ages of our planet. Professor Jameson soon saw that these investigations would also lead to much curious information in regard to the former physical and geographical distribution of plants and animals; and to the changes which the animated world in general, and particular genera and species, have undergone, and probably are still undergoing; and he would naturally be led to speculate on the changes that must have taken place in the climate of the globe during these various changes and revolutions. The writings of Blumenbach, Von Hoff, Cuvier, Brongniart, Steffens, and other naturalists, are proofs of what has been done by following up the views of Werner. Ami Boué, speaking of the services Professor Jameson has rendered to science, says: "He has spread valuable working pupils all over the world, and he was the electric spark which originated the beginning of true geology in Great Britain."

It is not much more than seventy years since Bishop Watson, a man of no mean abilities and of no slight distinction, turned the science of geology into open ridicule. He said that the geologists who attempted to speculate on the internal formation of the globe reminded him only of a gnat which might be perched upon the shoulders of an elephant, and might, by the reach of its tiny puncture, affect to tell him what was the whole internal structure of the majestic animal below.* Listen now to the language of an eminent man of the present day Sir David Brewster, on the same great subject: "How interesting must it be to study such phenomena—to escape for a while from the works of man—to go back to primeval times, and learn how its Maker moulded the earth—how He wore down the primitive mass into the strata of its present surface—how He deposited the precious metals in its bowels—how He filled it with races of living animals, and again buried them in its depths, to chronicle the steps of creative power—how He covered its surface with its fruit-bearing soil, and spread out the waters of the deep as the great highway of nations, to unite into one brotherhood the different races of his creatures, and to bless them by the interchange of their produce and their affections!" And again, referring to the discoveries of the great Cuvier in connexion with geology, he says: "In thus deciphering the handwriting of nature on her tablets of stone, the same distinguished naturalist discovered that all organised beings were not created at the same period. In the commissariat of Providence the stores were provided before the arrival of the host that was to devour them. Plants were created before animals, the molluscous fishes next appeared, then the reptiles, and last of all the mammiferous quadrupeds completed the scale of animal life." Such are the terms in which able men now refer to geological science.†

Fortunately, the science of Geology is an eminently popular one. The arguments which go to establish its leading doctrines require no long course of previous study to make them intelligible, and its professors, in this country at least, have been no way disposed to confine their teaching to the sanctuaries of learning. Wherever an audience can be gathered together, some eminent geologist is always ready to discourse for the benefit of the gentiles of science, who have rewarded their instructors by a larger share of popularity than is generally bestowed on the professors of other branches of physical knowledge. The consequence is, that a smattering of Geology is now very generally diffused amongst the upper and middle classes in this country—an excellent thing in itself, since even a smattering of natural science helps to enlarge and elevate the mind, but sometimes inconvenient, because few learn enough to get a

* Mr. Watson, among other qualities, which certainly contributed to his advancement in life, possessed a happy confidence in himself, and an opinion of his own fitness for any situation to which he should think proper to aspire, though totally destitute at the time of every qualification requisite to the discharge of its functions. On the 19th of November 1764, he informs us, "I was unanimously elected by the Senate, assembled in full congregation, Professor of Chemistry. At the time this honour was conferred upon me *I knew nothing at all of chemistry;* had never read a syllable on the subject, nor seen a single experiment in it."—*Quarterly Review*, vol. xviii. p. 233.

† Sir John Pakington, M.P.

correct idea of the extent of their own ignorance as compared with the smallness of their knowledge. In the interest of science, the main point to be gained is that, out of the large number who approach the threshold, a sufficient number should be induced to enter into her service, and that each of these should find work fit for his strength and his special faculties. Measured in this way, the progress of Geology seems to be sufficiently satisfactory.*

THE BEST EDUCATION.

Philip de Mornay enjoins: "The best thing to be instilled into the minds of children, is to fear God. This is the beginning, the middle, and the end, of wisdom. Next, they ought to be induced to be kind one to another. Great care ought to be taken to guard against speaking on improper subjects in their presence, since lasting impressions are made at a very early age; on the contrary, our conversation ought to be on good and instructive topics. Imperceptibly to themselves or others, they derive great benefit from such discourse; for it is quite certain that children take the tinge either of good or evil, without the process being discovered."

True excellence is only to be arrived at by the true Education; for in Education, as in all the rest of life, there are two ways of acting. "The one way, when the learner looks upon his powers as his own, and works them in a self-confident, hard spirit; which is by far the quickest way to temporary success. The other, when the learner, looking upon all his powers as given to him, works humbly in a tentative spirit, distrusting self, keeping the heart open to improvement, thinking that every body and every thing can teach him something; putting himself, in fact, in God's hand, as a learner, not as a judge. To such a spirit belongs the promise that he shall be led into all truth. Directly we imagine we know a thing, we close our stores, and shut the gates against fresh treasures; but whilst laying up truth, still think that all is incomplete, still humbly think, however broad and firm and deep the foundation we have laid may be, that eternity shall not suffice for the su-

* *Saturday Review.*

perstructure; in fact, still hold the vessel to be filled, and God will ever fill it; still use that fulness in His service, and at the right time the right thing shall come. Nothing but pride shuts out knowledge. Who is not conscious, taking only the merest intellectual work, how little really depends on himself, how many thoughts are direct gifts, how much precious material *comes* into his hands, is given—is given—not his own; who will not admit, if nothing more, that a headache, a qualm, may destroy his cherished hopes, so little can he rely on self?"*

The late Baron Alderson, writing to his son, says: "I have sent you to Eton that you may be taught your duties as an English young gentleman. The first duty of such a person is to be a good and religious Christian; the next is to be a good scholar; and the third is to be accomplished in all manly exercises and games, such as rowing, swimming, jumping, cricket, and the like. Most boys, I fear, begin at the wrong end, and take the last first; and, what is still worse, never arrive at either of the other two at all. I hope, however, better things of you; and to hear first that you are a good, truthful, honest boy, and then that you are one of the hardest workers in your class; and after that, I confess I shall be by no means sorry to hear that you can show the idle boys that an industrious one can be a good cricketer, and jump as wide a ditch, or clear as high a hedge, as any of them."

ADVICE TO THE STUDENT.

Dr. Arnold has given this sound counsel: "Preserve proportion in your reading, keep your view of men and things extensive, and, *depend upon it, a mixed knowledge is not a superficial one;* as far as it goes, the views that it gives are true; but he who reads deeply in one class of writers only, gets views which are almost sure to be perverted, and which are not only narrow but false."

It is a great mistake to suppose that full employment shuts out leisure. The secret of leisure is to have eight hours a day entirely devoted to business, and you will then find you have time for other pursuits; this for some time

* Thring's *Sermons delivered at Uppingham School.*

to come will seem to you a paradox; but you will one day be convinced of the truth, that the man who is the most engaged has always the most leisure.

KNOWLEDGE AND WISDOM.

That Knowledge is not True Wisdom cannot be too strongly urged upon youth. "There is a heaping up of knowledge just as amenable to this censure as the ignorance of the unlearned, not indeed so censured by man, but equally worthy of it in a true judgment. The intellectual fool, full of knowledge but without wisdom, whose way is right in his own eyes, is no less a fool, nay, more so, than the ignorant fool, and as far from true wisdom. For knowledge is a very different thing from wisdom; knowledge is but the collecting together of a mass of material at best, whilst wisdom is the right perception and right use leading to further riches. The mere heaper-up of knowledge digs, as it were, ore out of the earth, working underground in darkness; whereas the wise man fashions all his knowledge into use and beauty, praising and blessing God with it, and receiving from Him a fuller measure in consequence. Wisdom is knowledge applied to life and to the praise of God,—a thing of the heart, the heart controlling and using all the head gathers; knowledge by itself is a mere barren store of the head, quite separable from goodness and love,—a thing capable of being possessed by devils. For this we must mark, the humblest good heart which loves God alone can attain to the knowledge of God. No mere intellectual power and pride can do that. And hence we may see why the man whose way is right in his own eyes is a fool."*

Montaigne thus points out an educational error, common in our time as well as in that of this charming writer, whom a gentleman is ashamed not to have read:

> The care and expense our parents are at have no other aim but to furnish our heads with knowledge, but not a word of judgment and virtue. Cry out of one that passes by to our people, "Oh, what a learned man is that!" and of another, "Oh, what a good man is that!" they will not fail to turn their eyes and pay their respects to the former. There should then be a third man to cry out, "Oh, what blockheads they

* Thring's *Sermons delivered at Uppingham School.*

are!" Men are ready to ask, "Does he understand Greek or Latin—is he a poet or prose-writer?" But whether he is the better or more discreet man, though it is the main question, is the last; for the inquiry should be, who has the best learning, not who has the most. We only take pains to stuff the memory, and leave the understanding and conscience quite unfurnished. Of what service is it to us to have a bellyful of meat, if it does not digest—if it does not change its form in our bodies—and if it does not nourish and strengthen us? We suffer ourselves to lean so much upon the arms of others, that our strength is of no use to us. Would I fortify myself against the fear of death, I do it at the expense of Seneca; would I extract consolation for myself or my friend, I borrow it from Cicero; whereas I might have found it in myself, if I had been trained up in the exercise of my own reason. I do not fancy the acquiescence in second-hand hearsay knowledge; for though we may be learned by the help of another's knowledge, we can never be wise but by our own wisdom. Agesilaus being asked what he thought most proper for boys to learn, replied: What they ought to do when they come to be men.

EDUCATION ALARMISTS.

That a little learning is a dangerous thing, is an old saying, which has been fearfully repeated in these days; but a little learning every one will have, and the only way of averting the danger is, by providing the people with all facilities for acquiring more.

Lord Stowell was no admirer of the prevailing rage for universal education, and made a remark with which Lord Sidmouth was much struck: "If you provide," he said, "a larger amount of cultivated talent than there is a demand for, the surplus is very likely to turn sour."

Sir John Coleridge, in expressing his high sense of the obligations of the country to the University of Oxford for their recent aids to Middle-Class Education, says: "If the lower orders are to be raised in political power in this country, to make that a blessing you must cultivate the lower orders for discharging the duties to be thrown upon them. Therefore it is that I think the University of Oxford conferred the largest benefit that it had in its power to confer upon this country at large, when, passing simply from the education of the higher orders and those who were destined for the Church, it spread out its hands in a frank and liberal spirit to all classes of society, and offered to connect every body with itself, in a certain measure, who would only fit himself for it by proper application."

YORKSHIRE SCHOOLS.

The disappearance from our newspapers of strings of "Education" advertisements of Schools with low tariffs in Yorkshire, shows the effect of satiric humour in correcting abuses of our own time. The dietary of a school in Yorkshire, barmecide breakfasts and dinners, was often held up *in terrorem* to refractory boys, who heard the threat of "I'll send you to Yorkshire," with fear and trembling. Mr. Dickens gives an admirable exposure of this Spartan system in his tale of *Nicholas Nickleby*, in the preface to which he says:

I cannot call to mind now how I came to hear about Yorkshire schools, when I was not a very robust child, sitting in bye places, near Rochester Castle, with a head full of Partridge, Strap, Tom Pipes, and Sancho Panza; but I know that my first impressions of them were picked up at that time, and that they were, somehow or other, connected with a suppurated abscess that some boy had come home with in consequence of his Yorkshire guide, philosopher, and friend having ripped it open with an inky penknife.

Before the book was written, Mr. Dickens went into Yorkshire to look for a school in which the imaginary boy of an imaginary widow might be put away until the thawing of a tardy compassion in that widow's imaginary friends. Then some stern realities were seen; and we are told also, in the preface, of a supper with a real John Browdie, whose answer as to the search for a cheap Yorkshire schoolmaster was, "Dom'd if ar can gang to bed and not tellee, for weedur's sak', to keep the lattle boy from a' sike scoundrels, while there's a harse to hoold in a' London, or a goother to lie asleep in!"

BOOKS FOR THE YOUNG.

Great mistakes have been made in writing books for children. When Sir Walter Scott was about to write his *Tales of a Grandfather*, he remarked: "I am persuaded both children and the lower class of readers hate books which are written *down* to their capacity, and love those that are composed for their elders and betters. I will make, if possible, a book that a child shall understand, yet a man should feel some temptation to peruse should he chance to take it up. . . . . The grand and interesting consists in ideas, not in words." Again, "the problem of narrating history is at once to excite and gratify the curiosity of youth, and please and instruct the wisest of mature minds."*

THE ENGLISH LANGUAGE.

The treasures of our tongue, says Dr. Richardson, the lexicographer, are spread over continents, and cultivated among islands in the northern and the southern hemisphere, from "the unformed Occident to the strange shores of unknowing nations in the East." The sun, indeed, now never sets upon the empire of Great Britain. Not one hour of the twenty-four in which the earth completes her diurnal revolution, not one round of the minute-hand of the dial, is allowed to pass, in which, on some portion of the surface of the globe, the air is not filled with "accents that are ours." They are heard in the ordinary transactions of life, or in the administration of law, or in the deliberations of the senate-house or council-chamber, or in the offices of private devotion, or in the public observance of the rites and duties of a common faith.

Dr. Richardson's *Dictionary of the English Language*, the foremost work of its class, we owe greatly to the judicious energy of Mr. Pickering, the publisher, who laid out two thousand pounds in books, specially for this great labour, before it was commenced. If publishers would imitate Mr. Pickering's liberality oftener than is done, there would be fewer incomplete and abortive compilations than are yearly issued from the press. Dr. Richardson acknowledges this valuable aid in his Preface, where he justly makes his boast of bringing within the circle of his reading a large number of books which had never been employed for lexicographical purposes before; and Dean Trench acknowledges that the virgin soil which Richardson has tilled has often yielded him large and rich returns.

Of the uselessness of our legions of words to be found in dictionaries, a writer of the day observes:

Dictionary English is something very different not only from common colloquial English, but even from that of ordinary written composition. Instead of about 40,000 words, there is probably no single author in the language from whose works, however voluminous, so many as 10,000 words could be collected. Of the 40,000 words there are cer-

* Lockhart's *Life of Scott*.

tainly many more than one-half that are only employed, if they are ever employed at all, on the rarest occasions. We should any of us be surprised to find, if we counted them, with how small a number of words we manage to express all that we have to say either with our lips or even with the pen. Our common literary English probably hardly extends to 10,000 words, our common spoken English hardly to 5000. And the proportion of native or home-grown words is undoubtedly very much higher in both the 5000 and the 10,000 than it is in the 40,000. Perhaps of the 30,000 words, or thereabouts, standing in the dictionaries, that are very rarely or never used, even in writing, between 20,000 and 25,000 may be free of French or Latin extraction. If we assume 22,500 to be so, that will leave 5000 Teutonic words in common use; and in our literary English, taken at 10,000 words, those that are non-Roman will thus amount to about one-half. Of that half 4000 words may be current in our spoken language, which will therefore be genuine English for four-fifths of its entire extent. It will consist of about 4000 Gothic and 1000 Roman words.*

The Rev. Dr. D'Orsey has shown, by coloured charts and elaborate tables, the proportion of the Teutonic and Romanic elements in the spoken language of England, and in the writings of our great authors. Thus, out of 100,000 words, at least 60,000 were Teutonic, 30,000 Romanic, and 10,000 from all other sources.

It would be almost impossible to compose a sentence of moderate length consisting solely of words of Latin derivation. But there are many which can be rendered wholly in Anglo-Saxon. It would be easy to make the Lord's Prayer entirely, as it is in present use almost entirely, Anglo-Saxon. It consists of sixty words, and six of these only have a Latin root. But for each of them, except one, we have an exact Saxon equivalent. For "trespasses" we may substitute "sins;" for "temptation," "trials;" for "deliver," "free;" and for "power," "might." Dr. Trench proposes for "glory," "brightness;" but this we think is not a good substitute.

The gradual changes in language are very remarkable. Dean Trench, in one of his popular manuals, observes: "How few aged persons, let them retain the fullest possession of their faculties, are conscious of any difference between the spoken language of their early youth and that of their old age; that words, and ways of using words, are obsolete now which were usual then; that many words are current now which had no existence at that time. And yet it is certain that so it must be. A man may fairly be supposed to remember clearly and well for sixty years

* *Dublin University Magazine.*

back; and it needs less than five of these sixties to bring us to the period of Spenser, and not more than eight to set us in the time of Chaucer and Wiclif. How great a change, how vast a difference in our language, within eight memories! No one, overlooking this whole term, will deny the greatness of the change. For all this, we may be tolerably sure that, had it been possible to interrogate a series of eight persons, such as together had filled up this time, intelligent men, but men whose attention had not been especially roused on this subject, each in his turn would have denied that there had been any change at all during his lifetime. And yet, having regard to the multitude of words which have fallen into disuse during these four or five hundred years, we are sure that there must have been some lives in this chain which saw those words in use at their commencement, and out of use before their close. And so, too, of the multitude of words which have come into being within the limits of each of these lives."

WHAT IS "ARGUMENT"?

The origin and proper value of the word "Argument" has been thus explained by the Rev. Dr. Donaldson, in a paper read to the Cambridge Philosophical Society:

The author first investigated the etymology and meaning of the Latin verb *arguo*, and its participle *argutus*. He showed that *arguo* was a corruption of *argruo* = *ad gruo*; that *gruo* (in *argruo*, *ingruo*, *congruo*) ought to be compared with κρούω, which means "to dash one thing against another," especially for the purpose of making a shrill, ringing noise; that *arguo* means "to knock something for the purpose of making it ring, or testing its soundness," hence "to test, examine, and prove any thing;" and that *argutus* signifies "made to ring," hence "making a distinct, shrill noise," or "tested and put to the proof." Accordingly *argumentum* means *id quod arguit*, "that which makes a substance ring, which sounds, examines, tests, and proves it."

It was then shown that these meanings were not only borne out by the classical usage of the word, but also by the technical application of "argument" as a logical term. For it is not equivalent to "argumentation," or the process of reasoning; it does not even denote a complete syllogism; though Dr. Whately and some other writers on logic had fallen into this vague use of the word, and though it was so understood in the disputations of the Cambridge schools. The proper use of the word "argument" in logic is to denote "the middle term," *i. e.* "the term used for proof." In a sense similar to this the word is employed by mathematicians; and there can be no doubt that the oldest and best logicians confine the word to this, which is still its most common signification.

The author shows, by a collection of examples from the best English poets, that the established meanings of the word "argument" are reducible to three: (1) a proof, or means of proving; (2) a process of reasoning, or controversy, made up of such proofs; (3) the subject-matter of any discourse, writing, or picture. He maintains that the second of these meanings should be excluded from scientific language.

By this we are reminded of Swift's dictum, of much wider application—that "Argument, as generally managed, is the worst sort of conversation; as it is generally in books the worst sort of reading."

HANDWRITING.

The characters of writing have followed the genius of the barbarous ages: they are well or ill formed, in proportion as the sciences have flourished more or less. Antiquaries remark that the medals struck during the consulship of Fabius Pictor, 250 years before Augustus, have the letters better formed than those of the older date. Those of the time of Augustus, and the following age, show characters of perfect beauty. Those of Diocletian and Maximian are worse formed than those of the Antonines; and again, those of the Justins and Justinians degenerate into a Gothic taste. But it is not to medals only that these remarks are applicable: we see the same inferiority of written characters generally following in the train of barbarism and ignorance. During the first race of the French kings, we find no writing which is not a mixture of Roman and other characters. Under the empire of Charlemagne and of Louis le Débonnaire, the characters returned almost to the same point of perfection which distinguished them in the time of Augustus, but in the following age there was a relapse to the former barbarism; so that for four or five centuries we find only the Gothic characters in manuscripts; for it is not worth while making an exception for short periods which were somewhat more polished, and when there was less inelegance in the formation of the letters.

The being *able to write* has been taken by our statists as the best evidence of the progress of education. Thus, twenty years ago, only 67 in every 100 men who married in England signed their names upon the register, and 51 in every 100 women, and thirteen years later the percentage was but 69·6 of the men and 56·1 of the women; but in the last seven years, a period which probably shows in its marriages the result chiefly of the education of the years 1840-45 or thereabouts, the advance has been much greater, and the Registrar-General reports that in 1860 the proportion of men writing their names had risen to 74·5, and of women to 63·8. In the whole twenty years the proportion of men who write has risen from being only two-thirds to be three-fourths, and of women from being a half to be nearly two-thirds, which may be expressed with tolerable accuracy by saying that where four persons had to "make their mark" then, only three do so now. This is for all England; but the rate of progress has not been the same in every part of the kingdom.

In the reign of George III., when education had become more general, the crosses of those who could not write lost the distinction and artistic character of older times, and the large bold round-hand corresponds in style with the buildings and furniture then in use. This writing, although without much beauty, has, notwithstanding, the merit of distinctness. In these railway times, with the exception of book-keepers in banks and clerks in merchants' offices, few seem to have time to trim their letters. Few artists write a good hand. Physicians' prescriptions are often as difficult to decipher as ancient hieroglyphics; and it must be confessed that writers for the press are not generally remarkable for either the distinctness or beauty of their manuscript. As regards artists, the practice of handling the brush and pencil is not favourable to graceful penmanship; and in respect of the literary profession, it is generally difficult for the pen to keep pace with the thoughts, to say nothing of the fact, that time often presses.*

Short-Hand is of great antiquity; for Seneca tells us that in his time reporting had been carried to such perfection, that a writer could keep pace in his report with the most rapid speaker.

ENGLISH STYLE.

Style in writing has been well defined by Swift as "proper words in proper places." However, this is rarely seen.

To the unsettled state of our language, and owing to the want of proper training in composition, may be attributed the general corruption of English Style, which has scarcely ceased since Southey, in his *Colloquies*, wrote the following vigorous condemnation of it:

> More lasting effect was produced by translators, who, in later times, have corrupted our idiom as much as, in early ones, they enriched our vocabulary; and to this injury the Scotch have greatly contributed; for, composing in a language which is not their mother tongue, they necessarily acquired an artificial and formal style, which, not so much through the merit of a few, as owing to the perseverance of others, who for half a century seated themselves on the bench of criticism, has almost superseded the vernacular English of Addison and Swift. Our journals, indeed, have been the great corrupters of our style, and continue to be so; and not for this reason only. Men who write in newspapers, and magazines, and reviews, write for present effect; in most cases, this is as much their natural and proper aim, as it would be in public speaking; but when it is so, they consider, like public speakers, not so much what is accurate or just, either in matter or manner, as what will be acceptable to those whom they address. Writing also under the excitement of emulation and rivalry, they seek, by all the artifices and efforts of an ambitious style, to dazzle their readers; and they are wise in their generation, experience having shown that common minds are taken by glittering faults, both in prose and verse, as larks are with looking-glasses.
>
> In this school it is that most writers are now trained; and after such training, any thing like an easy and natural movement is as little to be looked for in their compositions as in the step of a dancing-master. To the views of style, which are thus generated, there must be added the inaccuracies inevitably arising from haste, when a certain quantity of matter is to be supplied for a daily or weekly publication, which allows of no delay,—the slovenliness that confidence as well as fatigue and inattention will produce,—and the barbarisms which are the effect of ignorance, or that smattering of knowledge which serves only to render ignorance presumptuous. These are the causes of corruption in our current style; and when these are considered, there would be ground for apprehending that the best writings of the last

* Communicated to *The Builder*.

century might become as obsolete as ours in the like process of time, if we had not in our Liturgy and our Bible a standard from which it will not be possible wholly to depart.

The days of sentences of one word, and of others without a verb, had not then arrived; nor had the spasmodic and sensation style been introduced. Southey's own style, whether for narrative, for exposition, or for animated argumentation, was perhaps the most effective English style of the time. It combines in a remarkable degree a somewhat lofty dignity with ease and idiomatic vigour. He was the most hard-working writer of his time, and left about 12,000*l.* in money, besides a valuable library.

Sir Thomas Browne satirises the strenuous advocacy of the classical style by saying: "We are now forced to study Latin, in order to understand English." And Pope ridicules that

Easy Ciceronian style,
So Latin, yet so English all the while.

It is no paradox to say that the perfection of style is to have none, but to let the words be suggested by the sentiments, unchecked by the monotony of a manner, and untainted by affectation.

How striking is this short passage in a speech of Edward IV. to his Parliament! "The injuries that I have received are known every where, and the eyes of the world are fixed upon me to see with what countenance I suffer." If actual events could often be related in this way, there would be more books in circulating libraries than romances and novels.

This lively and graphic style is plainly the best, though now and then the historian's criticism is wanted to support a startling fact, or to explain a confused transaction. Thus, the learned Rudbeck, in his *Atlantica*, four volumes folio, ascribing an ancient temple in Sweden to one of Noah's sons, warily adds, "'Twas probably the youngest."

A more practical definition of style may be gathered from what Fox said of his great antagonist, Pitt,—and therefore the more to be trusted,—that he always used *the* word; and each word had its own place, not regulated by chance, but by law.

To write a good Letter is a rare accomplishment. It is

owing to the want of proper training in the laws of composition that so few persons in England can write even a common letter correctly. We will give a familiar instance of a very frequent solecism which occurs in one of the most common acts of every-day life—the answer to a dinner invitation; and it is one in which, we are sorry to say, well-educated ladies are too often caught tripping. When "Mr. A. and Mrs. A. request the pleasure of Mr. and Mrs. B.'s company at dinner," the reply usually is, "Mr. and Mrs. B. *will* have the pleasure of accepting" the invitation. But the acceptance is already *un fait accompli* by the very act of writing it,—it is a present, not a future event; and the answer of course ought to be either "Mr. and Mrs. B. *have* the pleasure of accepting," or "Mr. and Mrs. B. *will have* the pleasure of *dining*."*

ART OF WRITING.

"He that would write well," says Roger Ascham, "must follow the advice of Aristotle, to speak as the common people speak, and to think as the wise think."

Coleridge says: "To write or talk concerning any subject, without having previously taken the pains to understand it, is a breach of the duty which we owe to ourselves, though it may be no offence against the law of the land. The privilege of talking, and even publishing, nonsense, is necessary in a free state; but the more sparingly we make use of it, the better."†

Much reading and good company are supposed to be the best methods of getting at the niceties and elegancies of a language; but this road is long and irksome. The great point is to acquire our most usual Anglicisms; all those phrases and peculiarities which form the characteristics of our language. Nearly eighty years since, Mr. Sharp took upon himself to say that we had no grammar capable of teaching a foreigner to read our authors; adding, "but of

* *Fraser's Magazine.*

† One fine morning, a stalwart anti-Newtonian, properly accredited, presented himself to Baron Maseres, in the library of his mansion at Reigate: "I am come to talk over my favourite subject," he said (it was. to overturn the universe!). "I am happy to see you," replied the Baron; "but before we commence, I must ask you if you consider yourself proficient in mathematics?" The anti-Newtonian was dumbfounded. "Then," rejoined the Baron, "it would be unprofitable for us to begin;" and he passed on to a more genial topic.

this I am sure, that we have none by which he can be enabled to understand our conversation."

What an annoyance are long speakers, long talkers, and long writers—people who will not take time to think, or are not capable of thinking accurately! Once when Dr. South had preached before Queen Anne, her majesty observed to him, "You have given me a most excellent discourse, Dr. South; but I wish you had had time to make it longer." "Nay, madam," replied the doctor, "if I had had time, I should have made it shorter."

Method in treating your subject is of great importance. Southey has well illustrated the absence of this quality. A Quaker, by name Benjamin Lay (who was a little cracked in the head, though sound at the heart), took one of his compositions to Benjamin Franklin, that it might be printed and published. Franklin, having looked over the manuscript, observed that it was deficient in arrangement: "It is no matter," replied the author; "print any part thou pleaseth first." Many are the speeches, and the sermons, and the treatises, and the poems, and the volumes, which are like Benjamin Lay's book: the head might serve for the tail, and the tail for the body, and the body for the head; either end for the middle, and the middle for either end; nay, if you could turn them inside out, like a polypus or a glove, they would be no worse for the operation.*

Free Translation is a rare accomplishment. Sir John Denham, who is declared by Johnson "to have been one of the first that understood the necessity of emancipating translation from the drudgery of counting lines and interpreting single words," gives the same praise to Sir Richard Fanshawe, whom he addresses thus:

> That servile path thou nobly dost decline,
> Of tracing word by word and line by line;
> A new and nobler way thou dost pursue,
> To make translations and translators too:
> They but preserve the ashes, thou the flame,
> True to his sense, but truer to his fame.

Dryden said, all the translations of the old school "want to be translated into English;" and verbal translation he compares to "dancing on ropes with fettered legs."

* *The Doctor.*

Education cannot do all that Helvetius supposes, but it can do much. *Elle fait danser l'ours,*—It makes a bear dance. It is said that some insects take the colour of the leaf that they feed upon. "I was common clay till roses were planted in me," says some aromatic earth, in an eastern fable.

To unlearn is harder than to learn, and the Grecian flute-player was right in requiring double fees from those pupils who had been taught by another master. "I am rubbing their father out of my children as fast as I can," said a clever widow of rank and fashion.

The Education of princes, or indeed the spoilt children of rich and distinguished parents, must be the *experimentum crucis* of teaching. "If Fénelon did succeed, as it is recorded he did, in educating the Dauphin, his success was little less than a miracle. How can any man, though of advanced age and of high reputation, perhaps also of a sacred profession and of elevated station, be expected to preserve any useful authority over a child (probably a wayward little animal), if he, the tutor, must always address the pupil by his title, or at least must never forget that he is heir to a throne?"

There is some truth in the following remarks by a writer in *Blackwood's Magazine*, upon information overmuch:

> We deal largely in general knowledge—an excellent article, no doubt; but one may have too much of it. Sometimes ignorance is really bliss. It has not added to my personal comfort to know to a decimal fraction what proportion of red earth I may expect to find in my cocoa every morning; to have become knowingly conscious that my coffee is mixed with ground liver and litmus, instead of honest chicory; and that bisulphuret of mercury forms the basis of my cayenne. It was once my fate to have a friend staying in my house who was one of these minute philosophers. He used to amuse himself after breakfast by a careful analysis and diagnosis of the contents of the teapot, laid out as a kind of *hortus siccus* on his plate. "This leaf, now," he would say, "is fuchsia; observe the serrated edges: that's no tealeaf—positively poisonous. This now, again, is blackthorn, or privet—yes, privet; you may know it by the divisions in the panicles: that's no tea-leaf." A most uncomfortable guest he was; and though not a bad companion in many respects, I felt my appetite improved the first time I sat down to dinner without him. It won't do to look into all your meals with a microscope. Of course there is a medium between these over-curious investigations and an implicit faith in every thing that is set before you.

Business-Life.

WANT OF A PURSUIT.

Such is the complicated constitution of human nature, that a man without a predominant inclination is not likely to be either useful or happy.

He who is every thing is nothing, is as true of our sensitive as of our intellectual nature. He is rather a bundle of little likings, than a compact and energetic individual. A strong desire soon subdues the weaker, and rules us with the united force of all that it subjugates.

Such being the force of human feelings, it must embitter our daily lives if our employments are unsuited to our talents and our wishes; yet how few, alas, are so fortunate as to be gaining either wealth or fame while gratifying an inclination!

In the best of all arts, the art of living, the greatest skill is not to wait; but, as you run along, snatch at every fruit and every flower growing within your reach; for, after all that can be said, youth, the age of hope and admiration, and manhood, the age of business and of influence, are to be preferred to the period of extinguished passions and languid curiosity. At that season, our hopes and wishes must have been too long dropping, leaf by leaf, away. The last scenes of the fifth act are seldom the most interesting, either in a tragedy or a comedy. Yet many compensations arise as our sensibility decays:

> Time steals away the rose, 'tis true;
> But then the thorn is blunted too.*

Life, without some necessity for exertion (says Mr. Walker†), must ever lack real interest. That state is ca-

* Richard Sharp.

† In *The Original*, a series of Periodical Papers, published in 1835, by Thomas Walker, M.A., one of the Police Magistrates of the Metropolis.

pable of the greatest enjoyment where necessity urges, but not painfully; where effort is required, but as much as possible without anxiety; where the spring and summer of life are preparatory to the harvest of autumn and the repose of winter. Then is every season sweet, and, in a well-spent life, the last the best—the season of calm enjoyment, the richest in recollections, the brightest in hope. Good training and a fair start constitute a more desirable patrimony than wealth; and those parents who study their children's welfare rather than the gratification of their own avarice or vanity, would do well to think of this. Is it better to run a successful race, or to begin and end at the goal?

THE ENGLISH CHARACTER.

Four and thirty years since, Sir Humphry Davy wrote: "The English as a nation are preëminently active, and the natives of no other country follow their objects with so much force, fire, and constancy. And as human powers are limited, there are few examples of very distinguished men living in this country to old age: they usually fail, droop, and die, before they have attained the period naturally marked out for the end of human existence. The lives of our statesmen, warriors, poets, and even philosophers, offer abundant proofs of the truth of this opinion: whatever burns, consumes; ashes remain. Before the period of youth is passed, gray hairs usually cover those brows which are adorned with the civic oak or the laurel; and in the luxurious and exciting life of the men of pleasure, their tints are not even preserved by the myrtle wreath or the garland of roses from the premature winter of time." If these characteristics were applicable to English life a third of a century since, how much has their fitness been strengthened by the rapidity of action, the excitement, and want of repose adding to the wear and tear of existence, since that period.

That the Englishman is one of the most noble species of the genus to which he belongs, seems to be generally conceded. The poet Southey expressed the opinion of more thinkers than himself when he said that the Englishman is the model or pattern man, at least of all the species at present existing. But even those who are most thoroughly convinced of this must admit that he has his peculiarities—foremost among which is his nationality; and one of the most striking peculiarities of that nationality is pride. Another potent element in the English character is its practical worth,—this word "practical" being the shibboleth by which we love to recognise ourselves; as the Greeks delighted to picture themselves as more wise, the French as more polite, than other nations.

Our genius has a most real, concrete, and altogether terrestrial tendency: there seems to be a considerable majority of Sadducees among us, or, as Plato calls them, "uninitiated persons, who believe in nothing but what they can lay hold of with their hands. These men will make railways, telegraphs, and tunnels, and build crystal palaces, and collect mechanical products from the ends of the earth, and exhibit in every possible shape and variety the sublime of what is mechanical and material; but for the supersensual ideas, they will have none of them."*

Nevertheless, if we look through the history of the world's genius, we shall find its greatest successes to lie in the practical. Homer begged; Tasso begged in a different way; Galileo was racked; De Witt assassinated,—and all for wishing to improve their species. At the same time, Raffaelle, Michel Angelo, Zeuxis, Apelles, Rubens, Reynolds, Titian, Shakspeare, were rich and happy. Why? because with their genius they combined practical prudence. This is the grand secret of success.

WORTH OF ENERGY.

A man with knowledge but without energy is a home furnished but not inhabited; a man with energy but no knowledge, a house dwelt in but unfurnished.

Mr. Sharp† counsels us: "Prefer a life of energy to a life of inaction. There are always kind friends enough ready to preach up caution and delay, &c. Yet it is impossible to

* Professor Blackie; *Edinburgh Essays*, 1856.

† Mr. Richard Sharp, F.R.S., and some time M.P. for Port-Arlington, in Ireland. He was celebrated for his conversational talents, and hence was known as "Conversation Sharp" At Fridley-farm, Sir James Macintosh, and other distinguished men of his day, were frequently Mr. Sharp's guests. Of his volume of *Letters, Essays, and Poems*, a third edition appeared in 1834.

lay down any general rule of a prudential kind. Every one must be judged of after a careful review of all its circumstances; for if one, only one, be overlooked, the decison may be injurious or fatal. Thus, there will ever be many conflicting reasons for and against a spirit of enterprise and a habit of caution.

"Those who advise others to withstand the temptations of hope will always appear to be wiser than they really are; for how often can it be made certain that the rejected and untried hazard would have been successful? Besides, those who dissuade us from action have corrupt but powerful allies in our indolence, irresolution, and cowardice. To despond is very easy, but it requires works as well as faith to engage successfully in a difficult undertaking.

"There are, however, few difficulties that hold out against real attacks: they fly, like the visible horizon, before those who advance. A passionate desire and an unwearied will can perform impossibilities, or what seem to be so to the cold and the feeble. If we do but go on, some unseen path will open among the hills.

"We must not allow ourselves to be discouraged by the apparent disproportion between the result of single efforts and the magnitude of the obstacles to be encountered. Nothing great or good is to be obtained without courage and industry; but courage and industry must have sunk in despair, and the world must have remained unornamented and unimproved, if men had nicely compared the effect of a single stroke of the chisel with the pyramid to be raised, or of a single impression of the spade with the mountain to be levelled.

* * * * * *

"Efforts, it must not be forgotten, are as indispensable as desires. The globe is not to be circumnavigated by one wind. 'It is better to wear out than to rust,' says Bishop Cumberland. 'There will be time enough for repose in the grave,' said Nicole to Pascal. In truth, the proper rest for man is change of occupation.

"The toils as well as risks of an active life are commonly overrated, so much may be done by the diligent use of ordinary opportunities; but they must not always be waited for. We must not only strike the iron while it is hot, but strike it till 'it is made hot.' Herschel, the great astronomer, declares that 90 or 100 hours, clear enough for observation, cannot be called an unproductive year.

"The lazy, the dissipated, and the fearful, should patiently see the active and the bold pass them in the course. They must bring down their pretensions to the level of their talents. Those who have not energy to work must learn to be humble, and should not vainly hope to unite the incompatible enjoyments of indolence and enterprise, of ambition and self-indulgence."

These lines of fair encouragement are the advice of a man of the world, but whose feelings had not become blunted by his intercourse with the world: he was one of the most cheerful, amiable, and happy beings it ever fell to our lot to know; his joyous manner was the true index to his large and sound heart.

TEST OF GREATNESS.

The true test of a great man (says Lord Brougham),—that at least which must secure his place among the highest order of great men,—is his having been in advance of his age. This it is which decides whether or not he has carried forward the grand plan of human improvement; has conformed his views and adapted his conduct to the existing circumstances of society, or changed those so as to better its condition; has been one of the lights of the world, or only reflected the borrowed rays of former luminaries, and sat in the same shade with the rest of his generation at the same twilight or the same dawn.

Nature seldom invests great men with any outward signs, from which their greatness may be known or foretold; and yet (says Lord Dudley) I own I share fully in that curiosity of the vulgar, which induces them to follow after and to gaze eagerly upon the mere bodily presence of persons that have raised themselves high above the common level.

Almost all great men who have performed, or who are destined to perform, great things, are sparing of words. Their communing is with themselves rather than with others. They feed upon their own thoughts, and in these inward musings brace those intellectual and active energies, the development of which constitutes the great character. Napoleon became a babbler only when his fate was accomplished, and his fortune was on the decline.

Boyle has this pertinent reflection: "There is such a kind of difference between vertue shaded by a private, and shining forth in a publick life, as there is betwixt a candle carri'd aloft in the open air, and inclosed in a lanthorn; in the former place it gives more light, but in the latter 'tis in less danger to be blown out."*

The real test of greatness is courage and respect for truth, generally the earliest precept of childhood, yet of comparatively rare observance through life. "Without courage," says Sir Walter Scott, "there cannot be truth; and without truth there can be no other virtue." And how nobly did Scott illustrate this in his own life-practice!

Truth was the redeeming virtue of one of the favoured men of our political history. The qualities which raised Fox high as a party leader were not merely his eloquence, his wit, his genius, but also his engaging warmth of heart and kindliness of temper. To these a strong testimony may be found in the memoirs of a great historian by no means blind to his faults, and by no means attached to his principles. On summing up his character, many years afterwards, Gibbon writes of Fox as follows: "Perhaps no human being was ever more perfectly exempt from the taint of malevolence, vanity, or falsehood."

CHOICE OF A PROFESSION.

Keep not standing fix'd and rooted,
  Briskly venture, briskly roam!
Hand and heart, where'er thou foot it,
  And stout heart are still at home.
In each land the sun does visit
  We are gay, whate'er betide;
To give space for wand'ring is it
  That the world was made so wide.

Wilhelm Meister: Carlyle.

We know of no more fertile source of crime than Idleness. It is the want of a due impression of the importance and legitimate employment of time, which is one of the main occasions of the luxury and profligacy of one order of

* *Occasional Reflections.*

society; and it is the same cause which vitiates and defiles the manners of another, and a subordinate rank, in the scale. It is inquired by an ancient poet, who was a keen and accurate observer of human character, why Ægisthus so grievously and wantonly deviated from the path of virtue? and he immediately rejoins the reply, "The cause is obvious,—he was idle!" And it is a circumstance worthy of remark, that when Hogarth wished to give a portrait of a veteran criminal, he made him commence his career as a boy lolling on the tombstones of the churchyard on a Sunday.

Mr. Ruskin has written these beautiful words of encouragement: "God appoints to every one of His creatures a separate mission; and if they discharge it honourably—if they quit themselves like men, and faithfully follow that light which is in them, withdrawing from it all cold and quenching influence—there will assuredly come of it such burning as, in its appointed mode and measure, shall shine before men, and be of service, constant and holy. Degrees infinite of lustre there must always be; but the weakest among us has a gift, however seemingly trivial, which is peculiar to him, and which, worthily used, will be a gift also to his race for ever."

'Know thyself' is an old precept; yet it is surprising how few are sufficiently acquainted with themselves to see distinctly what their own motives actually are. It is a rare thing, as well as a great advantage, for a man to know his own mind.

Were but a tithe of the time and the thought usually spent in learning the commonest accomplishments bestowed upon regulating our lives, how many evils would be avoided or lessened; how many pleasures would be created or increased!

In one of Steele's papers, No. 173 of the *Tatler*, are some admirable remarks upon the time lost by boys in learning that which, in after-life, is of little service to them. "The truth of it is," says Steele, "the first rudiments of education are given very indiscreetly by most parents. Whatever children are designed for, and whatever prospects the fortune or interest of their parents may give them in their future lives, they are all promiscuously instructed in the same way;

and Horace and Virgil must be thumbed by a boy as well before he goes to an apprenticeship as to the university. . . . . This is the natural effect of a certain vanity in the minds of parents, who are wonderfully delighted with the thought of breeding their children to accomplishments, which they believe nothing but the want of the same care in their own fathers prevented them being masters of. Thus it is that the part of life most fit for improvement is generally employed against the bent of nature; and a lad of such parts as are fit for an occupation where there can be no calls out of the beaten path, is two or three years of his time wholly taken up in knowing how well Ovid's mistress became such a dress, &c. . . . . However, still the humour goes on from one generation to another; and the pastrycook here in the lane, the other night, told me 'he would not take away his son from his learning; but has resolved, as soon as he has had a little smattering in the Greek, to put him apprentice to a soap-boiler.' These wrong beginnings determine our success in the world; and when our thoughts are originally falsely biassed, their agility and force do but carry us the farther out of our way, in proportion to our speed. But we are half-way on our journey when we have got into the right road. If all our ways were usefully employed, and we did not set out impertinently, we should not have so many grotesque professors in all the arts of life; but every man would be in a proper and becoming method of distinguishing or entertaining himself, suitably to what nature designed him. As they go on now, our parents do not only force upon us what is against our talents, but our teachers are also as injudicious in what they put us to learn."

The practice of the irresolute in deliberating without deciding is another parlous error. "What I cannot resolve upon in half an hour," said the Duc de Guise, "I cannot resolve upon at all."

Bacon has well described this irresolution in his complaint, "that some men object too much, consult too long, adventure too little, repent too soon, and seldom drive business home."

The strongest incentive to decision is self-dependence. Mr. Sharp writes to a young friend at college:

I have confidence in your capacity. However, my favourable

anticipations arise chiefly from your being aware that your station in society must depend entirely on your own exertions. Luckily, you have not to overcome the disadvantage of expecting to inherit from your father an income equal to your reasonable desires; for, though it may have the air of a paradox, yet it is truly a serious disadvantage when a young man going to the bar is sufficiently provided for.

Vitam facit beatiorem
Res non parta, sed relicta,

says Martial, but not wisely; and no young man should believe him.

The necessity for instant decision in life renders it often prudent to take the chance of being right or wrong, without waiting to balance reasons very nicely. In such cases, and sometimes even in speculation, this kind of credulity is more philosophical than scepticism; though authority in abstruse investigations should usually do little more than excite attention, while in practice it must guide our conduct.

It is unfortunate when a man's intellectual and his moral character are not suited to each other. The herses in a carriage should go the same pace and draw in the same direction, or the motion will be neither pleasant nor safe.

Bonaparte has remarked of one of his marshals, that "he had a military genius, but had not intrepidity enough in the field to execute his own plans;" and of another he said, "he is as brave as his sword, but he wants judgment and resources: neither," he added, "is to be trusted with a great command."

This want of harmony between the talents and the temperament is often found in private life; and, wherever found, is the fruitful source of faults and sufferings. Perhaps there are few less happy than those who are ambitious without industry; who pant foı the prize, but will not run the race; who thirst for truth, but are too slothful to draw it up from the well.

Now this defect, whether arising from indolence or from timidity, is far from being incurable. It may, at least in part, be remedied by frequently reflecting on the endless encouragements to exertion held out by our own experience and by example:

C'est des difficultés que naissent les miracles.

It is not every calamity that is a curse, and *early* adversity especially is often a blessing. Perhaps Madame de Maintenon would never have mounted a throne had not her cradle been rocked in a prison. Surmounted obstacles not only teach, but hearten us in our future struggles; for virtue must be learnt, though unfortunately some of the vices come, as it were, by inspiration. The austerities of our northern climate are thought to be the cause of our abundant comforts; as our wintry nights and our stormy seas have given us a race of seamen perhaps unequalled, and certainly not surpassed, by any in the world.

"Mother," said a Spartan lad going to battle, "my sword is too short." "Add a step to it," she replied; but it must be owned that this advice was to be given only to a Spartan boy. They should not be thrown into the water who cannot swim: I know your buoyancy, and I have no fears of your being drowned.

OFFICIAL LIFE.

The grand scramble for place was thus vividly painted by Mr. Sharp some eighty years since: "The young people of this country, in every rank, from a peer's son to a street-sweeper's, are drawn aside from a praiseworthy exertion in honest callings, by having their eyes directed towards the public treasury. The rewards of persevering industry are too slow for them, too small, and too insipid. They fondly trust to the great lottery, although the wheel contains so many blanks and so few prizes; hoping that their ticket may be drawn a place, a pension, or a contract; a living, or a stall; a ship, or a regiment; a seat on the bench, or the great seal.

"It is, indeed, most humiliating to witness the indecent scramble that is always going on for these prizes, the highest born and best educated rolling in the dirt to pick them up, just as the lowest of the mob do for the shillings or the pence thrown among them by a successful candidate at a contested election."

In this rush there must always be a host of genius and talent neglected or overlooked; and this from various causes, some of which have been thus sketched by a living novelist, accustomed to see far beyond most of his literary brethren:

In all men who have devoted themselves to any study, or any art, with sufficient pains to attain a certain degree of excellence, there must be a fund of energy immeasurably above that of the ordinary herd. Usually, this energy is concentred on the objects of their professional ambition, and leaves them, therefore, apathetic to the other pursuits of men. But where those objects are denied, where the stream has not its legitimate vent, the energy, irritated and aroused, possesses the whole being; and if not wasted on desultory schemes, or if not purified by conscience and principle, becomes a dangerous and destructive element in the social system, through which it wanders in riot and disorder. Hence, in all wise monarchies—nay, in all well-constituted states—the peculiar care with which channels are opened for every art and every science; hence the honour paid to their cultivators by subtle and thoughtful statesmen, who, perhaps, for themselves, see nothing in a picture but coloured canvas—nothing in a problem but an ingenious puzzle. No state is ever more in danger than when the talent which should be consecrated to peace has no occupation but political intrigue or personal advancement. Talent unhonoured is talent at war with men.*

Reliance upon family influence with persons in high

* Sir E. L. Bulwer Lytton's *Zanoni.*

stations is but a poor dependence.* We happen to know a large family of sons unprovided for, who have been calculating for years upon the influence of a maid-of-honour with her relative, the Premier. But ministers who have the good things to give away are often so pressed by their political supporters, that their own connexions are made to yield. The late Lord Melbourne was proverbially a good-natured man; but in a case of the above kind he acted with a sense of duty more stringent than might have been expected. It appears that Lord John Russell had applied to Lord Melbourne for some provision for one of the sons of the poet Moore; and here is the Premier's reply:

"My dear John,—I return you Moore's letter. I shall be ready to do what you like about it when we have the means. I think whatever is done should be done for Moore himself. This is more distinct, direct, and intelligible. Making a small provision for young men is hardly justifiable; and it is of all things the most prejudicial to themselves. They think what they have much larger than it really is; and they make no exertion. The young should never hear any language but this: 'You have your own way to make, and it depends upon your own exertions whether you starve or not.'—Believe me, &c. MELBOURNE."†

The foundation of the Sidmouth Peerage is traceable to one of those fortunate turns which have much to do with worldly success. It is related that while Lord Chatham was residing at Hayes, in Kent, his first coachman being taken ill, the postillion was sent for the family doctor; but not finding him, the messenger returned, bringing with him Mr. Addington, then a practitioner in the place, who, by permission of Lord Chatham, saw the coachman, and reported his ailment. His lordship was so pleased with Mr. Addington, that he employed him as apothecary for the servants, and then for himself; and, Lady Hester Stanhope tells us, "finding he spoke good sense on medicine, and then on politics, he at last made him his physician." Dr. Addington subsequently practised in the metropolis, then retired to Reading, and there married; and in 1757 was born his eldest son, Henry Addington, who was educated at Winchester and Oxford, and called to the Bar in 1784.

* Family reputation is generally considered but an insecure stock to begin the world with: nevertheless there is much truth in the experience of Lord Mahon (now Earl Stanhope), who says: "In public life I have seen full as many men promoted for their father's talents as for their own."

† This letter is quoted in Mr. Smiles's *Self-Help*.

Through his father's connexion with the family of Lord Chatham, an intimacy had grown up between young Addington and William Pitt when they were boys. Pitt was now First Minister of the Crown, and through his influence Addington entered upon his long political career, and became in very few years Prime Minister of England: his administration was brief; but he was raised to the Peerage in 1805, and held various offices until 1824, when he retired. Lord Sidmouth was an unpopular minister, and not a man of striking talent; but his aptitude for official business was great. He survived until 1844, when he was succeeded by his eldest son, the present Viscount, in holy orders.

The origin of Lord Liverpool is scarcely less striking. The father of this statesman was Mr. Robert Jenkinson, a man of no patrimony, but who, by his application and aptitude for State affairs, gave lustre to his name. In 1778 he succeeded Lord Barrington as Secretary-at-War: he rose at last to be Earl of Liverpool; and his son, the second Earl, to be fifteen years First Lord of the Treasury.

Another instance of successful integrity in Official Life is presented by the Right Hon. George Rose, one of the most valuable public servants which this country has known, —"an able, clear-headed, straightforward man of business, whose steady industry, devoted for years to the service of the State, won for him, and most deservedly, not only political importance, but the personal regard of his sovereign, and indeed of all who knew him."* He was, in early life, purser of a ship-of-war, where his abilities became known to the Earl of Sandwich, by whom he was recommended to Lord North, who gave him an appointment in the Treasury: he was a man of frugal habits, and often ate his mutton-chop at the Cat and Bagpipes tavern, at the corner of Downing-street; *pari passu*, he was one of the early encouragers of Savings-Banks. He was the sincere and devoted friend of Pitt, whose personal character and administrative zeal are nobly vindicated by the recent publication of Mr. Rose's Diaries and Correspondence. In 1777 he superintended the publication of the Journals of the House of Lords, in thirty-one folio volumes, from which time he rarely failed to be employed in a public capacity by successive administrations.

* *Notes and Queries.*

In the intervals of his heavy official duties, he was enabled to write several works upon political and administrative questions of importance.

John Barrow, born in a lowly cottage at Dragley Beck, in Lancashire, rose, by his own earnest industry, to the responsible post of a Secretary to the Admiralty, for forty years, under thirteen administrations. When sixteen years old, he made a voyage in a whaler to Greenland; he next taught mathematics in a school at Greenwich. He attended Lord Macartney in his celebrated embassy to China, and took charge of the philosophical instruments carried out as presents to the Emperor of China; of this journey Barrow subsequently published an account in a quarto volume. He was next appointed Secretary to Lord Macartney, Governor of the Cape of Good Hope; and during his leisure Mr. Barrow, in various journeys, collected materials for a volume of *Travels in South Africa*, which he published on his return to England. Throughout his Admiralty secretaryship he was indefatigable in promoting the progress of geographical or scientific knowledge, especially in recommending to the governments under which he served various voyages to the Arctic Regions. He was a man of untiring industry, and devoted his leisure to literature and scientific pursuits: he published various works; contributed 195 articles to the *Quarterly Review;* and at the age of eighty-three (one year before his death) wrote his Autobiography. His public services had been rewarded by a baronetcy in 1835; and shortly after his death, in 1848, upon the lofty Hill of Hoad, near to the humble cottage in which Sir John Barrow was born, there was erected, by public subscription, to his memory, a sea-mark tower, as a record of what noble distinction may be earned in this happy country by well-directed energy and strictly moral worth.

OFFICIAL QUALIFICATIONS.

Swift's happy illustration of a frequent cause of failure, drawn in the reign of Queen Anne,—whose administrators were principally eminent scholars,—is scarcely so applicable in our time. Men of great parts are often unfortunate *in the* management of public business, because they are apt to go out of the common road by the quickness of their imagination. This Swift once said to Lord Bolingbroke, and desired he would observe that the clerk in his office used a sort of ivory knife with a blunt edge to divide a sheet of paper, which never failed to cut it even, only requiring a steady hand; whereas, if they should make use of a sharp penknife, the sharpness would make it go often out of the crease, and disfigure the paper.

A model Court-letter has been preserved by singular accident. When Swift was looking out for the prebend and sinecure of Dr. South, who was then very infirm, he received the following letter from Lord Halifax, to whom Addison had communicated Swift's expectations:

"*October* 6, 1709.

"Sir,—Our friend Mr. Addison telling me that he was to write to you to-night, I could not let his packet go away without letting you know how much I am concerned to find them returned without you. I am quite ashamed, for myself and my friends, to see you left in a place so incapable of testing you; and to see so much merit, and so great qualities, unrewarded by those who are sensible of them. Mr. Addison and I are entered into a new confederacy, never to give over the pursuit, nor to cease reminding those who can serve you, till your worth is placed in that light it ought to shine in. Dr. South holds out still, but he cannot be immortal. The situation of his prebend would make me doubly concerned in serving you; and upon all occasions that shall offer, I will be your constant solicitor, your sincere admirer, and your unalterable friend.—I am your most humble and obedient servant, HALIFAX."

Sir W. Scott notes: "This letter from Lord Halifax, the celebrated and almost professed patron of learning, is a curiosity in its way, being a perfect model of a courtier's correspondence with a man of letters—condescending, obliging, and probably utterly unmeaning. Dr. Swift wrote thus on the back of the letter: '*I kept this letter as a true original of courtiers and court promises;*' and, on the first leaf of a small printed book, entitled *Poésies Chrétiennes de Mons. Jollivet*, he wrote these words: 'Given me by my Lord Halifax, May 3, 1709. I begged it of him, and desired him to remember it was the only *favour* I ever received from him or his party.'" Dr. South, it should be added, survived until 1716, and then died, aged 83.

Diplomatic Handwriting has been a point of some moment with ministers, but has been tested in some strange varieties. Lord Palmerston, who was so long Secretary of State for Foreign Affairs, was very particular as to handwriting, and the style in use in the Foreign-office is attributable chiefly to him, but partly to Mr. Canning, who laid down the rule that not more than ten lines should be put into a page of foolscap. The handwriting of the Foreign-office is peculiar: the letters are to be formed in a particular way, the writing to be large and upright, and the words well apart, so as to be easily legible; it is not what a writing-master would teach as a good hand, and a clerk has to acquire it in the Office. The Foreign-office has been able to boast of the best handwriting in the public service; but it is not so good as it was formerly, owing to the great pressure for quick writing in order to prepare papers that come down in the afternoon to go abroad the same evening. A question put by Mr. Layard implied that he had heard of despatches received from some of our ministers abroad so ill-written that the originals could not be sent to her Majesty, and copies had to be made for the purpose. Mr. Hammond, of the Foreign-office, states that this could certainly not have occurred of late years; but he has known two ambassadors of ours whose handwriting was the most difficult to read that it is possible to conceive.

PUBLIC SPEAKING.

The art of speaking well is unquestionably one of the showiest qualifications for public life; although the drawback of unsoundness may be as common now as when it was classically expressed: *Satis eloquentiæ, sapientiæ parum.* Little or no attention has been bestowed in modern times on oratory as a separate branch of study; and eloquence has come to be more admired as one of the rare gifts of nature, than sought after as one of the fruits of art. The diffusion of opinions and arguments by means of the press has perhaps contributed in some degree to the present neglect of oratory; for a speaker is mainly known to the public through the press, and it is often more important to him to be *read* than to be *heard:* the eloquence of the newspaper—that is, the accomplishment of reporting—is the best oratory of our times; but the following experiences may be useful.

First, of one of the greatest orators of antiquity—Demosthenes. Those who expect to find in his style of oratory *the fervid* and impassioned language of a man carried away by his feelings to the prejudice of his judgment, will be disappointed. He is said not to have been a ready speaker, and to have required preparation. All his orations bear the marks of an effort to convince the understanding rather than to work on the passions of his hearers. And this is the highest praise. Men may be *persuaded* by splendid imagery, well-chosen words, and appeals to their passions; but to convince by a calm and clear address, when the speaker has no unfair advantage of person or of manner, and calls to his aid none of the tricks of rhetoric,—this is what Cicero calls the Oratory of Demosthenes, the ideal model of true eloquence.*

Demosthenes laboured under great physical disadvantages: he was naturally of a weak constitution, had a feeble voice, an indistinct articulation, and a shortness of breath. To remedy these defects, he climbed up hills with pebbles in his mouth, he declaimed on the sea-shore, or with a sword hung so as to strike his shoulders when he made an uncouth gesture. He is also said to have shut himself up at times in a cave underground for study's sake, and this for months together.

Next, of a great master of eloquence in our own times—Charles James Fox, whom Lord Ossory describes as "one of the most extraordinary men that ever existed." He was very young when his father, Henry, Lord Holland, finished his political career; but hearing from his childhood a constant conversation upon political subjects and the occurrences in the House of Commons, he was, both by nature and education, formed for a statesman. "His father delighted to cultivate his talents by argumentation and reasoning with him upon all subjects. He took his seat in the House of Commons before he was twenty-one, and very shortly began to show the dawn of those prodigious talents which he has since displayed. He was much caressed by the then Ministry, and appointed a Lord of the Admiralty, and soon promoted to the Treasury. Lord North (which he must ever since have repented) was inclined to turn him out upon some trivial occasion or difference; and soon afterwards the fatal quarrel with America commenced, Mr. Fox constantly opposing the absurd measures of administration, and rising

* *Orat.* c. 7.

by degrees to be the first man the House of Commons ever saw. His opposition continued from 1773 to 1782, when the Administration was fairly overturned by his powers; for even the great weight of ability, property, and influence that composed the Opposition, could never have effected that great work, if he had not acquired the absolute possession and influence of the House of Commons. He certainly deserved their confidence; for his political conduct had been fair, open, honest, and decided, against the system so fatally adopted by the Court. He resisted every temptation to be brought over by that system, however flattering to his ambition; for he must soon have been at the head of every thing. But I do not know whether his abilities were not the least extraordinary part about him. Perhaps that is saying too much; but he was full of good nature, good temper, and facility of disposition, disinterestedness with regard to himself, at the same time that his mind was fraught with the most noble sentiments and ideas upon all possible subjects. His understanding had the greatest scope I can form an idea of, his memory the most wonderful, his judgment the most true, his reasoning the most profound and acute, his eloquence the most rapid and persuasive."

Scarcely any person has ever become a great debater without long practice and many failures. It was by slow degrees, as Burke said, that Fox became the most brilliant and powerful debater that ever lived. Fox himself attributed his own success to the resolution which he formed when very young, of speaking, well or ill, at least once every night. "During five whole sessions," he used to say, "I spoke every night but one; and I regret only that I did not speak that night too."

The model of a debate is that given by Milton in the opening of the second book of *Paradise Lost.*

Mr. Sharp tells of the first meetings of a society at a public school, in which two or three evenings were consumed in debating whether the floor should be covered with a sail-cloth or a carpet; and better practice was gained in these unimportant discussions than in those that soon followed,—on liberty, slavery, passive obedience, and tyrannicide. It has been truly said, that nothing is so unlike a battle as a review.

Sir E. Bulwer Lytton has well illustrated a defect even in great orators, namely, nervousness; he says: "I doubt whether there has been any public speaker of the highest order of eloquence who has not felt an anxiety or apprehension, more or less actually painful, before rising to address an audience upon any very important subject on which he has meditated beforehand. This nervousness will, indeed, probably be proportioned to the amount of previous preparation, even though the necessities of reply, or the changeful temperament which characterises public assemblies, may compel the orator to modify, alter, perhaps wholly reject, what, in previous preparation, he had designed to say. The fact of preparation itself had impressed him with the dignity of the subject—with the responsibilities that devolve on an advocate from whom much is expected, on whose individual utterance results affecting the interests of many may depend. His imagination had been roused and warmed, and there is no imagination where there is no sensibility. Thus the orator had mentally surveyed, as it were, at a distance, the loftiest height of his argument; and now, when he is about to ascend to it, the awe of the altitude is felt."

The late Marquis of Lansdowne one day remarked to Thomas Moore, that he hardly ever spoke in the House of Lords without feeling the approaches of some loss of self-possession, and found that the only way to surmount it was to talk on at all hazards. He added, what appears highly probable, that those *commonplaces* which most men accustomed to public speaking have ready cut and dry, to bring in on all occasions, were, he thought, in general used by them as a mode of getting out of those blank intervals, when they do not know *what* to say next, but, in the mean time, must say *something*.

Mr. John Scott Russell, the eminent engineer, gives the following practical hints: "In a large room, nearly square, the best place to speak from is near one corner, with the voice directed diagonally to the opposite corner. In all rooms of common forms, the lowest pitch of voice that will reach across the room will be most audible. In all such rooms, it is better to speak along the length of the room than across it; and a low ceiling will, *cæteris paribus*, convey the sound better than a high one. It is better, generally, to speak from pretty near a wall or pillar, than far away from it. It is desirable that the speaker should speak in the key-note of the room, and evenly, but not loud."

To be well acquainted with the subject is of prime importance. Malone relates an amusing instance of failure in this respect in one of our greatest orators. Lord Chatham, when Mr. Pitt, on some occasion made a very long and able speech in the Privy Council relative to some naval matter. Every one present was struck by the force of his eloquence. Lord Anson, who was by no means eloquent, being then at the head of the Admiralty, and differing entirely in opinion from Mr. Pitt, got up, and only said these words: "My Lords, Mr. Secretary is very eloquent, and has stated his own opinion very plausibly. I am no orator; and all I shall say is, that he knows nothing at all of what he has been talking about."

Mr. Flood, the Irish orator, being told that he seemed to argue with somewhat less of his usual vigour when engaged on the wrong side of the question, happily replied that he "could not escape from the force of his own understanding." This must be the origin of the shrewd observation, that some clever persons are "educated beyond their own understanding."

Mr. Brougham, writing to the father of Thomas Babington Macaulay when the latter was at Cambridge University, urged the following, with a view to the great promise for public speaking which Macaulay then possessed, and of which Lord Grey had spoken in terms of the highest praise. "He takes his accounts from his son," says Mr. Brougham; "but from all I know, and have learnt in other quarters, I doubt not that his judgment is well formed. Now, of course, you destine him for the Bar; and, assuming that this, and the public objects incidental to it, are in his views, I would fain impress upon you (and through you, upon him) a truth or two which experience has made me aware of, and which I would have given a great deal to have been acquainted with earlier in life from the experience of others.

"1. The beginning of the art is to acquire a habit of *easy speaking;* and in whatever way this can be had (which individual inclination or accident will generally direct, and may safely be allowed to do so), it must be had. Now, I differ from all other doctors of rhetoric in this: I say, let him first of all learn to speak safely and fluently; as well and as sensibly as he can, no doubt, but at any rate let him learn to speak. This is to eloquence or good speaking what the being able to talk in a child is to correct grammatical speech. It is the requisite foundation, and on it you must build. Moreover, it can only be acquired young: therefore, let it by all means, and at any sacrifice, be gotten hold of forthwith. But in acquiring it, every sort of slovenly error will also be acquired. It must be got by a habit of easy writing—which, as Wyndham said, proved hard reading; by a custom of talking much in company; by debating in speaking societies, with little attention to rule, and more love of saying something at any rate, than of saying any thing well. I can even suppose that more attention is paid to the matter in such discussions than to the manner of saying it; yet still to say it easily, *ad libitum*, to say what you choose, and what you have to say, this is the first requisite; to acquire which every thing else must for the present be sacrificed.

"2. The next step is the grand one: to convert this style of easy speaking into chaste eloquence. And here there is but one rule. I do earnestly entreat your son to set daily and nightly before him the Greek models. First of all, he may look to the best modern speeches (as probably he has already); but he must by no means stop here; if he would be a great orator, he must go at once to the fountain-head, and be familiar with every one of the great orations of Demosthenes. I take for granted that he knows those of Cicero by heart; they are very beautiful, but not very useful, except, perhaps, the *Milo*, *pro Ligario*, and one or two more: but the Greek must positively be the model; and merely reading it, as boys do, won't do at all; he must enter into the spirit of each speech, thoroughly know the positions of the parties, follow each turn of the argument, and make the absolutely perfect and most chaste and severe composition familiar in his mind. His taste will improve every time he reads and repeats to himself (for he should have the fine passages by heart); and he will learn how much may be done by the skilful use of a few words, and a vigorous rejection of all superfluities.

In this view I hold a familiar knowledge of Dante as being next to Demosthenes. It is in vain to say that imitation of these models won't do for our times. First, I do not counsel any imitation, but only an imbibing of the same spirit. Secondly, I know from experience that nothing is half so successful in these times (bad though they be) as what had been formed on the Greek models. I use a very poor instance in giving my own experience; but I do assure you, that both in courts of law and Parliament, and even in mobs, I have never made so much play (to use a very modern phrase) as when I was almost translating from the Greek. I composed the peroration of my speech for the Queen in the Lords, after reading and repeating Demosthenes for three or four weeks, and I composed it over twenty times at least; and it certainly succeeded in a very extraordinary degree, and far above any merits of its own. This leads me to remark, that though speaking with writing beforehand is very well until the habit of any speech is acquired, yet, after that, he can never write too much: this is quite clear. It is laborious, no doubt, and it is more difficult beyond comparison than speaking offhand; but it is necessary to perfect oratory, and at any rate it is necessary to acquire the habit of correct diction. But I go further, and say, even to the end of a man's life, he must prepare word for word most of his fine passages. Now, would he be a great orator or no? In other words, would he have almost absolute power of doing good to mankind in a free country or no? So he wills this, he must follow these rules.—Believe me truly yours, H. BROUGHAM."

A contemporary journalist* has well observed of the oratory of the present day: "With all its great defects, which are perceptible enough to any cultivated hearer, Public Speaking is one of the greatest treats you can provide for the middle and higher population of one of our towns. The extempore oration is of course often a rough production; it does not at all come up to our ideas of the perfection of language, but it fascinates and fetters attention as being extempore,—as displaying the energy of an actual creation on the spot. Lord Derby's is perhaps the best oratorical language we have,—we mean when he speaks his best; it

* The *Times*.

is properly different from book-language, and yet does not run into the technical inflation, and conventional bombast, and professional phraseology, which are the dangers of oratory. Mr. Gladstone's is Parliamentary English—a very surprising and brilliant creation, but one that has gone through a medium of technicality or conventionalism, and does not come straight from the fount of language. The Bishop of Oxford's oratory is open to the criticism that it is overstrained, and produces vivid pictorial effects at the cost of simplicity. This is no very severe or invidious criticism, because in nine cases out of ten an orator who selects an exaggerated phrase selects it because a simpler one does not come to hand. A ready and inexhaustible command of the simplest and truest words is, of course, the very triumph of oratory, and a most rare triumph. Still, with all its defects, oratory is oratory: it is an uncommon exhibition of power; it creates interest, and sustains attention as such; and we are not sorry that our provincial towns have now the opportunity of hearing most of our leading public speakers."

Akin to the present subject is the art of presiding over a festive company, for which Sir Walter Scott has left these few simple practical rules:

1st. Always hurry the bottle round for five or six rounds, without prosing yourself, or permitting others to prose. A slight fillip of wine inclines people to be pleased, and removes the nervousness which prevents men from speaking—disposes them, in short, to be amusing, and to be amused.

2d. Push on, keep moving! as young Rapid says. Do not think of saying fine things—nobody cares for them any more than for fine music, which is often too liberally bestowed on such occasions. Speak at all ventures, and attempt the *mot pour rire.* You will find people satisfied with wonderfully indifferent jokes, if you can but hit the taste of the company, which depends much on its character. Even a very high party, primed with all the cold irony and *non est tanti* feelings, or no feelings of fashionable folks, may be stormed by a jovial, rough, round, and ready præses. Choose your text with discretion—the sermon may be as you like. Should a drunkard or an ass break in with any thing out of joint, if you can parry it with a jest, good and well; if not, do not exert your serious authority, unless it is something very bad. The authority even of a chairman ought to be very cautiously exercised. With patience, you will have the support of every one.

3d. When you have drunk a few glasses to play the good fellow and banish modesty (if you are unlucky enough to have such a troublesome companion), then beware of the cup too much. Nothing is so ridiculous as a drunken preses.

Lastly, always speak short, and *Skeoch doch na skiel*—cut a tale with a drink.

OPPORTUNITY.

To *bide the time* is often the means, though slow, of reaping success. Late in the last century, a printseller settled in a leading street of the artistic locality of Soho: during the first six weeks he kept shop, his receipts were not as many pence; nevertheless he was civil and obliging to all callers and inquirers, to whom, in the printselling business, customers are a very small proportion. This obliging disposition was his main investment, and his shop grew to be the resort of print-collectors of all grades—from the rich duke to the hard-working engraver; he became wealthy, and died bequeathing to his family a considerable fortune, and the finest stock of prints in the metropolis.

Extraordinary instances have occurred of latent genius having been discovered by some lucky accident, and fostered to high position. Isaac Ware, the architect and editor of *Palladio*, was originally a chimney-sweeper, and, when a boy, was seated one day in front of Whitehall-palace, upon the pavement, whereon he had drawn in chalk the elevation of a building. This attracted the notice of a gentleman in passing, and led him to inquire who had chalked out the building. The boy replied, it was his own work; the unknown patron then took the lad to the master-sweeper to whom he was apprenticed, purchased his indenture, and forthwith had little Ware educated: he rose to be one of the leading architects of his day, and among other edifices he built Chesterfield-house, in South Audley-street, one of the handsomest mansions in the metropolis. Ware died in 1766; and, it is said, retained the stain of *soot* in his face to the day of his death.

MEN OF BUSINESS.

Our forefathers appear to have conveyed much of their instructions in Business Life by way of apophthegm. In the *Spectator*, No. 109, it is observed that " the man proper for the business of money and the advancement of gain, speaking in the general, is of a sedate, plain, good understanding, not apt to go out of his way, but so behaving himself at home that business may come to him. Sir William Turner, that valuable citizen, has left behind him a most excellent rule, and couched it in a very few words, suited to the meanest capacity. He would say, 'Keep your shop, and your shop will keep you.'" [Alderman Thomas, the mercer in Paternoster-row, made this one of the mottoes of his shop.] "It must be confessed, that if a man of a great genius could add steadiness to his vivacities, or substitute slower men of fidelity to transact the methodical part of his affairs, such an one would outstrip the rest of the world: but business and trade are not to be managed by the same heads which write poetry and make plans for the conduct of life in general."

However, Bacon thought otherwise. "Let no man," he says, "fear lest learning should expulse business; nay, rather, it will keep and defend the possessions of the mind against idleness and pleasure, which otherwise, at unawares, may enter to the prejudice both of business and pleasure."

The proper time—"*rerum est omnium primum.*" "To choose time," says Bacon, "is to save time; and an unseasonable motion is but beating the air. There be three parts of business: the preparation; the debate, or examination; and the perfection; whereof, if you look for despatch, let the middle only be the work of many, and the first and last the work of few."

Sir Robert Walpole had in his mind a man not apt to go out of his way, when he described Henry Legge, his Chancellor of the Exchequer, as having "very little rubbish in his head;" meaning that he was a practical, useful man of business.

There are few persons who have not met with cases of hypochondriacs who have been relieved and made more happy by useful and disinterested occupation in promoting the welfare of others. Dr. Heberden used to relate a striking case of this kind. Captain Blake was a hypochondriac for several years, and during that time every week or two he consulted the Doctor, who had not only prescribed all the medicines likely to correct disease arising from bodily infirmity, but every argument which humanity and good sense could suggest for the comfort of his mind; but in vain. At length Dr. Heberden heard no more of his patient, till after a considerable interval he found that Captain Blake had formed a project for conveying fish to London, from some of the seaports in the west, by means of light carts adapted for expeditious land-carriage. The arrangement and various occupations of the mind in carrying out this object entirely superseded all sense of his former malady, which from that time never returned.

Innumerable are the instances of men retiring from business in middle life, yet yearning to return to it,—so strong is the habit of occupation. We all remember the story of the city tallow-chandler, who retired into the suburbs, having sold his business, with the proviso that he should come to town on a melting-day. One of the partners of a large publishing house, some years since, retired into Wales; but did not long survive the change, to enjoy his well-earned fortune. Another instance occurs: a tradesman retired from business with a fortune, and travelled for some time to divert *ennui;* but this not succeeding, he returned to active life in manufacturing and patenting lamps and kettles, night-lights and potato-saucepans, and, in such small ingenuities, finds himself happy again.

The late Mr. Charles Tilt, the well-known publisher in Fleet-street, retired from business in middle life; travelled many years in each quarter of the world; and wrote a pleasant little book, entitled *The Boat and the Caravan.* He had been articled to Longman and Co.; then lived with Mr. Hatchard, in Piccadilly; and next established himself with great success. Notwithstanding his long retirement, his business habits never forsook him: he generously acted as trustee in the settlement of the affairs of his late partner, Mr. David Bogue, who had succeeded to the entire concern in Fleet-street; and he next officiated as executor to the estate of the late Mr. Hatchard, with whom he had formerly lived. Mr. Tilt died in 1862, leaving the large property of 180,000*l.*

CHARACTER THE BEST SECURITY.

"I owe my success in business chiefly to you," said a stationer to a paper-maker, as they were settling a large account; "but let me ask how a man of your caution came to give credit so freely to a beginner with my slender means?" "Because," replied the paper-maker, "at whatever hour in the morning I passed to my business, I always observed you without your coat at yours." Upon this Mr. Walker, the police-magistrate, observes: "I knew both parties. Different men will have different degrees of success, and every man must expect to experience ebbs and flows; but I fully believe that no one in this country, of whatever condition, who is really attentive, and, what is of great importance, who lets it appear that he is so, can fail in the long-run. Pretence is ever bad; but there are many who obscure their good qualities by a certain carelessness, or even an affected indifference, which deprives them of the advantages they would otherwise infallibly reap, and then they complain of the injustice of the world. The man who conceals or disguises his merit might as well expect to be thought clean in his person if he chose to go covered with filthy rags. The world will not, and cannot in great measure, judge but by appearances; and worth must stamp itself, if it hopes to pass current, even against baser metal:

> Worth makes the man, want of it the fellow;
> The rest is all but leather or prunello.—*Pope.*"

ENGINEERS AND MECHANICIANS.

"No man can look back on the last twenty or thirty years without feeling that it has been *the age of Engineers and Mechanicians.* The profession has, in that period of time, done much to change the aspect of human affairs; for what agency during that period, single or combined, can be compared in its effects, or in its tendency towards the amelioration of the condition of mankind, with the establishment of railroads, of the electric telegraph, and to the improvement in steam navigation?"

"The wide range of the profession of an Engineer requires the assistance of many departments of science and art, and must call into employment important branches of manufacture. He can perform no great work without the aid of a great variety of workmen; and it is on their strength and skill, as well as on their scientific direction, that the perfection of his work will depend. The personal experience of one individual cannot fit him for the exigencies of a profession which is ever extending its range of subjects, and is constantly dealing with new and complex phenomena,—phenomena which are all the more difficult to deal with from the fact, that they are generally surrounded by such variable circumstances as render them incapable of being submitted to precise measurement and calculation, or of being made amenable to the deductions of exact science. Consequently, nothing is more certain than that he who wishes to reach the perfection of his art must avail himself of the experience of others as well as his own, and that he will not unfrequently find the sum of the whole little enough to guide him. And let no inventive genius suppose that his own tendencies or capabilities relieve him from this necessity.

"There is no such thing as discovery and invention, in the sense which is sometimes attached to the words. Men do not suddenly discover new worlds, or invent new machines, or find new metals. Some indeed may be, and are, better fitted than others for such purposes; but the progress of discovery is, and always has been, much the same. *There is nothing really worth having that man has obtained that has not been the result of a combined and gradual progress of investigation.* A gifted individual comes across some old footmark, and stumbles on a chain of previous research and inquiry. He meets, for instance, with a machine, the result of much previous labour; he modifies it, pulls it to pieces, constructs and reconstructs it, and, by further trial and experiment, he arrives at the long-sought-for result."

Such were the emphatic words of Mr. Hawkshaw, F.R.S., in opening his Address on his election as President of the Institution of Civil Engineers, session 1861-62. It would not be difficult to illustrate the President's data by many bright instances of their truth. But we remember too well the sad story of Myddleton bringing the New River to our metropolis, a very early engineering labour, who, although he died not so poor as is usually represented, yet his family fell into decay. Almost equally familiar is the story of the life of George Stephenson, the maturer of the locomotive engine; and the career of his son, Robert Stephenson, the constructor of the London and Birmingham Railway, and second only to his father as a railway engineer. George learned to read and write at night-schools, and "figuring" by the engine-fires. As Robert grew up, his father was enabled to send him to Edinburgh University, where he acquired some knowledge in mathematics and geology: these acquisitions afforded subjects for comment and discussion between him and his father, and were of valuable use to both in their future joint avocations; and when the father had retired, in the sphere of railways Robert was recognised as the foremost man, the safest guide, and the most active worker. In the great railway mania of 1844, he was engineer for thirty-three new schemes; and his income was large, beyond any previous instance of engineering gain. His other great railway achievements were, the High-level Bridge at Newcastle; the Chester and Holyhead line; he constructed the Britannia and Conway tubular bridges, and designed the tubular bridges for Canada and Egypt. These intense labours brought him to his grave in his fifty-sixth year. It has been truly said of Robert Stephenson:

"He almost worshiped his father's memory, and said he owed all to his father's training, his example, and his character; and he declared in public: 'It is my great pride to remember that, whatever may have been done, and however extensive may have been my own connexion in the railway development, all I owe, and all I have done is primarily due, to the parent whose memory I cherish and revere.' Like his father, he was eminently practical, and yet always open to the influence and guidance of correct theory.

"In society Robert Stephenson was simple, unobtrusive, and modest; but charming, and even fascinating, in an eminent degree. Sir John Lawrence has said of him, that he was, of all others, the man he most delighted to meet in England, he was so manly, yet gentle, and withal so great.

"His great wealth enabled him to perform many generous acts in a right noble and yet modest manner, not letting his right hand know what his left hand did."*

In the life of Thomas Telford, we have another striking instance of a man who, by the force of natural talent, unaided save by uprightness and persevering industry, raised himself from low estate to take his stand among the master-spirits of the age. He was born in 1757, in Dumfriesshire, sent to the parish-school, and employed as a shepherd-boy; in his leisure, delighted to read the books lent him by his village friends. At the age of fourteen he was apprenticed to a stone-mason, and for several years worked on bridges and stone-buildings, village-churches, and manses, in his native district. In 1780 he went to Edinburgh, and for two years closely attended to architecture and drawing. He then removed to London, and worked upon the quadrangle of Somerset House, under Sir William Chambers, as architect. His next practice was in the construction of graving-docks, wharf-walls, and similar engineering works; and he built above forty bridges in Shropshire. His greatest works are, the Ellesmere Canal, 103 miles in length, with its wonderful aqueduct-bridges; the Caledonian Canal, which cost a million of money; the Bedford Level, and other

* Smiles's *Lives of the Engineers*, vol. iii.

important drainage works; 1000 miles of Highland roads and 1200 bridges; St. Katherine's Docks, London, constructed with unexampled rapidity; and the great road from London to Holyhead, and the works connected with it. The Menai Suspension Bridge is a noble example of his boldness in designing, and practical skill in executing a novel and difficult work; and it is related of him that, just previous to the fixing of the last bar, he knelt in private prayer to the Giver of all good for the successful completion of the great work. Telford left an account of his labours of more than half a century; yet he found time to teach himself Latin, French, Italian, and German. He was the first president of the Institution of Civil Engineers, in whose theatre is a noble portrait of him; and in Westminster Abbey, where he is interred, is a marble statue of the Eskdale shepherd-boy, whose works, in number, magnitude, and usefulness, are unrivalled.

John Rennie, who designed three of the noblest bridges in the world, in addition to other great engineering works, was born in 1761, in the county of East Lothian. He learned his first lessons in mechanics in the workshop of a millwright; before he was eleven years old he had constructed a windmill, a pile-engine, and a steam-engine; he next learned elementary mathematics and mechanics, and drawing machinery and architecture, and attended lectures on mechanical philosophy and chemistry. His greatest works are the Plymouth Breakwater; Waterloo, Southwark, and London bridges; the London, East and West India Docks; and great steam-engines; his principal undertakings having cost forty millions sterling. He was rarely occupied in business less than twelve hours a day; he seldom illustrated his information with any other instrument than a two-foot rule, which he always carried in his pocket. He owed his good fortune to talent, industry, prudence, perseverance, boldness of conception, soundness of judgment, and habits of untiring application: his works were indeed executed for posterity.

Sir Edward Banks, who built Rennie's three stupendous bridges, was a labourer at Chipstead on the Merstham railway, some sixty years since: by his own natural abilities, which had not been cultivated to any extent, and by his integrity and perseverance, he became contractor for public works, and acquired great wealth: and it shows the simplicity of his nature, that, struck with the retired picturesqueness of Chipstead churchyard, he chose it for the depository of his remains, where the tablet to his memory bears his bust, and an arch and the three great bridges,—the goal of his remarkable career.

The history of the life of the elder Brunel is strangely tinged with romance. He was born in Normandy in 1769, was early intended for the priesthood; but when at the college of Gisors, he would steal away to the village carpenter's shop, and draw faces and plans, and learn to handle tools; and one day, seeing a new tool in a cutler's window, he pawned his hat to purchase it. He was next sent to the ecclesiastical seminary of St. Nicaise at Rouen; there, in his play-hours, he loved to watch the ships along the quay; and seeing some large iron castings landed from an English ship, he inquired, Where had they come from? and on being told from England, the boy exclaimed, "Ah, when I am a man, I will go and see the country where such grand machines are made." On his return home, he continued his mechanical recreations; made musical instruments; and invented a nightcap-making machine, which is still used by the peasantry in that part of Normandy. His father now gave up all hope of his son for the priesthood, and had him qualified to enter the navy, and at seventeen he was nominated to a royal corvette; but while serving there he continued his mechanical pursuits, and made for himself a quadrant in ebony. His ship having been paid off in 1792, Brunel went to Paris, where he nearly fell a victim to the fury of the Revolution; but he escaped to Rouen, and thence fled to the United States, where he landed in 1793. While at New York, the idea of his block-machinery occurred to him. He now executed canal surveys, and designed the Park Theatre, and superintended its erection; he was next appointed chief engineer for New York, and there erected a cannon-foundry, with novel contrivances for casting and boring guns. He left New York in January 1799, and landed at Falmouth in the following March: there he met his early love, Sophia Kingdom, and the pair were shortly after united for life.

Brunel brought with him to England a duplicate writing and drawing machine; a machine for twisting cotton-thread and forming it into balls; a machine for trimmings and borders for muslins, lawns, and cambrics. The famous block-machinery was Brunel's next invention; then various wood-working machinery, and machines for manufacturing shoes; and next the Battersea saw-mills; but the failure of the two latter speculations brought Brunel into difficulties, from which he was extricated by a government grant of 5000*l.*, in consideration of the savings by the use of his block-machinery. He then improved the stocking-knitting machine and steam-engine; metallic paper and crystallised tinfoil; improvements in stereotyping and the tread-mill. In engineering, he designed suspension, swing, and other bridges, and machines for boring cannon. He next experimented with a boat on the Thames, fitted with a double-action engine, and made his first voyage in it to Margate in 1814, when he narrowly escaped personal violence from the proprietors of the sailing-boats. Marine engines and paddle-wheels were next improved by Brunel; and these were followed by his carbonic-acid gas engine, which proved too costly a machine. Then came the crowning event of his life, the construction of the Thames Tunnel, taking the idea of his excavating-machine from the boring operations of the *Teredo navalis*. In this formidable work he was assisted by his son, Isambard Kingdom Brunel, then only nineteen years of age; and after most perilous operations, the tunnel was completed, and opened March 25th, 1843. This was the engineer's last work: as a commercial adventure it proved disastrous, which preyed on the mind of Brunel; though he lived six years longer, until he had attained his 81st year.

The younger Brunel's first great work was the Clifton Suspension Bridge, followed by docks at Bristol and Sunderland, and several colliery tramways. In 1835, he was appointed engineer of the Great Western Railway, being then only about twenty-eight years of age, but skilful and ingenious, and anxious to strike out an entirely new course in railway engineering. He adopted the broad-gauge, then a great and novel enterprise, but now ascertained to be unnecessary: the works were unusually costly, and so novel that the line was called the Grand Experimental Railway;

while it rendered Brunel famous as a railway engineer. He next attempted the atmospheric principle; but this proved unsuccessful, and the loss exceeded half a million of money. His last and greatest railway engineering achievements were his "bowstring-girder" bridges at Chepstow and Saltash: the latter has two wrought-iron tubes, each weighing upwards of 1000 tons, and the viaduct and bridge are nearly half a mile, or 300 feet longer than the Britannia bridge. The central Saltash pier foundations, upon solid rock, 90 feet below the surface of the river, were laid within a wrought-iron cylinder 37 feet in diameter and 100 feet high, and the whole work involved six years' toil, anxiety, and peril.

Next, Brunel devised an iron-plated armed ship capable of withstanding the fire of the Sebastopol forts; but his grand triumphs as a naval engineer were, the *Great Western*, steam-ship, propelled by paddle-wheels; and the *Great Britain*, propelled by a screw; but these were thrown into the shade by his *Great Eastern*, combining the powers of the paddle-wheel and the screw; and which, with the aid of Mr. Scott Russell, its builder, was completed and launched,—the largest ship that has ever floated. But this stupendous labour had undermined Mr. Brunel's health; he was seized with paralysis, and died at the comparatively early age of fifty-three.*

Of Brunel's great engineering skill there can be no question; he loved difficulties and engineering perils: he has been styled "the Michael Angelo of Railways;" and his victory in "the Battle of the Gauges" gained him extraordi-

* He had more perilous escapes from violent death than fall to the lot of most men. He had two narrow escapes from drowning by the river suddenly bursting in upon the Thames-Tunnel works. During the Great Western Railway inspection, he was one day riding a pony rapidly down Boxhill, when the animal stumbled and fell, pitching the engineer on his head; he was taken up for dead, but eventually recovered. One day, when driving an engine through the Box-tunnel, he discerned some light object standing on the same line of road along which his engine was travelling; he turned on the full steam and dashed the object (a contractor's truck) into a thousand pieces. When on board the *Great Western* steam-ship, he fell down a hatchway into the hold, and was nearly killed. But the most extraordinary accident which befel him was, in showing a sleight-of-hand trick to his children, his swallowing a half-sovereign, which dropped into his windpipe, remained there for six weeks, when it was removed through an incision in the windpipe, by Sir Benjamin Brodie and Mr. Key; his body was inverted, and after a few coughs, the coin dropped into his mouth. Mr. Brunel used afterwards to say, that the moment when he heard the gold piece strike against his upper front teeth was perhaps the most exquisite in his whole life.—Abridged from the *Quarterly Review*, No. 223.

nary prominence in the railway world. His ruling passion was magnitude, without regard to cost: "he was the very Napoleon of engineers, thinking more of glory than of profit, and of victory than of dividends." Capitalists subscribed to his projects freely, and he put his own savings into the same risks; if shareholders suffered, he suffered with them; and it must be conceded that both railway travelling and steam navigation have been greatly advanced by the speculative ability of Mr. Brunel's Titanic labours.

The career of Joseph Locke, civil engineer, though less brilliant than that of Brunel, was one of more sterling worth. He was born in Yorkshire, in 1805, the son of a fellow-workman with George Stephenson at the pit. Locke had little schooling, and failing in two or three humble services, at the age of nineteen he became George Stephenson's pupil, and then his assistant, taking charge of the survey of railway lines; he was appointed engineer-in-chief of the Grand Junction and South-Western lines; and next initiated the Continental Railway system, promoting the rapid communication between London and Paris. He was made a chevalier and officer of the Legion of Honour, and sat in the British Parliament for Honiton. He died at the early age of fifty-five, leaving great wealth to his widow (a daughter of Mr. M'Creery, the literary printer), to form in the North a public park, and found a scholarship.

The high celebrity of Mr. Locke was not due to the fact of his making railways. It was, that he made them within the estimated cost, —an achievement which would sooner or later have been attained by the ordinary operations of capital. The Grand Junction Railway was eventually constructed for a sum within the estimate, and at an average cost of less than 15,000*l.* a mile. The heavy works on the Caledonian line were completed at less than 16,000*l.* a mile. This economical success was in a great measure owing to the adoption of a bold system of steep gradients—an expedient which Stephenson, it appears, disliked to the last, and which was a prevailing feature in his active rival's designs. Locke hated a tunnel, and with embankments and inclines would encounter any difficulty.*

Thomas Cubitt, the great metropolitan builder and contractor, was another remarkable man of this class. He was born at Buxton, near Norwich, in 1788. At the time of his father's death he was nineteen years old, and working as a journeyman carpenter. He next took a voyage to India

* *Saturday Review.*

and back, as captain's joiner; and, on his return to the metropolis, with his savings began business as a master-carpenter. Within six years he erected large workshops in Gray's-inn-road. One of his earliest works was building the London Institution in Moorfields. About 1824, he began to build Tavistock-square, Gordon-square, Woburn-place, and the adjoining streets; and next engaged to cover with houses large portions of the Five Fields, Chelsea, of which engagement Belgrave-square, Lowndes-square, and Chesham-place are the results.* He subsequently contracted to build over the large open district between Eaton-square and the Thames, now known as South Belgravia. He had completed most of his large engagements, and had just built for himself a mansion at Denbies, where he died in his sixty-seventh year, possessed of great wealth. Through life he constantly promoted the intellectual and moral improvement of his work-people. One of his brothers, and partner in business, is Mr. William Cubitt, M.P., who has twice served the office of Lord Mayor, and was, like his relative, originally a ship's carpenter.

Thomas Brassey, the railway contractor, is another remarkable instance of colossal labour. Born at Buerton in 1805, and educated at Chester, he commenced life as a surveyor at Birkenhead; and his first railway work was a contract to supply the stone for a viaduct of the Liverpool and Manchester line. From this period to the present hour, he has constructed, upon his own responsibility and credit, many hundred miles of railway in England, Scotland, France, Spain, and Canada, at the cost of millions of money. A striking instance of his energy and enterprise occurred in one of his French contracts. When the Barentine viaduct, of twenty arches, on the Rouen and Havre Railway, was nearly completed, the work gave way, and the casualty involved a loss of 30,000*l.* Mr. Brassey was neither morally nor legally responsible—he had repeatedly protested against the material used in the structure; but the viaduct was rebuilt entirely at Mr. Brassey's cost.

* This district was originally a clayey swamp; but Mr. Cubitt finding the strata to consist of gravel and clay of inconsiderable depth, the clay he removed and burned into bricks; and by building upon the substratum of gravel, he converted this spot from one of the most unhealthy to one of the most healthy—a singular adaptation of the means to the end.

Mr. George Bidder, the engineer, presents one of the few examples of early habits of calculation being matured to advantage. When about six years of age, he was first introduced to the science of figures. His father was a working man; his elder brother commenced instructing him to count up to 10, then to 100, and there he stopped. He repeated the process, and found that by stopping at 10, and repeating that every time, he counted up to 100 much quicker than by going straight through the series: he counted up to ten, then ten again=20, 3 times 10=30, 4 times=40, and so on. At this time he did not know one written or printed figure from another, nor did he know there was such a word as "multiply;" but, having acquired the power of counting up to 100 by ten and by 5, he set about, in his own way, to acquire the multiplication-table: he got a small bag of shot, which he arranged into squares of 8 on each side, and then, on counting them, found they amounted to 64; which fact once established, remained undisturbed in Mr. Bidder's mind until this day; and in this way he acquired the whole multiplication-table up to 10 times 10, which was all he needed. In a house opposite his father's lived an aged blacksmith, who allowed young Bidder to run about his workshop and blow the bellows for him, and on winter-evenings to listen to the old man's stories by the forge-hearth. By practice his powers of numeration were drawn forth, he was rewarded with halfpence, and thus he became more attached to arithmetic. The "Calculating Boy" has now matured as an eminent engineer; the process of reasoning, or action of the mind, by which, when a boy, he trained himself in Mental Arithmetic, having laid the basis of sound professional skill, which he has most beneficially exercised in various great engineering works.

James Walker, civil engineer, who died in 1862, aged eighty-one, was the oldest member of the profession. He was one of the earliest members of the Institution of Civil Engineers, succeeded Telford as President, and filled the chair fourteen years. Mr. Walker, through his long life, was associated with many of the greatest hydraulic works in England and Scotland, including lighthouses, harbours, bridges, embankments, and drainage. He had accumulated in personalty 300,000*l.*, which he took great pains to distribute by his will; for he was a kind-hearted, generous man, and considerate and liberal to those associated with him in his profession.

SCIENTIFIC FARMING.

Southey, in *The Doctor*, remarks: "It is a fact not unworthy of notice, that the most intelligent farmers in the neighbourhood of London are persons who have taken to farming as a business, because of their strong inclination for rural employments: one of the very best in Middlesex, when the Survey of that county was published by the Board of Agriculture, had been a tailor."

Scientific farming has of late years largely multiplied these amateur farmers; but, long before rural economy had taken this turn, we remember a curious instance. Some five-and-forty years since, when Davy's *Agricultural Chemistry* was the only work of its class, there lived in a town of Surrey a gentleman-tradesman, who loved to relieve the monotony of his own business by flying off to experimental pursuits. In politics he was a disciple of Cobbett, and year after year foretold a revolution in England,—an alarm which he raised throughout his household. He took extreme interest in new mechanical projects; and kept a chronological record of the progress of the Thames Tunnel. In wine-making he was a very experimentalist, and knew by heart every line of Macculloch on Wine from unripe fruit. Next, he turned over every inch of his garden, analysed the soil *à la Davy*, and *salted* all his growing crops, as well as the soil. But he soon flew from horticultural chemistry to real farming; and about the same time took to road-making and macadamisation, and became surveyor of the highways. He next bought the lease of a house in the neighbourhood for the sake of the large garden attached to it; and here he passed much of his time in its experimental culture. Had he lived to the days of Liebig, how he would have revelled in his theories!

We have a strong confirmation of Southey's remark in the present day in the case of Alderman Mechi, who has become a memorable man in this kind of experimental agriculture, and has transferred the *magic* of his Razor-Strop (by the sale of which, in ten years he realised a handsome fortune) to the barren heath-land of Essex. In 1840 he commenced his bucolic experiments by purchasing a small unproductive farm at Tiptree-heath; and here he tried what could be effected by deep drainage and the application of steam-power. The Essex farmers laughed at him as an enthusiast, and the country gentlemen kept aloof from him. Mechi, however, persevered, and brought his farm into such high productiveness that he realises annually an average handsome profit. We have seen his balance-sheet impugned: however, if public opinion is worth any thing, he has rendered great service to agricultural science by the exhibition of processes upon his model farm, Tiptree, which is known all over the European continent; for the Alderman has been presented with a 500*l.* testimonial of plate by noblemen and gentlemen interested in science and agriculture at home and abroad.

LARGE FORTUNES.

No single class can be pointed to in the present day as the first favourite of fortune. The loan-monger is still powerful, and so is the speculator; but bankers accumulate fortunes like those of the highest nobles, and a linen-draper left the other day cash which would purchase the fee-simple of the Woburn estates. The rate of fortunes has enormously increased. Pitt thought it useless to tax fortunes above a million, and now men die every day whose heirs chuckle over the saving produced by this want of foresight. A "plum" has ceased to be even a citizen's goal, and there are tradesmen in London whose incomes while in trade exceed "a great fortune" of the time of the second George. Very enormous realised fortunes, properties that are producing 50,000*l.* a-year, are, however, still very scarce. Only fifty-seven are returned to the English income-tax; and though that is a palpably erroneous account, it may be doubted if there are a dozen individuals with that amount in the world. There are none in France or Italy beyond a few working capitalists, a few remaining in Germany, a considerable number in Russia, and perhaps thirty individuals in America. There are perhaps ten private incomes in India of that amount, as many in South America, and a few officials in the Eastern world accumulate very considerable sums; but there the list ends.* Yet, how often are large fortunes wrecked by those who succeed to them!

Many a Londoner past middle age may recollect Thomas Clark, "the King of Exeter 'Change," who was long one of the most singular characters in the metropolis. He took a stall in the 'Change in 1765, with 100*l.* lent him by a stranger. By parsimony and perseverance he so extended his business as to occupy nearly one-half of the entire building with the sale of cutlery, turnery, &c. He grew rich, and once returned his income at 6000*l.* a-year. He was penurious in his habits: he dined with his plate on the bare board, and his meal, with a pint of porter, never cost him a shilling; after dinner he took a glass of spirits-and-water at the public-house opposite the end of the 'Change, and then returned to his business. He resided in Belgrave-place, Pimlico; and morning and evening saw him on his old horse, riding into town and home again—and thus he figured in the print-shops. He died in 1817, in his eightieth year, and left nearly half a million of money. His daughter was married to Hamlet, the celebrated goldsmith of Coventry-street, who, however, met with sad reverses; and, among other unsuccessful speculations, built the Bazaar and the Princess's Theatre in Oxford-street.

The wealth of the celebrated Mr. Beckford, the son of the demagogue Alderman, and Lord Chatham's god-child, proved the shoal upon which his happiness was wrecked. He succeeded to his father's enormous fortune at ten years of age. He was educated at home: he was quick and lively, and had literary tastes; he had a great passion for genealogy and heraldry; studied Oriental literature: in his seventeenth year he wrote a history of extraordinary painters. His father had left him, principally in Jamaica estates, a property which, on the conclusion of his minority, furnished him with a million of ready money and an income of 100,000*l.* a-year. He travelled and resided abroad until his twenty-second year, when he wrote *Vathek*, a work of startling beauty. At twenty-four he married; but the lady died in three years. He passed many years in travelling, princi-

* *Spectator* newspaper, 1862.

pally in Spain and Portugal, before he got sufficiently settled in mind to return to his family-seat, Fonthill in Wiltshire. He began to reside there in 1796, and immediately commenced the great squandering of his money. He had always a hundred, and often two hundred, workmen engaged in carrying out his wayward fancies. But he was haughty and reserved; and because some of his neighbours followed game into his grounds, he had a wall, twelve feet high and seven miles long, built round his home-estate, in order to shut out the world. He then began the third house at Fonthill, considering the second too near a piece of water. The new house was built in a sham monastic style, was called the Abbey, and cost a quarter of a million; but never put to any use, except on one occasion, to receive Lord Nelson. While Beckford was indulging these gigantic follies, he lost, by an adverse decision in a Chancery-suit, a considerable portion of his Jamaica property; he was also cheated out of large sums of money, and in the end was obliged to sell Fonthill; the purchaser was Mr. Farquhar, a rich but penurious merchant. In a few years the lofty tower of the Abbey fell down. The estate is now the property of the Marquis of Westminster. Mr. Beckford removed to Bath, and there built, on Lansdowne Hill, an Italian villa, with a lofty prospect-tower. While residing here he wrote an account of the travels which he had made half a century before; and having got through large sums of money in planting and building, he died in 1844, in his eighty-fourth year; and upon his tomb a passage from *Vathek* is inscribed.

Mr. Beckford was unquestionably a man of genius and rare accomplishments. "But his abilities were overpowered, and his character tainted, by the possession of wealth so enormous. At every stage of life his money was like a millstone round his neck. He had taste and knowledge; but the selfishness of wealth tempted him to let these gifts of the mind run to seed in the gratification of extravagant freaks. He really enjoyed travelling and scenery, but he felt it incumbent on him, as a millionnaire, to take a French cook with him wherever he went; and he found that the Spanish grandees and ecclesiastical dignitaries who welcomed him so cordially valued him as the man whose cook could make such wonderful omelettes. From the day when Chatham's proxy stood for him at the font till the day when he was laid in his pink granite sarcophagus, he was the victim of riches. Had he had only 5000*l.* a year, and been sent to Eton, he might have been one of the foremost men of his time, and have been as useful in his generation as, under his unhappy circumstances, he was useless."* It may be added, that he was worse: for he so threw about his money at Fonthill as to corrupt and demoralise the simple country-people. We remember three of his London residences: one on the Terrace, Piccadilly, on the site of the newly-built mansion of Baron Rothschild; another of Beckford's town residences was No. 1 Devonshire-place, New-road; and the third, No. 27 Charles-street, May Fair, a very small house, looking over the garden of Chesterfield-house.

The vanity of wealth is exemplified in the following anecdote, which Mrs. Richard Trench had from an ear-witness:

> The late Duke of Queensberry, leaning over the balcony of his beautiful villa near Richmond, where every pleasure was collected which wealth could purchase or luxury devise, he followed with his eyes the majestic Thames, winding through groves and buildings of various loveliness, and exclaimed, "Oh, that wearisome river! Will it never cease running, running, and I so tired of it?" To me this anecdote conveys a strong moral lesson, connected with the well-known character of the speaker, a professed voluptuary, who passed his youth in pursuit of selfish pleasures, and his age in vain attempts to elude the relentless grasp of *ennui*.

Now let us turn to some better uses of wealth earned by well-directed industry. Old Mr. Strahan, the printer (the founder of the typarchical dynasty), said to Dr. Johnson, that "there are few ways in which a man can be more innocently employed than getting money;" and he added, that "the more one thinks of this, the juster it will appear." Johnson agreed with him. Boswell also relates that Mr. Strahan once talked of launching into the great ocean of London, in order to have a chance of rising into eminence; and observing that many men were kept back from trying their fortunes there because they had been born to a competency, said, "Small certainties are the bane of men of talents;" which Johnson confirmed.

Mr. Strahan had taken a poor boy from the country as

* *Saturday Review.*

an apprentice, upon Johnson's recommendation. Johnson, having inquired after him, said, "Mr. Strahan, let me have five guineas on account, and I'll give this boy one. Nay, if a man recommends a boy, and does nothing for him, it's sad work. Call him down." Boswell followed Johnson into the courtyard behind Mr. Strahan's house, and there he heard this conversation:

"Well, my boy, how do you go on?" "Pretty well, sir; but they're afraid I a'n't strong enough for some parts of the business." *Johnson.* "Why, I shall be sorry for it; for, when you consider with how little mental power and corporeal labour a printer can get a guinea a week, it is a very desirable occupation for you. Do you hear; take all the pains you can; and if this does not do, we must think of some other way of life for you. There's a guinea."

Here was one of the many instances of Johnson's active benevolence. At the same time, says Boswell, the slow and sonorous solemnity with which, while he bent himself down, he addressed a little thick short-legged boy, contrasted with the boy's awkwardness and awe, could not but excite some ludicrous emotions.

Johnson appears to have been generally alive to the policy of getting money: we all remember when, as one of the executors of Mr. Thrale, he was assisting in taking stock of the brewery in Southwark, how its vastness impressed the doctor with "the potentiality of growing rich."

William Strahan, a native of Edinburgh, came to London when a very young man, and worked as a journeyman printer, having Dr. Franklin for one of his fellow-workmen. Strahan, industrious and thrifty, prospered, and purchased, in 1770, a share of the patent for King's printer; and he obtained considerable property in the copyrights of the works of the most celebrated authors of the time. He was a great friend to Johnson, and kept up his intimacy with Franklin. He died rich, bequeathing munificent legacies. He was succeeded in his business by his third son, Andrew Strahan, who inherited his father's excellent qualities, and died in 1831, aged eighty-three, leaving property to the amount of more than a million of money. Among his many generous acts, he presented to James Smith, one of the authors of the *Rejected Addresses*, the munificent gift of 1000*l*.

The vicissitudes of the Buckinghams, political as well as fiscal, can be traced through the long lapse of eight centuries. In our own times, two dukes have fallen from their high estate into neglect and poverty. Richard, first Duke of Buckingham and Chandos, lived at Stowe, with princely magnificence: his expenditure in rare books and works of art was enormous; and his entertainment of the Royal Family of France and their numerous retinues, upon one of his estates, not only drained his exchequer, but burdened him with debt. Neither Louis XVIII. nor Charles X., however, took the slightest notice of the obligation they had incurred,—apparently regarding such imprudent generosity as the natural acknowledgment of their exceeding merit. The Duke was, in 1827, compelled to shut up his house and go abroad, till his large estates could be nursed, so as to meet the heaviest and most pressing demands.* While abroad, he had a dream, which he has recorded in his *Private Diary*, published in 1862. He dreamed that he was at Stowe, his dear and regretted home: all was deserted—not a soul appeared to receive him. His good dog met him, licked his hand, and accompanied him through all the apartments, which were desolate and solitary,—every room as he had left it. He met his wife, who told him all his family were gone, and she alone was left. He awoke with the distress of the moment, and slept no more that night.

Mr. Rumsey Forster, in his piquant historical notice of Stowe, prefixed to the *Priced and Annotated Catalogue*, relates that, Louis Philippe being present when the Royal Family of France were enjoying the hospitality of the Marquis of Buckingham at Stowe, as they were seated together in the library, the conversation turned on events then enacting on the other side of the Channel; upon which Louis Philippe, recollecting his own position with the Revolutionists, threw himself upon his knees, and begged pardon of his royal uncle for having ever worn the tricoloured cockade. The anecdote is curious, when the subsequent career of the ex-monarch is borne in mind.

The Duke died Jan. 17, 1839, and was succeeded by his

* When the Duke and Duchess, in taking farewell of Stowe, had reached the flower-garden, they both burst into a violent fit of tears. They went through the two gardens, and left them in silent sorrow: as he passed along, the Duke gave the Duchess a rose, which she treasured as the last gift.

only son, Richard Plantagenet, who, though crippled in fortune by the paternal tastes, celebrated the coming of age of his son with profuse hospitality at Stowe, in 1844; and in 1845, entertained Queen Victoria and the Prince Albert with great sumptuousness. The mansion at Stowe was partly refurnished for the occasion, when the cost of the new carpets was 5000*l.* In 1848, the dream of the first Duke was strangely realised by the dismantling of Stowe, and the compulsory dispersion of the whole of the costly contents; the sale occupying forty days, and realising 75,562*l.* 4*s.* 6*d.* The Duke subsequently resided in the neighbourhood; and he often indulged his sadness at his fallen fortunes by walking to Stowe; and there, in one of the superb saloons in which kings and princes had held courts and been feasted with regal magnificence,—seated in a chair before a small table—the only furniture in the room—would Richard Plantagenet pass many an hour of "bitter fancy." He died July 30, 1861, at the age of sixty-four. Sir Bernard Burke, Ulster, writes of the Duke's lineage: "Of all native-born British subjects, his Grace was, after the present reigning family, the senior representative of the Royal Houses of Tudor and Plantagenet."*

"Day and Martin's Blacking," one of the inventions of the present century, realised a large fortune, which was mostly appropriated to beneficent purposes. Day is related to have been originally a hair-dresser; and, as the story goes, one morning a soldier entered his shop, representing that he had a long march before him to reach his regiment; that his money was gone, and nothing but sickness, fatigue, and punishment awaited him unless he could get a lift on a coach. The worthy barber, who, with his small means, was a generous man, presented him with a guinea, when the grateful soldier exclaimed, "God bless you, sir! how can I ever repay you this? I have nothing in this world except" (pulling a dirty piece of paper from his pocket) "a receipt for blacking: it is the best ever was seen; many a half-guinea have I had for it from the officers, and many bottles have I sold." Mr. Day, who was a shrewd man, inquired into the truth of the story, tried the blacking, and finding it good,

* See Ulster's *Vicissitudes of Families*, in three volumes, for many impressive narratives of the same class as the above.

commenced the manufacture and sale of it, and realised the immense fortune of which he died possessed in 1836; bequeathing 100,000*l.* for the benefit of persons who, like himself, suffered the deprivation of sight. The rebuilding of the Blacking Factory, in High Holborn, cost 12,000*l.*

Pianoforte-making has led to great money-making results. About the year 1776, Becker, a German, undertook to apply the pianoforte mechanism to the harpsichord, assisted by John Broadwood and Robert Stodart, then workmen in the employ of Burckhardt Tschudi, of Great Pulteney-street, London. After many experiments, the grand-pianoforte mechanism was contrived by these three. Messrs. Broadwood, from 1824 to 1850, made on an average 2236 pianofortes per annum; and employed in their manufactory 573 workmen, besides persons working for them at home. In 1862 died the head of the firm, Mr. Thomas Broadwood, sen., at the age of seventy-five, leaving 350,000*l.* personal property, besides realty.

James Morison, who styled himself "the Hygeist," and was noted for his "Vegetable Medicines," was a Scotchman, and a gentleman by birth and education. His family was of the landed gentry of Aberdeenshire, his brother being "Morison of Bognie," an estate worth about 4000*l.* a year. In 1816 James Morison, having sold his commission, for he was an officer in the army, lived in No. 17 Silver-street, Aberdeen, a house belonging to Mr. Reid, of Souter and Reid, druggists. He obtained the use of their pill-machine, with which he made in their back-shop as many pills as filled two large casks. The ingredients of these pills, however he may have modified them afterwards, were chiefly oatmeal and bitter aloes. With these two great "meal bowies" filled with pills, he started for London; with the fag-end of his fortune advertised them far and wide, and ultimately amassed 500,000*l.*

Such is the statement of a Correspondent of the *Athenæum.* Morison's own story was, that his own sufferings from ill-health, and the cure he at length effected upon himself by "vegetable pills," made him a disseminator of the latter article. He had found the pills to be "the only rational purifiers of the blood;" of these he took two or three at bedtime, and a glass of lemonade in the morning, and thus regained sound sleep and high spirits, and feared neither heat nor cold, dryness nor humidity. The duty on the pills produced a revenue of 60,000*l.* to Government during the first ten years. Morison died at Paris, in 1840, aged seventy.

The Denisons, father and son, accumulated two of the largest fortunes of our time. About 120 years ago, Joseph Denison, who was the son of a woollen-cloth merchant at Leeds, anxious to seek his fortune in London, travelled thither in a wagon, being attended on his departure by his friends, who took a solemn leave of him, as the distance was then thought so great that they might never see him again. He at first accepted a subordinate situation; but being industrious, parsimonious, and fortunate, he speedily advanced himself in the confidence and esteem of his employers, bankers in St. Mary Axe, and married successively two wives with property. He continued to prosper; and by joining the Heywoods, eminent bankers of Liverpool, his wealth rapidly increased. In 1787 he purchased the estate of Denbies, near Dorking in Surrey. By his second wife he had one son, William Joseph Denison; and two daughters—Elizabeth, married, in 1794, to Henry, first Marquis Conyngham; and Maria, married, in 1793, to Sir Robert Lawley, Bart., created, in 1831, Baron Wenlock.

Mr. Denison died in 1806; his son, succeeding to the banking business, continued to accumulate; and, at his death in his seventy-ninth year, in August 1849, left two millions and a half of money. He had sat in Parliament for Surrey from 1818. He was a man of cultivated tastes, possessed a knowledge of art and elegant literature; he feared to be thought ostentatious, and could with difficulty be prevailed on to have a lodge erected at the entrance to a new road which he had just formed on his estate, near Dorking. The Marchioness Conyngham was left a widow in 1832; she died in 1861, having attained the venerable age of ninety-two, and lived to see both her sons peers of the realm,—the one in succession to his father; the second, Albert Denison, as heir to her own brother's great fortune and estates, with the title of Baron Londesborough.

The career of George Hudson, ridiculously styled "the Railway King," was one of the *ignes fatui* of the railway mania. He was born in a lowly house in College-street, York, in 1800; here he served his apprenticeship to a linen-draper, and subsequently carried on the business as principal, amassing considerable wealth. His fortune was next increased by a bequest from a distant relative, which sum he invested in North-Midland Railway shares; and, under his chairmanship, they gradually rose from 70*l.* discount to 120*l.* premium. This led to the creation of new shares in branch and extension lines, often worthless, which were issued at a premium also: Hudson soon found himself chairman of 600 miles of railway, extending from Rugby to Newcastle; and he is stated in a single day to have cleared 100,000*l.* He was also elected M.P. for Sunderland; and served twice Lord Mayor of York. The sum of 16,000*l.* was subscribed and presented to him as a public testimonial; with which he purchased a mansion at Albert-gate, Hyde-park; here he lived sumptuously, and went his round of visits among the peerage. But the speculation of 1845 was followed by a sudden reaction: shares fell, the holders sold to avoid payment of calls, and many were ruined; then followed the unkingship of Hudson, who was hurled down like the molten calf; and he lost a vast fortune in the general wreck of the railway bubbles.

The most beneficial fortunes made in business are those by which, at the same time, permanent advantages are secured to the public. Henry Colburn, the well-known publisher, "was a man of much ability and extraordinary enterprise. His public career connected him intimately with the literature of the present century, and few are the distinguished writers, during the last forty years, whose names were not associated with that of Mr. Colburn. In one of Mr. Disraeli's novels a handsome tribute is paid to his acuteness of judgment and generosity of dealing. The publication of the Diaries of Pepys and Evelyn will rank among many sterling contributions to literature due in the first instance to his enterprise. He originated those weekly literary reviews which have since been so successful; he established more than one newspaper, and conducted for a great many years the Magazine which still bears his name; and was the original publisher of Sir Bernard Burke's *Peerage.* In private life he was known as a friendly, hospitable, kind man, and acts of the greatest liberality marked his course through life."* He died at an advanced age.

Mr. James Morrison, the wealthy warehouseman of Cripplegate, started in life as foreman to Mr. Todd, whose daughter he married; and succeeding to his large property, distinguished himself as a sound political economist, and for some years sat in Parliament. He obtained, by purchase, the fine estates of Basilden, in Berkshire, and Fonthill, in Wiltshire: at Basilden, in 1846, the Lord Mayor and Corporation, upon the View of the Thames, were entertained by Mr. Morrison, who then referred with much gratification to his having been brought up in the City of London, "connected with it in a mercantile point of view, and having, by his own industry, obtained every thing he could desire." He was a man of high commercial character; to which Mr. Edwin Chadwick, at the Meeting of the British Association at Cambridge, in 1862, bore this interesting testimony: "I had the pleasure," said Mr. Chadwick, "of the acquaintance of perhaps the most wealthy and successful merchant of the last half-century,—a distinguished member of our political economy club, the late Mr. James Morrison,—who assured me, that the leading principles to which he owed his success in life, and which he vindicated as sound elements of economical science, were—always to consult the interests of the consumer, and not, as is the common maxim, to buy cheap and sell dear, but to sell cheap as well as to buy cheap; it being to his interest to widen the area of consumption, and to sell quickly and to the many. The next maxim is involved in the first principle—always to tell the truth, to have no shams: a rule which he confessed he found it most difficult to get his common sellers to adhere to in its integrity, yet most important for success, it being to his interest as a merchant that any ship-captain might come into his warehouse and fill his ship with goods of which he had no technical knowledge, but of which he well knew that only a small profit was charged upon a close ready-money purchasing price, and that go where he would he would find nothing cheaper; it being, moreover, to the merchant's interest that his bill of prices should be every where received from experience as a truth, and trustworthy evidence so far

* The *Examiner*.

of a fair market-value. I might cite extensive testimony of the like character to show that the very labour and risks of continued deceits, however common, are detrimental to the successful operation of economic principles, and that sound economy is every where concurrent with high public morality."

With this brilliant exception before us, we must, however, admit the general truth of this experience: "The nobility of trade usually ends with the second generation. A thrifty and persevering man falls into a line of business by which he accumulates a large fortune, preserving through life the habits, manners, and connexions of his trade; but his children, brought up with expectations of enjoying his property, understand only the art of spending. Hence, when deprived of fortune, without industry or resources, they die in beggary, leaving a third generation to the same chances of life as those with which their grandfather began his career fourscore years before."*

CIVIC WORTHIES.

The state and dignity of the office of Chief Magistrate of the City of London have, during nearly centuries of its existence, pointed many a moral,—from the nursery-tale of Whittington to the accessories of Hogarth's pictures and a homelier illustration of our own days:

> Our Lord Mayor and his golden coach, and his gold-covered footmen and coachman, and his golden chain, and his chaplain, and great sword of state, please the people, and particularly the women and girls; and when they are pleased, the men and boys are pleased: and many a young fellow has been more industrious and attentive from his hope of one day riding in that golden coach.—*Cobbett.*

This is, however, but the bright side of the picture. Civic office is often a costly honour; not only by large expenditure, but by neglect of private business to attend to the public duties of the station.

All that we propose to do here is to record a few noteworthy Mayoralties of the *present century*, to show that the office continues to be filled by men of high character and moral worth.

Among the worthy citizens should be mentioned Sir

* *Golden Rules of Social Philosophy*, by Sir Richard Phillips.

James Shaw, born in 1764, in the humblest circumstances, and educated at the grammar-school of Kilmarnock. He settled in London as a merchant, by his own perseverance and integrity amassed a fortune, served as Lord Mayor 1805-6, sat in three parliaments for the City, and was subsequently Chamberlain. He was unostentatiously charitable, encouraged industrious poor men, and succoured the indigent, because he remembered his own unpromising infancy; and he was one of the first to assist the helpless children of Robert Burns. In commemoration of these estimable qualities, a marble statue of Sir James Shaw was erected by public subscription at Kilmarnock in 1848.

Sir Matthew Wood, Bart., the most popular Lord Mayor in the present century, began life as a druggist's traveller, and then settled in London in the ward of Cripplegate, for which he rose to be alderman: he served as Lord Mayor two successive years, and represented the City in nine parliaments; his baronetcy was the first title conferred by Queen Victoria shortly after her accession. He gained much popularity as the adviser of the ill-fated Queen Caroline; for which, and his general political conduct, a princely legacy was bequeathed to him by the wealthy banker of Gloucester of the same name. He died in his 75th year: his eldest son, the present baronet, is in holy orders; and his second son, Sir William Page Wood, is a sound equity lawyer and a Vice-Chancellor.

Alderman Birch, Lord Mayor in 1815, received a liberal education, and at an early age wrote some poems of considerable merit: he succeeded his father in business, as a cook and confectioner, in Cornhill. He produced several dramatic pieces, of which the *Adopted Child* is a stock favourite: he was a sound scholar, and wrote the inscription for the statue of George III. in the Council-chamber at the Guildhall, and took an active part in founding the London Institution.*

* Birch excelled in his art; and his *cuisine* was unrivalled in the City. Kitchiner immortalised his soups in print, and the Mansion-House banquets and Court dinners of the Companies attested the alderman's practical skill in his business. The shop in Cornhill was established in the reign of King George I. by Horton, who was succeeded by the father of Alderman Birch, whose successors, in 1836, were the present proprietors, Ring and Brymer. The premises present a curious specimen of the decorated shop-front of the early part of the last century.

Robert Waithman, Lord Mayor in 1823-24, was born of parents in humble life, in 1764, and, when a boy, was adopted by his uncle, a linendraper at Bath, and sent to a school where the boys were taught public and extemporaneous speaking. He was taken into his uncle's business, and subsequently came to London, and opened a shop at the south end of Fleet-market. In 1794 he began to take an active part in City politics, and was next elected into the Common Council, where his speeches, resolutions, petitions, and addresses, would fill a large volume. He sat in five parliaments for the City, made a popular Sheriff and Lord Mayor; and after his death, in 1833, his friends and fellow-citizens erected to his memory a granite obelisk upon the site whereon he commenced business. A memorial tablet was also placed in St. Bride's church, stating that "it was his happiness to see that great cause triumphant, of which he had been the intrepid advocate from youth to age." Curiously enough, this tablet is placed in the vestibule of the church, directly opposite a similar memorial to Mr. Blades, of Ludgate-hill, who was a fine old Tory, and a stanch opponent to Waithman throughout his stormy political life: as in life, so in death the great leveller has laid them here.

Waithman made his first political speech at Founders' Hall, "the caldron of sedition," when he and his fellow-orators were routed by constables sent by the Lord Mayor, Sanderson, to disperse the meeting. When Sheriff, in 1821, Waithman, in endeavouring to quell a tumult at Knightsbridge, had a carbine presented at him by a lifeguardsman; and, at the funeral of Queen Caroline, a bullet passed through the Sheriff's carriage, in the procession through Hyde-park. Latterly, the alderman grew too moderate for his Farringdon-ward friends, and he was defeated of being elected Chamberlain; he then withdrew to a farm near Reigate, and in this bucolic retirement passed away. He was an intrepid, upright man, but had been sparsely educated; and many of the Resolutions on the War with France, by which he gained political notoriety, were written by his friend and neighbour, Sir Richard Phillips.

In early life Waithman showed considerable genius for acting; and we once heard him relate that his success in the character of Macbeth led his friends to press upon him the stage as a profession; but he chose another sphere. He was uncle to John Reeve, the clever comic actor.

Alderman Kelly, Lord Mayor at the accession of her Majesty in 1837, was born at Chevening, in Kent, and lived when a youth, with Alexander Hogg, the publisher, in Paternoster-row, for 10*l.* a year wages. He slept under the shop counter for the security of the premises; but was reported to his master to be "too slow" for the situation: Mr. Hogg, however, thought him "a biddable boy," and he remained: this incident shows *upon what apparently trifling circumstances a man's future prospects in life depend.* Kelly succeeded Mr. Hogg in the business, became alderman of the ward, and lived upon the spot sixty years: he died in his eighty-fourth year.* He was a man of active benevolence, and reminded one of the pious Lord Mayor, Sir Thomas Abney.

Sir Chapman Marshall, Lord Mayor 1839-40, was also of humble origin, as he narrated in 1831, when Sheriff, in replying to the toast of his health: "My Lord Mayor and gentlemen, you now see before you a humble individual who has been educated in a parochial school. I came to London in 1803, without a shilling—without a friend. I have not had the advantage of a classical education; therefore you will excuse my defects of language. But this I will say, my Lord Mayor and gentlemen, that you witness in me what may be done by the earnest application of honest industry; and I trust my example may induce others to aspire, by the same means, to the distinguished situation which I now have the honour to fill." Here is a similar instance.

Sir John Pirie, Lord Mayor 1841-2, received his baronetcy on the christening of the Prince of Wales: at his inauguration dinner Sir John said: "I little thought, forty years ago, when I came to the City of London, a poor lad from the banks of the Tweed, that I should ever arrive at so great a distinction."

Alderman Wire, Lord Mayor 1858-9, was born 1801, and was one of the large family of a tradesman at Colchester; yet he had the advantage of a liberal education. He came to London and articled himself to a City solicitor, and by his intelligence and industry was advanced to be partner in the business, and ultimately became the head of the firm. He

* See *Life of Alderman Kelly,* by the Rev. R. C. Fell. 1856.

was elected Alderman of his Ward (Walbrook), served Sheriff in 1853, and then Lord Mayor. Early in his year of office he was afflicted with paralysis, of which he recovered; but died on Lord-Mayor's-day 1860! He was an active advocate of sanitary and educational movements, a liberal politician, and a man of cultivated taste, and made an able chief magistrate.

Alderman Mechi deserves a niche among these civic worthies, by the superior enterprise of his career. He is the son of a citizen of Bologna, was brought to England by his father, and, obtaining a clerkship in a house in the Newfoundland trade, he remained there eleven years. Whilst in this service, he turned the hour allowed for dinner to profitable account by selling, among his friends and acquaintance in the City, a small and inexpensive article, of which he had bought the patent. Mainly by these exertions, when in his twenty-fifth year, he commenced business as a cutler, with the success we have already intimated. He then studied how to remedy the defects of English farming by scientific processes; rose to be Sheriff and an Alderman; took an active part in the affairs of the Society of Arts, and was specially sent by her Majesty's Government to the Industrial Exhibition at Paris in 1854.

Addison, we know, says, "the City has always been the province for satire; and the wits of King Charles's time jested upon nothing else during his whole reign." Nevertheless, "the Merry Monarch" dined with the citizens no fewer than nine times in their Guildhall. Here also Whittington had feasted Henry V. and his Queen, when he threw the King's bonds for 60,000*l*. into a fire of spice-wood. But a still more memorable feast was that in 1497, when at the table of the Lord Mayor, William Purchase, Erasmus first met Sir Thomas More; whence sprung one of the most interesting friendships in literary history.

It has been well said that a dinner lubricates business; and it does more—it fosters charity and good works. The annual banquet on Lord-Mayor's-day, in the Guildhall, is mostly to be viewed as a festival of civic state: "the loving-cup and the barons of beef carrying the mind back to medieval times and manners."* The banquets at the Mansion House—one of the most palatial edifices in the kingdom—

* Cunningham.

are of a like stately description; and for the more direct benefits of civic festivity we must look to the Ward dinners, and the meetings of public officers at table, when they forget the cares and heartburnings incident to every grade of office, and enjoy with the feast the higher luxury of doing good.

WORKING AUTHORS AND ARTISTS.

Godwin, the novelist and political writer, used to say that an author should have two heads,—one for his books, the other for worldly matters. And Holcroft, Godwin's contemporary, made a similar remark on actors,—that they were so often filling other characters as to forget their own. These observations are, happily, of rare application in the cases of the present day.

We, however, remember the phrase of *Grub-street* in occasional use, and we find "the poor devil of an author" in one of Washington Irving's early works. But this species is now extinct; and authors build villas, give large parties, and keep carriages, like other successful professional men. Nor must it be forgotten that they do not receive their money for corrupt services, as did the hacks of former days; and a Grub-street Author would be now almost as great a rarity as a living gorilla.

We remember a specimen of "author and rags—author and dirt—author and gin,"—of forty years since. He lived in a garret,* in an old house at the top of Red Lion-court, Fleet-street: in one corner of the room, upon the floor, lay the bed; near the fire-place was an old chair; a box placed endwise served for a table; and these, with an almost spoutless coffee-pot, a maimed cup and saucer, a bottle for a candlestick, and an old chest, nearly completed the contents of the miserable apartment. The inmate was an old man turned of seventy, with shrunk shanks and loosely-fitting coat and breeches, and the conventional author's-nightcap; his scratch-wig being placed upon one of the uprights of his chair, which served as a block. Every portion of the room bore evidence of the *dirt;* and the atmosphere was redolent of *gin.*

* Such a room as Mr. Egg has painted in his masterly picture of "The Death of Chatterton;" and, curiously enough, the house above referred to was nearly upon the same spot.

He wrote a large black, sermon-like hand, upon paper of all sorts and sizes: his matter was as antiquated as his manner; his very talk was scholastic pedantry, and the room was strewed with scraps and shreds of his learning: but he lived within the classic shade of Valpy's printing-office. With all his labour and learning, whatever he wrote was not half so serviceable or so interesting as a short-hand report of an occurrence of yesterday.

Another humble practitioner of authorship had been driven to it by failure in business; and an undecided Chancery-suit had made him a pitiable, puling fellow; far less cheerful than the evergreen "Tom Hill," who, failing as a drysalter at unlettered Queenhithe, betook himself to the editorship of the *Monthly Mirror*, but had to part with a collection of book-rarities (chiefly English poetry), which he began to make in early life as some relief to drysalting, which was any thing but Attic work!

The life of this "merry bachelor" exemplified one venerable proverb, and disproved another: born in 1760, and dying in 1840, he was "as old as the Hills," having led a long life and a merry one. He was a remarkably early riser: but that which contributed more to his longevity was his gaiety of heart, and his being merry and wise: he had his cares and crosses, but when nearly ruined by an adverse speculation in indigo, he retired with the remains of his property to chambers in the Adelphi. His books were valued at 6000*l*. He had been a Mecænas in his time, and had patronised two friendless poets, Bloomfield and Kirke White. He was the Hull of his friend Theodore Hook's *Gilbert Gurney*, and suggested some of the eccentricities of Paul Pry.

Authorship and Trade are thought to be "wide as the poles asunder," though sometimes attempered by circumstances. David Booth, who wrote the *Analytical Dictionary* and a critical work on English Composition, was originally a brewer, then a man of letters; and late in life he realised much money by imparting to brewers the secret of preventing Acidification in Brewing.

Among the strange successes of authorship may be mentioned the popularity of works published anonymously, which their authors have not cared to claim. The accomplished Dr. William Maginn wrote the tragic story of the Polstead murder, in 1827, in the form of a novel, entitled the *Red Barn*, the sale of which extended to many thousand copies; yet no one suspected it to be the work of an elegant scholar, critic, and poet.

Literary Fame, Lord Byron affected to despise, in the following entry in his entertaining *Ravenna Journal*, January 4th, 1821:

> I was out of spirits—read the papers—thought what *fame* was, on reading in a case of murder that Mr. Wych, grocer, at Tunbridge, sold some bacon, flour, cheese, and, it is believed, some plums, to some gipsy woman accused. He had on his counter (I quote faithfully) a book, the *Life of Pamela*, which he was *tearing* for *waste* paper, &c. &c. In the cheese was found, &c., and a *leaf* of *Pamela wrapped round the bacon*. What would Richardson, the vainest and luckiest of *living* authors (*i. e.* while alive)—he who, with Aaron Hill, used to prophesy and chuckle over the presumed fall of Fielding (the prose Homer of human nature), and of Pope (the most beautiful of poets)—what would he have said could he have traced his pages from their place on the French prince's toilets (see Boswell's *Johnson*) to the grocer's counter and the gipsy murderess's bacon? What would he have said—what can any body say—save what Solomon said long before us. After all, it is but passing from one counter to another—from the bookseller's to the other tradesman's, grocer or pastry-cook. For my part, I have met with most poetry upon trunks; so that I am apt to consider the trunk-maker as the sexton of authorship.

The Letters of Southey afford some of the most truthful experiences of an author to be found in any record of human life and character. At the age of thirty, when struggling with the world, he wrote thus reverentially:

> No man was ever more contented with his lot than I am; for few have ever had more enjoyments, and none had ever better or worthier hopes. Life, therefore, is sufficiently dear to me, and long life desirable, that I may accomplish all which I design. But yet, I could be well content that the next century were over, and my part fairly at an end, having been gone well through. Just as at school one wished the school-days over, though we were happy enough there, because we expected more happiness and more liberty when we were to be our own masters, might lie as much later in the morning as we pleased, have no bounds, and do no exercise,—just so do I wish that my exercises were over, that that ugly chrysalis state were passed through to which we must all come, and that I had fairly burst my shell, and got into the new world, with wings upon my shoulders, or some inherent power like the wishing-cap, which should annihilate all the inconveniences of space.

How lifelike also is the following passage upon Southey's meeting his friend and schoolfellow, Combe! "It is about six years since I saw him. Both he and I have grown into men with as little change as possible in either; and yet, after a few minutes, there was a dead weight upon me which was not to be shaken off. We met with the heartiness of old and thorough familiarity,—something like a family feeling,—but it was necessary to go back to school; for the moment we ceased to be schoolboys there was nothing in common between us. We had no common acquaintance or pursuit; and I feel that of all things in the world there is nothing more mortifying than to meet an old friend from whom you have had no weaning, and to find your friendship cut through at the root."

The life of John Britton, the topographer and antiquary, presents a remarkable instance of a man born to trouble, yet so successfully struggling with difficulties of all kinds, as to attain a respectable position in life, and to be honoured in his declining years with a public testimonial of esteem. He was born at Kington, Wilts, in 1771: his father, through failure in trade, became insane; the boy learnt his letters from a hornbook, but received little further schooling. He came to London, and, until manhood, worked hard in wine-cellars; but his health breaking down in this employment, he engaged himself at fifteen shillings a week as clerk to an attorney. He had grown fond of reading, but could only get snatches at book-stalls from books, having no money to buy them. However, he at length succeeded in getting a few, read early and late, and made some attempts at authorship, which led him to an enterprise that may be said to have indicated his future fortune. He projected publishing a description of his native county, Wiltshire, and with this view waited upon the Marquis of Lansdowne, at Bowood, to solicit his patronage.* He had neither card nor prospectus; but he told his early struggles and his love of reading so artlessly, that the kind-hearted nobleman directed his librarian to provide young Britton with books and maps; to allot him a bedroom; and depute a person to show him over the house and pleasure-grounds. He re-

* This was William, first Marquis of Lansdowne, who, as Earl of Shelburne, was Prime Minister in 1782; the date of Mr. Britton's visit was 1798. By the Marquis's kindness, he tells us that he left Bowood for Chippenham loaded with books, and a copy of a large Survey of Wiltshire, in eighteen folio sheets. The Marquis was a liberal patron of Art, and commenced at Bowood and Shelburne House the formation of a gallery of modern art; and his fine taste was amply inherited by his son Henry, the third Marquis, who died at Bowood in January 1863.

mained at Bowood four days, much of which time he passed in the well-stored library. All this kindness* Mr. Britton gratefully acknowledges in his Autobiography, adding that, had he been coldly repulsed by Lord Lansdowne, "it is probable that the *Beauties of Wiltshire* would never have appeared before the public, nor its author become known in literature." He wrote, edited, and published nearly one hundred works, and in this way laboured for some sixty years. This success we attribute to his great energy of character, nurtured by the kindness with which he was received at Bowood; and aided in after-life by qualities which we rarely see associated in the same individual. Mr. Britton was not only industrious and persevering, but cheerful under defeat; his evenness of temper was very remarkable; yet he was not cold in his attachments. He tells us that from his boyhood he was ambitious to be in the company of his elders and superiors in knowledge: we can testify that he was well-behaved, though not obsequious; well-ordered and accurate in business and money-matters; always living within his means, from youth, when he read books in bed to save the expense of fire,—to his green old age of comfort in his quiet and elegant home in Burton-street: "years had not blunted his sympathies, but to the last his heart overflowed with genial kindness and benevolence;" and he passed away peacefully and resignedly in his eighty-sixth year, on New-Year's-day, 1857. It will thus be seen that John Britton possessed qualities which, if less striking than his industry, were equally essential to his success in life, although they were but fully known to his more immediate circle of friends and acquaintance.

The career of Mr. Britton's friend and neighbour, Francis Baily, the astronomer, presents a memorable instance of a well-spent life, although commenced with a mistake. He was apprenticed to a London tradesman; but disliking the business, at the expiration of the term, his taste

* We remember a similarly gratifying incident in early life. We had scarcely reached twenty-one, when we had occasion to wait upon Mr. Chamberlain Clark, to request of him some particulars of the house of Cowley the poet, at Chertsey, which was then in Mr. Clark's tenancy. The bland old Chamberlain inquired if we had ever written a book; to which the reply was, that we had a volume of topography in the press. "Then please to put down my name for a copy," kindly rejoined the Chamberlain, although the work was merely of local interest. What kindness in one who was the chastener of refractory apprentices and the terror of evil-doers!

for science having already been developed, at the age of one-and-twenty he made a very remarkable tour in the unsettled parts of North America. Returning to England, he became a member of the Stock Exchange, wrote some important papers upon subjects connected with commercial affairs, and applied himself to astronomy in his leisure-hours. In 1820 he took a conspicuous part in the foundation of the Astronomical Society. After realising a competent fortune, he retired from business, and devoted himself to his favourite pursuits. He died in 1844, in his seventieth year, after performing a vast amount of valuable work, of which his labours in the remodelling of the *Nautical Almanac;* in the fixation of the standard of length, involving more than 1200 hours' watching the oscillations of the pendulum; in the determination of the density of the earth; and in the revision of catalogues of the stars,—were only a part. He passed away with these memorable words almost upon his lips: "My life is nearly closed. I leave life with the same tranquillity and equanimity which I have generally felt and acted on in my personal intercourse with friends and strangers. I have been blessed with uninterrupted health. In short, I have had more than my share of terrestrial happiness, and leave it, as fulfilling an inscrutable law of animal nature, with thankfulness and resignation." "Among Mr. Baily's friends," says Prof. de Morgan, "there is surely not one who will venture to say positively that he ever knew *a better or a happier man.*"

The rise of Chantrey, the sculptor, from peasant-life was nobly earned. He was born in the village of Norton, Derbyshire, in 1781, of parents in humble circumstances. When a boy carrying milk to the next town, he would stop to form grotesque figures of the yellow clay; and he moulded his mother's butter on churning-days into various forms. From his fondness for drawing and modelling he was apprenticed to a carver and gilder at Sheffield. Thence he came to London, and began to work at carving in stone, not having received a single lesson from any sculptor; and he laboured for eight years without earning 5*l.* in his profession. At length, a single bust brought him 12,000*l.*-worth of commissions, and he rose to be the first sculptor of his day. He died in 1841, and was buried in a tomb which he had built for himself in the churchyard of his native village, where a granite obelisk has been raised to his memory. He was ever mindful of his lowly origin; for when he had become famous, and had received knighthood, at a party given by his patron, Mr. Thomas Hope, Sir Francis Chantrey was observed to notice a piece of carved furniture; on being asked the reason, he replied, "This was my first work."

It is scarcely possible to name Chantrey without being reminded of his friend, "honest Allan Cunningham," who, born in the county of Dumfries, in 1784, received but scanty education, and at the age of eleven was apprenticed to a mason. In the intervals of his laborious occupation, "he sought knowledge wherever he could obtain it," and drew his earliest poetic inspiration from the dear country of Burns—the wilds of Nithsdale, and the lone banks of the Solway. Here he earned his daily bread as a common stonemason until his twenty-sixth year, when he came to London, wavering between labour and literature. He chose the latter, in reporting for the newspapers; but, soon tired of its perplexities, he resumed his first calling, and by a fortunate opportunity, to which his own excellent character recommended him, he became foreman of the works of Chantrey, in which honourable employment he remained until the sculptor's death, in 1841. In his intervals of business, by untiring industry, Allan Cunningham produced a succession of works noteworthy in the poetry and general literature of his day. His first poetry was printed in 1807: he also wrote stirring romances; and in collecting Tradition Tales of the Scottish Peasantry, by the light of an evening fire, he sweetened many an hour of remission from daily labour. Later in life he became a critic of the Fine Arts, and wrote with amiable feeling, honesty, and candour, and mature and liberal taste: it was well observed of him in his lifetime: "He needs no testimony either to his intellectual accomplishments or his moral worth; nor, thanks to his own virtuous diligence, does he need any patronage." His genius and artistic judgment have been inherited by his third son, Peter Cunningham, the well-known critic, topographer, and antiquary.*

* Mr. P. Cunningham, in the *Builder*, Feb. 14, 1863, writes as follows: "Chantrey died so suddenly that an inquest was held upon his body. I was

The greatest author of the present century, whether we regard the beneficial influence of his writings, or its extent, is Sir Walter Scott. We have already spoken of his diligence and economy of time; his characteristics as an author have been ably sketched as follows:

With far less classical learning, fewer images derived from travelling, inferior information on many historical subjects, and a mind of a less impassioned and energetic cast than other writers of his time, Sir Walter is far more deeply read in that book which is ever the same—the human heart. This is his unequalled excellence: there he stands, without a rival since the days of Shakspeare. It is to this cause that his astonishing success has been owing. We feel in his characters that it is not romance, but real life, which is represented. Every word that is said, especially in the Scotch novels, is nature itself. Homer, Cervantes, Shakspeare, and Scott, alone have penetrated to the deep substratum of character, which, however disguised by the varieties of climate and government, is at bottom every where the same; and thence they have found a responsive echo in every human heart. Every man who reads these admirable works, from the North Cape to Cape Horn, feels that what the characters they contain are made to say, is just what would have occurred to themselves, or what they have heard said by others as long as they lived. Nor is it only in the delineation of character, and the knowledge of human nature, that the Scottish novelist, like his great predecessors, is but for them without a rival. Powerful in the pathetic, admirable in dialogue, unmatched in description, his writings captivate the mind as much by the varied excellences which they exhibit, as by the powerful interest which they maintain. He has carried romance out of the region of imagination and sensibility into the walks of actual life.*

Isaac Disraeli, who died in 1848, at the age of eighty-two, was "a complete literary character, a man who really passed his life in his library. Even marriage produced no change in these habits: he rose to enter the chamber where he lived alone with his books, and at night his lamp was ever lit within the same walls." His father destined him for business; but this he opposed so strongly as to compose a long poem against commerce, which he attempted to get published. In spite of all his father could say or do, young Disraeli determined to become a literary man. His first

present. It was a solemn sight, not to be effaced whilst unimpaired remembrance reigns. In an exquisite little gallery built for him by Sir John Soane, lay (seen by many lighted tapers) the breathless body and torpid hand that had given life to helpless clay and shapeless stone. Around the body in its winding-sheet were ranged some of the finest casts from the antique that money and taste could procure. Calm and solemn was the scene. My father kissed the cold forehead of his friend with these words: "My dear master." I looked into his eyes as we left together; they were full of tears."—*New Materials for the Life of Chantrey.*

* Sir Archibald Alison.

efforts were in poetry and romance; but he soon found out that his true destiny was literary history; and in 1790 he published anonymously *Curiosities of Literature*, the success of which led him to devote the remainder of his long life to literary and historical researches, which he prosecuted partly in the British Museum, where he was a constant visitor when the *readers* were not more than half a dozen daily: he also worked in his own library, which was very extensive. His *Curiosities* reached eleven editions; and in acknowledgment of his *Life and Reign of Charles I.* he was made D.C., &c. by the University of Oxford. He is thus personally described by his gifted son:

> He was fair, with a Bourbon nose, and brown eyes of extraordinary beauty and lustre. He wore a small black-velvet cap, but his white hair latterly touched his shoulders in curls almost as flowing as in his boyhood. His extremities were delicate and well formed, and his leg, at his last hour, as shapely as in his youth, which showed the vigour of his frame. Latterly he had become corpulent. He did not excel in conversation, though in his domestic circle he was garrulous. Every thing interested him; and blind, and eighty-two, he was still as susceptible as a child. One of his last acts was to compose some verses of gay gratitude to his daughter-in-law, who was his London correspondent, and to whose lively pen his last years were indebted for constant amusement. He had by nature a singular volatility, which never deserted him. His feelings, though always amiable, were not painfully deep, and amid joy or sorrow the philosophic vein was ever evident. He more resembled Goldsmith than any man that I can compare him to: in his conversation his apparent confusion of ideas ending with some felicitous phrase of genius, his *naïveté*, his simplicity not untouched with a dash of sarcasm affecting innocence—one was often reminded of the gifted and interesting friend of Burke and Johnson. There was, however, one trait in which my father did not resemble Goldsmith: he had no vanity. Indeed, one of his few infirmities was rather a deficiency of self-esteem.

Mr. Disraeli had the pride and happiness to see the writer of the above, Benjamin Disraeli, not only achieve high distinction in literature, but become a minister of the Crown. We remember him in his twenty-fifth year. "Who is that gentleman with a profusion of hair, whom I so often see here?" was our inquiry of a publisher in Oxford-street. "That is young Disraeli," was the publisher's reply; "and he would be glad to execute any literary work for a guinea or two." He had already produced a piece of piquant satire, an *Account of the Great World*,* with a Vocabulary; and shortly after there was announced for publication a periodi-

* Published by Ridgway, Piccadilly, 1829.

cal to be called *The Star-Chamber*, to have been edited by Mr. Disraeli. He published his first novel, *Vivian Grey*, in 1825; *Coningsby*, a work of fiction and political history, he wrote chiefly at Deepdene, in Surrey, the seat of his friend, Mr. H. T. Hope. Mr. Disraeli entered Parliament in 1837: he succeeded Lord George Bentinck as the Conservative leader; was Chancellor of the Exchequer under Lord Derby's administrations of 1852 and 1858-9; thus exemplifying that the highest political honours are attainable in this country by intellectual qualification for public life.

Lord Macaulay, the brilliant essayist, historian, and orator, exemplifies in his successful career how genius may be most profitably nurtured by systematic education. Of quick perception and great power of memory, when a boy he would tell long stories from the *Arabian Nights* and Scott's novels; but the familiar books of his home were the Bible, *Pilgrim's Progress*, and a few Cameronian divines; and he was fond of Scripture phraseology throughout his writings. He appears to have been a great favourite of Hannah More, who thought him a little prodigy of acquisition, and wrote of him, when on a visit to her in his boyhood:

> The quantity of reading that Tom has poured in, and the quantity of writing he has poured out, is astonishing. We have poetry for breakfast, dinner, and supper. He recited all *Palestine* (Bishop Heber's poem), while we breakfasted, to our pious friend, Mr. Whalley, at my desire, and did it incomparably. . . . . I sometimes fancy I observe a daily progress in the growth of his mental powers. His fine promise of mind, too, expands more and more; and, what is extraordinary, he has as much accuracy in his expression as spirit and vivacity in his imagination. I like, too, that he takes a lively interest in all passing events, and that *the child* is still preserved; I like to see him as boyish as he is studious, and that he is as much amused with making a pat of butter as a poem. Though loquacious, he is very docile; and I don't remember a single instance in which he has persisted in doing any thing when he saw we did not approve it. Several men of sense and learning have been struck with the union of gaiety and rationality in his conversation.

More remarkable was the prevoyance of Macaulay's power as a writer, which Hannah More almost literally predicted: he cherished a warm recollection of his obligations to her, and the influence she had in directing his reading. He received his peerage in honour of his valuable services to literature: he will long be remembered by his grasp of mind, descriptive picturesqueness, strong feeling and vivid fancy, life-like portraiture, and marvellous scenic skill. In his mastery of the art of writing he was unrivalled.

It may take the reader by surprise to be told that, astounding as the career of Lord Brougham has been, the rise of this distinguished man to the highest honour of the realm appears to have been predicted thirty years before its attainment. At the Social Science dinner at the Crystal Palace, Sydenham, on June 14th, 1862, at which Lord Brougham presided, Mr. J. W. Napier, Ex-Chancellor of Ireland, related that he remembered, some years previously, meeting an old and respected lady in the north of England, who was present at a party when the first writers in the *Edinburgh Review*, including Henry Brougham, dined together at Edinburgh, after the publication of the Second Number of the Review (in 1802). On that occasion, the lady's husband, Mr. Fletcher, remarked that the writer of a certain paper in the Review, of which he knew not the author, was fit to be any thing. Mr. Brougham hearing this, observed, "What! do you think he is fit to be Lord Chancellor?" The reply was, "Yes; and I tell you more: he will be Lord Chancellor;" and the old lady had the happiness to live thirty years after this, and to see her friend Lord Chancellor of England. Lord Brougham well remembered old Mrs. Fletcher, and corroborated the accuracy of Mr. Napier's anecdote. Mr. Napier then proposed, in an affectionate manner, the health of Lord Brougham, whose answer was, as he said, but a repetition of words he had spoken thirty years ago elsewhere. But on the present occasion they were perhaps even more appropriate, and in themselves singularly beautiful: "When I cease from my labours, the cause of freedom, peace, and progress will lose a friend, and no man living will lose an enemy." The noble lord was much affected, and it is needless to tell of the applause which followed the sentiment.

Henry Brougham was born in Edinburgh in 1779: his father was no extraordinary man, but his mother is described as a woman of talent and delightful character. The son was educated in Edinburgh, which, in 1857, he declared in public he looked upon as a very great benefit conferred on him by Providence. He was *dux* of the Rector's class at the Edinburgh University in 1791; and he was preëminent in mathematics and natural philosophy, in law, metaphysics, and political science. When not more than seventeen, he contributed to the Royal Society a paper on the Inflection and Reflection of Light; and next, a paper of Porisms in the Higher Geometry. He chose the Scottish Bar as his profession; and, with Horner, Jeffrey, and other Scottish Whigs, joined the renowned Speculative Society for the sake of extemporaneous debate. He for some time edited the *Edinburgh Review*, and was for five-and-twenty years the most industrious and versatile of the contributors. In 1808 he was called to the Bar at Lincoln's Inn, and began to practise as an English barrister. In 1810 he entered Parliament, and soon distinguished himself on all the great questions of the day. His application to law, literature, and science was alike intense. Sir Samuel Romilly said, he seemed to have time for every thing; and Sydney Smith once recommended him to confine himself to only the transaction of so much business as three strong men could get through. Hazlitt, in a portrait-sketch taken about 1825, says:

> Mr. Brougham writes almost as well as he speaks. In the midst of an election contest he comes out to address the populace, and goes back to his study to finish an article for the *Edinburgh Review*, sometimes indeed wedging three or four articles in the shape of *rifacimenti* of his own pamphlets or speeches in Parliament in a single Number. Such indeed is the activity of his mind, that it appears to require neither repose nor any other stimulus than a delight in its own exercise. He can turn his hand to any thing, but he cannot be idle. He is, in fact, a striking instance of the versatility and strength of the human mind, and also, in one sense, of the length of human life: *if we make good use of our time, there is room enough to crowd almost every art and science into it.*

It is now nearly forty years since this was written, and it is almost as applicable as ever. In 1828, in a debate in Parliament, Mr. Brougham used the memorable words, "The schoolmaster is abroad." He next, in a speech of six hours' delivery, moved for an inquiry into the state of the Law; the Repeal of the Test and Corporation Acts, Catholic Emancipation, and the Charities Commission, were next advocated by him; and then, Parliamentary Reform, the Abolition of Punishment of Forgery by Death, Local Courts, and the Abolition of Slavery. In 1830 he was raised to the high office of Lord Chancellor. Mechanics' Institutes, and the foundation of University College, and the Diffusion of

Useful Knowledge, were next advocated by Lord Brougham. His Chancellorship was brief. But he continued to labour for the next thirty years in Law Reform and Social Science, and in aiding the progress of liberal opinion.

The universal energy which has marked Lord Brougham was thus ably summed up, on the publication of his volume of scientific Tracts, in 1860:

> If the fact of his scientific researches were less well known, there would be something quite startling in the announcement of a volume of mathematical tracts from the hand of a man who has had half a score of other occupations, each sufficient to engross the whole mind of an ordinarily constituted mortal. To be great as a circuit leader, all-powerful as a popular chief, triumphant as a reforming Chancellor—to be the prominent figure in the Anti-Slavery movement, the promoter of education, the concocter of law-reforming statutes almost without number—the statesman of all parties, the citizen of two countries, and the orator of a thousand platforms—might have sufficed most ambitions, without the renown of literary success and scientific effort. But, not content wich the public achievements of his life, or the obscure glory of anonymous literature, Lord Brougham has striven to reproduce in an English dress the eloquence of Demosthenes, and to correct the real or supposed errors of no less a philosopher than Newton himself. . . . Philosophical theories may survive Lord Brougham's attacks, and *savans* may forget his speculations; but generations of Englishmen will long remember the career of a man who has exhibited in a thousand forms an amount of mental vitality which it would be difficult to parallel in the history of the most restless and eager aspirants to the glory of universal genius.

It is impossible to reflect upon the politico-legal position of Lord Brougham when he sat upon the woolsack, without remembering that Brougham and Denman, at the trial of Queen Caroline, attacked with virulence, then generally condemned, the Prince from whose hands, as sovereign, ten years later, both received high legal office. This change in feeling is alike creditable to all.

One of the most remarkable men of our day was Professor Wilson, the Editor of *Blackwood's Magazine*, in the pages of which he is thus characterised, from his bust in the Crystal Palace at Sydenham: he was born at Paisley, in Scotland, in 1785; and died at Edinburgh, in 1854.

> The head tells the story of the whole man. It is the head of an athlete, but an athlete possessing a soul, the grace of Apollo sitting on the thews of Hercules. Such a man, you would say at once, was none of your sedentary *litterati*, who appear to have the cramp in their limbs whenever they move abroad, but one who could, like the Greeks of old, ride, run, wrestle, box, dive, or throw the discus at need, or put the stone like Ulysses himself, or one who could do the same things,

and in addition to them steer, pull an oar, shoot, fish, follow hounds, or make a good score at cricket, like a true Briton of modern times, in spite of all our physical and intellectual degeneracy, about which, indeed, we have a right to be sceptical, when we know that such an unmistakable man as Wilson was living in the reign of Queen Victoria. It is an honour to Scotland that she produced such a critic on Homer, only second to that which is hers in having produced that poet who, of all the moderns, has composed poetry the most Homeric—even Walter Scott.

WEAR AND TEAR OF PUBLIC LIFE.

The sudden death of Lord George Bentinck, the political leader, in 1848, in his forty-seventh year, showed how the most ardent intellect and the noblest frame are alike broken down by the turmoil of public life. After a late debate in Parliament he would travel by rail many miles to hunt, and return in time to attend the sittings of the House in the evening; throwing a wrapper over his scarlet hunting-coat, and exercising indefatigably the office of "whipper-in" in the House, and subsequently leader of "the country party." He had during these political avocations continued his attention to racing and race-horses, declaring on one occasion that the winning of the Derby was the "blue-ribbon" of the turf. In August 1848 he retired to Welbeck Abbey for relaxation; he, however, attended Doncaster races four times in one week, at which a horse of his own breeding won the St. Leger stakes, to his great gratification. On September 21st he left Welbeck on foot, soon after four o'clock in the afternoon, to visit Earl Manvers, at Thoresby-park, and sent his servants to meet him with a carriage at an appointed place. He appeared not; the servants became alarmed; search was made for him; but it was not till eleven at night that he was found quite dead, lying on a footpath in a meadow about a mile from the house: his death having been caused by spasms of the heart. In Cavendish-square has been set up a colossal statue of this remarkable man: the pedestal simply bears his name; his political and sporting celebrity has waned with time; had the awful circumstances of his death been inscribed upon the memorial, it would have been a constant monition—a "siste viator"—of far greater value than a political monument.

Home Traits.

LOVE OF HOME.

ENGLAND is, above all other countries, favourable to individual industry, and that energy of character which, developed and well directed, succeeds in the world. Still, failure neither is nor ever has been rare; and private munificence and public benevolenee have provided " many happy ports and havens" for those whose evening of life is clouded with storm. We have visited not a few of these sacred places—these palaces of philanthropy; we have gone about their buildings—their noble halls glowing with comfort, and their tables beaming with good cheer. We have for a brief hour enjoyed the quiet of these retreats, and thought how their decayed brethren, jaded with adversity and buffeted with misfortune, may find here that consolation and repose which the outside world has denied them. These may be found in the fellowship of the dining-hall, the social walk in the garden, and the assembling for worship in the chapel. All this, however, is but the bright side of this mode of life; and when the time arrives for the brethren to retire, each to his solitary chamber, then comes the pang of isolation from the world—even the ungrateful world! And, perchance, they look from the casement upon the larger foundation-buildings, and are by them still more forcibly reminded that this noble place is *not their own*—in short, that it presents not the joys nor the delights which are conveyed to the sensitive heart by that brief but touching word —HOME!

It is scarcely possible to overrate the importance of this love of home in our scheme of earthly happiness. Southey has well observed: " Whatever strengthens our local attachments is favourable both to individual and national character. Our home, our birthplace, our native land; think, for a while, what the virtues are which rise out of the feelings connected with these words."

Then, how is man, in the loneliness we have referred to, parted from the sweet solace he most needs in his hour of woe! Such consolation has been thus picturesquely bodied forth by one of our happiest writers on domestic life: "As the vine, which has long twined its graceful foliage about the oak, and been lifted by it into sunshine, will, when the hardy plant is rifted by the thunderbolt, cling round it with its caressing tendrils, and bind up its shattered boughs; so it is beautifully ordered by Providence, that woman, who is the mere dependent and ornament of man in his happier hours, should be his stay and solace when smitten with sudden calamity; winding herself into the rugged recesses of his nature, tenderly supporting the drooping head, and binding up the broken heart."*

FAMILY PORTRAITS.

We remember reading a humorous sketch entitled, "The late Mr. Smith," whose portrait after his death was removed by his widow to the lumber-room, lest it should be displeasing to her second husband: occasionally the children would bring out the portrait, and with a rusty foil run "the ugly old man" through the eyes.

Here we have one of the reasons why family portraits are so often thrust aside; but there are several others. The Rev. Mr. Eagles relates the following, in *Blackwood's Magazine:* "I remember, when a boy, walking with an elderly gentleman, and passing a broker's stall, there was the portrait of a fine florid gentleman in regimentals. He stopped to look at it—he might have bought it for a few shillings. After he had gone away—'That,' said he, 'is the portrait of my wife's great uncle—member for the county, and colonel of militia: you see how he is degraded to these steps.' 'Why do you not rescue him?' said I. 'Because he left me nothing,' was the reply. A relative of mine, an old lady, hit upon a happy device; the example is worth following. Her husband was the last of his race, for she had no chil-

* Washington Irving.

dren. She took all the family portraits out of their frames, rolled up all the pictures, and put them in the coffin with the deceased."

Sheridan has turned an incident of this class to admirable account, in his *School for Scandal*, in the reservation of Uncle Oliver's portrait from sale.

Sometimes a good picture has unpleasant associations. "That is an excellent portrait of Ireland, the Shakspeare forger," said a collector to a picture-dealer in Wardour-street; whose ready reply was, "Will you buy it, sir? it is but half a guinea." "No," answered the other; "it would seem either that I admired Ireland's dishonest ingenuity, or that I had been his friend."

HOW TO KEEP FRIENDS.

When Goldsmith once talked to Johnson of the difficulty of living on very intimate terms with any one with whom you differed on an important topic, Johnson replied: "Why, sir, *you must shun the subject as to which you disagree.* For instance, I can live very well with Burke; I love his knowledge, his genius, his diffusion, and effulgence of conversation; but I would not talk to him of the Rockingham party."

Mr. Helps, in his admirable work, *Friends in Council*, well observes: "A rule for living happily with others is to avoid having stock subjects of disputation. It mostly happens, when people live much together, that they come to have certain set topics, around which, from frequent dispute, there is such a growth of angry words, mortified vanity, and the like, that the original difference becomes a standing subject for quarrel; and there is a tendency in all minor disputes to drift down to it. Again: if people wish to live well together, they must not hold too much to logic, and supposing every thing is to be settled by sufficient reason. Dr. Johnson saw this clearly with regard to married people when he said, 'Wretched would be the pair, above all names of wretchedness, who should be doomed to adjust by reason every morning all the minute detail of a domestic day.' But the application should be much more general than he made it. There is no time for such reasonings, and nothing that is worth them. And when we recollect how two lawyers, or two politicians, can go on contending, and that there is no end of one-sided reasoning on any subject, we shall not be sure that such contention is the best mode for arriving at truth. But certainly it is not the way to arrive at good temper."

The most gifted men are least addicted to depreciate either friends or foes. Dr. Johnson, Mr. Burke, and Mr. Fox were always more inclined to overrate them; your shrewd, sly, evil-speaking fellow is generally a shallow person; and frequently he is as venomous, as false when he flatters as when he reviles. He seldom praises John but to vex Thomas.

SMALL COURTESIES.

How much politeness and winning of the affections exist in small courtesies, is well exemplified in the following anecdote related by a lady of a gentleman who had been the politest man of his generation. On returning once from school for the holidays, she had been put under his charge for the journey. They stopped for the night at a Cornish inn. Supper was ordered, and soon there appeared a dainty dish of woodcocks. Her cavalier led her to the board with the air of a Grandison, and then proceeded to place all the legs of the birds on her plate. At first, with her school-girl prejudices in favour of wings and in disfavour of legs and drumsticks, she felt rather angered at having these (as she supposed) uninviting and least delicate parts imposed upon her; but in after years, when gastronomic light had beamed on her, and the experience of many suppers brought true appreciation, she did full justice to the memory of the man who could sacrifice such *morceaux* as woodcocks' thighs to the crude appetite of a girl, and who could thus show his innate deference for womanhood even in such budding form.

LASTING FRIENDSHIPS.

The man who ill-naturedly said that the church would not hold his acquaintance, but the pulpit would contain his friends, cannot be congratulated upon the disproportion.

"Who is your friend?" is an every-day question, probably never better answered than in the following forcible and eloquent rebuke by a modern writer:

Concerning the man you call your friend, tell me, will he weep with you in the hour of distress? Will he faithfully reprove to your face, for actions which others are ridiculing or censuring behind your back? Will he dare to stand forth in your defence, when detraction is secretly aiming its deadly weapons at your reputation? Will he acknowledge you with the same cordiality, and behave to you with the same friendly attention, in the company of your superiors in rank and fortune, as when the claims of pride or vanity do not interfere with those of friendship? If misfortune and losses should oblige you to retire into a walk of life in which you cannot appear with the same distinction, or entertain your friends with the same liberality as formerly, will he still think himself happy in your society, and, instead of withdrawing himself from an unprofitable connexion, take pleasure in professing himself your friend, and cheerfully assist you to support the burden of your afflictions? When sickness shall call you to retire from the gay and busy scenes of the world, will he follow you into your gloomy retreat, listen with attention to your "tale of symptoms," and minister the balm of consolation to your fainting spirits? And lastly, when death shall burst asunder every earthly tie, will he shed a tear upon your grave, and lodge the dear remembrance of your mutual friendship in his heart, as a treasure never to be resigned? The man who will not do all this may be your companion,—your flatterer,—but, depend upon it, *he is not your friend.*

Southey has left this charming picture of Friendship which ceases but with existence:

It may safely be affirmed that generous minds, when they have once known each other, never can be alienated as long as both retain the characteristics which brought them into union. No distance of place or lapse of time can lessen the friendship of those who are thoroughly persuaded of each other's worth. There are even some broken attachments in friendship, as well as in love, which nothing can destroy, and it sometimes happens that we are not conscious of their strength till after the disruption. There are a few persons known to me in years long past, but with whom I lived in no particular intimacy then, and have held no correspondence since, whom I could not now meet without an emotion of pleasure deep enough to partake of pain, and who, I doubt not, entertain for me feelings of the same kind and degree—whose eyes sparkle when they hear, and glisten sometimes when they speak of me, and who think of me, as I do of them, with an affection that increases as we advance in years. This is because our moral and intellectual sympathies have strengthened, and because, though far asunder, we know that we are travelling the same road towards our resting-place in heaven. "There is such a pleasure as this," says Cowper, "which would want explanation to some folks, being perhaps a mystery to those whose hearts are a mere muscle, and serve only for the purpose of an even circulation."*

* *The Doctor.*

And Professor Wilson has written these words of sweet consolation for the loss of friends:

Friends are lost to us by removal—for then even the dearest are often utterly forgotten. But let something that once was theirs suddenly meet our eyes, and in a moment, returning from the region of the rising or the setting sun, the friend of our youth seems at our side, unchanged his voice and his smile; or dearer to our eyes than ever, because of some affecting change wrought on face and figure by climate and by years. Let it be but his name written with his own hand on the title-page of a book; or a few syllables on the margin of a favourite passage which long ago we may have read together, "when life itself was new," and poetry overflowed the whole world; or a lock of *her* hair in whose eyes we first knew the meaning of the word "depth." And if death hath stretched out the absence into the dim arms of eternity, and removed the distance away into that bourne from which no traveller returns—the absence and the distance of her on whose forehead once hung the relic we adore—what heart may abide the beauty of the ghost that doth sometimes at midnight appear at our sleepless bed, and with pale uplifted arms waft over us at once a blessing and a farewell!

It rarely happens that broken friendships can be repaired or renewed. Mrs. Richard Trench, in her Journal, relates this remarkable instance of a failure:

At last, after an interval of twenty-four years, which succeeded a tolerably intimate acquaintance of seven weeks, I saw Count Münster of Hanover again. We met like two ghosts that ought to have been laid long since. I witnessed the whole process of the difficulty of persuading him that I was I; and I thought him as much changed in his degree as he could have found me. When we conversed, all the persons we referred to were dead and gone; and our interview added another link in my mind to the chain of proofs that, after a very, very long interval, neither friends nor acquaintance ought to meet in this world. He was kindly anxious to renew our acquaintance, and visited me next day; but still it seemed as if seeing me had renewed some painful associations.

TRUE TONE OF POLITE WRITING.

Sir James Mackintosh, who has sometimes been unfairly characterised as a writer of drawing-room essays, has left the following able view of what may be termed "the True Tone of Polite Writing,"—a rare accomplishment even in these days of assumed facility and literary pretension:

When a woman of feeling, fancy, and accomplishment has learned to converse with ease and grace, from long intercourse with the most polished society, and when she writes as she speaks, she must write letters as they ought to be written, if she has acquired just as much habitual correctness as is reconcilable with the air of negligence. A moment of enthusiasm, a burst of feeling, a flash of eloquence, may be allowed; but the intercourse of society, either in conversation or in letters, allows no more. Though interdicted from the long-continued use of elevated language, they are not without a resource. There is a part of language which is disdained by the pedant or the declaimer, and which both, if they knew its difficulty, would approach with dread; it is formed of the most familiar phrases and turns in daily use by the generality of men, and is full of energy and vivacity, bearing upon it the marks of those keen feelings and strong passions from which it springs. It is the employment of such phrases which produces what may be called colloquial eloquence. Conversation and letters may be thus raised to any degree of animation, without departing from their character. Any thing may be said, if it be spoken in the tone of society. The highest guests are welcome if they come in the easy undress of the club; the strongest metaphor appears without violence, if it is *familiarly* expressed; and we the more easily catch the warmest feeling, if we perceive that it is intentionally lowered in expression, out of condescension to our calmer temper. It is thus that harangues and declamations, the last proof of bad taste and bad manners in conversation, are avoided, while the fancy and the heart find the means of pouring forth all their stores. To meet this despised part of language in a polished dress, and producing all the effects of wit and eloquence, is a constant source of agreeable surprise. This is increased, when a few bolder and higher words are happily wrought into the texture of this familiar eloquence. To find what seems so unlike author-craft in a book raises the pleasing astonishment to its highest degree. I once thought of illustrating my notions by numerous examples from "La Sevigné." And I must, some day or other, do so; though I think it the resource of a bungler who is not enough master of language to convey his conceptions into the minds of others. The style of Madame de Sevigné is evidently copied, not only by her worshiper, Walpole, but even by Gray; who, notwithstanding the extraordinary merits of his matter, has the double stiffness of an imitator and of a college recluse.

PRIDE AND MEANNESS.

Rousseau has well described this association of Pride and Stinginess, which is very common: "We take from nature, from real pleasures, nay, from the stock of necessaries, what we lavish upon opinion. One man adorns his palace at the expense of his kitchen; another prefers a fine service of plate to a good dinner; a third makes a sumptuous entertainment, and starves himself the rest of the year. When I see a sideboard richly decorated, I expect the wine to be very indifferent. How often in the country, when we breathe the fresh morning air, are we not tempted by the prospect of a fine garden! We rise early, and by walking gain a keen appetite, which makes us wish for breakfast. Perhaps the domestic is out of the way, or provisions are wanting, or the lady has not given her orders, and you are tired to death with waiting. Sometimes people prevent your desires, or make you a very pompous offer of every thing, upon condition that you accept of nothing. You must fast till three o'clock, or breakfast with the tulips. I remember to have walked in a very beautiful park, which belonged to a lady who, though extremely fond of coffee, never drank any but when at a very low price; yet she liberally allowed her gardener a salary of a thousand crowns. For my part, I should choose to have tulips less finely variegated, and to drink coffee whenever my appetite called for it."

HOME THOUGHTS.

There is much to be learned from domestic annals. Southey has well observed: "The history of any private family, however humble, could it be fairly related for five or six generations, would illustrate the state and progress of society better than could be done by the most elaborate historian."

Cheerfulness and a festival spirit fills the soul full of harmony; it composes music for churches and hearts; it makes and publishes glorifications of God; it produces thankfulness, and serves the ends of charity; and when the oil of gladness runs over, it makes bright and tall emissions of holy fires, reaching up to a cloud, and making joy round about: and therefore, since it is so innocent, and may be so pious, and full of holy advantage, whatever can minister to this holy joy does set forward the work of religion and charity.*

In how delightful a strain has the same writer said: "There is some virtue or other to be exercised, whatever happens, either patience or thanksgiving, love or fear, moderation or humility, charity or contentedness; and they are, every one of them, equally in order to his great end and immortal felicity: and beauty is not made by white or red, by black eyes and a round face, by a straight body and a smooth skin, but by a proportion to the fancy. Whatever we talk, things are as they are; not as we grant, dispute, or hope, depending on neither our affirmative nor negative; but upon the rate and value which God sets upon things."

* Jeremy Taylor.

Lord Macaulay, too, has left us this touching picture:

Children, look in those eyes, listen to that dear voice, notice the feeling of even a single touch that is bestowed upon you by that gentle hand! Make much of it while yet you have that most precious of all good gifts—a loving mother. Read the unfathomable love of those eyes; the kind anxiety of that tone and look, however slight your pain. In after-life you may have friends—fond, dear, kind friends—but never will you have again the inexpressible love and gentleness lavished upon you which none but a mother bestows. Often do I sigh in my struggles with the hard, uncaring world, for the sweet, deep security I felt when, of an evening, nestling to her bosom, I listened to some quiet tale, suitable to my age, read in her tender and untiring voice. Never can I forget her sweet glances cast upon me when I appeared asleep; never her kiss of peace at night. Years have passed away since we laid her beside my father in the old churchyard; yet still her voice whispers from the grave, and her eye watches over me as I visit spots long since hallowed to the memory of my mother.

We pass from these traits of sweet simplicity to a lesson for riper age, by a living writer of sterling humour:

It is better for you to pass an evening once or twice a week in a lady's drawing-room, even though the conversation is slow, and you know the girl's song by heart, than in a club, tavern, or the pit of a theatre. All amusements of youth to which virtuous women are not admitted, rely on it, are deleterious to their nature. All men who avoid female society have dull perceptions and are stupid, or have gross tastes and revolt against what is pure. Your club-swaggerers, who are sucking the butts of billiard-cues all night, call female society insipid. Poetry is uninspiring to a yokel; beauty has no charms for a blind man; music does not please a poor beast who does not know one tune from another; but as a true epicure is hardly ever tired of water, sancey, and brown bread and butter, I protest I can sit for a whole night talking to a well-regulated, kindly woman about her girl Fanny or her boy Frank, and like the evening's entertainment. One of the great benefits a man may derive from woman's society is, that he is bound to be respectful to her. The habit is of great good to your moral men, depend upon it. Our education makes of use the most eminently selfish men in the world. We fight for ourselves, we push for ourselves, we yawn for ourselves, we light our pipes and say we won't go out, we prefer ourselves and our ease; and the greatest that comes to a man from a woman's society is, that he has to think of somebody to whom he is bound to be constantly attentive and respectful.—*Thackeray.*

Every virtue enjoined by Christianity as a virtue, is recommended by politeness as an accomplishment. Gentleness, humility, deference, affability, and a readiness to assist and serve on all occasions, are as necessary in the composition of a true Christian as in that of a well-bred man. Passion, moroseness, peevishness, and supercilious self-sufficiency, are equally repugnant to the characters of both, who differ in this only, that the true Christian really is what the well-bred man pretends to be, and would still be better bred if he was.—*Soame Jenyns.*

The Spirit of the Age.

PROGRESS OF KNOWLEDGE.

THE zeal which Albert, Prince Consort, evinced in furthering good works,—his sympathy with the wants of the poor, their bodily health and comfort, and their intellectual and moral culture,—will long endear his memory to the grateful people of the country of his adoption.

It was a characteristic of his genius that he would never consent to take the lead in any movement until he had, as far as possible, satisfied himself of its proper object and practicability. That he fully understood and appreciated the requirements of the age, is evident from the following passage in one of his manly Addresses:

"Whilst formerly the greatest mental energies strove at universal knowledge, and that knowledge was confined to the few, now they are directed on specialities, and in these again even to the minutest points; but the knowledge acquired becomes at once the property of the community at large; for, whilst formerly discovery was wrapped in secrecy, the publicity of the present day causes, that no sooner is a discovery or invention made, than it is already improved upon and surpassed by competing efforts. The products of all quarters of the globe are placed at our disposal, and we have only to choose which is the best and the cheapest for our purposes, and the powers of production are intrusted to the stimulus of competition and capital. So man is approaching a more complete fulfilment of that great and sacred mission which he has to perform in this world. His reason being created after the image of God, he has to use it to discover the laws by which the Almighty governs His creation, and, by making these laws his standard of action, to conquer nature to his use; himself a Divine instrument. Science discovers these laws of power, motion, and transformation; industry applies them to the raw matter, which the earth yields us in abundance, but which become valuable only by knowledge. Art teaches us the immutable laws of beauty and symmetry, and gives to our productions forms in accordance to them." Again: "To the human mind nothing is so fascinating as progress. It is not what we have long had that we most prize. We highly prize new accessions; but we enjoy almost unconsciously gifts, of far more value, we have long been in possession of. This is our nature; thus we are constituted. It is not surprising, therefore, that we should have a peculiar relish for new discoveries. The interest of discovery, however, is not permanent. For a time we are dazzled by its brilliancy; but gradually the impression fades away, and at last is lost entirely in the splendour of some fresh discovery which carries with it the charm of novelty. When we reflect upon this, we cannot help perceiving in how very different a state the world would be from what it is if mankind in the beginning had been in the possession of all the knowledge we now have, and there had been no progress ever since."

There is no royal death within memory of the present generation which has caused such grave and regretful reflection as the sudden manner in which the Prince Consort was taken from our beloved Sovereign and her family, at the close of the year 1861. The nearest approach to the public sorrow upon this melancholy occasion was the universal sympathy expressed on the loss of the Princess Charlotte, in 1817, when the mother and offspring were at once swept by the hand of death into the same grave! But widespread as was the lamentation of the people for their hopes being thus crushed, it differed in this respect from the sorrow for the Prince Consort,—that in the one case expectation was blighted, but in the other realisation was extinguished when the fruits of superior intelligence were fast ripening into the maturity of true greatness.

Since the death of the Prince the country has learned the full extent of its loss by this sad event. Yet it was plainly asserted in the *Leader* newspaper, ten years ago, that the Prince was "becoming the most popular man in

England;" and the reader was assured that the above paper was written to put the Prince's "position and his services in the point of view in which we may comprehend him, and be grateful to him." This statement was unheeded at the time it was made; but, in the year following, other journalists had discovered that the Prince had some voice in English foreign policy,—a charge which was admitted to be true by Ministers in Parliament. Public attention was then turned, in an entirely different direction, and the Prince resumed his powerful popular position. Yet his weighty influence, as we have said, was not fully made known until recently. We have seen but one acknowledgment of the service of the well-informed and far-seeing writer in the *Leader*, and to this was not attached his name. We therefore add, in justice to the memory of a man of rare talent, and the right spirit of independence, which is the best characteristic of a public journalist, that the writer in question was the late Mr. E. M. Whitty, who reprinted the above in *The Governing Classes of Great Britain.*

SPECIAL PROVIDENCE IN SCIENCE.

The records of science furnish us with examples in which complicated causes have operated through vast periods of duration anterior to man's existence, or even anterior to that of the existence of any of the more perfect animals, in order to provide for the wants and happiness of those animals, especially of man. Laws, apparently conflicting and irregular in their action, have been so controlled and directed, and made to conspire, as to provide for the wants of civilised life untold ages before man's existence. In those early times, vast forests, for instance, might have been growing along the shores of estuaries; and these dying, were buried deep in the mud, there to accumulate thick beds of vegetable matter over huge areas; and this, by a long series of changes, was at length converted into coal. This could be of no use whatever till man's existence, nor even then, till civilisation had taught him to employ the substance for his comfort, and for a great variety of useful arts.

Dr. Hitchcock illustrates this position as follows: Look, for instance, at the small island of Great Britain. At this day 15,000 steam-engines are driven by means of coal, with a power equal to that of 2,000,000 of men; and thus is put into operation machinery equalling the unaided power of 300,000,000 or 400,000,000 of men. The influence thence emanating reaches the remotest portions of the globe, and tends mightily to the civilisation and happiness of the race. And is all this an accidental effect of nature's laws? Is it not rather a striking example of special protective providence? What else but divine power, intent upon a specific purpose, could have so directed the countless agencies employed through so many ages as to bring about such marvellous results?*

SCIENTIFIC PROGRESS.

School-learning is, undoubtedly, the best foundation: "In all industrial pursuits connected with the natural sciences, in fact in all pursuits not simply dependent on manual dexterity, the development of the intellectual faculties, by what may be termed 'school-learning,' constitutes the basis and chief condition of progress and of every improvement. A young man with a mind well stored with solid scientific acquirements will, without difficulty or effort, master the technical part of an industrial pursuit; whereas, in general, an individual who may be thoroughly master of the technical part is altogether incapable of seizing upon any new fact that has not previously presented itself to him, or of comprehending a scientific principle and its application."

Lord Stanhope has thus strikingly illustrated the subject:

See how the field of human knowledge is extended. Within the last fifty years there is scarce a branch of knowledge, even in those which have been explored for hundreds of years—classical learning, for example—which has not received some new and important additions. But not only this; it may be said that new sciences have been discovered. Who, seventy or eighty years ago, thought or heard of the name of geology, or of men like Cuvier, who by their genius have brought back to us the forms of long-extinct animals, and the state of the earth as it must have existed thousands of years ago? Who could have imagined that in art such vast resources should have been opened up to us, as, for instance, the now-familiar science of photography supplies? Who would have imagined that railways, which have enabled us at so quick a rate to have communication with all parts of the country, would become a study of well-regulated curiosity; or that the instantaneous

* *Religious Truth illustrated from Science.*

power of transmission which we possess in the electric telegraph should be imparted to the whole of the people who now crowd these busy shores?

Some of the noblest triumphs of science, however, do but show the shortsightedness of man, and seem to dictate to him that great results can only be obtained by gradual and patient labour, as if to keep in check his overweening conceit. This is illustrated in the discovery of Voltaism. "When Galvani," says Lord Brougham, in his powerful manner, "observed the contortions of the muscle in a dead frog, or even when Volta gave an explanation of them, how little could it be foreseen that the discovery would lead not only to the decomposition of bodies which had resisted all attempts to ascertain their constituent parts, and bring us acquainted with substances wholly unlike any before known, as metals that floated in water and took fire on exposure to the air; but, after having thus changed the face of chemical science, should also impress a new character upon the moral, judicial, and political world! Yet this has undeniably been the result of the discovery made by Volta."

The histories of invention present many instances of "the slip between the cup and the lip." New modes of lighting have been very productive of such disappointments. About thirty years since was patented a light by the admixture of the vapour of hydrocarbons with atmospheric air, so as to produce an illumination equal in brilliancy to that of the purest gas; the power of light from a ten-hole burner equalling that of 22⅛th wax-candles. This invention had been a long and costly labour; a single set of experiments having cost 500*l.* At length the patent was sold to a company for the large sum of 28,000*l.*; a plant was established, licenses were advertised for sale, and, among the confident promises, it was held out that the gas-pipes and mains of the existing companies might be bought up for the requirements of this new light! But the working of the invention did not succeed in detail (indeed, it had been purchased with the knowledge that it was incomplete); and the entire capital invested, some 40,000*l.* or 50,000*l.*, was lost!

TIME AND IMPROVEMENT.

The Rev. Dr. Temple, in his glowing Essay, "Education

of the World," thus maintains that all human improvement is the result of the accumulations of Time:

To the spirit all things that exist must have a purpose, and nothing can pass away till that purpose be fulfilled. The lapse of time is no exception to this demand. Each moment of time, as it passes, is taken up in the shape of permanent results into the time that follows, and only perishes by being converted into something more substantial than itself. Thus, each successive age incorporates into itself the substance of the preceding,—the power whereby the present ever gathers itself into the past, transforms the human race into a colossal man, whose life reaches from the Creation to the Day of Judgment. The successive generations of men are days in this man's life. The discoveries and inventions which characterise the different epochs of the world's history are his works. The creeds and doctrines, the opinions and principles of the successive ages, are his thoughts. The states of society at different times are his manners. He grows in knowledge, in self-control, in visible size, just as we do. And his education is in the same way, and for the same reason, precisely similar to ours. All this is no figure, but only a compendious statement of a very comprehensive fact.

EVIL INFLUENCES.

It has been asked by a great author, "What does it signify whether you deny a God or speak ill of Him?"—a question well answered by another sage, when he declares, "I would rather men should say that there never was such a man as Plutarch, than that Plutarch was an ill-natured, mischievous fellow."

Nearly eighty years ago Mr. Sharp wrote, "There can be no reasonable doubt that it is better to believe too much than too little; since, as Boswell observes (most probably in Johnson's words), 'A man may breathe in foul air, but he must die in an exhausted receiver.'"

Much of the scepticism that we meet with is necessarily affectation or conceit; for it is as likely that the ignorant, weak, and indolent should become mathematicians as reasoning unbelievers. Patient study and perfect impartiality must precede rational conviction, whether ending in faith or doubt. Need it be asked, how many are capable of such an examination? But whether they come honestly by their opinions or not, it is much more advisable to refute than to burn, or even to scorch them.

It has been shrewdly remarked by a contemporary:

All the voices which have any real influence with an Englishman in easy circumstances combine to stimulate a low form of energy, which stifles every high one. The newspapers extol his wisdom by assuming that the average intelligence which he represents is, under the name of public opinion, the ultimate and irresponsible ruler of the nation. The novels which he and his family devour with insatiable greediness have no tendency to rouse his imagination, to say nothing of his mind. They are pictures of the every-day life to which he has always been accustomed,—sarcastic, sentimental, or ludicrous, as the case may be,—but never rising to any thing which could ever suggest the existence of tragic dignity or ideal beauty. The human mind has made considerable advances in the last three-and-twenty centuries; but the thousands of Greeks who could enjoy not only Euripides, but Homer and Æschylus, were superior, in some important points, to the millions of Englishmen who in their inmost hearts prefer Pickwick to Shakspeare. Even the religion of the present day is made to suit the level of commonplace Englishmen. There was a time when Christianity meant the embodiment of all truth and holiness in the midst of a world lying in wickedness. It afterwards included law, liberty, and knowledge, as opposed to the energetic ignorance of the northern barbarians. It now too often means philanthropic societies—excellent things as far as they go, but rather small. Any doctrine now is given up if it either seems uncomfortable or likely to make a disturbance. It is almost universally assumed that the truth of an opinion is tested by its consistency with cheerful views of life and nature. Unpleasant doctrines are only preached under incredible forms, and thus serve to spice the enjoyments which they would otherwise destroy.*

WORLDLY MORALITY.

Professor Blackie, in his eloquent Edinburgh Essay, has these stringent remarks upon the lax morality of the day:

There is in the world always a respectable sort of surface morality,—and nowhere more than in this British world at the present hour,—a morality of convenience and utility, which pays respect to the principles of right and wrong when generally formalised, but which recognises them practically only in so far as local customs and decencies, proprieties, etiquettes, and the round of certain "inevitable charities," are willing to recognise them. This morality many a consumer of beefsteaks and swiller of porter in this lusty and material land accepts, after eighteen hundred years of Gospel preaching, as quite sufficient for all the purposes of a respectable English life. But the perverse maxims and vicious practices with which our British society is rank, make it evident to the most superficial glance how far the current morality of our trades and parties is from seeking to accommodate itself to the principles of extreme moral purity laid down in every page of the New Testament. A sermon may be a very proper thing as Sunday work, and may help to bridge the way to heaven, when a bridge shall be required; but on Monday a man must attend to his business, and act according to the maxims of his trade, of his party, of his corporation, of his vestry. Then the respectable sporting-man will stake his last thousand on the leg of a race-horse, and think it quite like a Christian gentleman to allow his tailor's bill to be unpaid for another year; then the respectable Highland proprietor will refuse to renew the lease to the industrious poor cotter on his estate, that the people, for whom he cares nothing, may make way for the red-deer, which it is his only

* *Cornhill Magazine.*

passion to stalk; then the respectable brewer, instead of preparing wholesome drink from wholesome grain, will infect his brewst with deleterious drugs in order to excite a factitious thirst in the stomach of his customers, and increase the amount of drinking; then a respectable corporation, to maintain their own "vested rights," will move heaven and earth to prevent the national parliament from acting on the plainest rules of justice and common sense in a matter seriously affecting the public well-being; and the respectable members of society shall flutter round the gilded wax-lights of aristocracy, and perform worship at Hudson's statue, and have respect to men with gold rings and goodly apparel, and do every thing that is expressly forbidden in the second chapter of the Epistle of James, which they profess to receive as a divine rule of conduct. These are only one or two of the more glaring points in which our commonly-received maxims and practice of respectable British life run directly in the face of that highest morality, which the most religious and church-going Englishman professes to acknowledge as his rule of conduct.

Professor Blackie concludes with the gospel text, "What shall it profit a man, if he gain the whole world and lose his own soul?" which the Professor applies in the plain practical question: "What will it profit England to spin more cotton, to pile more money-bags, to set more steam-coaches a-going, if Mammon is to be worshiped every where, rather than virtue and wisdom?" &c.

SPEAKING THE TRUTH.

One of the sublimest things in the world is plain Truth. Indeed it is so sublime as to be entirely out of the reach of many people.

The ancients said many fine things of Truth; but nothing to exceed in practical worth the love of Truth shown by the great Duke of Wellington in every phase of his wonderful career, of which the majority of us have been, more or less, contemporary witnesses.

"The foundation of all justice," said this truly great man, "is Truth; and the mode of discovering truth has always been to administer an oath, in order that the witness may give his depositions under a high sanction."

Elsewhere he said, when advocating the cause of the Church of England, "I am resolved to tell plainly and honestly what I think, quite regardless of the odium I may incur from those whose prejudices my candour and sincerity may offend. I am here to speak the truth, and not to flatter the prejudices of any man. In speaking the truth, I shall utter it in the language that truth itself most naturally suggests. It is upon her native strength—upon her own truth—it is upon her spiritual character, and upon the purity of her doctrines, that the Church of England rests."

When, upon the death of Sir Robert Peel, the Duke of Wellington sought to express what seemed to him most admirable in the character of his friend, he said that he was *the truest man he had ever known;* adding: "I was long connected with him in public life. We were both in the councils of our sovereign together, and I had long the honour to enjoy his private friendship. In all the course of my acquaintance with Sir Robert Peel, I never knew a man in whose truth and justice I had a more lively confidence, or in whom I saw a more invariable desire to promote the public service. In the whole course of my communication with him I never knew an instance in which he did not show the strongest attachment to truth; and I never saw, in the whole course of my life, the smallest reason for suspecting that he stated any thing which he did not firmly believe to be the fact."

It was the instinct of a man, himself as true as he was great, thus to place the regard for truth in the front rank of human qualities. On that simple and noble basis his own nature rested. Wellington could not vapour, or even utter a lie in a bulletin. Every thing with him was simple, direct, straightforward, and went to the heart of its purpose, if any thing could. In all that has singled out England from the nations, and given her the front place in the history of the world, the Duke of Wellington was emphatically an Englishman. His patience, his probity, his punctuality in the smallest things, in every thing the practical fidelity and reliability of his character, we rejoice to regard as the type of that which has made us the great people that we are. It has indeed been well said that the Duke's whole existence was a practical refutation of all falsehood.

RESTLESSNESS AND ENTERPRISE.

An anxious, restless temper, that runs to meet care on its way, that regrets lost opportunities too much, and that is over-painstaking in contrivances for happiness, is foolish, and should not be indulged.* If you cannot be happy in one way, be happy in another; and this facility of disposition wants but little aid from philosophy, for health and good-humour are almost the whole affair. Many run about after felicity, like an absent man hunting for his hat while it is on his head or in his hand. Though sometimes small evils, like invisible insects, inflict great pain, yet the chief secret of comfort lies in not suffering trifles to vex one, and in prudently cultivating an undergrowth of small pleasures, since very few great ones, alas, are let on long leases.

Nothing will justify, or even excuse, dejection. Untoward accidents will sometines happen; but, after many years' experience (writes Mr. Sharp), I can truly say, that nearly all those who began life with me have succeeded, or failed, as they deserved:

Faber quisque fortunæ propriæ.

Though you may look to your understanding for amusement, it is to the affections that we must trust for happiness. These imply a spirit of self-sacrifice; and often our virtues, like our children, are endeared to us by what we suffer for them. Conscience, even when it fails to govern our conduct, can disturb our peace of mind. Yes, it is neither paradoxical nor merely poetical to say:

That seeking others' good, we find our own.

This solid yet romantic maxim is found in no less a writer than Plato; who, it has been well observed, sometimes in his moral lessons, as well as in his theological, is almost, though not altogether, a Christian.

The passion for enterprise and adventure is the shoal upon which high hopes are constantly being wrecked. We remember, some thirty years since, a merchant of London, who inherited a princely fortune, which he embarked in speculations of almost astounding magnitude. He was a large-minded and generous man; and among other instances of his liberality, was his aid to scientific explorations, in acknowledgment of which he received an honorary Fellowship of the Royal Society. He published upon political economy and monetary questions; and with that fatality which often

* Such a person knows as much of what true felicity consists as did Horace Walpole's gardener, who thought it "something of a bulbous root."

attends those who aspire to public business, our merchant, in some measure, out-ventured his own. Before the problematical economy of vast steam-ships had been settled, he invested large sums in this class of speculation. He was rather athirst for fresh fields than for the gold itself; and with this view he and his family ceded to a chartered company a group of islands discovered some forty years previously through their enterprise, and which the Government had granted them in consideration for their services in more recent discoveries of the southern continent. It was then resolved to colonise the islands as the head-station of the southern whale-fishery; our merchant receiving the appointment of lieutenant-governor. Troops of friends and well-wishers attended the leave-taking; the voyage out was fair and auspicious, and the governor and his little staff planted their bare emblem of authority upon the islands.

The scheme was reasonable; for whale-fishing was rife in the neighbouring seas, and sperm-whales even came into the anchorage. The country is luxuriantly wooded, the flowering plants abound; and the climate is mild, temperate, and salubrious. But the fishery failed, and the horizon soon grew dark with gathering clouds of discontent among the colonists; and there arose cabals, the usual consequence of defeated hopes: as success brightly colours all things in life, so failures darken them. After many months of suffering from indignities heaped upon him by exasperated adventurers, and the confusion which follows such mischances, the governor's brief authority was respected only by *two* individuals among the six-score colonists. Such heartless desertion in a land upon whose storm-beaten shores human foot had rarely set, would have made many a stout heart quail: not so our almost friendless representative of authority; and at length the many closed their cruel indignities by determining that he should leave the islands by the first ship which should touch there. This stern resolve was carried into effect; and our merchant-prince, solitary in all respects save hope, returned to the home which he had left amid a choir of aspirations. He memorialised the Government for redress, and besought parliament-men to assert his wrongs; but the only result was the usual official coldness and disinclination to interfere in troublesome matters;

although the enterprise was, at the commencement, fully recognised by the colonial authorities at home.

This is a painful story of a few years' misadventure and wrecked fortune, and ingratitude to a man whose honour and integrity, in the face of misfortune, should at least have shielded him from insult. Yet how forcibly does it illustrate the perils which so often beset the restless spirit!

THE PRESENT AND THE PAST.

Sharon Turner, a man of sound, practical sense, as well as a reverential and reflective writer of history, has these pertinent remarks upon the tendency of historians to magnify the Present at the expense of the Past:

Nothing is a greater reproach to the reasoning intellect of any age than a splenetic censoriousness on the manners and characters of our ancestors. It is but common justice for us to bear in mind that in those times we should have been as they were, as they in ours would have resembled ourselves. Both are but the same men, acting under different circumstances, wearing different dresses, and pursuing different objects; but neither inferior to the other in talent, industry, or intellectual worth. The more we study biography, we shall perceive more evidence of this truth.

Disregarding what satire might, without being cynical, lash in our own costumes, we are apt to look proudly back on those who have gone before us, and to regale our self-complacency with comparisons of their deficiencies, and of our greater merit. The retrospect is pleasing, but it offers no ground for exultation. We are superior, and we have in many things better taste and sounder judgment and wiser habits than they possessed. And why? Because we have had means of superiority by which they were not assisted. But a merit which owes its origin merely to our having followed, instead of preceding, in existence, gives us no right to depreciate those over whom our only advantage has been the better fortune of a later chronology. We may therefore allow those who have gone before us to have been amused with what would weary or dissatisfy us, without either sarcasms on their absurdities, or contemptuous wonder at their stately childishness and pompous inanities.

One of our most popular historians indulges to excess in these brilliant antitheses, which in his pages remind one of poppies in corn.

CIRCUMSTANCES AND GENIUS.

This episode in man's history,—this stage in the great struggle of life,—has been thus powerfully painted by a contemporary:

We presume there can be little doubt that circumstances have an effect upon the lives and characters of men; to say any thing else would be to contradict flatly the ordinary opinion of the world. Notwithstanding, if one will but look at one's private experience among the most ordinary and obscure actors in the life-drama, how wonderfully, one must allow, character, temper, heart, and spirit, assert themselves beyond the reach of all external powers! How triumphantly the poor prodigal, to whom Providence has given the fairest prospects, and whose steps are guarded by love and kindness, can vindicate his own instincts against all the virtuous force of circumstance surrounding him, and go to destruction in its very face! Who needs to be taught that ever-recurring lesson? Who can be ignorant that scarcely a great career has ever been made in this world otherwise than in the face of circumstances—in strenuous defiance of all that external elements could do to overcome the unconquerable soul? In the face of such examples, what are we to say to the theory that adverse circumstances can excuse a man born with all the compensations of genius for an unlovely and ignoble life, a bitter and discontented heart, a course of vulgar vice and sordid meanness? Never was genius more wickedly disparaged. That celestial gift to which God has given capacities of enjoyment beyond the reach of the crowd, is of itself an armour against circumstance more proof than steel, and continually holds open to its possessor a refuge against the affronts of the world, a shelter from its contumelies, which is denied to other men. He who reckons of this endowment as of something which gives only a more exquisite egotism, a finer touch of selfishness, a sublimation of envy and self-assertion, and dependence upon the applause of the crowd, forms a mean estimate, against which it is the duty of every man who knows better to protest. Outside circumstances, disappointment, neglect, dark want and misery, have plagued the souls and disturbed the temper of great men before now, but have never, so far as we are aware, polluted a pure heart, or made a noble mind despicable. The bitter soreness of unappreciated genius belongs proverbially to those whose gift is of the smallest; and the man who excuses a bad life by the pretence that this divine lymph contained within it has been soured by popular neglect and turned to gall, speaks sacrilege and profanity.*

OUR UNIMAGINATIVE AGE.

We have now no great poets; and our poverty in this respect is not compensated by the fact, that we once had them, and that we may, and do, read their works. The movement has gone by; the charm is broken; the bond of union, though not cancelled, is seriously weakened. Hence our age, great as it is, and in nearly all respects greater than any the world has yet seen, has, notwithstanding its large and generous sentiments, its unexampled toleration, its love of liberty, and its profuse and almost reckless charity, a certain material, unimaginative, and unheroic character, which has made several observers tremble for the future. . . . . That something has been lost is unquestion-

* *Quarterly Review.*

able. We have lost much of that imagination which, though in practical life it often misleads, is, in speculative life, one of the highest of all qualities, being suggestive as well as creative. Even practically we should cherish it, because the commerce of the affections mainly depends on it. It is, however, declining; while, at the same time, the increasing refinement of society accustoms us more and more to suppress our emotions, lest they be disagreeable to others. And as the play of the emotions is the chief study of the poet, we see in this circumstance another reason which makes it difficult to rival that great body of poetry which our ancestors possessed. We quote the above from the second volume of Mr. Buckle's *History of Civilization*. We would add, that the suppression of emotions to which the author refers is one great cause of the difficulty of getting persons to speak the truth in the present day: they are ever disguising their feelings, until hypocritical caution becomes habit, and it requires a stronger light than the old cynic possessed to find honest men. The low standard of commercial morality, and the time-serving expediency which so greatly regulates the actions of our rulers and those who make the laws, is traceable to this over-refinement.

MARVELS OF THE UNIVERSE.

Nothing is more startling, or more likely to be received with incredulity by minds unprepared for their reception, than what are, in common parlance, termed the Marvels of the Universe. The philosophical writers of our day have strikingly illustrated this fact, which should be taken into account in writing of the *impedimenta* to the progress of science even in our own day. Sir John Herschel has thus forcibly stated the case:

> What mere assertion will make any one believe that in one second of time, in one beat of the pendulum of a clock, a ray of light travels over 192,000 miles, and would therefore perform the tour of the world in about the same time that it requires to wink with our eyelids, and in much less than a swift runner occupies in taking a single stride? What mortal can be made to believe, without demonstration, that the sun is almost a million times larger than the earth? and that, although so remote from us that a cannon-ball shot directly towards it, and maintaining its full speed, would be twenty years in reaching it, yet it affects the earth by its attraction in an appreciable instant of time?

Who would not ask for demonstration, when told that a gnat's wing, in its ordinary flight, beats many hundred times in a second; or that there exists animated and regularly-organised beings, many thousands of whose bodies laid close together would not extend an inch? But what are these to the astonishing truths which modern optical inquiries have disclosed, which teach us that every point of a medium through which a ray of light passes, is affected with a succession of periodical movements, regularly recurring at equal intervals, no less than five hundred millions of millions of times in a single second! That it is by such movements communicated to the nerves of our eyes that we see; nay, more, that it is the difference in the frequency of their recurrence which affects us with the sense of the diversity of colour. That, for instance, in acquiring the sensation of redness, our eyes are affected four hundred and eighty-two millions of millions of times; of yellowness, five hundred and forty-two millions of millions of times; and of violet, seven hundred and seven millions of millions of times per second. Do not such things sound more like the ravings of madmen than the sober conclusions of people in their waking senses? They are, nevertheless, conclusions to which any one may most certainly arrive who will only be at the trouble of examining the chain of reasoning by which they have been obtained.

Professor Airy, however, considers this difficulty to be over-estimated. He observes, that "persons who take great interest in Astronomy appear to regard the determination of measures, like those of the distance of the sun and moon, as mysteries beyond ordinary comprehension, based perhaps upon principles which it is impossible to present to common minds with the smallest probability that they will be understood; if they accept these measures at all, they adopt them only upon loose personal credit; in any case, the impression which the statement makes on the mind is very different from that created by a record of the distance in miles between two towns, or the number of acres in a field."

Now, the measure of the moon's distance involves no principle more abstruse than the measure of the distance of a tree on the opposite bank of a river; and the Professor shows that the methods used for measuring astronomical distances are, in some applications, absolutely the same as the methods of ordinary theodolite-surveying, and are in other applications equivalent to them; and that, in fact, there is nothing in their principles which will present the smallest difficulty to a person who has attempted the common practice of plotting from angular measures.*

The habit of beholding the spectacle of the sun gradually sinking, to disappear after a time below the level of

* See Prof. Airy's *Six Lectures on Astronomy.*

the sea,—this habit, we say, and our astronomical knowledge, have long since familiarised us with the phenomenon which, undoubtedly, would appear inexplicable were we to witness it for the first time, and without being prepared. Who has not in childhood felt this wonder? The ancients were far from being able to account for it: some Greek philosophers regarded the sun as an inflamed mass, which plunged itself every night into the waters of the sea: and they pretended to have heard a hissing noise! We have found the same idea lingering among the credulous peasantry of Sussex. We remember our first nurse, a native of Battle, used to relate that, from the cliffs at Eastbourne, she had seen the comet of 1769 dip its tail into the sea, and that she had distinctly heard the "hissing noise." Such is the persistence of certain impressions, which, monstrous as they are, can only be explained away by reasoning.*

PHYSIOGNOMY.

Sir David Brewster, in his introductory Address to the University of Edinburgh, 1862-3, remarked that one of the characteristics of the age in which we live was its love of the mysterious and marvellous.

I refer (said Sir David) to the so-called science of physiognomy, but more especially to that morbid expansion of it called the physiognomy of the human form, which has been elaborated in Germany, and is now likely to obtain possession of the English mind. In want of any other arguments, our physiognomists assert that it is simply probable that the outer form would be designed on purpose to represent the mental character, and on this ground they dogmatically declare that the expressions of rage, or grief, or fear have been "divinely designed on purpose that the inner mind may be known to those who watch the outer man." The persons who use such arguments and have recourse to such assumptions never propose to make any inductive comparison of a certain number of well-measured forms with the well-ascertained mental phases with which they are associated. Were such experiments made, they would yield no result. No two physiognomists, acting separately, would agree in measuring and characterising the forms and indications of the head, the features, the hands, and the feet of the patient; and no two men—neither the sagacious judge on the bench, nor the shrewd counsel at the bar—could determine his real character were they to conjure with all the events of his life. In this new physiognomy, a head large in the mid region indicates a predominance of the feelings over the other faculties; a proneness to superstition and fanaticism is shown by a little increase in the elevation; and a head large behind evinces practical ability; and, as Dr. Carus says, characterises a race which will give birth to great historic names! Small

* See *Things not Generally Known*, First Series, p. 11.

heads, however, are not to be despised. They indicate talent, but not genius; while very small ones belong, he says, to the excitable class, from whom "a great part of the misery of society arises." In the varying expressions of the human face physiognomists find a better support for their views. That the emotions of the past and the present leave permanent traces on the human countenance is doubtless true, and to this extent we are all physiognomists, often very presumptuous ones, and, excepting accidental coincidences, always in the wrong, when we infer from any external appearance the character and disposition of our neighbour. In every class of society we encounter faces which we instinctively shun, and others to which we as instinctively cling. But how frequently have we found our estimates to be false! The repulsive aspect has proved to be the result of physical suffering, of domestic disquiet, or of ruined fortunes; and under the bland and smiling countenance a heart deceitful and vindictive, and "desperately wicked," has often been found concealed.

TRADE AND PHILANTHROPY.

In the Memoirs of Bulstrode Whitlocke, the following anecdote is told as illustrative of the erroneous notions formerly entertained as to the Employment of Machinery for purposes of economy. "The advantage of free competition, and the inexhaustible resources of new inventions, contrivances, and appliances were," it is observed by the editor at that time (1658), "utterly ignored. The Swedish ambassador" (to the court of Oliver Cromwell) "seems to have had a gleam of the truth, a dawning consciousness of how desirable it was to economise human labour by introducing machinery whenever practicable. He told a pleasant story of the Czar and a Dutchman; and how the latter, observing the boats passing upon the Volga to be manned with three hundred men in each boat, who, in a storm and high wind, held the bottom of the sails down with their hands, offered to the former a mode of manning each boat quite as efficiently with thirty men instead of the three hundred, by which the cost of transport would be lessened. But the Emperor called him a knave; and asked him if a boat that now went with three hundred men should be brought to go as well with thirty only, how were the other two hundred and seventy men to get their living?"

Cromwell, it will be remembered, protected by Act of Parliament a sawmill erected in his time, it is imagined, on the site of the Belvidere-road, Lambeth; in which locality at this day there is probably more sawing by machinery than in any other part of England.

World-Knowledge.

MISCELLANEA.

ENERGY and force of character are among the first requisites essential to success in business. A man may possess a high degree of refinement, large stores of knowledge, and even a well-disciplined mind; but if he is destitute of this one principle, which may be termed resolution of soul, he is like a watch without a mainspring—beautiful, but inefficient, and unfit for service.

Never do too much at a time, is a good practical maxim. Sir Edward Bulwer Lytton gives the following history of his literary habits: Many persons, seeing me so much engaged in active life, and as much about the world as if I had never been a student, have said to me, "When do you get time to write all your books? How on earth do you contrive to do so much work?" I shall surprise you by the answer I make. The answer is this: "I contrive to do so much by never doing too much at a time. A man, to get through work well, must not overwork himself; or, if he do too much to-day, the reaction of fatigue will come, and he will be obliged to do too little to-morrow. Now, since I began really and earnestly to study, which was not till I had left college, and was actually in the world, I may perhaps say I have gone through as large a course of general reading as most men of my time. I have travelled much, and I have seen much; I have mixed much in politics, and the various business of life; and, in addition to all this, I have published somewhere about sixty volumes, some upon subjects requiring much research. And what time, do you think, as a general rule, I have devoted to study—to reading and writing? Not more than three hours a day; and when Parliament is sitting, not always that. But then, during those hours, I have given my whole attention to what I was about."

Sir Benjamin Brodie says that "humility leads to the

highest distinction, because it leads to self-improvement." He adds—and the advice cannot be too often repeated—"study your own characters; endeavour to learn and supply your own deficiencies; never assume to yourself qualities which you do not possess; combine all this with energy and activity, and you cannot predicate of yourselves, nor can others predicate of you, at what point you may arrive at last."

Among the empiric arts of gaining notoriety, that by engraved portraits has led to some curious results. When the late John Harrison Curtis, the aurist, came to town to seek his fortune, he had his portrait engraved in large handsome style, and offered the same to a printseller to publish. He demurred, as the original was unknown; but recommended Curtis to leave his prints at the different printshops "on sale, or return." The sudden appearance in the shop-windows of a large portait of the great unknown led to the question, "Who is *this* Mr. Curtis?" The repeated inquiries laid the foundation of his fortune, and led to his living in good style for many years in Soho-square, and numbering royalty and nobility among his patients; but he outlived his professional reputation, and died in reduced circumstances.

Silence, says Boyle, discovers Wisdom and conceals Ignorance; and 'tis a property that is so much belonging to Wise Men, that even a Fool, when he holdeth his peace, may pass for one of that sort.

It is one thing to see that a line is crooked, and another thing to be able to draw a straight one. It is not quite so easy to do a good thing as those imagine who never try.

One of Sir Thomas Wyat's common sayings was, that there were three things which should always be strictly observed: "Never to play with any man's unhappiness or deformity, for that is inhuman; nor on superiors, for that is saucy and undutiful; nor on holy matters, for that is irreligious."

A little grain of the romance is no ill ingredient to preserve and exalt the dignity of human nature, without which it is apt to degenerate into every thing that is sordid, vicious, and low.*

* Swift.

One very common error misleads the opinion of mankind,—that, universally, authority is pleasant, submission painful. In the general course of human affairs, the very reverse of this is nearer the truth. Command is anxiety; obedience, ease.*

Lamartine has well observed: "Travelling is summing up a long life in a few years; it is one of the strongest exercises a man can give his heart and his mind. The philosopher, the politician, the poet, should all have travelled much. Changing the moral horizon is to change thought."

"Begin at the Beginning" is an excellent maxim. The laborious pursuit of first principles brings its own reward. To begin at the beginning in the sciences, as well as in matters of fact, is the nearest and safest road to the end. Even sensible men are too commonly satisfied with tracing their thoughts a little way backwards, and they are, of course, soon perplexed by a profounder adversary. In this respect, most people's minds are too like a child's garden, where the flowers are planted without their roots. It may be said of morals and of literature, as truly as of sculpture and painting, that, to understand the outside of human nature, we should be well acquainted with the inside.

Such is the Waywardness of Fate, that one man sucks an orange, and is choked by a pip; another swallows a penknife, and lives: one runs a thorn into his hand, and no skill can save him (a fact of recent date); another has a shaft of a gig passed completely through his body, and recovers: one is overturned on a smooth common, and breaks his neck; another is tossed out of a gig over Brighton cliff, and survives: one walks on a windy day, and meets death by a brickbat; another is blown up into the air, like Lord Hatton, in Guernsey Castle, and comes down uninjured. The escape of this nobleman was indeed a miracle. An explosion of gunpowder, which killed his mother, wife, some of his children, and many other persons, and blew up the whole fabric of the castle, lodged him and his bed on a wall overhanging a tremendous precipice. Perceiving a mighty disorder (as he might expect), he was going to step out of his bed to know what was the matter, which, if he had done, he would have been irrecoverably lost; but, in the instant

* Paley.

of this moving, a flash of lightning came and showed him the precipice, whereupon he lay still till people came and took him down.*

There is an almost prophetic meaning in the following passage from Berkeley's "Essay towards Preventing the Ruin of Great Britain," written soon after the affair of the South-Sea Scheme: "All projects for growing rich by sudden extraordinary methods, as they operate violently on the passions of men, and encourage them to despise the slow moderate gains that are to be made by an honest industry, must be ruinous to the public; and even the winners themselves will at length be involved in the public ruin."

Theodore Hook was one of the most experienced exponents of the Town Life of his day: in habits, a bachelor, notwithstanding his industry as a man of letters, he saw more of the outside world than the majority of idle men. He has left many of these experiences in his novels, which, as pictures of life, are valuable.

Thus, in *Gilbert Gurney*, he gives this admirable bit of club criticism: "People who are conscious of what is due to themselves never display irritability or impetuosity; their manners insure civility—their own civility secures respect: but the blockhead or the coxcomb, fully aware that something more than ordinary is necessary to produce an effect, is sure, whether in clubs or coffee-houses, to be the most fastidious and factious of the community, the most overbearing in his manners towards his inferiors, the most restless and irritable among his equals, the most cringing and subservient before his superiors." No man could utter such criticism with more complete safety from being answered with a *Tu quoque*.

PREDICTIONS OF SUCCESS.

A few noteworthy incidents have occurred in the early lives of great men, which have singularly accorded with their success in after-life.

The first notice of Lord Chancellor Somers as a boy is exceedingly curious. In Cooksey's *Life and Character of Lord Somers*, the following is stated to be well authenticated.

* *New Monthly Magazine.*

It is to the effect that the boy was walking with one of his aunts, under whose care he was placed at the time, when "a beautiful roost-cock flew upon his curly head, and while perched there crowed three times very loudly." The occurrence was instantly viewed as an omen of his future greatness.

Pope, writing to Lord Orrery, after first witnessing Garrick's performance of Richard III., said, "That young man never had his equal as an actor, and will never have a rival." As yet the prophecy is unshaken.

A few weeks before Lord Chatham died, Lord Camden paid him a visit. Chatham's son, William Pitt, left the room on Lord Camden's coming in. "You see that young man," said the old lord; "what I now say, be assured, is not the fond partiality of a parent, but grounded on a very accurate examination. Rely upon it, that young man will be more distinguished in this country than ever his father was." His prophecy was in part accomplished. At the age of twenty-four he was Chancellor of the Exchequer; and before he had attained his twenty-fifth year, had been offered, and refused, the place of First Minister.

When Horatio Nelson was a weakly child, he gave proofs of that resolute heart and nobleness of mind which, during his whole career of labour and of glory, so eminently distinguished him. When a mere boy, he strayed a bird's-nesting from his grandmother's house, in company with a cow-boy; the dinner-hour elapsed, he was absent, and could not be found; the alarm of the family then became very great, for they apprehended that he might have been carried off by gipsies. At length, after search had been made for him in various directions, he was discovered alone, sitting composedly by the side of a brook which he could not get over. "I wonder, child," said the old lady when she saw him, "that hunger and fear did not drive you home." "Fear! grandmamma," replied the future hero; "I never saw fear—what is it?"

Arthur Wellesley, when at school at Chelsea, was a boy of indolent and careless manner, and rather than join in the amusements of the playground delighted to lean against a large tree, observing his schoolfellows when playing around him. If any boy played unfairly, Arthur quickly apprised those engaged in the game: on the delinquent being turned out, it was generally wished that he should supply his place; but nothing could induce him to do so: when beset by a party of five or six, he would fight with the utmost courage and determination until he freed himself from their grasp; he would then retire again to his tree, and look about him, as observant as before. Such was the love of fair play in the boy who became the great Duke of Wellington.

An incident in the life of Parry, the intrepid Arctic navigator, may also be related here. He left Bath, accompanied by an old and faithful servant of the family, with whom he travelled to Plymouth, and who did not leave him till he saw him finally settled in the *Ville de Paris* man-of-war. To Parry all was new. He had never before beheld the sea, and his experience of naval matters had been confined to the small craft on the river Avon. He seemed almost struck dumb with astonishment at his first sight of the ocean and of a line-of-battle ship; but, after a while recovering himself, he began eagerly to examine every thing around him, and to ask numberless questions of all who were inclined to listen. While so engaged, he saw one of the sailors descending the rigging from aloft; and in a moment, before the astonished servant knew what Parry was about, he sprang forward, and, with his wonted agility, clambered up to the mast-head, from which giddy elevation he waved his cap in triumph to those whom he had left below. When he regained the deck, the sailors, who had witnessed the feat, gathered round him and commended his spirit, telling him he was "a fine fellow, and a true sailor every inch of him." We can well imagine with what gratification the various members of his family would receive the account of this and every other incident connected with his first entry on his new career, and how eagerly they would hail his conduct on this occasion as a happy omen of future success.*

* *Memoirs of Sir E. W. Parry.*

Conclusion.

EASE OF MIND.

In order to enjoy Ease of Mind in our intercourse with the world, we should introduce into our habits of business punctuality, decision, the practice of being beforehand, despatch, and exactness; in our pleasures, harmlessness and moderation; and in all our dealings, perfect integrity and love of truth. Without these observances we are never secure of ease, nor indeed taste it in its highest state. As in most other things, so here, people in general do not aim at more than mediocrity of attainment, and of course usually fall below their standard; whilst many are so busy in running after what should procure them ease, that they totally overlook the thing itself.

Ease of mind has the most beneficial effect upon the body, and it is only during its existence that the complicated physical functions are performed with the accuracy and facility which nature designed. It is, consequently, a great preventive of disease, and one of the secret means of effecting a cure when disease has occurred; without it, in many cases, no cure can take place. By ease of mind many people have survived serious accidents, from which nothing else could have saved them, and in every instance is much retarded by the absence of it. Its effect upon the appearance is no less remarkable. It prevents and repairs the ravages of time in a singular degree, and is the best preservative of strength and beauty. It often depends greatly upon health, but health always depends greatly upon it. The torments of a mind ill at ease seem to be less endurable than those of the body; for it scarcely ever happens that suicide is committed from bodily suffering. As far as the countenance is an index, "the vultures of the mind" appear to turn it more mercilessly than any physical pain; and no doubt there have been many who would willingly have exchanged their mental agony for the most wretched existence that penury could produce. From remorse there is no escape. In aggravated cases probably there is no instant, sleeping or waking, in which its influence is totally unfelt. Remorse is the extreme one way; the opposite is that cleanliness of mind which has never been recommended any where to the same extent that it is by the precepts of the Christian religion, and which alone constitutes "perfect freedom." It would be curious if we could see what effect such purity would have upon the appearance and actions of a human being—a being who lived, as Pope expresses it, in the "eternal sunshine of the spotless mind." Goldsmith has beautifully said:

> How small of all that human hearts endure,
> That part which laws or kings can cause or cure!
> Still to ourselves in every place consign'd,
> Our own felicity we make or find.

Shakspeare observes: "There is nothing either good or bad but thinking makes it so."*

Charles James Fox, who was, from infancy, a spoiled child, would spend night after night in gambling, and wasting his sweet nature in the orgies of Bacchus. Then he would flee away to the delightful scenery and refreshing air of St. Anne's Hill, and there betake himself to gardening, in a blue apron; or to the learned leisure of his study, in the bosom of conjugal felicity and friendship.

THE LIFE OF MAN.

It is impossible to say what analogy exists between the race and the individual, and attempts to explain the history of the one by the stages which mark the life of the other are at best more ingenious than satisfactory; but almost every fact with which we are acquainted seems to suggest that some such analogy exists, though its particulars are altogether unknown, and though we cannot even say whether mankind ought to be compared to one individual or to several. It may, however, be allowable, in dealing with a subject which, after all, appeals rather to the feelings and to the imagination than to the reason, to point out the fact that the cessation of human society would present a striking analogy to the death of individuals; and that there would be the same contradictory mixture of completeness and incompleteness about a society eternally renewed, as there would

* *The Original.* By Thomas Walker, M.A.

be about a human being who never died. That the life of a man forms a moral whole, is a conviction which is so thoroughly worked into our minds and our very language, that no one doubts it. That it is a mysterious and utterly contradictory thing at its best estate, is the experience of every person who has even ordinary powers of reflection. It is hard to imagine the degree in which these mysteries and contradictions would be heightened if man were immortal. If, after arriving at that average degree of prudence and self-restraint which almost every one attains comparatively early in life, people lived on and on for centuries and millenniums, carrying on the same sort of transactions, settling the same difficulties, enjoying the same pleasures, and suffering from the same vexations, the question why they ever were sent into the world at all (which is even now sufficiently perplexing) would become altogether overwhelming; and the faith which people at present maintain in the Divine government of the world would have to be based on entirely different grounds, if it survived at all. It is perhaps not merely fanciful to suggest that a somewhat similar difficulty would exist if human society, after a long and laborious education, were to attain to a stationary state, and were then to go on indefinitely enjoying itself. Such a heaven on earth would be at best a sort of high life below stairs.

The celebration of the triumphs of civilisation, which is at present in full bloom, produces on many minds an effect not unlike that which Robespierre's feasts to the Supreme Being produced on his colleagues. "You and your nineteenth century are beginning to be a bore," is the salutation which many a philosopher would receive in these days from a sincere audience. Weigh and measure and classify as we will, we are but poor creatures, when all is said and done. It would be a relief to think that a day was coming when the world, whether more comfortable or not, would at least see and know itself as it is, and when the real gist and bearing of all the work, good and evil, that is done under the sun, should at last be made plain. Till then, knowledge, science, and power are, after all, little more than shadows in a troubled dream—a dream which will soon pass away from each of us, if it does not pass away at once from all.*

* *Saturday Review.*

THE GOOD MAN'S LIFE.

Some are called *at age* at fourteen, some at one-and-twenty, some never; but all men late enough, for the life of a man comes upon him slowly and insensibly. But as when the sun approaching towards the gates of the morning, he first opens a little the eye of heaven, and sends away the spirits of darkness, and gives light to a cock, and calls up the lark to matins, and by and by gilds the fringes of a cloud, and peeps over the eastern hills, thrusting out his golden horns, like those which decked the brows of Moses when he was forced to wear a veil, because himself had seen the face of God; and still while a man tells the story, the sun gets up higher, till he shows a fair face and a full light, and then he shines one whole day, under a cloud often, and sometimes weeping great and little showers, and sets quickly: so is man's reason and his life. He first begins to perceive himself to see or taste, making little reflections upon his actions of sense, and can discourse of flies and dogs, shells and play, horses and liberty; but when he is strong enough to enter into arts and little institutions, he is at first entertained with trifles and impertinent things, not because he needs them, but because his understanding is no bigger, and little images of things are laid before him, like a cockboat to a whale, only to play withal: but before a man comes to be wise, he is half-dead with gouts and consumption, with catarrhs and aches, with sore eyes and a worn-out body. So that if we must not reckon the life of a man but by the amounts of his reason, he is long before his soul be dressed; and he is not to be called a man without a wise and an adorned soul, a soul at least furnished with what is necessary towards his well-being: but by that time his soul is thus furnished, his body is decayed; and then you can hardly reckon him to be alive, when his body is possessed by so many degrees of death.

* * * * * *

But if I shall describe a living man, a man that hath that life which distinguishes him from a fool or a bird, that which gives him a capacity next to angels, we shall find that even a good man lives not long; because it is long before he is born to this life, and longer yet before he hath a man's growth. "He that can look upon death, and see its face with the same countenance with which he hears its story; he that can endure all the labours of his life with his soul supporting his body; that can equally despise riches when he hath them, and when he hath them not; that is not sadder if they lie in his neighbour's trunks, nor more brag if they shine round about his own walls; he that is neither moved with good fortune coming to him, nor going from him; that can look upon another man's lands evenly and pleasantly as if they were his own, and yet look upon his own, and use them too, just as if they were another man's; that neither spends his goods prodigally and like a fool, nor yet keeps them avariciously and like a wretch; that weighs not benefits by weight and number, but by the mind and circumstances of him that gives them; that never thinks his charity expensive if a worthy person be the receiver; he that does nothing for opinion sake, but every thing for conscience, being as curious of his thoughts as of his actings in markets and theatres, and is as much in awe of himself as of a whole assembly; he that knows God looks on, and contrives his secret affairs as if in the presence of God and his holy angels; that eats and drinks because he needs it, not that he may serve a lust or load his belly; he that is bountiful and cheerful to his friends, and charitable and apt to forgive his enemies; that loves his country, and obeys his prince, and desires and endeavours nothing more than that they may do honour to God:"* this person may reckon his life to be the life of a man, and compute his months not by the course of the sun, but the zodiac and circle of his virtues; because these are such things which fools and children and birds and beasts cannot have; these are therefore the actions of life, because they are the seeds of immortality. That day in which we have done some excellent thing, we may as truly reckon to be added to our life, as were the fifteen years to the days of Hezekiah.†

* Seneca, *De Vita Beata.*
† Jeremy Taylor's *Holy Dying.*

PREDICTIONS OF FLOWERS.

To what excellent account have our thoughtful old writers turned these prophetic indications of changeful flowers! Bishop Hall, in his *Occasional Meditations*, has the following "On the Light of Tulips, and Marigolds, &c. in his Garden:" "These flowers are the true clients of the sun; how observant they are of his motion and influence! At even, they shut up, as mourning for his departure, without whom they neither can see nor flourish; in the morning, they welcome his rising with a cheerful openness; and at noon, are fully displayed in a free acknowledgment of his bounty.

"Thus doth the good heart turn unto God. '*When thou turnedst away thy face, I was troubled,*' saith the man after God's own heart. '*In thy presence is life; yea, the fulness of joy.*' Thus doth the carnal heart to the world: when that withdraws its favours, he is dejected; and revives with a smile. All is in our choice. Whatsoever is our sun will thus carry us.

"O God, be Thou to me such as Thou art in Thyself: Thou shalt be merciful in drawing me; I shall be happy in following thee."

The use of Perfumes in the last century exceeded that in the present day. Possibly the old notion that they were employed to mask the exhalations from diseased persons may have driven perfumes out of fashion in our day; we recollect *musk* to have been specially so considered. Bishop Hall, in his *Occasional Meditations*, adverts to this use of perfumes in a meditation illustrative of a custom which is associated with the symbolic character of "flowers and redolent plants, just emblems of the life of man, which has been compared in Holy Scriptures to those fading beauties, whose roots, being buried in dishonour, rise again in glory."* The Bishop's meditation is "On the Sight of a Coffin stuck with Flowers:"

"Too fair in appearance is never free from just suspicion. While there was nothing but wood, no flower was to be seen here; now that this wood is lined with an unsa-

* Evelyn.

voury corpse, it is adorned with this sweet variety. The fir, whereof that coffin is made, yields a natural redolence alone; now that it is stuffed thus noisomely, all helps are too little to countervail that scent of corruption.*

THE WORLD'S CYCLES.

There is a Revolution of History as of Knowledge: who does not remember how often the same succession of events has happened in his memory! Dr. Newman has well expressed this truth in a poem in the *Lyra Apostolica*, entitled "Faith against Sight," with the motto, "As it was in the days of Lot, so shall it be in the days of the Son of Man:"

> The World has Cycles in its course, when all
> That once has been, is acted o'er again:
> Not by some fatal law which need appal
> Our faith, or binds our deeds as with a chain;
> But by men's separate sins, which blended still
> The same bad round fulfil.

DEATH ALL-ELOQUENT.

> Death and I have met in full, close contact;
> And parted, knowing we should meet again;
> Therefore, come when he may, we've looked upon
> Each other far too narrowly for me
> To fear the hour when we shall be so join'd,
> That all eternity shall never sever us.—*F. Kemble.*

What solemnity is there in the following passage, with which Sir Walter Raleigh concludes his *Marrow of Historie!* "O eloquent, just, and mighty Death! whom none could advise, thou hast persuaded; what none have dared, thou hast done; and whom all the world have flattered, thou only hast cast out of the world and despised: thou hast drawn together all the far-stretched greatness, all the pride, cruelty, and ambition of man, and covered it all over with these two narrow words, HIC JACET."

* See "Flowers on Graves," in *Mysteries of Life, Death, and Futurity.*

Finis.

APPENDIX.

Generations (page 71).

MR. HATSELL TO LORD AUCKLAND.

Morden Park, Sunday, Nov. 23, 1813.

MY DEAR LORD,—I must correct the conclusion of your last letter, "and so the world goes on," to "and so the world goes off." In the same Marlborough family I have lived to see eight* generations:

1. Sarah Duchess of Marlborough.
2. Lady Sunderland.
3. Jack Spencer.
4. The first Lord Spencer.
5. The present Lord Spencer.
6. The Duchess of Devonshire.
7. Lady Morpeth.
8. Her children (the present Lord Carlisle and Duchess of Sutherland).

I saw Sarah in Lincoln's-inn consulting Mr. Fazakerly, who stood close to her Grace's chair; so, you see, I beat history out and out.† . . —From the *Auckland Correspondence*, vol. iv. p. 401.

Memory (page 75).

Professor Faraday, at the close of a Lecture on Gas Glass-house Furnaces, delivered at the Royal Institution in 1862, alluded, in an affecting manner, to his increasing loss of memory. There was a time, he observed, when he inclined to think that Memory was a faculty of secondary order; but he now feels its great importance; and the deficiency of that power, he said, would prevent him from again bringing before them any thing that was new; for he was often unable to recollect even his own precious researches, and he could no longer trust himself to lecture without notes.

Great Ages (page 114).

An old woman who died in 1858 in St. Patrick-street, Dublin, at the age of 110 years, distinctly remembered and described the appearance of Dean Swift, and added, that he never went outside the Deanery-house that he was not attended through the streets by a vast crowd of washed and unwashed admirers.

Mrs. Keith, of Newnham, Gloucestershire, who died in 1772, aged 133, left three daughters, aged 111, 110, and 100.

In 1862, a lady residing at Cheltenham received a second donation of 5*l.* from her Majesty the Queen, for an old man of 107 years of age, named William Purser, a native of Redmarley, but living in Cheltenham.—*Worcestershire Chronicle.*

In 1862, a curious fact occurred at Downton, showing how few individuals are required to connect distant periods of history with the present time. A man was buried in this parish whose father was born in the reign of William III., and that father lived in three centuries, having been born in 1698 and died in 1801.—*Salisbury Journal.*

In 1853, the Irish newspapers announced the death of Mrs. Mary Power, aunt of the celebrated Mr. Shiel, at the Ursuline Convent, Cork, at the age of 116 years; but this statement lacks legal evidence to prove it.

* Only seven; the name of the second Lord Spencer ought to be omitted.

† Mr. Hatsell died 1820.

The obituary of the *Times* of January 21, 1863, records the decease of persons who had attained the following advanced ages, viz.: 92, 90, 82, 82, 82, 80, 78, 78, 76, 74, 72, 72, 72, and 70 years respectively.

Dr. Mead, grandfather of the celebrated physician and antiquary, died at Ware, in Hertfordshire, 1652, aged 148.

In Scawen's *Dissertation on the Cornish Tongue,* written in the reign of Charles II., is mentioned a woman recently deceased, who was "164 years old, of good memory, and healthful at her age; living in the parish of Gwithian. She married a second husband after she was 80, and buried him after he was 80 years of age."

A Philadelphia Correspondent of *Notes and Queries,* No. 213, 1853, records the death of "Aunt Polly" (Mary Simondson), near Shippensburg, Pennsylvania, at the age of 126 years.

Among the legacies bequeathed to the Middlesex Hospital in 1863, was one which is deserving of special notice, inasmuch as the donor, Mr. Cropper, exhibited a singular instance of rigid economy in his personal expenditure, combined with a bountiful and almost princely benevolence towards the poor. Mr. Cropper, who was 90 years old when he died, had, it appears, survived all his relations. He was a barrister-at-law, and lived in the most frugal manner in his chambers at Gray's-inn. The amount of his property at the time of his decease is estimated at about 4000*l.* per annum, and 10,000*l.* in money, the whole of which he has bestowed on London charities, selecting Middlesex Hospital as his residuary legatee.

In the *Express* of February 11, 1863, it is recorded: Two octogenarians, named Joseph and John Fitzwalter, brothers, lived together with their sister in a house in Parliament street for a great number of years. The brothers had been brought up to the business of lace-designing, and the sister had acted in the capacity of housekeeper. Joseph, the elder one, was a short time ago attacked with bronchitis, under which he lingered for some time in much pain. On Wednesday last (February 4), however, he died, at the ripe old age of 84 years. The brother and sister of the deceased were much affected by his death, the brother showing excessive signs of grief. His grieving, however, was not long, for he expired in one hour after his brother. The death of two brothers, to whom she was devoutly attached, was a shock which the sister was unable to withstand; and on the morning fixed for their interment she also expired, at the age of 88 years.

Baron Maseres (*page* 149).

Baron Maseres long resided at Reigate, in a fine old brick mansion, about midway between the church and town. His remains rest in a vault in the churchyard towards the north-east; upon the tomb over which Dr. Fellowes has inscribed an epitaph in elegant Latinity, terminating thus: "Vale, vir optime! amice, vale, carissime; et siqua rerum humanarum tibi sit adhuc conscientia, monimentum, quod in tui memoriam, tui etiam in mortuis observantissimus Robertus Fellowes ponendum curavit, solitâ benevolentiâ tuearis."

On Sundays the Baron, bent with age, might be seen advancing up the nave of Reigate church; for he was a sound churchman, and testified his sincerity by making an Endowment for an Afternoon Sermon to be preached on Sundays, with this proviso, that, in case of non-observance of the bequest, the endowment should be given in bread to the poor. The chancels, with their faded pomp of effigied monuments, hatchments, and armorial glass, have little attraction compared with this interesting memorial of practical piety.

INDEX.

CPSIA information can be obtained
at www.ICGtesting.com
Printed in the USA
LVHW100445110522
718424LV00003B/241

9 783375 003197